Conscience isn't something all people are born with...

Gabriel Church is a portrait in contrast. It would be easy to get lost in his pale-blue eyes, ache with the need to feel the strength of his masculine frame. He appears to be nothing but animal and instinct. The only people who know the full depth of that truth are dead, murdered, or two thousand miles away.

Gabe is a serial killer, and for the first time in his life, he has more on his mind than his own survival. This time he is running from Seattle to protect the only person he thinks innocent in his laundry list of crime and murder: Christian Maxwell, his biographer and unexpected lover.

Drawn to a place he never thought to return, Gabe finds new and different realities. Realities that insist he let go of his tragic past, those incredible perceptions of God, and his own divinity. He must open his eyes to what the love of a good man can do to heal a broken soul.

Torn and Frayed

The Gabriel Church Tales, Book Two

Rodd Clark

A NineStar Press Publication

Published by NineStar Press
P.O. Box 91792,
Albuquerque, New Mexico, 87199 USA.
www.ninestarpress.com

Torn and Frayed

Printed in the USA
First Edition
July, 2018

Print ISBN: 978-1-949340-26-6

Also available in eBook, ISBN: 978-1-949340-22-8

Warning: This book contains sexually explicit content, which may only be suitable for mature readers, and depictions of graphic violence.

This is for those who've ever loved someone whom they knew they shouldn't—but who never seemed to find the sufficient strength to leave those soul mates in their wake. You all know who you are, and for TSK whom I hope to see on the other side.

Also dedicated to Richard DeVoe and the family he gifted me.

"Conscience isn't something all people are born with, Gabriel. Sometimes we find it during our journeys through life—and usually in places we never thought to look."—Father Albert Kait, Diocese of San Antonio

Chapter One

WHEN THE KILLER Gabriel Lee Church pulled into town, the day was like any other. The traffic was heavy as morning commuters filled the routes and teemed into service roads like ants traveling in long foraging lines. As the vehicles inched forward and jockeyed and broke for entry into those faster lanes, one might've assumed there was a chaotic order to it all, a symphony of instruments working in tandem like a reflex arc operating without direction of a maestro. It seemed every car was speeding along at a harried pace to reach their jobs and appointments, but as hectic as it appeared, it never stopped the drivers and passengers from reaching for their cell phones, or tuning radios, or stuffing their faces with fresh, powdery donut treats while sipping their Starbucks coffees.

To his continued frustration, Gabe noticed the one thing drivers rarely used during their morning commute was blinkers, with few acting as if they remembered they even had them. He, on the other hand, always obeyed the rules of the roadway. No point evading police for murder if you were going to allow yourself to be hauled away because of a simple reckless driving charge. His stereo was on like many others, playing tunes from the eighties, which he'd grown to enjoy more than other shit he'd heard today. He didn't like the rap influence in today's pop hits. *Give me an old James Taylor or Glen Campbell song. Now those were memorable.* He didn't have the radio tuned to any local station either, because he didn't need to the hear traffic reports since he had nowhere pressing to be, nor anyone requiring an audience with him.

Gabe rarely had second thoughts about his nomadic lifestyle, although he regretted putting the Pacific Northwest in his rearview for more reasons than simply loss of beautiful scenery and the lonely, yet lovely stretches of endless highway. Leaving Seattle was harder than other cities he'd passed through because he had been forced to leave his writer behind. He hated abandoning Christian Maxwell. He'd actually grown quite fond of the man—someone who'd successfully slipped quietly into his life, and as surreptitiously into his bed, once he'd figured the story Chris was supposed to write was never, in fact, going to see the light of day. For all the good he'd found there, Seattle turned up only death and bad memories for him.

Or maybe it was another lie to tell one's self. Another justification to say he needn't make apologies, particularly when he knew Chris would be waking up alone in his bed. Clearly the writer wanted a relationship, but he would never understand the ramifications and the danger in that. Gabe never settled for too long anywhere, or with anyone. It seemed he was forever bound to be running from the law, as much as he was his own past.

Gabriel Church possessed a driver's license, but it'd expired some ten years earlier. If the police stopped him, he'd flash it or one of the many false documents he'd gathered together over the long haul. They were simple guarantees for all the checkpoints and traffic stops he knew he'd have to make it past. But the Glock 9 mm really worried him more. He didn't use guns very often, but one never knew what challenges lay in the path ahead, and he'd have been foolish not to carry something for every contingency. He acquired the weapon years earlier and carried it in his Dodge, snuggly buried under a corner of the interior's loose nylon mat which'd come unglued at a spot just under his dashboard.

Amazingly, he'd successfully traveled across the United States many times in long, lazy passes headed nowhere in particular, and he'd never been arrested. He'd managed to talk his way out of every awkward intervention by the police. If they'd known who he was or what he was guilty of, their guns would have been pulled and stances taken in readiness of the kickback. He imagined he'd hear the screams from shaky officers demanding he drop to his knees atop the black asphalt as they withdrew handcuffs from tiny holders strapped to their belts. But Church had never been caught and always smiled back at the officers who ticketed him under his makeshift aliases. He would wave as he'd pull back into traffic and resume his speed, only to toss the crumpled tickets out his window a few miles farther down the highway. They were remnants of another warrant issued on his Joe Dirt personas from Idaho and Wyoming, supposedly traveling on business when they'd found the misfortune of changing lanes without a proper signal.

Gabe left the New Mexico border behind him the night before and was now traveling through San Antonio. Every joint in his body ached because he'd been stuck behind the wheel for over six hours. Leg muscles screamed at him over tiny twinges, alerting him he needed to stop soon and stretch his legs. He saw the fuel meter nearing empty and knew he needed to gas up as well. Just as his legs were begging for relief, his stomach began rumbling to life. Gabe needed to look for the nearest interstate diner. He'd been living on fast food burgers and convenient store burritos for far too long.

Seeing the familiar red roof of a Howard Johnson's in the distance, he maneuvered his pickup to the far right and looked for the nearest exit off I-151. *What do you get the man who has everything?* Certainly his answer was fried clams. But then he realized the time of day. Too early for fried clams, so he chose instead to have a cup of coffee and a thick slab of chicken-fried steak. When he walked inside, the smell of food on the grill hit his nostrils, and he salivated. He'd forgotten how long it'd been since he'd had a good meal that hadn't been served through a window.

As he waited near the entrance, a tiny waitress came bounding from the kitchen, stopping in her tracks when she spotted Gabe. Her mouth dropped open as she sized him top to bottom. Seeing an attractive man with no wife or babies in his arms must have given her some hope, he figured. Hope that the tip he left her was in direct relation to the number of flirtatious efforts she expended to receive it.

"Only one, darlin'?" she asked as she rushed up with another table's meal teetering on her tray.

"Sure," he said, nodding politely as she ushered him to what he'd assumed was one of her prized tables in the rear of the restaurant.

"Be right back, hon," she said, passing busboys in the aisles. By the time she came back, she was already carrying a carafe of coffee with a single glass of ice water. Gabe mentioned with a grin how he didn't really need a menu, and she leaned in just enough to allow her perfume to filter in.

"I only want chicken fried steak with whatever sides you think I deserve," he said with a grin. His charm with the ladies came easy for him, and because it did, he'd gotten laid more in his lifetime than the typical male could boast too. And since he'd met Christian, he was no longer married to the notion of a single gender in the sack.

Christian Maxwell was the first man he ever fucked, but the experience felt natural in hindsight. It felt genuine in a way that should've surprised him more, though it didn't; the bucking sweaty pleasure and explosive release of seed. Ever since he left Seattle, he'd been afforded the time to think how nice it could've been to have him reclining in the passenger seat beside him. If only for the company and long conversations they could've had.

"Right away darlin'," she said as she slipped back toward the kitchen.

Gabe watched her walk away and saw how his waitress, Alethea, pointed him out to nearby female staffers by the area where the coffee makers sat. He winked and heard faint girlish laughter issuing from behind the counter as each one surveyed him. He knew his eyes and his physique attracted women. He wasn't metrosexual and cultivated, so he wasn't always sure why others found him so sexually attractive. Gabe wore faded flannel and dusty work boots in lieu of the polished, esthetic sensibilities of a man obsessed with his own image.

TRACING A FINGER along the rim of his cup, he was pulled back to another time. He'd been sitting at the Cherry Street Grinder in Seattle when he'd met Christian formally for the first time. They'd discussed his origin story and the murders he'd committed. It'd come as a quite a surprise for him anyone would want to place his life on paper, but Christian Maxwell was surely the exception to most rules, Gabe suspected.

He'd offered to write Gabe's story from beginning to the present, in an unadulterated fashion. He agreed not to alert the police, or to inform the authorities in any way. Not before the killer could slip out of town like being given a five-minute head start before the race ensued. Maxwell's initial condition was that Gabe remained silent and never alluded to any crimes he might have committed from any point when the two men became introduced. Like some carefully crafted legal wrangling that didn't seem to insulate anyone from being charged as an accessory by Gabe's perception. Their arrangement was an oddity from the jump, but it worked, however tenuously. At least until his biographer began to develop strong feelings for him during their interviews.

It seemed simple enough. A writer who wants to make a name for himself by interrogating a serial killer—trying to learn the breaking point or isolate an unknown defect, as if he possessed some mental acuity others did not. The first time Gabe sat across from Christian he'd seen the writer's nervousness. He'd witnessed the unsure way he began scribbling notes on a legal pad, like an employer learning basic facts about a potential employee in some twisted interview process. Gabe enjoyed making others squirm and fidget while in his company. It proved the power he maintained over others and defined who he was. Particularly in the presence of other males, where he fully exercised his dominion and proved he was greater in all aspects.

It only took a minute or so before he guessed Christian was queer. He didn't need to see the absence of a ring on his finger to confirm what he already knew. He sensed it. Even over coffee with a complete stranger, he knew his companion was a homosexual although everything seemed copacetic and exceedingly professional during their first encounter. He survived alone and on his wits for too long not to have recognized it. As a survivor, Church utilized every skill at his command and most of those came in his ability to read others. He learned quickly how to expose someone's weakness to his advantage, though with the writer that was hardly a gift. Christian seemed unable to hide his weaknesses and spilled them on the floor at Gabriel's feet from the very first moment they met.

Gabriel enjoyed watching others. He tried to understand their makeup and the lack of similarities to his own life. It became a game for him, of tearing down the mechanism and reassembling it so he would be able to understand its clockwork precision and it fascinated him.

At the time, seeing the beads of perspiration beginning on the writer's brow, he guessed it hadn't come from the writer being in the company of a killer; in so much as he was trying to disguise his own brewing attraction. But Gabe had seen it before—a typical reaction from women, and even a few men he'd come across in his many travels through backwoods towns and tiny hamlets.

Christian's voice cracked ever so slightly as he opened their conversation with the edict: *"Tell me your story."* Gabe knew it hadn't been the first question the writer wanted an answer for, and this was his way of sidestepping the obvious. Gabe expected the first questions hanging on his lips should have been: *"Who was your very first victim, and why did you choose to murder them?"* How can someone sit in a crowded café, killer mere feet away, and not ask the obvious questions? But this was the game, and Gabe had been intent on allowing the writer his eccentricities. After all, he'd agreed to be interviewed.

That had been the hardest part of his relationship with Christian. Trying to explain why Church murdered in the first place. He wasn't a writer himself and lacked the words to describe the dark motivations behind his actions. No matter how he tried, the writer always looked back with glassy-eyed wonderment and disbelief. He'd seen Christian's jaw muscle tighten and twitch as he fumbled over his words, desperately trying to bring the writer around to his way of thinking. He'd said it was his calling. That every victim hadn't been a random isolated attack and that

God had chosen each murder, not him, with the exception of his first and his last.

What he understood best, was when others believe you're crazy it's easy to accept their reality than to merely shrug it off. But Christian had been the first, and more importantly, the only living individual where his perceptions mattered. And more than anything, Gabe needed to understand *why*. He was driven to making the writer understand him and his actions; the pull of the radiance, the cold stillness of seeing a white-lighter suddenly revealed before his very eyes. He didn't want Chris to fall into the same trap though; he wasn't going to allow him to breathe in the contamination and become the same kind of killer that he was. And in his gut, Church knew he wasn't crazier than anyone else. *It's God who's off the beam for making me the sole proprietor of His mission to cleanse a dirty world and free the righteous.*

Their next discussion came in a hotel suite, which Maxwell rented for privacy. The underlying purpose was supposedly so Gabriel Church might feel more comfortable telling his tale or hashing out his childhood isolated from prying eyes and the occasional conversant ear. No one else needed to hear details of his serial killer's rampage across several states or those people he murdered in them. But it also had another effect when it pitted the two men in luxurious surroundings alone and in close proximity. Their house of cards was guaranteed to fall as long as Church was as charming and irresistible as he'd been at the café.

The relationship Gabriel Church and Christian Maxwell shared was based on a period that overshadowed any real emotional bond. If the situation had been *normal,* Christian might've learned how Gabriel used gallows humor far too frequently, or he had a cruel streak buried under his handsome exterior. As much as they thought they cared for each other, neither looked closely enough at the *reasons* and the *whys* regarding the draw each one felt for the other. Gabriel was a serial killer running on an uneasy apprehension of arrest, and he'd never allowed himself to get close to anyone, particularly a stranger like Maxwell. But paramount to that, he was a man who hadn't had a friend in more years than he could count. They'd somehow formed a connection, and the result had been greater than Gabriel ever thought he'd achieve. Their friendship had turned sexual, but it had more to do with the evolution of simple human contact and a desire to have something neither man could have guessed would become their future.

The allure which bound them was based on something bent and unconventional. This distinction outshone all else and was the only thing that might've remained standing. A Romeo and Juliet tragedy in the making: two souls who'd shared a single foxhole, yet neither saw clearly enough in those earlier days.

Christian had all the "tells" of someone who was distrustful of Gabe from the beginning. It may have been his bent smile and the shadow of a killer underneath such an attractive façade, or possibly just the blossom of the writer's sexuality and the heat generating between them. Theirs had been a strange relationship, more parasitical than not. Chris wanted to learn everything possible about the mind of a serial murderer, and Gabe hungrily fed off the man's undeniable devotion. Even before they'd fucked the first time, Gabe felt the odd stirrings in his jeans. He'd disregarded the titillation at the time, and later he wrote it off as some type of control, knowing that whatever he had the writer wanted in spades. Christian's eyes had told the truth, his crystal gaze lapping up the image of the man across the room. In some twisted satisfaction, Gabe likened the writer to a puppy, trying desperately to please a stern owner and the clearly visible desire to lick at the stubble on his cheeks.

AS CARS PULLED up and parked outside the plate glass diner front, it broke apart Church's dreamlike trance. About the same time, the pretty waitress who had taken a shine for him showed up with his chicken fried steak and a fresh pot of coffee. She gently touched his shoulders as she leaned in to refill his cup, and he felt electricity course through his body. With the smell of her perfume wafting to his nose, he knew he'd be able to have her. He even considered it. She wasn't bad-looking, and she was clearly signaling interest. He'd grin at her with his crooked half smile and ply the twinkle that closed so many deals before. He'd promise he'd stop by after her shift. Then he'd take her to an inexpensive motel along the interstate and fuck her hard for hours. But it would be nothing more than a simple distraction for him, despite the urgent release his body was telling him he needed.

Gabe locked up, recoiling as he looked closely at the waitress. There was something about her, something he couldn't quite put his finger on, but it reminded him of the woman who'd been a catalyst for his latest flight—Shea Baltimore.

Shea was innocent and kind and was never supposed to be one of his victims; she didn't fit the pattern or his calling. But he'd made a single mistake when he allowed himself to be taken in by the moment. He'd slept with her, though only once, and because of that error, she'd learned he wasn't who he claimed to be. She then knew all too quickly everything about his criminal past and suddenly she'd become a real threat to his survival. This was when his instincts kicked in with their usual vengeance.

The aftereffect became the final, broken straw in the deterioration of his relationship with Christian. With the dead girl lying in her apartment, Church was forced back onto the blacktop and racing out of town right ahead of the police. Part of him wanted the writer to come along with him, but he knew that part of the dream was impractical. So he hardly glanced backward when he made haste outta the city, leaving Chris behind and wondering on his lover's fate, as well as his own involvement in Shea's murder.

This time he looked at the waitress without the twinkle and the heavily laden seduction he usually employed. As she walked back toward the kitchen, he stood staring out the window at the flow of cars on the highway, wondering how much he'd changed lately to have given up so easily.

In the weeks since pulling out of Washington, he'd had no human contact. Driving aimlessly, he'd crisscrossed interstates and rural roads in a pattern to keep others off his scent. It had been a blur of small towns and cheap motels. Gabe never allowed himself to get close to anyone in those weeks, stealing when possible, Hustling pool for cash and staying in one cheap dive after another; all to put the city of Seattle behind him and try hard to forget the writer who'd inadvertently changed his life in ways he'd hadn't imagined.

Gabe shoved forkfuls of steak and gravy into his mouth. *Strange, how in all my travels across this United States, this is the first through San Antonio that I can remember.* So after his meal, he jumped back into his truck and hit the streets to survey his surroundings. It became an instinctual pattern, to drive into a town and immediately begin exploring like an archeologist at a dig site. It was more than intellectual curiosity though; he was appraising every route out of the city, every possible escape and proper hiding spot. Gabriel was always working the angles, trying to ensure his own survival and freedom. It'd become second nature by then and born from a hobo existence and his desire to remain secreted beneath the shadows and away from prying eyes of the stalwart authorities, or even a deputy who just luckily stumbled onto him in one catastrophic turn of events.

Under the azure sky, he weaved through traffic, driving close to the world-famous canals and trendy shops overflowing with overweight tourists with screaming kids clutching souvenirs like security blankets. *In a different life*, he'd told himself, but after an hour behind the wheel, he decided he needed to find a hole to crawl into for the remainder of his stay. He pointed his Dodge in the direction of the interstate and the lines of inexpensive motels he'd noticed on his initial drive into town.

Chapter Two

EVEN THOUGH THE office was state governed, there was nothing sterile or briskly efficient inside the halls of the CID, or Criminal Investigative Division for the Washington State Police. As Detective Scott Keen could attest, the CID was nothing more than peeling paint and cracked linoleum, where an inescapable odor of testosterone and stale brewed coffee wafted out of every office he passed along his route to reach his desk.

He imagined it as pledging a fraternity, where on listless Sunday mornings, each man paid a toll for a previous night's party, or where feet were dragged and men stumbled through their morning routines like recovering freshmen hauling their bodies through a.m. classes. The type of men who only appeared revitalized whenever an opportunity arose where they might goad or bait another weaker, unsuspecting colleague.

"Hey, Autumn Boy..." someone yelled behind his back as he passed, "are you making headway on the schoolgirl murders yet?"

Like most detectives, Keen had been given a nickname by his brothers and sisters in blue. The moniker of Autumn Boy was a double reference. *Autumn* being that subset category of cases applied to those with very little chances for any resolution or arrest. The seasonal terminology became an ideal description of a cold case around the office—one where a hard freeze seemed imminent. But as everyone knows, was no single guarantee itself, a simple idiom used by cops to illustrate a particular investigation was nearing its pinnacle. The added *Boy* was originally intended as an insult because Keen was well-known for his baby-faced features, even though he'd graduated from the academy years earlier and was actually about the same age as most of his coworkers and current roster of detectives on the force.

"Certainly more than you, Simmons, so screw ya!" he shouted over his shoulder without slowing down or glancing back to even acknowledge his detractor.

Keen didn't mind the childish taunts from his coworkers. He did, however, require their respect. He'd worked hard to achieve what status he attained, and his reputation for solving cold cases had become a trait few questioned. He did the necessary legwork and viewed every suspect with fresh and critical eyes. And, more often than not, he brought life back to his dead or dying files. But for him, more than the satisfaction of bringing closure to victim's families, winding up a case where others before had failed the task became the primary reason for his tenacious efforts and gave him a reason to use every available resource at his disposal.

And when he was successful and the potentiality of arrest whispered above the horizon, he'd walk the corridors in the Belltown Station like a king who sported a crown of gold. He was always smugly confident when he headed to his captain's office, clutching a once dead file now breached with surprisingly new life. He counted every triumph as a personal achievement above his associates, which may not have made him the most highly regarded among his peers but certainly a man worthy of recognition. And that became the coin Keen treasured above all others as he shuffled through his daily grind.

One of his open cases was fast becoming known around the station as "The Schoolgirl Murders" and was justifiably big news at the moment—the subject of great interest to families, reporters, and the politicians currently soapboxing on that very issue. It began with the abduction of two young girls, who'd been taken in broad daylight and on a public street. Regrettably the term *Schoolgirl Murders* was first coined by a beat officer before sadly being picked up later by the press. Keen particularly hated the practice of giving nicknames to a killer or their victims. He knew it might be easier to categorize when working in closed groups, such as investigators, but it minimized the tragedy when "cute" monikers were given to unsubs or their act or even as in this case, the victim profile. Keen knew how widespread nicknaming was, particularly with male serial killers. The public had been doing that since before there was even a term, serial killer, remembering a time in the mid-1800s when the public titled Edward Rulloff, *"the educated murderer."*

Keen had been given the case only after the girls' bodies were recovered in a field in the city's industrial section of town. With almost no physical evidence and an absence of eyewitnesses, the case was proving to be difficult for Keen. And since his former partner had been recently reassigned, it meant he would be working alone. Keen worked cold cases primarily, but when a case was as hot as the murders of two young girls, it became an all hands on deck sort of time.

So with the double homicide drawing public scrutiny, Keen was juggling more than he'd have liked. He used to tell his wife Carol, that by the time he got a case, most of the witnesses died, moved out of state, or were currently incarcerated for other unrelated charges. Typically, that was the type of problem he enjoyed tackling. He had only recently transferred from Homicide to the CID, and even though his solve rate had dipped during the interim, he was finally catching his footing—until he was bestowed the more noteworthy double homicide to close.

Keen knew he had the general perception of being an amiable enough fellow around the water cooler. But his often brusque exterior and single-minded focus could be a tad off-putting to some detectives. It contributed to how his diminutive title came into being and then later stuck after others saw how much their newcomer loathed it. In part, it had been their way of drawing him and even welcoming him into their collective, while simultaneously and subtly reminding him that his age didn't bother them, but his lack of tenure in the group did. Keen understood all that, though he'd hoped to have been given a much cooler nickname. Autumn Boy seemed so haphazard. But like jet fighter pilots, no one gets to choose their call sign, and around the station, Keen was simply Autumn Boy. He hoped to outgrow the handle as quickly as possible.

"There you are, Scott. Been looking for you," a female detective said when she encountered him in the hallway.

Where Keen's baby-faced features may have inspired his most hated epithet, it also proved to be an equal draw for the women at his precinct. All of them knew Keen was married. Some had even met Carol when she'd visited the station on occasion. But it never stopped the female gaze from admiring and coquettishly batting their long lashes should there be a chance there were troubles in paradise which Keen wasn't divulging.

"What's up, Erin?" Scott asked cordially. "Did you need me downstairs?"

Erin Franks was a second tier Lieutenant, currently assigned to the high-tech unit of the CID. Besides being attractive, smart, and flirtatious, she was an excellent contact for Keen and had become invaluable as a resource whenever he needed record searches or IP traces. He'd allowed her artful advances and, oftentimes, over-the-edge teasing to get slightly out of hand. But he knew the importance of balancing a favorable connection with someone in her skillset. Though, out of all the detectives on site, Erin was the one he wouldn't have liked Carol to meet or become acquainted with.

"Well, not yet," she said with a suggestive lilt in her words. "I have the vehicle records printout you requested. Of course Keen, you'll need to drop by and get it at your leisure, since I don't carry it around in the hope I'll simply bump into you."

Laughing to shatter the mood, Scott said, "Sure thing, Detective. I'll stop by later when I can." Then as quickly as she'd met him, she was gone and leaving with the fragrant scent of soft perfume in her wake. She'd smiled briefly before she sauntered off, her shoes clicking across the tile. Erin's reputation always preceded her wherever she went, mainly because she was one of the few females on the force who had the chutzpah to wear fashionable, yet impractical heels to work. And much like all the male detectives at the station, Scott saw her as one highly attractive woman. Though in his head, he had to wonder how she thought her choice in footwear might've enabled her to race after a fleeing suspect.

Keen was an old school detective. He still utilized a murder board even in these technical times. His familiar whiteboard, with its green and blue scrawled notes, represented every possible suspect and timetables relating to each crime. He only erased the board completely after he'd presented a suspect to the pretty law grad in the DA office. Her name was Connie, and she saw every file prior to submitting it to the District Attorney or his associate attorneys.

Keen just sat down at this desk when his captain popped his head around the corner and knocked on his open door. "Hey, Detective, can you squeeze in one more cold case? That is if you can get to it sometime before your next public appearance?" His captain was gruff as he dropped a sheet assignment on his desk and walked out, not waiting for an answer.

Scott knew he was referring to the media for the Schoolgirl Murders he'd been tasked to solve. His superiors didn't like giving away the types of cases that brought the most notoriety to the precinct. At least, not until they were personally involved in the outcome and were able to stand center stage during a press announcement or generally take their sizeable chunks of credit for everything the detectives finished prior to an arrest.

The sheet the captain had given him was informational. It coded to a particular banker's box held in storage, where every box consisted of old investigative notes and minor evidence packets. Each cardboard box comprised the sum of a particularly stale homicide that hadn't been closed to date. Detective Keen's primary claim to fame and his most stalwart commission inside the CID was solving cold cases.

After retrieving the evidence box and skimming the contents, Keen learned of the murder of a young woman who'd lived in a rundown apartment in a less than reputable quarter of Seattle. Her name was Shea Baltimore, he read. Her lifeless corpse had been discovered in her own residence, and the attached crime scene photos displayed her limp and frail figure positioned on a bright-red sofa, which he presumed had to be hers.

Immediately, Keen was seized by the way her tiny frame was placed in the photos. Even though her head was slumped awkwardly to the right, in her final moments of death, she almost appeared as if she were sitting on her couch comfortably. Keen suspected she'd been positioned in that manner and possibly situated there postmortem. Which suggested another possibility, one where she might've been killed at another location then moved there. But whoever sat her upright in her seated position, with her back against the pillows, had done so with seemingly kind and gentle hands. Or it was possible the body was staged in a gesture to show a killer's remorse. And if true, would spoke volumes about her assailant. Even without the particulars of the investigation, Keen was already defining his suspect pool. One he knew would chiefly consist of all the victim's friends, family members, and lovers.

The young woman's death was initially thought to be a sexual attack gone awry. But it was only *supposition*, first responders suggested to officers after seeing no telltale clues to suggest otherwise. It wasn't a robbery, they'd said, and there hadn't been any sign of a break in, with nothing disturbed at the scene as far as anyone could ascertain. Sexual assault was quickly discarded from their line of possible inquiry when the medical examiner's office found no evidence of rape. Miss Baltimore's remains were absent the necessary DNA which might've resolved the case more quickly, and there were no physical signs of assault still lingering on her body. This was why the case went tragically awry, Keen figured—first responders weren't detectives. Even those seasoned investigators previously assigned to the case, failed their victim, in Keen's opinion. He wouldn't be burning through his afternoon, elbow deep and buried in a cold case evidence box if they hadn't. He also wouldn't be trying to decipher through the hen-scratched notes of their early investigation with reports strewn across his desk.

Neighbors were questioned and coworkers interviewed, but there was a decided lack of physical evidence and absent markers of a robbery-homicide. That, combined with new proof the murder hadn't been the typical sexually motivated killing, meant the file was relegated to the back burners until, eventually, it reached a final apex for investigators and quickly turned ice cold.

Shea Baltimore's grisly resolution had yet to be transcribed onto a new murder board, but it appeared it would be necessary. Sometimes seeing a photograph of a victim taken by CSI sparked an outrage that worked to skewer the case directly into a detective's head. But looking at a candid photo of the victim always worked best for Keen. It served as his motivation by keeping the outcome of that nearing finish line somewhere within reach. He knew what investigators learned over time: that it's difficult not to remain driven when you see the victim's face staring back at you, judging and imploring you for a quick resolution.

Such was the case with his latest acquisition still perched on the corner of his desk. So he flipped his whiteboard over to the clean side and begrudgingly put the Schoolgirl Murders on a temporary hold. The detective began taping photographs to the top of the board, and he jotted down the highlights of the analysis under a double-underlined title he'd written in capital letters: THE SHEA BALTIMORE HOMICIDE. And next to that declaration he included the date and time of death he'd found listed in the ME's report.

Sometimes, family presented law enforcement with a photograph of the deceased to use during their investigations, because it wasn't only detectives who understood what the sight of a fresh face smiling bright with vitality could do to drive and inspiration. The very first connection, more often than not, became forged between a family in grief and the champions they turned to in their search for their loved one's killers. But Keen didn't find any real photos of Shea Baltimore when he rifled through his evidentiary contents. He did find an old high school picture buried inside near the bottom of the box, which for his purposes was fairly useless, but he found nothing more recent to use on his murder board, making him strangely curious.

Skimming through the investigative notes, Keen read Miss Baltimore already lost her mother and was survived by her only living relative, her father. From the scrawled assessment the investigating detective made of DeWayne Baltimore inside the margin edges of his notepad, their first meeting had been less than promising. He'd already been informed of his daughter's death by the black-and-white units who first arrived on the scene. Keen wondered right off the bat why it'd been police officers who made the death notice visit and not the investigative agents who arrived next. His question wasn't addressed in the notes he currently possessed, so he quickly decided to investigate the anomaly the following morning.

This was only one of the many discrepancies he wanted to address. The notes went on to describe the father as being a heavy drinker due to the number of empty, crushed aluminum cans surrounding his chair when they stopped by for their initial visit. Protocol was to meet the family to establish their relationship and learn any new facts about the victim, while surreptitiously asking about their own alibis, under a guise of concern and compassion in those heartbreaking, worst of moments. Keen knew he, too, would be introducing himself to DeWayne Baltimore in the very near future, because he wanted to know why the man hadn't given police a photo of his daughter that wasn't years before she'd been murdered—only a question, but the first of many in a long line of puzzling incongruities.

His concentration was broken when Detective Gilroy peeked around the corner to ask, "Hey there, Scott, whatcha doing?"

"Messing around with photos of dead folks," Keen replied over his shoulder.

"Well, do you have to do that now?"

"Well, when I do it at the park, people stare," Keen said with a light chuckle.

Then Gilroy chimed back, "No, buddy, I mean the captain wishes to see you."

Putting his murder board aside, Keen turned to the big man and asked, "So now you're a messenger for him? Well, congratulations on the promotion, Dennis. Let's hope with the small pay increase, you can finally afford the stomach staples." His smile was warm yet cutting as he patted the man's belly. Then he whisked up his suit jacket and headed down the hall for his meeting.

THE PALMETTO INN was visible from the highway, leaving Gabe to pull through the parking lot to gauge each access road in and out of the motel. His instinct turned to second nature, and he wasn't always even aware he was performing the tasks that might one day save his life. He was always checking for exits whenever he entered somewhere new. And whether conscious of it or not, it became a habit he'd taken for granted for far too long. When he was satisfied with the layout, he parked his truck and grabbed the duffel he kept behind the seat. After pulling out a phony ID, he headed inside to rent his room.

The desk clerk appeared to be of Indian descent. He spoke with a broken English dialect of someone not born on these shores. And since Gabe grew up in the hills of Kentucky and the sticks of Tennessee, it wasn't possible to imagine any more awkward an exchange. He'd always presumed he was as white bread as was possible to bake. Their exchange was awkward, and with some effort, he made it more so in his attempt to distract the clerk from inspecting the phony ID for flaws. Even a hillbilly like himself had a fair degree of charm which he used to dazzle and much as conceal.

Gabe convinced him to accept cash but left a copy of his stolen credit card to ensure the deposit. He'd asked for a room to the rear of the parking lot, and he chose to back into a space before heading off to locate his room.

He found it surprisingly spotless, bright, and airy, at least as far as cheap motels along the highway tended to be. Tossing his duffel on the bed, he closed the curtains and immediately began undressing. It'd been two days since his last hot shower, and he figured he was going to take full advantage of one immediately. Ever since he'd left Seattle, showers and clean linens was a luxury he could rarely afford. But the memories of that drew him back to his time at that fancy schmancy Mayflower Park Hotel, where Chris and he stayed. It may have been the weird sensation he felt holding the same tiny bar of Ivory soap or the clean tiles under his bare feet, but he felt yanked backward in time to where the two of them spent all their time fucking and drinking and discussing Church's childhood back in Tennessee. He remembered always waking up slower than usual, naked and still wrapped around Christian like a cocoon. His whole adult life had been comprised of wasted, empty moments of time—those long strings of nothingness stretching through his days, and the thing he worked diligently to kill before it'd take his mind. But that time with the writer felt different; it somehow had purpose without a purpose.

For the first time in his life, that freedom felt more like he was relaxing on a beach somewhere without any care in the world. But prior to meeting Christian, it'd been nearly unbearable as an existence. The sluggish periods between the killings felt endless, as if he were actually sleepwalking through his days like a zombie. The weighted gaps of days were like stones tied around his neck, dragging him down and burying him in that black, empty abyss. Gabe knew how real people lived. Some would probably have been envious of his life, no ties or responsibilities to hold him down or imprison him, but he knew better. He'd lived his life and knew the consequences of those freedoms. Some might be envious or think it would be emancipation, but for him it was different. It might as easily steel his mind and make him seriously insane.

There was a difference with Chris. He knew to acquire that transformation all he had to pay him was his time. In exchange for feeling whole again, he'd only have to suffer through the spilling of his details and the examination of his soul. Though at times it felt exhausting, having to dissect his childhood and expose its weaknesses, in the end he didn't mind.

He liked watching Chris as he excitedly wrote down his notes, forgetting he was naked and still sitting on the floor, the bottle of 90 Proof sitting beside him, which they both were sharing. He stacked his little notes like firewood and eagerly begged for more. And even when it felt invasive, like he'd been strip-searched, and cavities explored, *it was still a bargain nonetheless*. He was beginning to realize how much he would've traded just to keep those moments flowing.

Even though he'd set out to have his story told, there were times when he regretted it. Reliving parts of his childhood was embarrassing and damned near impossible to explain his motivation. He knew there were those who he sought to tell who'd only stare back at him with astonishment, their eyes frozen wide in fright and disgust. Or merely sit there perplexed and blank, as the horrors of his life were spilling off his tongue. But Christian urged him forward, and he was able to see how the writer tried not to judge him as he scrawled out notes, which as it occurred to him, he'd never gotten to read after it was said and done.

"I need a drink," he said one afternoon, crawling out of the hotel bed they shared. He gave a resounding slap to Christian's bare ass cheek before plodding off naked into the front room to find the bottle of bourbon the writer brought with him.

"And I would support that notion," Christian muttered as he left the room. Apparently, his way of asking for a cocktail, Church smiled his faint half grin as he walked away. He liked this man.

At the time, probably neither of them knew how truly those emotions were ingrained into his life. It's the small gestures, the ones the others didn't see, that cemented their attraction. Like the secret pleasure Gabe felt every time the writer said something astute or clever. But real men didn't talk about their feelings like prepubescent schoolgirls. They were just there and remained as something unsaid and somehow understood.

But standing in the tiny shower at the Palmetto Inn Motel, as Gabriel rubbed a soapy washcloth over his hairy frame, he suspected if anyone ever wrote out his obituary, Christian's name would surely have to be there. Then he became morose at the prospect that the only person able to write his obit *was* Christian, and he doubted he'd ever see the writer again, despite the fact he wanted to.

Leaning back and allowing the spray to hit his chest and face, he rested against the tile and wallowed in the hot mist. Not that he deserved that much relaxation. But it did help him to forget. He had considered a nap before clubbing but thought also about hitting a gym for an hour or so and working out his kinks. He knew San Antonio wasn't that big and saw how eventually all roads led to Mecca. If someone wanted sex, they headed to the bars and to the gyms. The presence of a military base meant that there were always strapping young men eager to get their rocks off. Gabe presumed he knew their blueprint well.

They would labor under the pretense of pumping iron, as seductions began with long, lingering glances from across the floor. They'd nod and smile when they noticed one another in the locker room heading to and from the showers, with the steam and sweat making slick mirrors along their muscular builds.

They'd strut around like proud fighting cocks with towels draped around oversized necks, wearing only olive drab military-issued boxers, or nothing at all with their privates bouncing erotic and free under the white cotton fabric in a hint of promise of grander things to come. Time would seemingly stand still then; the males loitering uneasily as they slowly changed into, and out of, their street clothes. And whether straight or gay, it didn't matter to most, as long as each man drowned in that sea of overstuffed jocks, perfectly round cherry-tomato asses, and testosterone sinew stretched across overworked frames. The game was one of understanding, even with contrived and methodic gestures as they meticulously shaved or primped their hair. There was always finite comprehension to an endgame they both shared. Both knew to gap the minutes from one departure and the next. But each knew they'd end up in the parking lot where a better introduction would culminate in them sharing a bed somewhere, for an afternoon of furious bare-assed fucking as their reward. It would be over as quickly as it began, but at least they carried their salacious memories with them as they headed back to their jobs and offices.

Before he stepped out from under the showerhead, he'd already decided the best defense against old memories was to make newer ones. First a nap, then he was determined to hit the nearest club or dive bar and order a tall drink, then many others to follow. He felt reasonably confident there would be someone that'd strike his fancy wherever he ended up. And whoever got the lucky nod would be dragged back to his room at the Palmetto because Gabe was certain he'd get his wick wet sooner than later, and residents in the adjoining rooms would be hearing his raucous fucking and taste the bitterness of envy on their salivating tongues.

Chapter Three

CHURCH RESTED BEFORE heading out. But his nap was fitful, even with the rare sensation of cool, clean sheets wrapping his naked thighs. His dreams were spinning out of control; it felt as if he were caught in a river's rapid current, pulling him every which way, bouncing against the water's edge and smashing on the rocks. There were pictures of faces from his past, but they stayed for only a second before swirls and eddies took him to someone new from his memory. His head was reeling from the dance, and Gabe rolled and wrestled from under the thin comforter. Waking after a fitful sleep felt like he never rested at all, and his first inclination was to get bourbon in his stomach. He knew that at least would settle his mind and push back images to a place where they belonged.

Slipping behind the wheel of the old Dodge, he pointed his truck to the service roads because cheap drinking holes sat in abundance there. He passed buildings without signage, simply painted brick with odd names like the Circus Lounge and Night & Ale's. He decided it would take something slightly more upscale if he intended to get laid, and he did. He pulled back onto Loop 410 to circle around San Antonio to reach the downtown area. He knew there were always better clubs in downtown, like in any other city he'd passed through lately.

Gabe wasn't in a hurry, so he meandered through the business district until he came to the urban, cosmopolitan streets where he knew trendy bars and eateries would be established with regulars. Well after dusk he saw a sign with the name Crash Landing. He smiled when he saw the building's roof displayed a beat-up Cessna plane, appearing as if it'd just taken an unexpected tailspin and collided there in some awful accident of fate. With a grin, he pulled into the parking lot. He wanted to see the inside since from the exterior was so odd.

Who could afford to buy an old sixties-era, dilapidated Cessna simply to be used as mere decoration? *Whoever had, they'd certainly done something cool.* Passing through the doors, he was amazed at how intricately the theme had been carried. He was like a kid at Disneyland, amazed with each elaborate detail. Whoever the owners were of Crash Landing, they'd certainly gone batshit crazy with their idea. *But it all worked.* The bar staff were wearing T-shirts which carried the colors of a crime scene tape and were emblazed with the words: *I SURVIVED THE CRASH.* The music was old-school club tunes from before the travesty of techno house. This was another promising aspect. Men and women danced on the floor together under a cloud of fog machine smoke. Because of this, Gabe hadn't realized from his initial walk-through that the Crash Landing was a gay bar. Not that it much mattered anyway, given his history. The unique, faded, and crumpled roof accessory was what'd first drawn his attention.

Stepping toward the bar, he saw crash test dummies hanging from the black tin ceiling tiles. They were crammed like deceased air travelers between professional DJ light fixtures with their color LEDs and strobe light flashes from the UV cannons perched in dark recesses. A single parachute was tacked open across a far back wall and luggage—duffel bags and suitcases—was suspended in nets above the bartending stations. He had to admit though it had resembled the scene of some horrific aviation nightmare. But in crisp disparity, there were chic people drinking and dancing under the cloud of pretend carnage. Gabe liked everything about the place from the first moment he entered through their doors.

The one place a man is usually found alone is a sports bar. Often meeting his buds and coworkers or prowling for company on a weekend night. But when a studly figure like Gabriel Church entered a gay bar alone, he tended to draw attention. Heads turned to examine the fresh presence of man meat, and eyes loitered longer than necessary as everyone scoped the big man from his tousled hair to his brown work boots. Reaching the bar, he saw his server was a tank-top-wearing muscle twink, which was all the indication he needed for the bar he'd chosen. No wonder people were staring when he walked in.

Even *he* found the bartender attractive and the image of him skull fucking the young man brought satisfaction to his mind. "Bourbon and Coke," he said with confidence, as the server turned to grab a clean glass. He figured he'd explore each corner of the club, but he'd probably head out soon to find something more in tune with his usual speed. Although charming and intelligent, even in his own head, he'd spent too many miles alone and behind the steering wheel, away from the bustle of strangers or the need for idle conversation. He slipped over to an empty table and stared at the hodge-podge of partiers on the dance floor, feeling more awkward than usual. Gabriel began tapping his foot to the unfamiliar music, but he was becoming antsy standing alone. He began fidgeting and lifted his drink to drain the last remnants from his glass. *Christian would've liked this kind of bar.* Then he was pulled back to wondering what the writer would be doing right about then.

Regardless of gender, every head turned to fixate on the big man at the table alone. Salacious desires hung like overgrown Spanish moss from every angle of the bar. And for the brave and self-assured few, he represented quite the challenge. That was if there was one fearless enough to engage him in conversation. They did not know his background or upbringing...and most did not care. There wasn't a single person in the bar that night who might have understood how pretty the devil can appear, and how nice the package he can create whenever he chooses to. The image was made even more mysterious and beckoning because glycerin vapors from the smoke machine started rising from the dance floor to circle and engulf him, making him appear angelic and surreal.

Church was a portrait in contrast. Colored lights flickered across the stubble of his jaw, and even standing in the shadows, there were those getting lost in his pale-blue eyes and aching with the need to feel the strength of his masculine frame. He appeared to be nothing but animal and instinct. The only ones who knew the full depth of that truth were dead, murdered, or were two thousand miles away.

COLE LAWRENCE STOOD a few yards away from the newcomer to the bar, watching him, sizing him up from a distance. He was an experienced hunter in these parts, and his experience was telling him the big man's movements suggested his prey was about to bolt. Cole knew with a certainty his train was running out of track and decided to take the plunge and risk rejection or lose the opportunity altogether. Dragging a palm across his wet lips, he nodded once to the small group of males he was standing next to then turned and headed toward the big man he'd been spying.

Cole understood how to move without showing interest. If you hesitated too long when approaching a potential trick, you took the risk they'd get bored and walk away. In an ocean of possibilities, one convenient fish was just as attractive as another prettier one. In his opinion gay men were more opportunistic in their hunting rituals. He envisioned it like a lion stalking a gazelle through the tall savanna grass. You inched closer, pretending not to even notice your quarry. You didn't want to spook the birdlike friends who circled around him, waiting to scavenge off someone else's kill. And this creature possessed real meat and a strong swagger that indicated potential between his thighs. It'd make for a satisfying meal by the way he moved through the crowd, Cole surmised.

"I HOPE YOU'RE enjoying the music" whispered a dulcet, honeyed voice in Gabriel's ear. "Something tells me you don't enjoy dancing all that much, though," said the uninvited stranger who'd wandered to his table.

"Two left feet here," Gabe said, "and no, the music's only okay."

"You from outta town?" he asked. "I haven't seen you around the Landing before."

"Not my usual hangout," Church said, evading his question completely.

He surveyed the younger man with a distracted smile. He'd had the courage to step up to his table. That was something he had to give him anyway. He appeared to be in his early thirties. Only a puppy in Church's eyes, but he had an air of wholesome decency and civility about him. But civility wasn't in Gabe's vocabulary. He didn't do civilized and polished well. Christian Maxwell had been the exception, but even he had changed during their brief time together. The stranger was tall without being lanky, his brown hair was shaved close, reminiscent of a military cut, and he had the hint of a beard and mustache bordering slightly above a five-o'clock shadow. He worked out, that was evident by a physique which had seen regular workouts at the gym. To Gabe, the man's greatest assets were his depthless brown eyes and his voice. He was worthy of further scrutiny.

"What should I call you?" Gabe asked abruptly.

"Cole," he said as he extended his hand. "Cole Lawrence."

"Well the pleasure's mine, Cole. When they call me, they ask for Gabriel."

"Like in the..."

"Like in the Bible, yes," Church finished for him.

"I bet you get that a lot, people wanting to blow Gabriel's horn."

"Actually, the Bible says it's God who blows the horn. I think Gabriel is an archangel or something. He carries it around for the big guy. At least, if I still remember my Sunday school lessons."

"Well, I'm sure you're right. My parents weren't religious folk, and I think I only ever went into our family church for weddings or funerals."

Cole looked down and cleared his throat as if embarrassed about the turn the conversation had taken. When he looked back up again, he changed the subject. "Can I buy you a cocktail? I'm getting one for myself."

Gabe nodded with a smile, thinking how nice it might feel to have Cole's cock-flavored spit drizzling down his shaft. "Sure, bourbon and Coke, and thanks."

Together, they walked to the tank-topped gym rat serving behind the bar. Cole ordered two drinks, and as the bartender poured, he gave Cole a twinkle of recognition and a wry smile. Gabe almost felt the "Attaboy" slapped on Cole's shoulder with a rowdy, "You go, boy, you lucky, sonofabitch!" They knew each other, Gabe guessed. They'd probably even fucked in the past.

Church didn't give a shit whether they'd fucked or not, but he didn't like the feeling of being displayed as anyone's next conquest or trophy, so he gave the bartender a cold glance as he accepted his glass then turned and walked away. He considered leaving and finding another bar. ussy was easier, and he didn't like the grand ballet performed by gay men. As he was about to turn and thank Cole for the drink and then disappear, Cole touched him on the shoulder.

"Sorry about that. He's an old friend," Cole said before leaning in and saying under his breath, "Hey, we don't know each other very well, but why not drop the façade crap; we are both aware of what we want here. I was thinking about heading out and hoping you wanted to accompany me, possibly to get naked and sweaty. Whatcha say?"

There, thought Gabe. The way it's supposed to work when men go out to acquire some sexual gratification. His pale eyes sized up Cole again as he considered his offer without even a hint of any emotion cracking his cool exterior. "Know this though... I don't get fucked, *ever*," he said in a flat detached tone. "But I wouldn't mind doing you. That is if you're up for it."

Cole raised an eyebrow but offered nothing except his smile, which might've been a personal gift from the devil himself. Gabe drained his glass in one swig and turned his back and headed for the door, expecting his new trick to follow.

They worked out Cole's place was the quickest to get to and both men jumped into his new red Nissan Rogue and then pulled from the parking lot. Gabe saw his trick was edgy with excitement. He could tell by the way he'd nervously played with his car stereo buttons and scanned for a good station using twitchy fingers. The Nissan was roomy and still had that new car odor. Gabe wondered how the man was able to afford such a pricey car, given his youthful age, and he found it hard to contain his jealousy. *My own life might've been different, had I a better chance with a proper education and the choices that Bennett and Sissy didn't give me.* But he had to consider how Cole wanted him, and not the other way around. Whatever gifts he had been bestowed were in demand by others, and as it seemed then, everything was relative in the bitter end.

"How long you in town for?" Cole asked, breaking the heavy silence into manageable shards.

Gabe was distracted, staring at the dials and lights on the Nissan's console, comparing another's life by the dissimilarity of the fourteen-year-old Dodge he was forced to drive. "Not sure," he said, once again evading the finer points of his life. He'd made such mistakes before. In a hotel suite with Christian, when he tossed everything out onto the table and together they rummaged through the carnage of a life he'd much rather have put behind him. *This was a testament to Christian, because knowing a writer had consequences, and one needed to keep some secrets close to the vest or risk seeing them printed on paper one day, exposed for the whole world.*

COLE TRICKED MANY times with strangers who wanted it simple and to keep it unattached. He was used to the curt responses and awkward dances of those who hated offering too much information on a first encounter. How odd, that even though a man could be so guarded—not really knowing the stranger in the bed across from him—it never mattered once he found his dick growing hard and he was breathy with excitement to shove it in any available orifice. Funny how some people wouldn't eat a banana if there were black bruises on its skin, Cole thought, but they'd certainly jump at a chance to lick a stranger's cockhead without a care in the world.

He wondered what Gabe's story was. Typically, those who hid their secrets were usually married, or already had a lover at home they were cheating on. The silence, if questioned, was clear indication. It might as well have been a bright yellow safety sign on the side of the road saying CAUTION and showing a stick figure with falling rock dangers ahead. Some people enjoyed the danger affiliated with quick anonymous fucking. In the end, it's supposed to be about the sex anyway. Men didn't care about their fuckbuddies' dreams or aspirations, or favorite songs or colors, all that was nonsense unless it got them closer to the climax. Cole was one of those men. He told himself to accept the silence and simply enjoy the view of Gabriel's muscular frame stuffed into the seat next beside him. He knew that he was going to be a real firecracker in the sack.

They pulled up to a gated condo complex close to the main road, and in a rather self-congratulatory way Cole announced, "Well, this is my place."

IT APPEARED NICE enough, but then again in Gabe's rational white bread upbringing, every gay man's esthetic seemed alien to his own. Driving through, as the gate's arm swung up, the Nissan passed a stone façade archway. Quite an imposing entrance, Gabe thought, but only artificial pretense. Never the real display of security it should have shown. Still, it'd make their residents feel safer behind its rock and brick exterior. But it could never fully protect anyone. Even for a blind burglar, it offered zero challenges. He smiled as they pulled into a nearby parking space. He knew he'd never be caught dead living in a place like that. He couldn't exactly do normal.

He naturally felt a shade of envy when confronted with how the other half lived. He couldn't even begin to imagine how his life might've turned out if he'd been granted the same gifts as Cole. Gifts like the younger man's new shiny red Rogue with its showroom polished exterior and multitude of glowing dials and knobs that looked like the flight deck of a 747. The leather seats were pristine. Absent the worn patches, holes, and stains of the Chevy he'd been forced to drive when he left home as a boy, or the trusty Dodge pickup he drove now, currently held together by baling wire, rubber bands, and simple prayer. The truck was nothing but a constant reminder that he'd never have the same beautiful things others seemed to have in abundance and take for granted.

But an accumulation of nice things, as well as the efforts people expended to maintain them were the very things that made them weak and useless. They were destined to become fat, lazy, and unfocused. Like that parable of a lion yanked from the Serengeti Plains and locked away inside a cage, denied his all-consuming fight for food and jurisdiction of his own pride. Because that image was so crystal clear for him, he was able to release some of the resentment he felt inside, each one disappearing like smoke into the ether. Cole no doubt worked at some boring middle-management job, a life of mundane sojourns under the harshest of fluorescent lighting, where the walking dead ran their tedious mazes driven only by their blind and stupid instinct.

Gabe's life was adventurous, frequently testing his skills of survival in ways which only made him stronger. The truth of the matter was he didn't have all that this asshole had, but he was clearly the better man. If he was forced to step into this man's shoes and carry his burdensome life for even a single day, Gabe knew it wouldn't take long before he snapped. He pictured himself pulling out his old Glock 9mm from under his jacket and spraying bullets in all directions, taking out everyone on his floor before he was taken down by security. All before enjoying his first morning cup of coffee. No, his life may not be as grand as others, but he knew to feel pity for the driver of the shiny new Nissan Rogue.

Manicured grounds and freshly painted doors met him after he lumbered out of the vehicle. He followed Cole to his unit, and once the door opened, he saw that this was assuredly a gay man's residence, pristine and organized. It could've been a spread right out of *Better Homes and Gardens*. Civility was the word he'd first described Cole by and that came echoing back as they entered the home. But he wasn't fixated on the Berber carpeting, or the expensive modern objects de art poised throughout. He was looking for the bedroom. He was horny and didn't give one rat's ass about Cole's station in life. He just wanted to see that round ass perched on a bed primed for fucking. Nothing else mattered in that moment. "Want a bourbon and Coke? I recall that was your drink of choice," Cole asked as he clicked on a kitchen light.

There was the expectation of the dance he hated. "Maybe later," he said as he craned his head in a not so subtle indication he was spying for the bedroom.

"Then later it is," Cole replied as he began pulling the hoodie over his head. The words Penn State were emblazed on the back, and Church wondered if he'd graduated from there but asking would only instigate further conversation and that seemed unnecessary. Tossing the shirt aside, Cole walked past Gabriel and led him into the bedroom as his hands fumbled with the snaps of his loose-fitting jeans.

Gabe saw he'd been right about Cole's physique. He maintained the athletically toned and tanned body of a university senior. And, as the denim slipped below his ass cheeks, Gabe knew he'd been right about a lot of things. A meticulously made queen-sized bed awaited them, and as Gabe passed a bureau, he saw their reflection in the mirror mounted above. Cole turned and wriggled like a snake escaping its skin until he was as naked as the day he was born. But this one was no infant recently freed from the womb; he had a sizable erection pointing skyward. His cock was fatter than one might've expected, and a faint dotting of precum covered the head, visible only in the scant light from the hall.

COLE WONDERED IF his was the type of date who enjoyed kissing. Most tricks didn't, he found, but he did. He wanted to feel Gabriel's rough five-o'clock stubble scraping across his cheeks as much as he desperately wanted to feel it raking across his inner thighs. That raw burn of passion it created when his wet breathing made the flesh sting. And as abruptly as the question arose, it became instantly resolved. Gabriel reached over and forcibly yanked him closer with his open arm and drove his tongue deep into Cole's mouth, invading it like he needed to taste every wet space hidden inside.

With a large hand tightly holding the back of his neck, Cole was restrained. Like Gabriel was pressing him, pushing him to stand there and to willingly acquiesce to every command he might decide to utter. Cole felt a satisfying feeling of letting go, without ever really losing power or his control.

"I CAN'T WAIT to get inside you," Gabe whispered between breathy kisses.

After a few moments of exploration, the anticipation became overpowering, a feeling beyond anything either man was able to bear. Gabriel pushed him back a few feet; it showed only a modicum of Gabe's strength, not enough to unbalance him, but it did allow him room. He needed space so he might rip off his shirt and finally escape his Levi's, which were becoming tighter and more uncomfortable with every passing minute.

"Get naked," Gabriel ordered as he began to strip.

As Cole kicked off his shoes and wrestled out of his clothes, he was witness to what he now thought was the apex of every masculine dream and image from his childhood. And that masculinity was displayed rather wholly and in a very pleasing fashion. He stood there wide-eyed and respectful.

Watching Gabriel get undressed, he decided his was the epitome of what it's like to be the total male package; the way his muscles danced seductive under his chest hair and inched it's way southward. Cole then noticed the semi-erect cock as it bounced free while Gabriel wriggled out of his jeans. His first instinct was overwhelming, that desire to drop to his knees and wordlessly worship at the altar of such a supremely beautiful god.

In bed Cole felt a stiff, weighty cock at his abdomen, twitching in anticipation. Their kissing slowed the pace and created a different rhythm to their encounter. Running his fingers along the ridges of Gabriel's spine, he felt the sticky wetness of perspiration, and without even breaking stride, he reached over and allowed his fingers to disappear into the nightstand. After fumbling for a second, they emerged with a condom held in his fingertips, which he then tossed nonchalantly on the comforter for later.

GABE ALWAYS HATED using rubbers. Most times he didn't even make the pretense. He simply didn't see the point. He supposed his life would end in a flurry of bullets, and if he had to admit it to himself, he knew he didn't really much care what types of things his partners worried about. He never thought about pregnancy, and sexual diseases never really crossed his mind. For all his catting around, he'd been fortunate. And he'd never once had to pull into a town and accept those shots he'd heard that were given at the free clinics. He'd been blessed with cleaner tricks than most, he guessed. So why rock the boat now? But he didn't want a heavy discussion with Cole to ruin the mood, so he grabbed the condom and begrudgingly bent his will to someone else's.

This was different than with Chris—someone he had fabricated as being one of a kind. And although he'd gotten his wick wet a few times since they'd first met, he never allowed any real intimacy to intrude. This was something he reserved for Chris alone. How the hell had he permitted his life to become so fucking corrupted, he wondered?

That was his invading picture then, bursting in to cloud his mind when he knew that it shouldn't be there. All he could do was keep reminding himself: this was only an act of sexual release, nothing more. Still, he squinted hard—enough to cause his brain slight discomfort. And it worked temporarily to banish those thoughts and then he positioned Cole in such a way as to force his legs apart and burrowed down, intent on completing the task of sucking this man's dick. Come hell or high water, he'd get through it. He'd worry about it later, if a later came to pass where any of this sounded as important as it had before.

Before he could ravage his partner, Gabe sat up abruptly. He watched as Cole's hand palmed at the bedspread until he found the condom nearby and ripped it open with his teeth. Cole's fingers shook with excitement as he pushed the rubber down and covered Gabe's rigid shaft. He knew what his partner needed, so with one deep and sustaining rush of air, he took the plunge inside, never taking his eyes from Cole's, watching as he arched his back against the thrust, as if his parry had been meant to say *"What a lovely pain this is."*

THEY FUCKED FOR the next half hour as the younger man bucked and bent against Gabe's thrusts, amid furious perspiration and the grunting sounds of pleasure and pain. Gabe took him once atop the mattress before moving to the shower. They wrestled under the hot spray of the running water and screwed until the mirror was covered by the steam. Neither whispered any obligatory words of sweetness in the other's ears, nor was there the holding of hands or the gentle rake of fingers along the other's cheek. This time there was masculine energy and forcible sex, with the only words being phrases like "Suck, fella. And don't lose eye contact." This sex was an act for indulgence alone and plenty satisfying to both. Gabe considered later how Cole didn't need any training as a worthy bottom boy.

Lying back spent and happy, Gabe rested his head atop his interlocked fingers and stared at the ceiling quietly. Cole already jumped up to collect himself and had disappeared into the bathroom to rinse off. He thought about spending the night, and even though he hadn't been invited, he knew Cole was fairly smitten by then. And besides, sometimes simply having someone close had its own way of keeping bad memories at bay.

But bad memories were all he had left those days. And with the sound of running water as Cole showered alone, he was taken back to the beginning, to where it began. Gabriel never learned how to completely shut his brain down after sex, like most men did. All the energy he expelled only spurred old memories back to life. This was his hell, he surmised, reliving every dark place and corner of his life in his attempt to understand them. It reminded him of those ghosts he'd watched on TV shows, those who were trapped inside the void, unable or unwilling to reach the light and simply disappear. He was as imprisoned as they were, destined to perform the same tasks over and over again, like a machine. It also provided his reflection, his examination of the life he led, so he would see its causes. Trying to understand that exact point where it all shifted out of his control.

Chapter Four

BORN IN KENTUCKY and later raised in the hills of Tennessee, Gabriel Church grew up under the tutelage of a bitter father and weak-willed mother. Bennett Church was a tyrant of a man, evil and harsh. Gabriel learned quickly to hate his father and spent his childhood under the misconception that he would grow up and be nothing like the man. He had to consider now, as an adult, how much he'd failed in that respect.

Bennett showed himself as a twisted man, but only in the confines of his family home. To the world, he was the picture of civility. An honorable blue-collar worker with a lovely, churchgoing family, but behind the walls of their modest three bedrooms, the rules changed drastically. The beatings were frequent, and more often than not, out of proportion for the crime committed. The house had been his prison and his purgatory. But then he came of age and left home, setting out to make a life of his own—one that didn't include Bennett or those dried up little backwater towns he remembered from his childhood.

The leaves were turning pale yellow, the color of oxidized iron, by the time he'd found the courage to drive away that autumn of his sixteenth birthday. He expected a fight to be initiated as he loaded up his Chevelle with all his scarce possessions. Gabe figured Bennett might've raised his hands in anger before ever allowing his boy to up and leave home and abandon his responsibilities and family. He expected his mother would cry and plead for him to stay, as she cowered beneath Bennett's shadow, afraid to watch as her only son disappeared down the driveway and onto that long country road headed east. But she hadn't.

He was slightly surprised when she stoically wiped the faintest of tears from the corner of her eyes while hovering over his little sister, who'd been quietly standing like a statue in her modest floral dress and black patent-leather shoes. She appeared more like a doll than a living, breathing reminder. This was a picture that he knew would change him forever. Something he'd never fully be able to liberate from his life. Sissy nodded only once as she drew her daughter into an even tighter embrace.

Run! Her eyes implored. *Get out while you can, Gabe. Run far—run fast. Don't bother looking back. You needn't worry about either of us anymore. We'll be all right...I promise.*

He saw yearning plastered across her face, that subtle desire to scoop up her daughter in her arms and make a sprint for the Chevelle herself. To land her own escape with someone she'd raised who mercifully possessed more strength than anything she could've mustered on her own. Instead, she just stood there silently, a balled tissue in her hand and a faint smile appearing to be sadness mixed with unfathomable relief.

Bennett screamed out what a pussy his son was, coughing out the edict that he'd fuck up soon enough and he'd come crawling back to huddle under his mama's apron before long. He seemed not to want to watch as Gabriel pulled out of the driveway, so he sulked back inside even before Gabe's fingers turned the ignition key. In his rearview, the boy saw the living room curtains being pulled aside and realized how much he wanted to see Bennett's face as he drove away. But the only movements he saw were the curtains and his mother and sister waving and crying from the front yard. Even now, all he was able to remember was the sense of sadness and freedom he'd felt driving down the hilltop, realizing that however much he thought he loved his mother and sister, he knew with stone-carved certainty he'd never see any of them ever again.

He'd bailed on crazy and decided any life he made for himself would surely be better than the one he'd left behind. With little funds and a vehicle that'd already seen too many miles on the road, he should've been more worried. But instead he was confident in his wherewithal to survive any adversity. And for the most part, he had. He'd traveled through no-name towns not much bigger than a spit stain on the highway. He found legitimate work whenever possible and resorted to theft when he couldn't. His biggest challenge by far was in keeping his car running smoothly. In more than one city, Gabe forced the Chevy to limp from one place to another, held together by prayers, duct tape, and wire.

Church never spoke to his father again, nor did he ever learn what became of him. And with God's mercy, some destinies are occluded from us for good reason...*and this was one.* Gabriel hadn't seen how his father's excessive drinking only grew worse after Sissy successful escaped. He hadn't known that one of the Church's closest land neighbors, old man Farenthold, as little Gabe often called him, on that day and on a whim decided to stop in as a welfare check and would discover Bennett dead in his house all alone. Farenthold wasn't a kind man but the absence of seeing Bennett's work truck barreling down their shared country roads for days piqued his interest. Plus, he knew the stories; knew how things spiraled out of control for his neighbor during those last months. Everyone in those parts knew the gossip. He found Bennett still sitting in that same ugly old easy chair which'd become his throne. There were piles of bent aluminum cans and an empty bottle which once held a fifth of bourbon scattered around his feet. The television was still on, playing in the background when he gingerly opened the kitchen door and called out for Bennett. He'd passed away several days earlier by the looks of him, and not unsurprisingly the medical examiner listed the cause of death as severe cirrhosis of the liver. If Gabe had been privy to that knowledge, he might've disputed it.

It wasn't disease that killed his old man, he believed, it'd been his abject failure to hold his family intact.

His father's death hadn't counted as a tragedy in his life since Gabriel was unaware it occurred. But the true, vicious calamity was how it affected his relationship with his mother and younger sister. Not wanting to stand in the shade of his father's shadow also meant never seeing them again either, and secretly, even Church was left wondering if he saw Bennett in the face of all his future victims.

EVERY KILL GABE committed was born from his twisted devotion to an unknowable God, save for the first. That one occurred early on, barely a few weeks after he left home when he was just learning about himself and verging on his own manhood at the unseasoned age of twenty-one. It all began on a desolate gravel road on the outskirts of Dallas, Texas. It was the first of many of his trips cutting across our country, and the first of many times he'd see the neon of the city's glorious night skyline. There'd been no white radiance to direct him then, and nothing to show him his part in a grander plan. He'd been a faceless nobody and there'd been no mission to occupy Church at the time. He was an overweight fucker who smoked fat stinky cigars and possessed shitty poker manners. No, that particular violence was bred out of nothing more than his frustration and anger. To a world he felt he'd been tossed into as casually as Bennett once tossed a tow sack filled with screaming newborn kittens into the Caney Valley River.

He'd chosen to dispose of them before his children stumbled onto them, knowing their old pregnant barn cat was about to drop her litter. He didn't need them finding them or growing instantly attached. But Gabe did see. He'd been hiding behind the stacks of timber and half-empty cans of house paint they stored in the barn. He watched Bennett scooping them up and stuffing them in the tow sack and then followed as he headed toward the water. He never said anything as the sack went under, never tried to stop his father or rescue the helpless creatures. But it did leave a noticeable scar. And in many ways the wound had never scabbed over, it altered Gabe forever...particularly with how he saw death and betrayal. He hadn't intervened with his father, knowing his backside would've felt the sting of Bennett's belt. And in the end, the kittens would've still been drowned. He couldn't have changed a thing. But his anger grew and was directly linked to why he chose to beat that particularly unpleasant man to death just outside Dallas. At least he'd not have to suffer through his stale cigar smoke any longer, he thought as blood flew off his knuckles and scattered in all directions.

And the last, many years later, was the murder of Shea Baltimore. Out of all the killings he committed, he knew hers would be the one he'd have to eventually pay the dearest for. And he knew that cost was fast approaching a much-needed reimbursement. But then, in the heat of it, Shea represented a tangible threat to both Christian and himself. And so, he made a cold, calculated decision to stifle the danger—thereby saving the only other thing he'd ever found a value for in his life.

With so many white-lighter kills under his belt, Gabe no longer pictured the faces of every victim. But Shea was different. He still easily recalled how her throat felt in his hand and how she struggled, with flaying arms and the wide-eyed surprise on her face. Even now he felt the tears streaming down her cheeks and falling like raindrops on his wrist. And like a nightmare, it came back many times to haunt him. Of how fragile she'd been, like a broken-winged bird trapped inside his massive fingers. He played the scene over and over in his mind, mostly because she wasn't supposed to die. There'd been no booming voice directing him to end her as it had before. Hers was simply another sad necessity and far from the perfect crime. In the end, killing her only backfired and placed Christian in even greater peril than if he'd just let her live. It was just regret in a litany for his collection.

At first, it'd been his criminal past which instigated his first meeting with Chris. But the death of Shea united them in ways that neither of them could've foreseen. His part-time lover had become his accomplice, without either of them ever intending it, a mortal sin they shared together. As if being around each other only allowed the writer to inhale the contagion of Gabriel's worst parts. But he understood how there was no turning back now. The deed was already done and couldn't be taken away so easily. But, that single mistake had more ramifications than any other kills he remembered. This was a murder he felt tied to and one destined to change his fate...or at least one he hoped to have with Christian one day.

Later that same morning after the sun was up, Cole drove them both back to the bar to retrieve Gabe's truck. They drove in silence as Gabe stared out the passenger window and watched a parade of buildings pass by, seeing his own reflection in the glass staring back at him. Gabe was lost in thought because after years of being alone he discovered he was finding comfort in looking back as much as forward. He'd never felt guilt and he wasn't feeling it now. He wasn't consumed by those types of emotions as most men might be after having fucked a man. He'd once considered himself straight, he now figured he was straight but had a tendency to lean when the right winds blew – *so to speak*. Gabe saw Christian Maxwell's face in his mind, and he wondered what his former lover might think of him if he saw him now.

Cole pulled up next to Gabe's truck, which was still sitting alone in the back of the Crash Landing parking lot. The fresh light of morning might turn casual moments awkward. They were two strangers who'd tricked with a minimum of words and found themselves fumbling over what to say next.

Cole handed him a business card as he opened the car door. "Uh, give me a call, yeah? We should do this again."

Gabe smiled back as he accepted the offer. He knew the rules, and there wasn't any doubt in Gabe's mind they'd never meet again. Their passions were exhausted, and the tank was running on fumes. He never played games with strangers because he couldn't manipulate their civilities. He didn't much care what others thought, so he shoved the car door closed with his hip, gave another nod, then turned and walked to his truck, pulling keys from his pocket. He was grateful to be finally alone in the light of day, and as he watched Cole pull out into the street, ostensibly heading to his job, he wondered what his next step would be after driving back to the Palmetto to check out.

A crisp breeze through his open window slapped at his face, bringing him back to reality even more. The music from his truck stereo was playing Bob Seger's "The Famous Final Scene," and it reminded Gabe of his relationship with Chris. He turned up the volume, his way of clouding his brain from those thoughts, but it only served to open a crack in the floodgates and a barrage of memories to wash through. His life on the road was an existence spent completely alone, and it'd done a number on him. He lived in the shadows with his secrets and his crimes, and he could honestly say through all his travels there hadn't been a single soul who had truly known him...at least not until Christian. *I am becoming quite the pussy.* He was spending all that wasted energy thinking about love, and nearly becoming obsessed, he feared...like some schoolgirl content to glue the photos of her latest crush inside her journal late at night.

And that wasn't him, Goddamn it!

He wondered how he'd allowed this man to infect his brain as much he had. A chill ran down his spine before he realized it couldn't be the temperature outside; this was San Antonio, after all. He rolled the window up, nonetheless, and hoped no one who passed him in traffic could tell he was mouthing the words to the Segar song and bobbing his head to match the music.

Before Chris, he'd always been certain of his purpose—to eliminate the white-lighters revealed for his benefit. But now he was in purgatory, a dead man walking through life without a proper course. He had to escape Seattle and Chris because he'd allowed his desires to get the better of him. He'd been forced to commit a murder that was outside of his usual divine and sacrificial targets. Shea was young and pretty, and she'd offered herself freely. So why wouldn't he accept it? Possibly he was thinking with his cockhead more than he should have, but how was he to know the writer would spill his guts in jealousy? Whatever his reasoning, Chris put them both at risk, forcing Gabe to take action to silence Shea. That was the cause behind the rift, the thing that would divide them forever. *Damn, so many regrets.*

And he did miss the man. He couldn't escape that reality despite his best efforts. And surprisingly the idea of a life together in Costa Rica, which Chris painted for his benefit, was certainly alluring. But now it felt like waking up late on judgment day and missing the invitation for the free ride upstairs, and another bitter pill to swallow.

From childhood, Church maintained a strong religious conviction despite what others may have incorrectly presumed. He fully expected the rapture to happen one day, probably not in his lifetime, but it had been foretold. Or at least that's what their priest warned them all from his perch behind the altar. Young Gabe always assumed even a real sinner such as his father somehow knew when God was watching. That he could look down and see an image of a loving traditional family and forgive them their faults. But as it turned out for him, God wasn't any different than any of the others in his congregation. No one ever wanted to examine deeper, or to even try to learn where those dangerous fissures first began.

If anyone had ever asked, they might have learned how important those windows were to Gabriel's story. The stained-glass windows of St. Ignatius were lovely and showed righteous depictions of figures swathed in robes, resting in radiant circles of amber lights spotlighting down from the heavens. Even as a small boy he'd been captivated as he stared at them with austere fascination. This was the instant when such a focused mind, like Gabe's, first became fixated on all the questions that would one day plague him. Staring at the saints and angels, it strangely became all jumbled and disordered in his mind. The holiness and reverence he saw were suddenly twisted into a new and an unexpected sensation. This was in that pivotal moment while archaic to him, he'd become an effective killing machine, operating on a bent ideology of mercy.

They were unprecedented incidents, which by themselves should hold no gravity. But somehow, they had. Even the smallest and most obscure flashes can bear a mark, and for Gabriel, it was the stained-glass windows with their beautifully colored splinters of light dancing around his feet. It all began one Sunday morning when Sissy leaned down to her son and pointed to a window up above. In the glass, Gabe saw an illustration of an angel hovering over the ground and blowing a long horn. Every cut shard surrounding the angel seemed gilded and radiated with shades of gold and yellows the color of summer squash.

"That's how you got your name, son," Sissy whispered in his ear. "He is the angel Gabriel, and your daddy let me name you after him. Not at this place, but back in Kentucky at our old church when I saw a similar window there. You were named after an arc angel, my love... Isn't it wonderful?"

Little Gabe was transfixed, but not on the window with his namesake, but on the others that showed great figures bathed in a glow of celestial light. One window showed the traditional image of St. Francis of Assisi; another showed St. Peter of Canterbury standing in a pool of water, no doubt a catholic rendition of his life before drowning as he crossed the English Channel. Each figure was bathed in that same radiance, and as the priest told him in one Sunday sermon, they were special and therefore chosen by God for a divine purpose. The moment when Gabe first saw the light shining down on people and was blinded by its brilliance, his career in murder began. And although bright for him, it'd been a special kind of light, one which others couldn't always see. He remembered trying to explain it to Christian as they were lounging in that posh hotel back in Seattle. Somehow it seemed reasonable to him, *clear as day*, he remembered saying. How every stranger had potential for radiating that unusual glow to show their divinity. It became an invitation for his eyes alone, and whether it came from God or somewhere else, it still felt like a solid belief he could find comfort in. An unwavering rock he could stand upon and know he wasn't about to tumble into a chasm

When he explained this to his biographer, he expected to get "that" look returned. And he had. Gabe wasn't crazy, though he knew how crazy it sounded. He understood how others might hear his story and gingerly rise from their chairs and back out of the room slowly, a look of cautious uncertainty and fear upon their faces...but he knew he wasn't crazy. This was why Gabriel never told a living soul about his visions, at least not until Christian wanted to write it down for posterity, somehow making it sound necessary.

Because Gabe was sane, he was able to see the inevitable outcomes as clearly as he did. He knew his future settled somewhere between the pages of his capture and redemption, or that split second of cold reality when everyone understood he wouldn't allow himself to be taken alive by force. Then his only available recourse would become his suicide by cop. He'd always pictured being confronted by police on some tiny inner-city street. He saw the hail of bullets and knew there would be men who'd lose their lives that day.

Then again, that became an image he'd recalled watching in old black-and-white gangster flicks, and in truth had no basis in reality. But he'd pictured the scene in his mind nonetheless. Once the pungent aroma of nitroglycerin-soaked gunpowder dispersed into the air and the screams of passersby caught in the fray eventually died down, Gabe would hope it might be him lying face down on the asphalt. He wasn't a murderer, not by his sick reckoning. Though he rarely considered the immense, sweaty poker player back in Texas whom he murdered at the tender age of twenty-one. He refused to ruminate over that one because, in his mind, the shithead got everything he deserved. Gabe considered his work missionary in nature, and the only one he had to face for his crimes would be the man upstairs, not the FBI and certainly not the local authorities.

When the realization overtook him that his work would end and his life would be forfeit, he'd reached the sad conclusion no one would ever know his story but him. And this knowledge had its own hidden tragedy. But then he met Christian. A failed writer with kind eyes who wanted to tell his personal insights to the world and explain away the madness and the killings and the motivations behind each and every seemingly random murder. It didn't exactly go as planned.

It'd been a strange beginning, for an even stranger relationship. One built by questions from Gabe, like *why would anyone want to write about the horrors bouncing inside my skull?* Or *why would someone take the legal risk of writing about a serial killer and not contacting the police after learning his identity?*

There were a lot of questions Christian never really answered, but somewhere in the first few conversations, they shared it no longer mattered. Because Gabe got to tell his outlandish story for the first time in his life and Christian got to spend some time with a very interesting and dangerous man.

There were days spent together in the hotel suite, where the writer asked about Gabe's childhood and how he felt about those he'd killed. Christian wrote down everything he said for a book that might never be written. It was the origin of their relationship and there had been a purpose for each interview, but after their relationship changed to one of lovers, it altered the course of what they were doing. Christian would never have been able to capture Church's story without admitting to his involvement in a questionable relationship. If a story of their relationship became public, the authorities would immediately pick up Christian, possibly only to learn what involvement he'd had in a young girl's murder, or maybe to ascertain why he hadn't contacted police when he suspected the murders had continued. Either way, he was truly fucked.

San Antonio was a long way from Seattle and Christian. Eight-lane interstates now replaced its expansive plains where cattle used to graze, and cars dotted the landscape that once held only blackjack trees and scrub oak saplings, a place in Gabe's mind should have been an absence of activity, save for the occasional dart of a rabbit or a coyote in the distance behind rolling sagebrush tumbleweeds. Instead, it seemed immeasurable, particularly from the highest overpasses with the city stretching far to the horizon. And though he hated it, he had to admit it had some features he wanted to see more of, like the Riverwalk and the chic touristy bars in the arts district.

After reaching the Palmetto Inn, Church showered one last time and cleaned up before heading out. The opportunities for better hygiene and restful sleep were scarce when money was his greatest issue. He would have to do something about that later, he figured, but for now, all he wanted to do was take a tour of the Riverwalk before he left, just to see all he could see, as his mother was fond of saying.

Chapter Five

EVEN FROM WHEN he was very young, Gabe believed in destiny. It'd been heavily ingrained into his life via every Christian parable he'd ever been taught along the way, crafted by those years he sat hunkered in the pews, silently pretending to pray while shrinking beneath Bennett's scornful gaze. And even with as many reasons as he had to not keep his convictions, he'd never wavered in his faith. Not on that single point anyway.

He was a boy who might've easily stirred his doubts into hatred, but even despite his many odds, he felt there must be something more out there…something more for him. Even in the steadfast belief his God existed, he wondered, *why is everyone free and running through those silly mazes, so unaided, unprotected, and alone?* Was he watching from the heavens with a smile? Did mortal man represent comical amusement? *God might have simply been trying to see some value in the microbes in the glass*, he'd thought, but if that was the case, as Gabriel suspected, he may be sorely disappointed in the end.

So his belief in the Almighty was unassailable. But he believed just as fiercely in the idea of fatalistic destiny. He remembered mentioning it once to the writer back in Seattle, prior to them crawling like horny thieves across the carpeted floor and screwing there in the center of Maxwell's suite inside the luxurious Mayflower Park Hotel.

He remembered Christian looking at him quizzically, almost as if Gabe didn't understand the contrast of his own words. Only a fool believed two such opposing ideologies, because they had a tendency to cancel each other out in the end. But Church was adamant in his belief that both could coexist simultaneously. His theories may have been born in his Catholic days at St. Ignatius, but since escaping Bennett and his family, he'd seen a significant absence of God in the minutia of mortal survival. He figured God wasn't too interested in what puny, insignificant humans did on this insignificant blue planet, because Fate handled that division…and in Gabe's opinion God and Fate weren't the types to get along.

Church had been constructed by unusual notions from the get-go. He believed his Lord directed him to kill and still believed Fate put every divine soul in his path to complete that cycle. He believed his life and story had already been prewritten, that he was only running lines on stage, like a dress rehearsal before the opening. If that were true, he had to consider himself a terrible actor, because he'd only scanned the script, reading ahead to see how much dialogue he still had left. Although he couldn't see the future, he felt confident he had a part to play and a tragic ending as his ultimate and final death scene; another reason Christian had become so important from the outset. He was like a prophet sent to record Gabe's tale so all the weak-willed cannon fodder around him might comprehend his mission and appreciate how much he wasn't crazy. For those who considered him unbalanced, well, they'd have to face the grand deity themselves with all their slanderous accusations. They'd find no support, and they would risk being hollowed into an empty husk by some hellacious inferno of God's wrath.

Gabe never asked himself what happened to the souls he sent to heaven. He wasn't sure if it was cleansing incineration for wickedness committed or a calling he'd yet to divine. But it never mattered, because after his mother bled him out, long after he'd seen the beautiful stained-glass windows in St. Ignatius, he'd decided Fate and the Almighty worked specifically through him. He didn't remember if Christian had ever given his opinion of his rather odd viewpoints, because all he remembered was fucking on the floor, and then again in the shower before heading downstairs and into the streets to find a nearby café for dinner.

Cars weaved dangerously onto onramps as everyone was frantically trying to make it to offices, day jobs, or the nearest shopping malls. Everyone was out to make a living, but for him life was different. In the burbs, Gabe made a living with a towel and a pair of shorts. Stopping in at motel pools, appearing like any other guest out for a swim. His true intention was spying for purses sitting open by the women tanning themselves on chaise lounges.

Gabriel wasn't vain, but he knew what catnip a strong physique might be for a lonely female traveler, and he knew how to work the tourist trade even better than the brown-skinned boys from the beaches of Puerto Vallarta. But it was more than loose change he'd be begging for. Motel pools were ideal because husbands rarely swam with their families, but mothers knew the importance of getting screaming children out of tiny motel rooms and into pools. It meant they'd sit in quiet solitude, possibly reading and tanning their alabaster skins as urchins on sugar highs splashed and frolicked at their feet. It was the perfect savanna for hunting when you had a build like Gabriel's. And if his target was a lone single woman, he often used his skills to get her to draw him to her room for sweaty sex between the sheets.

Purses and pocketbooks were easy, and when they weren't available, there were pool for money and poker with betting. He considered his petty theft something few would miss, and his efforts enabled him to stay off the grid and under anyone's radar. He'd never been arrested or ticketed for any of his minor crimes for cash because he was that good. A tempting smile went a long way for him, and he could be charming and self-effacing whenever he needed. Christian had chuckled and called him *whore* when he'd explained how he maintained his existence back in Washington. Remembering that incident brought a faint grin to his face and he found pleasure in the fact the writer hadn't judged him harshly, as others might've.

"You do what you have to if you want to survive, little buddy," Church had offered over Christian's raucous laughter. It had been one of the first times they'd discussed his manner of survival or money during one of their many frequent interviews in the Mayflower. He had to admit they'd been a little drunk by then after Maxwell had purchased a bottle of premium bourbon and carried it back to their suite as entertainment and distraction. They were inebriated more often than he cared to admit, but a necessary evil when Christian was asking him to reveal his deepest, darkest secrets. The only way he'd get to the impervious truth was by laced libation and longing looks of sympathy and interest. One of Gabe's fondest memories came from them sitting on the sofa in the spacious suite at the Mayflower in their underwear, close enough that their knees were touching. They were already high on bourbon and colas, laughing and joking with one another well into the night. Something Gabriel never expected or experienced before, as unfathomable as they may've sounded to anyone with a normal upbringing.

The last friend he remembered having was long before he left home. He was a neighborhood kid and they'd been about ten years old. He couldn't remember the boy's name anymore, but he remembered hating it when he heard the boy's family was moving away. By the time Gabe had sped off in his Chevelle and put Tennessee in his rearview, he'd lost any opportunity of having a friend. Life on the road was often harsh and lonely, and the first person he'd taken the time to get become acquainted with Christian. He knew Chris was unable to comprehend that, such an awful, inconceivable truth for most normal folks. But when running from the police and living like an abandoned dog on the run and rummaging for scraps to survive, having a BFF isn't even in the scope of consideration.

GABRIEL STEERED HIS pickup onto the overpass so that he might make the Riverwalk before San Antonio's humidity made it unbearable. While Cole had been in the shower, Gabe had lifted the cash from his wallet, about ten singles and a couple of twenties. But regardless of how little he'd pocketed, he thought the whole encounter had turned into a nice distraction. He smiled when he realized what a fucking whore he'd become, screwing anything and anyone, just to get the fuel money the Dodge required.

What would my mother think of me now? Not that Sissy Church would have understood his life, or what he'd become. But he still thought of her fondly, sitting with her hands folded in a pew at St. Ignatius. Dressed in her prettiest finery and looking so prim and proper. *Quite the façade, so very different than the woman at home who always appeared to be hiding from Bennett by spending time in the kitchen. Her hands forever drenched in a sudsy sink.* Gabe had watched his mother like she was an enigma, something he couldn't quite fathom completely, but still he tried.

Sissy always kept a vigilant eye out for little Claire, who Gabe remembered was always playing on the bare linoleum floor of the kitchen like a cat transfixed by the whirling dust bunnies. She was frail and weak, but he loved his sister, nonetheless. It had been a reward leaving his father, and it hadn't been that traumatic leaving his mother, but he'd always regretted leaving Claire to the life he'd successfully escaped. Still, any true feelings he had for family would never have been sufficient cause to keep him tethered there. Like a gangrened limb, he cut it from his life and never looked back; the necrosis of dead tissue no longer necessary to maintain. He wouldn't have survived Tennessee if he hadn't made the hard decisions in those early years and how he'd managed to make other choices later, difficult ones...ones that had devastating and lasting resolutions.

He'd seen the look in his mother's eyes; saw the weariness staring back at him as if he was just another reminder of Bennett Church. He understood her fear, felt her wonder if he too would someday develop the same idiosyncratic ticks and penchant for volatile, angry outbursts that Bennett had. He hadn't always been that way, she recalled. In the beginning, he'd been a very kind and patient man. But sadly, Gabe was beginning to see how his mother was distancing herself from him. Saw how she was losing faith that she'd be able to even keep him safe for much longer. Like she'd found strange writing on the wall and felt dread as she dutifully sponged it off with soap and water. She did, however, retain a certain amount of hopeful optimism when it came to her daughter. There's no way for him to know that she thought. Just as her son had done when he pulled out that last ugly weed and drove away at aged twenty-one and never looked back.

There were things Church would never learn because he never went back to Tennessee. He'd never called home or cared enough to inquire. Sissy would eventually leave Bennett, mostly to salvage a life with little Claire. She would pack her bags one afternoon without any indication of trouble and she would take her daughter's tiny hand in hers and phone for a taxi. She would make her own escape and travel upstate to her sister's place. She would simply disappear from her husband's life one day, without ever speaking a word in regards to it. Bennett would accept his new situation with a gruff *who gives a shit* exclamation and wallow away in his beer and bourbon and his television until he was nothing more than a shell of pissed-off personality disorders. Many years later he would succumb to cirrhosis and show signs of a failing heart while still sitting in that same comfy chair Gabe had watched him sit in when he was a boy. But he never heard those details, and even if he had, it wouldn't have made a difference in how he lived his life or the choices he made. The damage was irreparable and nothing but dead tissue already excised from Church's life completely. In his mind, this was how it's supposed to work.

Chapter Six

GABE SAW FACADES from trendy restaurants in the distance and realized he was closing in on the Riverwalk district. He took the Commerce Street exit and maneuvered his truck into the far lane. With his window down, he almost smelled the water rising from the canals; as if he'd crossed a European border into another unique country with its own scents and cultures. He had the same reaction he walked onto Bourbon Street in N'awlins; an alien disconnect of a city unlike any other he'd experienced before. He'd seen every aspect of city life in his travels, trudged through countless towns, boroughs, and counties. He'd been a ghost in most places, a whisper of a passerby and forgettable stranger by most he encountered as a tourist. This became just another ideal quality separating Church from other murderers: his ability to move deftly through a crowd whenever he needed. He had become a deft killer with a fastidious attention to the smallest of details.

In his mind, he was no boogeyman, no evil incarnate reaping carnage on the victimless. He had a calling and only murdered to complete a goal. And always only when he encountered someone bathed in the glow of radiance told him that was his next target. He stalked and followed because he was good at it. He watched and waited with patience because that was something he had learned. When the opportunity presented itself, he would take a life, but he never relished the act. He never felt hatred or deep-seated emotions for the ones he was called to dispatch. He did it because it had become his cause, his mission, and it originated from the colored glass windows of the old St. Ignatius Cathedral, while in the company of his family.

He rarely killed with a pistol. Choosing instead to use whatever might be at hand as if it had been designed with God in mind. At the moment of each predestined death, whatever light that emanated from them always seemed to be shared. Like an explosion Gabriel couldn't determine was real or a simple fabrication of his brain; the two figures, killer and victim, were awash in the same glowing radiance. After the fireworks of yellows and pale greens had subsided, Gabe felt every sin that he as well as his victim had ever experienced, being yanked from their bodies, and then pulled magnetically upward. Although he didn't relish the killing per say, he did find the rapture of the act itself exhilarating. Once the afterglow had become nothing but cinder and the clean, pristine wash had overtaken him, he'd drop the body and then walk away.

Even though he had never attempted to dispose of a body, or hide his crime in any way, he'd never even gotten close to getting caught. This was a fact not lost on Gabriel. He trusted this was sufficient proof that what he was doing was some form of ecclesiastical enterprise. Walking away from a lifeless corpse, he'd never felt remorse. For him, a simple unadorned truth, and as he'd told himself many times before, this was God's will, and his target was no doubt carried up to heaven on wings of angels. Wings like his. Doing what they were commanded in some twisted salvation of the human soul.

He had taken many lives, across many states, but never felt the brutality of killing touch his soul. He had become a master hunter, skilled with taking a life both mercifully and quickly. Like field dressing a stag, it carried the same emotional baggage, just another task done with blind rote purpose to see it through to completion. Because he rarely killed in the same city or same state, he didn't think local authorities had ever made a connection to a traveling serial killer. His modus operandi varied greatly; the victims followed no specific profile, and there was no robbery or malice. There was a significant absence of any linking relationship of victim to killer, and if the FBI had made the correlations from body to body, they would not, or could not, suspect Gabriel Church as the killer. He was a man who lived as far off the grid as humanly possible. He was a drifter without cause, floating as aimlessly as a leaf might on a windy day.

No witness had ever stepped up or described him to police, nor had he ever left any DNA behind to stain his crime scenes, at least not to his knowledge. But even if he had, he knew none of his genetic markers had ever been typed before then. Hell, he'd only ever been arrested on a public intox charge, and that occurred when he was still a kid in a small Kentucky backwater town and years before the term DNA had ever crept into the vocabularies of the police, reporters, or their judicial counterparts.

It'd been a difficult life for sure. He didn't possess anything as normal as a cell phone. Not that prior to Chris he'd ever even found someone he needed to talk to with any regularity. Once he did find himself fighting that urge to hear his friend's voice on the line, he knew locating a pay phone along the interstate was becoming a thing rarer than gold. He lacked many amenities, but he was a survivor. During the long lonely spells of driving, whenever he really needed to hear Christian giving him another of his many encouraging little speeches, he had to find a diner with a working pay phone outside. He wondered how life had ever existed before the advent of cellular technology.

He always hoped Chris would tell him he'd been thinking about Gabe as much as he was thinking about him. What else can a man ponder over when trapped behind the steering wheel for hours on end with the country music blasting from the speakers, reminding him of all the things he'd left behind? Chris was his only true connection to those things which were supposed to feel normal. Like a late-night call on a near-empty parking lot of some no-named truck stop in Kansas? He didn't exactly know if his writer even wanted to hear his voice. Things had been left badly, and the last killing might've been the one Christian found it too difficult to be able to handle. He also had to consider the police might have tapped Christian's phone by then, possibly after connecting somehow to Shea's murder.

Suddenly the thought of meandering through crowds of tourists amid expensive shops and cafés sounded like a very unappealing plan. Too fucking hot for that to be fun, he determined. So, turning the wheel, Church decided to leave the Riverwalk tours behind, choosing instead to locate the nearest bar that would be dark, quiet and where there were far too many neon signs and stale nicotine clouding the walls. He wanted the kind of establishment built solely for the lonely, a place where they could meet up at night and drink fistfuls of major jar served beer—a place where the alcohol poured liberally and was strong enough to wash even the blackest of memories clean.

Gabe had always known how things around him were destined to crumble, how everything decayed and eventually turned to dust. That had been a lesson learned first at St. Ignatius, then later as he drove out from his parents' drive with his tires burning rubber while he made his great escape. He'd also learned it in every life he'd taken and seen it on the faces of the corpses as their lights became extinguished. It made his a fatalistic personality with every step. It seemed preordained his friendship with Christian would come to an end, but he'd been the only living soul who knew Gabe best. Not since he was a boy trailing Sissy Church as she shopped at the local grocer or prepared their family meals had anyone taken the time to get to know him as a person. But he didn't confuse Christian with his mother, Sissy, because in his heart Gabe only loved one.

Scanning the streets for the closest open bar, Gabe passed a small Catholic parish cathedral sitting off Grand Street that caught his eye. It's possible it reminded him of his family church back in Tennessee, or it only looked inviting, but he turned back on the next block to make another pass. The building was old, but not dilapidated. It had a tall ornate spire roof topped with a white cross reminiscent of the Christmas trees from his childhood. Bennett had long insisted on having a cross atop their holiday tree. In lieu of the more atypical Christmas angels, Gabe might've preferred. You didn't argue with your father with those kinds of battles, they weren't the hills you wanted to die on.

The top spires were gray with overlapping shingles, but the church itself was a bland taupe-brick structure, smaller than his St. Ignatius recollection, but its architecture gave a haughty appearance of something bigger than its mass. As he passed it again, driving his truck slower, he noticed the signage out front. It read, "St. Joseph's Church of the Acclaimed," and below that, "est. 1907." It sat on the corner of Grand and bordered an empty lot but seemed comfortably nestled in, as if it had always been there, simply watching as the city grew up around it. It surprisingly only had one tree on the property, besides the small insignificant shrubbery at its ostentatious entrance. A tall yellow poplar sat beside the church in full bloom of bright buttery foliage. It made a stark ecclesiastic image in Gabe's perception. A single blazing bush like the one Moses was confronted with in those old Sunday-school lessons. It beckoned him for reasons he didn't understand, and even with his desire for a drink still wet on his tongue, he pulled over to stare in amazement. Thin arched windows were cut into the brick façade embossed with the multicolored glass he remembered so well from his youth. Dirty asphalt streets and weathered buildings around the corner gave the little parish a disjointed feeling but a welcoming one for all to enter. And Gabe decided he would.

Turning off the ignition, the engine rumbled down, and the driver's side door creaked loudly when he opened it, reminding him he was in need of newer transportation. Clouds came from nowhere and quickly made the skies overcast as he walked slowly up the steps to the large double-door entrance. Being later in the morning and midweek, he couldn't be sure if he'd see anyone in the chapel. But he felt as if he needed to see inside, to refresh his memories of St. Ignatius. He noticed an elderly woman seated behind a glass-encased office at the farthest point of the foyer. But before he could ask, he saw a doorway marked Winslow Chapel, and brazenly he strolled in. He wasn't a parishioner there at St. Joseph's and anyone might have stopped him he worried. But this was a church, and all were supposed to be welcome inside.

The tiny chapel was empty, but candles were still burning in the corner, marking the last visitors seeking solace there. The altar up front was a contrast of unpretentiousness, at least in relation to the ornate architecture of the building itself. The lectern where the priest spoke his sermons was nothing more than modest mahogany with a single red sash hanging as its only decoration. Gabe could almost smell the history in the line of pews, bringing flashes of childhood memories back to the forefront.

What the hell am I doing here? He asked himself. He was a killer after all, and he knew that…but how odd it felt being back inside such a haunting recollection of his past. *Are all churches simply mirrored reflections of the ones from my childhood?"*

As he soaked in the quiet atmosphere, a noise from behind startled him. He turned and saw a priest entering from the rear of the chapel. He was about sixty or so, Gabe figured. He appeared to be a wise and paternal presence, calm and devout, and the embodiment of the kind of man his parishioners might find comfort in.

"Excuse me, young man," the priest whispered as he brushed past Gabe and headed to the altar. He was carrying a lush potted ivy, which he placed on a shelf against the back wall under a faded wooden crucifix figurine hanging as their represented deity. *He must be preparing for the next service,* so he turned on his heel to leave before old ladies with big handbags might block his escape.

"You don't have to leave son…" the priest called out. "I'm not familiar with your face, but all are welcome here in St. Joseph's. Sit a spell and let me get to know you."

Even with the memory of his recent fuck still lingering and the unquenched desire for hard booze present, he turned back to face the older man and seemed frozen by the kind eyes staring back at him.

What the hell. Why not?

But deciding to remain in the church, when every fiber was screaming at him and shouting how this was the occasion when he needed to run most, wasn't exactly as easy as one might assume. Ignoring every instinct, Gabe rushed quickly to the front and hastily made the sign of the cross against his heart, like Bennett had instructed so many years before. Then he slipped nervously into the closest pew and bowed his head as if in silent prayer.

He certainly had ample time, so why not stick around and check it out? Later he'd tell himself it had been those kindly priest eyes that had held him so firmly. That, somehow, they'd drawn him in as if they possessed some secret truth twinkling beneath the blue.

AFTER PLACING THE ivy where he wanted it, Father Albert Kait ambled over and took a seat in the pews, directly in front of the newcomer.

"I'm Father Kait," he said quietly, his head facing forward. He didn't turn around to engage his visitor. He knew what things might draw a sinner into a house of God and knew the deference it took to be an effective clergyman.

"Father," the man said as a baritone-voiced introduction.

"Are you looking for comfort or salvation, my son?"

The question surprised Gabe at first, but he grinned widely, his eyes still trained on the floor in obedient fashion. "Both I suppose," he said softly.

"Confessional is always free, son," the priest said.

"I don't think you have enough hours before your next service to hear my all my confessions, Father," Gabe said with a twinge of honest despondency.

"No service this afternoon, young man, so I'd guess you'd be mistaken." With that, the old man rose and headed toward a booth without looking back. He then secured the door to wait for what Gabe assumed was his way of offering a welcoming gesture. Before he could thoroughly process the idea, he stood and walked to the booth. *Why not? I have the time and a lot of sin to ask forgiveness for.* The chapel was still vacant when he looked back, then gingerly closed the door to await that familiar sound of a sliding screen under the latticed square.

Chapter Seven

SAN ANTONIO NATIVES were restless and beginning to stir in those later evening hours as some prepared for dinner and some for socializing out on the town. But hours seemed to whittle away with Gabriel still inside the sacrament of the confessional. Regular members of the congregation entered and left in relative silence as Father Kait sat behind closed doors and heard what Church offered as fact.

Gabe never lied to Father Kait, but he held most of his sins under wraps, not wanting to shock the old man into a fast coronary. For the second time in his life, Gabe was becoming close to a stranger. And being the second only time, he found a comforting lack of judgment as his reward. Sidestepping his brutal acts of murder, Gabe talked about Bennett and upbringing. He then labored on about all his travels through small towns as the priest listened, kindly never interrupting as he talked. It felt like shedding some heavy burden for him, and he rattled on about a wide variety of subjects. Father Kait may have recognized how long it had been since he'd talked with a friend because he let him prattle on without halt, and unlike a therapist telling him his time was over, he allowed him to continue talking as the floodgates opened and as all the dark inklings found their own ray of illumination.

He talked about Christian; leaving his gender absent from his tale, though he'd already gathered Kait had seen through his deception and glaring absence of feminine pronouns. He washed clean some of the regrets he'd had driving out of Seattle. He talked about his desire to remain with the writer, and his longing to whisk his lover up inside his truck and head down the highway satisfied that everything he wanted was sitting alongside him in the light of a hot afternoon. And he talked about his skewered belief in God and what damages the Catholic Church had left as scars in his life, but still the priest said nothing.

The single trail of a tear wet his cheek before falling from Gabe's face, bringing him back to his surroundings and forcing him to remember who he was. Out of instinct, he pulled a ball cap out of his back pocket. He'd stuffed it there when he entered St. Joseph's but now he needed it to shield his face, as if he wasn't alone in the cubicle. Having it on relaxed him and brought him peace.

Nice being in another's company, and someone he had no desire to fuck or fuck over with petty robbery, and with Christian only a ghost in his mind, Father Kait was the best anyone could've offered. Finally, he sat in silence, slightly ashamed about how long he'd occupied the priest's time. But then he saw a shadow lean in and heard Father Kait whisper, "Sounds like you needed to talk, son. And something tells me there's more waiting behind those big walls of yours." *You couldn't be more right.*

"How 'bout we plan on you visiting again soon. We can always talk further."

"Sorry, but I don't live in San Antonio," was all Gabriel could offer to say.

"You're here for a while, I trust. At least try, for the short time you might be with us. I kinda enjoy your company, young man...and I'm eager to learn more."

That was a strange sentiment indeed, Gabe thought. Before, it'd only been Christian who ever gave an indication he wanted to spend some quality time in Church's company. But life on the road made that his one greatest impossibility. Yet surprising for even him, he'd found someone other than the writer whom he could talk with and open up to. Someone willing to listen to his rambles and help him find the clarity he'd lost along the way. But as gentle as Father Kait appeared to be, there was no way he could take some of the stories Gabriel had stored up in his past. No one could be that forgiving or nonjudgmental, he assumed. For a split-second he considered unleashing one of the horrors of his more recent killings, knowing the old man's hair would've turned suddenly and miraculously icicle white if it hadn't already turned that shade of pale.

"I can stop by, but I'm only interested in confessing to you, Father."

"It's a small church and we only have one pastor, so I guess it means personal service with a smile. But there might be lines," he warned. "We all have sin, my boy. But some sins are greater encumbrances for a select few...and you are always welcome here."

He heard the rustle of heavy cloth as the priest leaned in closer to the screen. "I'm going to break all bonds of propriety here and ask what I can call you on your next visit."

"Gabriel...my name is Gabriel," he stammered out without thinking.

"I'm familiar with your namesake," Kait whispered back. "We should talk about him next time. Something tells me you have a story there as well."

Flashes of his long conversations with his mother came flooding back, and he smiled. It was like stepping back in time to St. Joseph's, he thought. It'd be nice to hear an unfamiliar voice instead of the booming echoes normally rattling around his skull. And as a change of pace, seemed more appealing. With it resolved, he bowed his head and waited for the traditional blessing and delivery of the penance.

He felt amazing, like he'd just stepped out of the shower only to witness the dirt which stained his humanity as it circled the drain. Refreshed and clean, and ready for another day on the road. *By what means could I have forgotten how such a simple act could feel so rewarding?* The priest's side door never opened, and he knew he'd been given ample time to leave, out of an idiotic sense of anonymity. But lifting his hand, he absently palmed Father Kait's door with loving respect, before he walked out of the chapel and back to his truck and forgetting what drew him there in the first place. At least until he reached the Dodge and remembered how all he'd really wanted at the time had been a cold beer.

Taking the next exit, Church scanned for any motel signs. It'd turned humid and he hoped the heat wouldn't keep guests locked inside their dingy rooms. Then he noticed a bright La Quinta sign and steered his truck into a vacancy in the lot. Though he had some crumpled folding money still left in his jeans, he thought it better to make hay while the sun was still shining, as he remembered his father saying on more than one occasion. He stripped out of his shirt and grabbed a pair of old sunglasses from the console. He then pulled a towel from a spot under his seat, and shorts from a duffel bag. Looking around to see who might be watching, he jumped out and wriggled free of his jeans, standing there naked beside his open door like some redneck men's changing room. Though bare-assed for only a few seconds, he still hoped someone had the pleasure of witnessing his transformation. Then he confidently and briskly headed to where he suspected the motel's pool should be.

Fortune shone down on him because he observed a lone woman lying in a lounge chair at the water's edge. She was wearing a black bikini and listening to an iPod. She wore dark shades too big for her small face and masked her delicate features and hiding her eyes. He was grateful to see she was pleasingly thin with petite, yet adequate, breasts. Beside her, Gabe noticed a spare towel and a summer hat laying to her left. Ride alongside an oversized carry-all invitingly open and unsecured.

When he entered the enclosure, the metal-on-metal clang of the gate closing caused her to turn slightly and start looking him up and down as he entered her very private domain. The first thing he noticed was her abundance of costume jewelry and the gaudy hoop earrings dangling from her ears. It became clear for him at least, this was no child's mother. The smell of chlorine hit his nostrils when he sidled up next to the woman and rested his hand on the back of her lounge chair.

"Excuse me, is this one free?" he asked, flashing his enamel seductively.

"Help yourself, handsome," the woman said before turning back to her iPod to indicate she was above being interested. Gabe laid out the towel in meticulous fashion on the open chair next to her. It gave him the opportunity of scoping out her body and imagining her straddled over him in one of the moderately priced rooms upstairs.

"I heard it's supposed to reach over a hundred today," he said flatly. Making idle conversation was step one.

"Is it?" she asked with bland neutrality. *She is going to be tough, what a bitch.* He smiled with the thought of an untested challenge.

"I gotta be honest; I didn't watch the weather this morning...I was only trying to make conversation. Ya see I'm in town on business, and I guess I've been spending too much time behind the steering wheel...and well, seeing a pretty woman brings out the idiot in me."

He smiled pleasantly wide as he ran his hand along an unshaven chin. To gain her confidence, he knew he'd have to give her something...and to him that only meant a lie. A lie built upon a stack of lies if need be. Gabe recognized a woman's trust was a fragile thing, with a tensile strength of spider's silk. And to illustrate he wasn't a creepy interloper, he needed to become a very thing he wasn't. So he set his goals to appear kind and seemingly unthreatening—just another predictable encounter with a man whose only base intention came from flirting with an attractive stranger in the hopes of seeing something hidden behind impenetrable walls.

Turning her head to look at him fully, she had to raise her hand to shield her eyes from the bright sunlight. But even in the shadow of her palm, Church saw her lingering gaze as she slowly traveled from his smile down to his massive, hairy chest. All the way down, eventually, to his strong calves, and he noticed a smirking, satisfied curl to her ruby lips. To further seal her interest, he turned his back and adjusted his chair, which he knew would give her ample view of his round ass cheeks even in those god-awful bathing shorts he'd regrettably grabbed last minute.

Sitting down next to her, he leaned back as if he wanted the sunlight to bathe him in radiance.

"So, where's home and what business brings you to San Antonio?" she asked. The amazing part of casual conversation was in how many of your privacies you had to divulge just to play. But he intended on playing to win.

"Tennessee, originally, and I buy and sell mineral rights. San Antonio is only a hop from some private acreage I have to visit." Gabe often used land and oil rights as a cover story. It'd been his experience those who didn't know much about it didn't want to hear about it. And those who might be familiar with the occupation hated discussing it with any great detail. Ms. Black Bikini simply nodded her approval, and he knew that was the last word they'd share on the subject. "What about you? Here on business or pleasure?" he asked as he repositioned his head over his interlocked fingers to better show off his build.

"Girlfriend's wedding," she said. "But that was yesterday, and I decided to take a couple of free days before heading back home. And why not?" she said with a shrug of her shoulders and a pout to her mouth. "The flight and room were already paid for, so why not make a holiday out of it?"

Gabe never understood why people gave away so much information to strangers. For example, this woman had mentioned she was traveling alone and offered that it could be several days before she may be missed if anything tragic were to befall her. He knew she was traveling with cash, as most ladies might, and she appeared to be all but begging that a killer should find her. But fortunately for her, he saw no halo of light surrounding her, and she never quite understood how close to her own demise she'd been dancing.

"My name is Dalton, by the way," Gabe lied, his grin exposing a more practiced bravado. He was a true hunter with an eagle eye, knew every calculation necessary to find and take down a target. Not wind speed or where the sun was positioned above or the hours of hunting time he had left in the day could hinder him. Leaning over, he extended his hand in a warm greeting, more to complete the need for physical contact and guarantee his new friend should trust him explicitly.

"Leah..." she offered with a nod.

He saw that she was still cautious about the man who'd approached her, but even through her dark shades, he could see that her interest was piqued.

"First time in San Antonio?" she asked.

"Actually, it is. I was considering hitting the Riverwalk later. I can't believe I've never made it through here before now, and I've always wanted to see it. If only to see if the fuss I'd heard was true or not."

Gabe had gifts other than his smoldering sensuality. He'd grown skilled in becoming a chameleon, assuming the roles others expected him to play. He needed to appear simply to her as an attractive and age-appropriate man. A stranger who'd recently arrived in town and nothing more. When they shook hands, he made sure to turn his wrist around for her benefit, all to display the absence of any wedding band, and no tan line where a ring might've been. It'd been important that she connect all the dots herself, anything less might allow the dominoes to drop and begin a chain reaction that resulted in failure. She had to engage him with an offer of intercourse, not the other way around. His only mission was to remember to scoop up her any available cash and loose jewelry or any other valuables he could pawn later.

"The Riverwalk is nice, but I prefer to escape most of the touristy areas when I travel," she offered. "I'm sure you'll find parts of it to be lovely," she said. Leah readjusted her shades then swatted the air as if annoyed by a flying insect Gabe failed to see.

He leaned over and allowed her to turn to see his devil-may-care smile and asked, "So where do the pretty ladies from out of town choose to go when hitting the streets of San Antonio?"

The game had begun and now raced near completion. Such an attractive woman was surely used to getting hit on. That much was obvious. But Leah presented as one who wanted to be the one in control. That was evident by the tiny gestures she sent rippling through the air in his direction. Gabriel knew a thing about manipulation. He could tell she thought her new poolside companion was coming off bolder than other men who had the courage to make advances on her. He didn't need a drink in his hand to secure the courage necessary to approach a pretty woman and didn't need the background music of a smoke-filled bar to mask his desires. But he wasn't Gabe in those first minutes of their meeting, he'd become the persona of *Dalton*, the fabrication he was quickly forming in his head as a disguise. He had to remind himself to rein himself in from his usual methods of attracting a partner.

She'd turned slightly to reveal a polished, artificial smile across red-tinted full lips. Even from beneath the dark amber of her oversized shades, he could see she was captivated by the color of his irises, or decided lack thereof. That, and the seductive way he flashed his pearly whites meant as a bonfire signal to any woman in the room that he was interested. She was probably picturing herself riding him in her empty motel room, atop that very chaise lounge or even fucking poolside for any and all to bear witness. He could almost imagine the quiver of her insides, that tactile twitch from a few tiny orgasms all being fired in rapid succession.

ALTHOUGH LEAH WAS all but baking in the muggy San Antonio afternoon, she wasn't sure how much to blame on the heat and how much to blame the stranger she'd just encountered. He at least seemed partially responsible, and she surmised that his sexy grin and those lovely eyes of his had to at least be a contributing factor for the damp dewiness she'd noticed in her bikini bottoms. She was falling into the idea of melting even further and knew it'd be futile to even try to appear disinterested at that point. He was already staring at her in his confident knowledge of where their exchange was headed.

He was brutishly sexy, she noticed. And despite a boring sales job, he didn't show the usual dull traits of any salesman she'd ever met before. Leah saw a dangerous quality surrounding him like a halo. Not to mention those immense arms and fur-covered chest of his. He all but turned her skin to gooseflesh and started the faint ringing of bells to go off inside her skull. Maybe womanly intuition or possibly the anticipation building as she only hoped he would offer to take her back to his room and then ravage her for hours. He had a certain "bad boy" feel. Having him was the very thing to finish off a near perfect vacation and escape from the tedium of her life. It would be the story she'd share gloriously with girlfriends over drinks. The perfect memory to use as her fingers traced the wet linings of her pussy when she masturbated. It would be something she'd treasure for years to come. So, was this the end product of a rebellious youth once he'd grown and become a man, she questioned.

"ACTUALLY, DALTON, FUN can be found anywhere...given the right company."

"Well, a woman after my own heart," Church stuttered happily, before leaning back to absorb every inch of the sun's rays. Normally he wouldn't have spent this much effort on the insignificant gas money he was sure he'd get by all the subterfuge. He would have waited until she was distracted and reached inside her purse grabbed her wallet and then been gone within minutes. But he had to admit she was attractive, and she exuded sex at a time he needed some. Besides, he was relaxed for the first time in a while and didn't need to be anywhere in particular. It became a cleansing experience; taking in the sun and forgetting about the late-night bars and multitude of miles spent on highways. They chatted for about twenty minutes or so, saying nothing important or earthshattering. Both knew the ping-pong of subtle innuendos and sexual wordplay was a requirement women needed and men were forced to deal with to get what they wanted. Gulping down the last of the drink Leah had carried from her motel room, she turned the glass upside down with a comical bent of her head.

"Aw drinky all gone," she said through pouty lips.

"Well that's a shame," he said, inching closer to pull her in. "Know anyplace you can get a refill? Someplace close where I can join you in a glass?"

"Well I brought mine from my room. I always carry vodka when I travel because a girl never knows when a party is gonna break out."

He thought it funny when she'd referred to herself a girl, mainly because it'd been so apparent she was farther from her school years than she might've enjoyed admitting. She was a cougar, nothing more.

"I do have extra glasses in my room, but I don't usually invite strange men to my boudoir," she said coquettishly as she batted her lovely lashes.

Well, this is going to be easier than I originally guessed, he thought as he grinned back at her.

"A good policy for anyone, I'm sure," Church said with a seductive leer. "Your momma must have taught you well."

With that, he leaned back in his chair to ignore her and take in additional sun. She needed to work for it. It made his part easier in the end.

Seeing a cloud of doubt engulf her pupils, Gabe recognized an immediate need to make Leah feel more comfortable with the prospect, so he reached down and picked up her bottle of tan lotion and her empty glass. "Allow me," he said with a congenial smile so as not to intimidate. He followed her dutifully out of the pool area and felt her nerves titter and jangle in the space between them as he traipsed behind her up the concrete steps to her room. As Leah slid the keycard into the lock, she looked first right and then left down the terrace walkway, probably to ensure no one was witness to her indiscretions. With a timid smile, she opened the door with a flurry and allowed Gabe—or Dalton, the traveling salesman he was pretending to be—to enter her rented sanctum.

Gabe might easily have killed the woman, just as he had others. But he wasn't called for murder on that sunny afternoon. Leah had not been bathed in the familiar white radiance that he saw on all those who'd been gifted him. In truth, she was not in danger of anything more than petty robbery because all that Gabe was thinking about at the time was fucking her then lifting her purse whenever the first opportunity arose. With him wearing only shorts and Leah in a bikini, half the work was already done, and as the door closed behind them, Gabriel whisked her up in his arms not wanting to carry the façade further and kissed her deeply.

Leah looked stunned for a moment but then accepted his embrace readily as he bent down to kiss her again. He ran an open palm along her back, tracing her spine with his fingers. As his reach went upward, his digits deftly unsnapped her bikini top. As a gesture, it appeared insignificant, but she melted into him just as her top hit the carpet. Her breasts were smallish but pert, and when he brought his fingers up to cup one gingerly, she liquefied in his arms like warm butter atop hot flapjacks.

Church liked any sex he could get, but he found it strange that women rarely went to his dick as quickly as the men did. The testosterone-driven need of a gay always meant the cock was one of the first prizes they reached for, whereas women loved deep embraces and hot breath blowing in their ears or the gentle biting of their lobes or nape. Leah's time was far different than that with Cole, but to Gabe, everyone he bedded had their own special flavor to enjoy. Maybe it came with the harsh commands he blurted such as, "Come on baby, this big ole dick isn't going suck itself."

A RAY OF sunlight hit Gabe's face from a whispered gap in the closed blinds and forced him back into reality, reminding him he'd come for more than simple sexual satisfaction. He brought the tip of his fingers up and traced along Leah's lips gently, close enough to bask in the warmth of their combined breathing. "How 'bout you start the shower, and I'll meet you in there 'cause we are far from done, lover."

Even as he said the words, he wanted to choke. It made him sound like a bad actor from a seventies porn show, and he hated the words before they even hit the air. But Leah hadn't seemed to notice and kissed him sweetly on the mouth before jumping up and heading to the bathroom. Then he noticed a bottle of vodka on the bureau in her room, and realizing he needed an extra few seconds, he called out to Leah, "Mind if I make us a drink? I see that bottle you were referring to...and it's just sitting here begging for me to make us a cocktail."

"Go ahead, please," she called out. "But hurry, I don't want to be in here alone for long."

Gabe grabbed his shorts and slipped back into his tennis shoes before reaching under the bed and finding Leah's pocketbook and that spare condom. He was quiet when he slipped out the door and sauntered self-assuredly to the parking lot to find his pickup truck.

He never considered what might've gone through Leah's mind when she stepped out of the shower in shock and amazement in finding herself alone in the room. She wouldn't think about having her purse taken, not at first. She would have been sad before it turned into acrid bitterness. Bitter even before her anger at being discarded so casually, hating all men for their wicked ways and how they treat the gentler sex. But the anger would turn once again, when she would think that all her Harlequin romance memories would now be tainted and spoiled like unattended picnic food growing rancid in the summer sun, already speckled with bad memory flies.

Chapter Eight

THE LORD SOMETIMES occludes us from seeing the things we cannot change, such as a growth of cancerous cells in the making, or another hidden patrol car parked a tad too unobtrusively behind a screen of trees. People stumble onto this axiom like they do all things…by chance, or by destiny. If one ever needs to make God laugh, as the old truism went, one need only to mention all the big plans one had in mind.

Such became Gabe's evening. Sitting at a bar he'd found off Euclid, he stared up at the black and white portable resting in the upper corner of the room and currently tuned to a college game that no one was particularly paying attention to. The music from a nearby jukebox droned out any chance to hear the game's colorful commentary. It was early in the evening and this was the type of dive where drunks came to wallow in the singular joy of alcohol, calling it self-medication, or reward for another day's labors.

Gabe enjoyed these types of bars. They were ideal for his *drinking alone time.* He hated having to compete with his environment when he wanted nothing more than quality solitude and a chance to relish the booze and quiet. There was melancholia in bars of this ilk, all of which seemed as pervasive as the cigarette smoke that once hung in the air before the laws changed and smoking became banned from any and all public areas.

Lighting was always dim in these familiar haunts, broken only by the neon beer signs and the illumination from a jukebox or television monitor. The clink of glasses broke the solitude and any chatter from other patrons seemed to come in small, insignificant waves. This was a place one could lose one's self. Not the type of establishment where one makes new friends. Gabe looked down along the long mahogany to see every face staring blankly over their drinks like androids. They were a simple line of automatons, each lifting a glass to their lips in bizarre unison, and with the regular mechanical gestures of a robot, and not another walking corpse in the making. It was like being awoken from a deep sleep in the center of zombies who'd chosen to forgo their usual munching of brains for a liquid diet of scotch and vodka. And thank God none of them had an interest in him.

Christian would've hated this place. He seemed to need the fanfare of swankier surroundings whenever he got dressed to take an evening out on the town.

But not him; because Gabe reached his maturity in similar beer halls and pool bars. They were familiar for him and he chose to visit one in every tiny town he traveled through. He hustled games of poker or pool for gas money, so these places became his bread and butter. He learned how to interact with strangers over draft, or an occasional dart game. They were his school, his church, his summer camp. And it was those types of places that'd one day make him the man he was destined to become. He learned fast how roadhouses were always more rewarding than trendy clubs and fancy discos. They made him feel as if he'd stepped back inside his youth, and more than highway dust was washed clean when he entered the dark mysteries of some nameless, anonymous bar that typically dotted the interstate and farm communities. He understood better than most how monsters like him loved small towns—just as they loved the places where its residents spent their nights and meager paychecks.

Drinking alone at the bar, he had little else to do but contemplate his long list of regrets. It seemed he wasn't that different than the rum jockeys sitting down the line in glassy-eyed repose. What he sat in deep contemplation with was Christian, wondering why the man's eyes had always seemed to follow him around a room. Like panning for gold in a California river and scrutinizing for those flecks of rocks with gilded veins, he seemed to see something of value hidden below the surface. But Gabriel knew he wasn't a good man; he'd always known that. He didn't understand why Chris didn't see it. He wasn't going to change anytime soon because had he been capable, they might still be together as friends. Not there, in Washington, but somewhere.

A strange friendship origin story for sure, he thought; a killer and the writer penning his biography. And, of course, there was the unexpected sexual relationship that developed during those interviews. When he had put Seattle in the rearview, it occurred to him there would be no book now. Chris had tripped up, fallen into his own subjective tale and become more than a mere plot point. He had become, by association, a guilty participant to every prior bad act Gabe had committed, and whom no one could say wasn't directly or indirectly responsible for the death of Shea Baltimore. He'd been quite the pussy, Gabe thought, telling a stranger about Gabe's past like some jealous bitch.

But what Chris hadn't understood was Gabe hadn't done it for himself. He could've outrun the law. He'd always remained one leg ahead of any authorities before. But he had to stop her from confessing anything to the police...because of Christian Maxwell. When they first met at the café to discuss the book, Gabe hadn't considered drawing another person into his nightmare. But once he knew Chris better, once they'd become friends, the seeds of doubt began to sprout and the realization that he might destroy that friendship seemed unbearable, even for one as cold as he.

Squeezing his eyes shut, Gabe rubbed his eyelids harshly, until imaginary flashes gouged in his brain. He wasn't tired. He wanted to take bitter memories between his thumb and forefinger and smash them into black nothingness, to make them go away. It served no one's purpose to rehash this shit. Tossing a few bucks on the bar for his last unpaid drink, Gabe stood and headed for the door. He needed to find a hole for the night and didn't have sufficient funds for another expensive motel. It looked like he'd have to hunker down in the pickup again, only to wake with stiff muscles and in wrinkled clothes and a blinding Texas sun as his alarm clock.

KEEN HAD BEEN working on summary reports for previously closed cases for hours that afternoon. Investigations meant paperwork above everything and generated more from the dead than the living. He didn't mind though; he considered himself a profiler as much as he thought of himself as a detective. And reading through old cases was a great way of testing his suppositions against facts. The suspect in every case fit a mold; he'd drawn his own conclusions, even when the case was not assigned to him. He read through the details and used it against what he'd already guessed. Did the occupation or age match up to what he'd originally presumed when the murder was fresh news? Was the boogeyman he crafted in his mind anything like the suspect they eventually convicted?

Wrapping up old cases meant his mind was distracted from more recent homicides. But occasionally, his eyes would dart across the room to a newly-formed whiteboard and CSU images of Shea Baltimore's lifeless body. The city's latest murder was the strangulation of a young artist in a rundown apartment and although the schoolgirl murders were just as important, he was reminded Shea Baltimore was also someone's daughter, someone's sister. Just like those young victims, everyone left someone behind. He wanted to be assigned to that homicide, because the schoolgirls, like Shea, had a name and were more than the mere numbers they represented. *How many killers were currently walking free on Seattle streets?*

Keen would've spotted another homicide detective from a mile away. They had this look of "God, the horrors and shitty things I've seen" in their glassy-eyed expressions. They were beaten down with all the constant reporting—that minutia of their jobs that had little to do with catching a killer. The court appearances, the typing of endless forms, the daily meetings, and the meticulous way they were required to maintain a professional demeanor. The police called it "distance," like when doctors joked about a patient's illness and it seemed crass to anyone outside the field. But Keen called it a curse, and even though he was saddled with the same gallows humor because of his job, the deadpan pupils gazing out from the fixed images of Ms. Baltimore reminded him he had a mission-like calling for answers. So, for him, being a detective wasn't that bad a life.

Keen moved to the coat rack by the door, where he placed his shoulder holster and suit jacket as he walked into his office every morning. He had clocked in enough time working the old and needed to focus on the new. Shea Baltimore's murder lacked any connection to other murders according to the file. But the detective didn't have all the facts...not yet anyway. Nothing linked to the young artist's homicide or any individual currently topping his radar. He had received the file for that reason alone, even taking into account it'd been incorrectly assessed as being a sex crime from the beginning. He'd deduced nearly instantly that had been a bullshit assumption.

The victim's former residence wasn't far from the station, and he'd learned the name of the witness who'd made the initial 911 call from the flimsy file tossed on his desk. Keen began by rote; interviewing the sole name in the file outside of the victim's, and that was a landlord questioned by officers and then detectives at the scene. After a short jaunt across town, he was walking up to the manager's office and passing a "For Rent" sign weathering in the elements of an untended courtyard. Had they only recently ripped down crime tape and thrown a rental notice in the yard, he wondered. Probably not but before he left, he decided to check out the unit where Shea Baltimore met her last, just to make sure it was still secure.

Someone had loved the place once, Keen mused. The property was lined by an ornate wrought-iron gate, breaking up the grounds from the street, and as one entered the waist-high gate and the metal clanged shut behind, the eye was drawn along the stone walkways that lead to the cracked pavement of the sidewalks leading up to each unit. It had been a Grande Dame years before, but as the building and area around it fell into disuse, crime and poverty swept in and soiled the dame's gown, turning her into some faded glory living off past memories of when she'd once shone— *I'm ready for my close-up, Mr. Deville.*

It presented as one of those courtyard-style apartment buildings where every unit had a window facing the interior grounds. It had a faded Italian villa ambiance with its old fountains and once lush grounds. But that was long ago. When those who'd owned the property saw its grandeur and cared. It had long since fallen into disrepair, with the flowerbeds overgrown with weeds and the ornate fountains cracked and whitewashed and silent with the absence of the water that once bubbled from its spouts. Any vestige of life that the courtyards once possessed had long since perished beneath its peeling paint and weathered awnings...and though grand at one time, it presently sat as simply another sad, lonely building living in the shade of its better days.

Following the path, Keen found a unit marked unobtrusively as "Manager." The man who answered didn't seem to fit the part in the play working through his mind. The supervisor was obese and his wifebeater top was stained and wrinkled. Chest and arm hair poked from every tattered hole, and he made an odd picture chomping down on an apparently old, wet cigar butt. He saw surprise in the man's eyes: obviously this wasn't an interested party for any of the currently open units.

"Excuse me, I'm Detective Keen, and I presume you are the manager?" He waited for a reply, but the ghastly figure only smiled broadly without speaking.

"I'd like to ask you some questions about the recent homicide of Miss Shea Baltimore."

The portly man seemed without shame, smiling as he stepped aside to allow the detective entrance even though he hadn't requested one. "I thought I'd be done with all this by now. It's not like it happened last week."

"These investigations take time. I'll try to be brief."

Scanning the room, Keen drew a wealth of information about the man. He was lazy. A large faded comfy chair faced the television head-on, next to it was a small side table where the ashtray was overflowing with butts and littered with small papers. A half-filled glass, still dusty from languishing there for a while, sat next to that. *How the hell did this asshole get this job?*

"You are Mr. Von Stroheim, I presume? Can you tell me how long you've been onsite manager here?"

"Too damned long." the man offered from his faux-leather throne. "At least four years now," he said in a humph, expelling labored breaths as he positioned his girth into the lounge chair.

"But we never had a murder here. This was the first."

Keen stared down at him in disgust, thinking he seemed less surprised than a normal sane person should be at this turn of events. He surely must be the owner's brother-in-law, or an out of work uncle hidden away with a promise of a petty job, hoping that he wouldn't show up unannounced somewhere. That odd, impoverished distant relative we all seem to have crawling out from our family woodwork.

As the man tried to relight his dead cigar, Keen continued his interview because he wanted to make this quick. "What can you tell me about Miss Baltimore?"

"You mean visitors?" he began. "I don't keep up with my tenants, but that one seemed pretty shy. She was young and pretty, though; would've guessed her to have boys creeping up to taste her juices...but not her, never really saw she had any visitors; 'tis a shame." As he said this, Von Stroheim got a faraway gaze on his face, and Keen suspected he was contemplating more that she hadn't gotten laid enough and less about the pity of her murder.

"So, no visitors that you recall? There were no neighbors or friends in the complex that you saw her interact with?"

"Like I said, that one was a shy one. She was nervous when she rented the shit hole, almost like she was afraid of being around a man."

The detective jumped to the conclusion it had to be this man's presence which had unnerved Shea.

"Felt sorry for her, but she never chatted with anyone I ever saw... although I do recall one fella showing up sniffing around her door. It must've been the day before she died or thereabouts, but I told this to the detectives that showed up when I found her dead."

Keen had read the file completely; he was certain, and there weren't any indications in the notes alluding to a suspect. He presumed the original investigator was either an idiot or couldn't make enough of a connection about a stranger visiting a murder victim and the sincerity of the fat fuck he was forced to interview at the scene.

"Refresh my memory, sir," he said with a chilly detachment.

"I think I remember him because he didn't look like anyone who usually visits one of my tenants, looked outta place, ya know? He might've been wearing a nice a jacket or some such shit. I don't rightly remember. But I did recall the way he looked right and then left, like he didn't know exactly where he was going; kinda lost."

"So a stranger, someone you'd never observed before?"

"Nah, he didn't look like he knew where he was going. I don't think I'd even know how to describe him. He didn't strike me as unusual or anything. Ya know what I mean?"

Apparently it did, thought Keen. *Maybe if I close my eyes, this idiot will disappear.*

"Did you happen to notice the vehicle he arrived or left in?"

"Now that was one thing I did see." He said without even the slightest hint of irony. "A newer model Mercury sedan, grayish blue I think."

"Well that's something," Keen offered. "Why is it you remember damn near next to nothing about the stranger but you do remember his car?"

"I don't much care for dudes…I like cars," was all he said with a smack from the wet cigar butt under a trail of wispy smoke. The detective shuddered with the thought of all the pretty female tenants who had to visit this asshole once a month to pay rent. They probably waited until his living room light was extinguished, then crept across the courtyard on shaky legs with an envelope.

"I even remember the first three numbers of the tag: NP, then 9, but I think the NP was some kinda city code designation or sumptin. I remember the old plates used to be three numbers then three letters, but the new ones are seven random mixes."

Von Stroheim wasn't without a glimmer, Keen suspected. As a former patrol officer himself, he knew that up until 2009 the three-digit-three-letter designation occurred on all tags, and all were produced by prisoners from upstate in the Walla Walla Pen. Tags after that held the newer style, which meant the tags on the Mercury were at least from after 2009, making a search from the database easier. Plus, the NP wasn't a city code but a tag designated for a plate chosen for Washington's National Park Fund, which might help even further to ID the owner. It's about all the small victories, the detective mused, and something was better than nothing for having to put up with this fat fuck for even such a short while.

Through clenched teeth, he begrudgingly offered, "You've been very helpful, sir. Thank you."

And he had, he thought, since he had a new lead to pursue. But such a gift from such a man was a bitter pill to swallow. He bade Von Stroheim a good day and started to head out to his car but quickly turned and asked. "By the way, I wasn't working the murder when it occurred. Do you suppose I could bother you to open up the unit for a fast walk-through?"

Lumbering out of his chair like a sleep-deprived bear coming out of hibernation, the rolls of fat threatening to escape his shirt any second, Von Stroheim stood up and yanked a ring of keys from a pegboard by a dusty unused desk. "Might as well. I haven't actually been in it since they allowed it to be opened and rentable. But I still have to get in there with a cleaning crew."

"But you do have a rental sign out front already. Is that for this unit or another one?"

"Oh, that's for another unit." He was lying, Keen was certain. "I have more than one

A shadow of shame slithered over the fat fucker's face, like a kid too close to the cookie jar, crumbs still splattered across his chin. The man tried to appear casual, a disguise to an untruth tossed out too carelessly. Clearly he had no scruples. His intention may've been to pocket any money allocated on cleaning the unit, even after the horrors of a violent crime being committed there. A shit hole after all and he knew it. He'd probably get some oblivious renter, even without having to run up a painting bill or pull carpet. He was the type of landlord who'd even show a unit with the white tape diagram of a recently deceased renter still glued to the floor, saying nothing as he stepped over the spot where the prior tenant had lain. He'd even try to highlight the apartment's stunning city skyline views, which couldn't be seen from there either. The kind of presence that begged the thought, *Pay no attention to that man behind the curtain. He doesn't matter anyway.*

Chapter Nine

DEATH WAS SOMETHING Gabe thought a great deal about...his as well as others. When you walk away from a dumpster after depositing a corpse there, or when you crawled from a bedroom window late one night, having left some lifeless white-lighter crumpled in their sheets, you tend to look at death in a more accommodating fashion. No one escaped death, Jesus didn't...and in the end Gabe wouldn't. Just as it would come for Chris as easily as it had come for Shea back in Seattle.

Gabriel had few illusions about his death. He knew it would likely come with a hail of bullets whizzing past his ears as he ducked and weaved to escape gunfire from overzealous highway patrol officers or FBI agents who'd finally run him successfully to ground. His mission would be complete whenever God decreed, so he didn't need to worry about the resolution. Some things were simply out of his hands.

He had woken in his truck again, which was an all too frequent event for someone who was a killer on the lam. After driving out of the city last night, he'd found the lights of San Antonio fading in his rearview. This was Texas, and even with the vast sprawl of people, there were endless rural areas one might get lost in—remote farm-to-market roads where very few farmhouses dotted the landscape. It had been late when he'd finally found a spot on a sloping bend on a rarely traveled dirt road, miles from where he'd last seen black asphalt. He'd hunkered down in his seat and pulled his LSU ball cap down over his eyes. The sounds of crickets chirping outside his truck window mixed with the swishing noise from a breeze hitting the tall kudzu grass. It had been relaxing, and he'd drifted off slowly while images of the faces of all the white-lighters he'd killed flashed through his brain.

There was no protection from the morning sun, and at daybreak, he was squinting into the rearview from the blinding light coming into his truck from every angle. He yawned and ran his hands over the scruff on his face. He'd always maintained a dark five-o'clock shadow, but it was becoming too thick and unruly and needed attending to soon. Rubbing the crust from his eyes, his stomach rumbled. He needed food, so he turned the key and revved the engine, breaking the pastoral quiet of the countryside, and then turned his truck down the same red dirt road he'd traveled on the night before.

As he drove back into the city with the radio playing and his window down, he decided to visit the priest at St. Joseph's again. But not until he'd grabbed some cheap drive-thru meal and filled his belly. He enjoyed having someone to talk with since his own isolation kept him far removed from *normal* people. That may have had some bearing as to why he'd hit it off with Christian from the onset. Or, his emotions had been all jumbled up because he'd simply been fucked-up and lonely and the writer listened without judgment, like Father Kait had done. A crooked smile hit his face as he remembered he'd taken out his sexual frustration on Chris in the end. Did that mean he was supposed to screw the old priest as well? A chuckle escaped his mouth under that fanciful notion, right before a shiver ran down his back at the boner-killing picture he'd made for his brain.

BACK AT THE precinct, Detective Keen was loading the vehicle tag information he'd learned from the slovenly landlord into the police database. Tag readers were positioned on all patrol cars, as was the case with the majority of law enforcement vehicles, but not for homicide detectives, so he had to go back to the station to get that done. Doing this would produce a lengthy report he knew more than one man could run down. But he knew he'd have to work smart and profile the names down to a manageable suspect list. However even that would take time.

As he clicked away at his keyboard, Detective Jackson Conley of Vice came sauntering up. He didn't much care for Conley who always entered a room like a swinging dick with a bellowing voice that didn't much fit his frame. Overcompensation, Keen suspected, for a witless man with nothing substantial below the belt but his need to be seen and a childish desire for respect.

"Hey there, Autumn Boy, how's tricks in cold case? You solve any big homicides lately?"

"Not sure..." Keen said without looking back over his shoulder. "Have you busted any hundred-dollar poker games or arrested any school bus drivers beating their meat from the glow of their computer monitors?"

Conley gave a hearty laugh as he approached the desk then laid a conciliatory hand on the back of Keen's chair. Leaning in, he said, "Now, Scott, I have the greatest respect for all that you do." His words were breathy, and an aroma of a recent coffee came wafting out.

"Whatever it is you want, Jax, I don't have the time. I'm busy working a new case at the moment."

"Now there, detective, it's not like I was asking you to join me in blowing a few lines and then jumping on your parent's bed. I only wanted to see if you had a few minutes to help me run through a few surveillance tapes."

Conley was a grade-A Asshole. "I think not buddy..." Keen barked out indelicately. "I can tell by your tone that a *few* means at least six to eight hours of endless monitor viewing, and all because you think you can con some poor sap into doing your work for you."

"Well, worth a shot. Had to try at least," Conley said as he turned to go. "Sorry for the intrusion. I thought catching a suspect would be good for the whole team."

"I call that malarkey bullshit! What you meant to say is whatever increases your solve ratio and brings that much-needed pat on the back from your supervisor...the one you so desperately seem to need."

"Now, now, detective, don't get all your tiny hairs standing on end! It's just a friendly request."

He patted Keen on the back before walking away almost as if he were making some amends, but Keen knew his own reputation at the CID. What he hated more than anything was losing a day of fruitful investigation for a *pretentious wannabe* like Conley. He also knew that at if he'd helped Jackson with the video; he'd still have taken all the credit for the hours spent scrutinizing the grainy black-and-white footage. At least he didn't have to spend the time sitting next to that asshole while he chomped and crunched through the snacks he always seemed to have around his desk, and he preferred to skip another crappy conversation he knew he must endure.

With his own search parameters for the vehicle finally loaded into the official database, he knew it would take time to generate a printout. He could wait it out but decided to go through the file again and go over the notes the first detectives had made regarding their interviews with the victim's friends and family. Keen knew how Miss Baltimore had died, and he'd seen the grisly images captured in CSI photos. But what he didn't know was what made his victim tick. A quick trip across town might allow him to understand her better, or whether a possibility existed that she might have known her assailant after all. Within minutes Keen had grabbed his holstered gun and suit jacket, and armed with the names he retrieved from her file, he was heading toward the parking lot.

FROM A DISTANCE, Gabe saw the black crested spires of St. Joseph's even before he reached the intersection. It reminded him of some sad and lonely paragon, dedicated to a simpler time where there was strength in the same religious history that had built it, out of place against the backdrop of neighboring storefronts, with their modern architecture of glass and neon. As he pulled to the front of the church, he was pleased to see that solitary poplar tree again, the one that had caught his eye earlier, emblazoned in the color of summer squash and the only item separating St. Joseph's and the barren, empty lot next door. It emerged as a stalwart and dependable warden of the grounds. St. Joseph's own celestial guardian, he mused, protecting the building, and all those who chose to worship there.

Gabe had found some measure of comfort at St. Ignatius, and he figured this was why he'd been drawn there initially. Like revisiting an old haunt, or lovingly running his fingers over the dark mahogany wood of a stair railing in a house he once called home. It was a chance not only to revisit but to possibly alter destiny from that point when it first derailed and spiraled off the tracks. But Gabe knew that God didn't offer up opportunities for those types of changes, not really. He just offered bitterness and sorrow, reminding people that they never had a chance to change anything because it's always beyond reach.

Before entering the church, Gabe took a long look at the simple, unadorned cross perched atop the tallest of the many spires. It seemed to reach all the way to the clouds. Then he remembered suddenly he was still wearing his ball cap, and he yanked it from his head and crammed it into a back pocket of his faded Levi's. As he reached the concrete steps, he ran a palm over his heavily bearded face and wished he'd taken the time for a quick shave before arriving. He had changed shirts in the truck, though, while at the fast food joint he'd driven through earlier, but only because the funk of sleeping in his clothes had become unbearable, even for him. He still felt unkempt, and it seemed strangely inappropriate to pass those double doors dressed as he was, a throwback to his childhood, when Bennett required everyone in the family to be spit-shined and polished every Sunday. Every member had to be in their best attire before being allowed to pile into the station wagon and head to weekly mass to receive communion from the Holy See. Unlike most boys his age, little Gabe rather enjoyed his weekly visits to St. Ignatius. He didn't even mind those unkind pews that sometimes made his butt ache, as long as he was able to observe the early morning light as it transformed into a multicolored exhibition of fantastical visions as they broke through the stained-glass windows and then made interesting shapes dance across the hardwoods. He particularly liked hearing his sometimes longwinded, but always charismatic, priest rally his sermons around stories of heaven and hell, with all its fiery retribution awaiting every sinner.

Entering the vestibule, he first noticed the scent of incense colliding with the chemical odor of recent Pine-Sol. He caught sight of an aging janitor with white hair backing his way down a long hallway, mop swishing back and forth across the linoleum floor. Catholic churches always seem to have long mazelike hallways in them, he remembered. There were countless doors leading to supply closets, offices, tiny libraries, and chapels with their varied sizes. It occurred to him that only the Catholic parishioners seemed to feel the need to have small, intimate chapels as well as expansive ones used for Sunday services. When he was a boy, he thought such places were where the help went to worship. No doubt he'd foolishly assumed this when he saw Latino maids and housekeepers entering the smaller chapel during the day. But as he got older, he figured it's nothing more than wasted space, and the perfect illustration of how much money churches collected in donations.

Before he could make it to the chapel marked *Winslow*, he heard a voice behind him.

"So you decided to visit again, young man. What a pleasure."

Turning too abruptly, he spun to find Father Kait coming up on his heels. "Well, yes..." Church said quietly. "But I wasn't sure you'd be here," he lied.

"Always...like I said earlier, tiny church, one priest, no waiting." As Kait came close enough, he placed a hand on Gabe's shoulder and in a paternal fashion he whispered discreetly, "Are you here for some private conversations with God, or is it confession you require today?"

He really liked this old guy. But when his own father figure was Bennett Church, one didn't have to look too far or too high for any patriarchal improvement. Not that he had. He'd actually learned great pride in being self-reliant. He lived with mementos, all of which had taught him that all he'd ever learned by those object lessons were those he had discovered on his own. He knew that statement would have sounded sad once confessed out loud, but Gabe kept his realities securely guarded in his chest. A lesson like many others, self-taught and learned early in his life. This was his reality, and his alone. Something he'd learned to accept a long time ago.

No one ever taught him how to drive or how to shave or how to hunt game or the proper way to carry a rifle as most fathers might've done. But he didn't feel pity in that. And no one ever slapped him on his back or offered him advice on sex and the need to protect himself from unwanted pregnancy or any of the facets of being a man. While his friends may have gone to the proms and the dances and played out the traditional conventions of growing up a small town, he denied himself that by choosing to remain preserved in his self-imposed isolation.

More often than any of his peers, Gabe could be found drinking six-packs alone and at the old *Indian Graveyard* on the outskirts of town. It may have been the same spot where others experimented with drugs or alcohol, and where kids his age smoked their first cigarettes or had their first awkward sexual encounters. But that wasn't the case for him. He'd spend his afternoons there, whenever he was able to ditch an early class unnoticed. He'd spend the day walking around the woods or skipping stones across the water, never wanting to go home or to whatever fresh hell he knew was waiting there. He'd also spend his free evenings at the graveyard, lying face up on the hood of his car and staring into the vastness of starry skies. A plan being formulated where he would run as far and fast as possible; to forget about those inevitable consequences for his actions, or those he'd be leaving in his wake.

"I wouldn't mind confessing, Father...that is if I'm even within the allotted time."

"You're not, and yet you are," the priest said with a grin. "Give me a couple of minutes and I'll *not see you* in the booth." Kait turned and headed down another hallway to parts unknown, and Gabe dropped his head and entered the tiny chapel. Father Kait gave the impression of a wise and caring man. He sort of reminded him of his former priest at St. Ignatius who seemed to stare at him as if he knew all his secrets.

Gabe wasn't sure why he'd been drawn back to St. Joseph's. He began by sidestepping his brutal acts of murder, and instead, he spoke about his lonely upbringing in Tennessee and of how he truly felt about his life, both then and now. He also spoke about Bennett Church and tasted the bile on his tongue when he dredged through those old memories. But speaking to the priest was comforting, and he was able to unburden himself without ever realizing how desperate he was to make another human connection. He didn't see how powerful it'd been or how necessary it became to keep his sanity in check.

What he did see was the substitution and how his quiet conversations with the priest kept him fighting back the urge to make another, more important call. He'd been struggling with it for days when that desire crawled into his belly and refused to leave. It whispered constantly from its new residence, telling him he should pick up the damned phone and reach out to the man. He had to admit he wanted that as well, but he resisted, because the thought of dragging Chris back into his unending drama only worked to put them both at further risk.

If he'd learned one thing lately, like how much danger he represented; not for the general public, but for the white-lighters who had the misfortune of walking past him and for those he cared about. He didn't need to get Maxwell tangled up inside his shit, and he knew he might be swapping that preferred time with Chris for that of a stranger, but better than keeping everything bottled inside. Or even the threat that his secrets might escape, only to rise to the surface, as secrets often have a tendency to do. It may be true that some things were better buried in the sticky mud at the river's bottom...but awful hard to keep them there.

Chapter Ten

AT SIXTY-ONE, Father Albert Kait still had a couple of years of preaching the gospel ahead of him, but in the back of his mind, he always feared the specter of doubt creeping in. The one that made him feel ultimately useless and surrounded by a world that was quickly passing him by unnoticed. And unlike the pontiff, he hadn't been bestowed a lifetime position of authority, and he knew that even the church had their limits. He understood that one day, probably a day very soon, he feared, he'd get a visit from the cardinal, or possibly one from his trusted entourage. Or he'd receive a lengthy private call while resting in his office, minutes before he was to step out for one of his sermons. They'd be kind; that much was certain. They'd show all kinds of concern, mostly about his health and well-being. But they'd talk as if he'd been magically transformed into a child who might not understand their words. And even with their gentlest of ways, they'd still be suggesting his retirement. And that was something he knew would force him into sudden realization that his age meant he wasn't necessary any longer, not to God and not to his congregation. Yes, Father Kait knew the speech was coming, that much was imminent, like he knew the words when heard would fairly drip with syrupy respect. And despite the saccharine sweetness, the words never sounded that way to him. It would be a sad and sour day, one he dreaded all the time.

Albert Kait attended his seminary at Regent College in Vancouver, from the age of twenty-five. Regent College had not long been incorporated at the time, and when Albert attended, there was a smattering of groundbreakings and buildings in various stages of construction. Even with concrete being poured and chapels being erected throughout the grounds, he'd thought it lovely surroundings. And even more beautiful today with the foliage completely filled in and paved sidewalks that crisscrossed the manicured green.

After completing courses in evangelical studies and Christian counseling, he was chosen quickly by the diocese to be assigned to a small church in San Antonio, Texas. Father Kait had been there from the beginning of his priestly duties, and he had never given a reason for reassignment, as was the typical papal subterfuge for other priests with less than savory behavior.

There were only two confessional booths available in the chapel, and both were empty that afternoon when Gabe slid the screen open and made the sign of the cross over his chest in anticipation. The anonymity of the confession seemed odd to him, given his relationship with Father Kait was already sealed with their conversations outside the sanctuary of the booth, but he'd been raised in Catholicism and knew how much they loved ritual and secrecy. Much to keep clutched to the chest for, he thought, and more for the church than the sinners they counseled.

After a minute, he saw the light from the open door announcing Father Kait arrived, and Gabe began with "In the name of the Father and of the Son and of the Holy Spirit. My last confession was...well, recent."

"Well, Gabriel, it's been very recent. You can't have committed sin of any substance," Kait addressed him. "Tell me plainly, son, what brings you here today?"

After a few painful seconds of contemplation, Gabe finally stuttered out, "Well, Father, I guess it's guidance I need." Expecting the priest to follow-up with a question, he only heard the rustle of cloth as Kait settled in quietly to allow the younger man to begin.

"I've committed many sins, some of my own choosing, some for God. At least I recognize those as being sins in the eyes of mortal men. I have also loved a man, but I'm not sure anymore where the church stands on that issue. I'm not sorry for it, though...for me it is not a sin."

The voice from the screen interrupted him quickly. "Regardless of the church's stance on that...issue, I can't offer forgiveness without contrition, as you're already aware."

"And that's not a sin I'm asking forgiveness for; then again, I'm not here for penance."

"Yes, it's guidance I can tell. I remember that you mentioned that." And with unexpected civility and kindness, given his confession, the priest added, "So how is it that I can assist you today, son?"

"It's about killing in God's name," he blurted out, then quickly added, "it's been going on for hundreds of years, and I was wondering if you thought that it'd ever really end?"

Gabe was met with a long pause that made him question what Kait's reaction was going to be. He felt cold reality washing over him, laying waste to any words he'd already spilled, ones that might yet minimize his declaration and not out him as what he truly was, a killer, pure and simple. All those years of isolation skewered the way he dealt with others, and he understood he'd overstepped and had to fight the growing urge to run from the confessional and escape St. Joseph's and never look back.

THE PRIEST FELT a chill enter his body and every hair along his forearms rose to immediate attention. He'd heard many things during confessionals through the years, but nothing nearly as enigmatic and foreboding as what Gabriel was asking then. It had nearly taken his breath away, and caught in that surprise, he leaned closer to the screen that divided them and whispered, "Son, Isaac was a blessed covenant. But he didn't die by Abraham's hands, which makes me all but wonder if there's something greater you need absolution for, my boy?"

"Maybe the Bible is still being written, Father. What if there's more to add?" It came as a statement from a mind obviously turning over ideals and finding no ground to stand upon.

"No, Gabriel! It's already a done deal. What was written was done so long ago. It is not being added to, there are no new chapters, and God's final decree is that killing is wrong, a mortal sin...but even one that can be forgiven...if there is contrition and a request for salvation."

"I'm not asking for any, Father. I was only wondering."

Kait had heard it over the years, but the words coming from this burly, yet handsome fella seemed out of place. He'd already guessed the man had weighty concerns he needed to unburden. But he couldn't have even begun to imagine it might be the worst of the worst in quality of mortal sin. The priest heard about infidelity, overly charged stories of masturbation, petty criminal offenses like stealing a twenty from a cash register, or a maid who had lied to her employer about breaking some bric-a-brac item in her daily cleaning ritual through broken English and sobs of clear regret. Nothing prepared him for the hint of murder, and Gabriel didn't outwardly seem the culprit who'd do such a thing. That was, if he fully understood the words coming through the screen behind that black huddled mass of the confessional booth.

"You haven't done anything like that have you, young man?"

"Never *taken*, Father, but possibly *released*," Gabriel said in a measured cool fashion, sending chills down Kait's spine with the lack of remorse he heard in every word.

"Why don't we discuss the events of that incident, my child? We can ask for redemption together...reconcile with our shepherd."

"I'm not here for forgiveness!" Gabriel shot back, showing impatience. "I'm here for guidance and a single question about whether you knew when it could be over, I mean, coming from a man of the cloth."

In the privacy of his booth, Kait began to realize his confessor wasn't speaking about a particular incident alone. He was making it sound like an ongoing sin, and that prospect chilled his blood and he grew paler with the knowledge. He'd never encountered anything of this gravity before. He sat horrified until the silence became too much of a tomb not to acknowledge. If what the stranger said was true, then he was not only sick and delusional, it meant that the priest had a killer in his cathedral. Nothing could've ever have prepared him for this type of test of his morality. Not unless it'd been discussed in a divinity seminar he'd mistakenly skipped one day. He thought hard about what he was going to say because anything less made him feel like a coconspirator in any future crime, he thought.

"If you're not here for redemption, would you prefer to discuss how you *release* a soul instead?"

The priest's hands began to tremble slightly, but it wasn't his proximity to danger, rather it was the palsy, nothing more than proof of long mileage and the sin of growing older. For him it became a price for all his learned wisdom. He didn't believe his visitor might've done a mortal crime like murder. In his eyes, there was nothing to fear. *And regardless, one should reflect on their personal sin and utter the words before begging for contrition. I can't begin any absolution without first beginning there.* Father Kait had never faced the dilemma of convincing a member of his congregation to turn themselves into any authorities, at least for anything greater than petty vandalism. It may've been his lack of experience in such matters that prevented him from seeing Gabriel as anyone actually dangerous, and the reason his kindness never wavered during their time together.

Some words a person hears during their lifetime can seem too unreal to be authentic, like a phone call in the night from someone informing them of a recent or unexpected death. A single long-distance conversation standing apart from all the others because it's the one they know instantly that they'll never fully forget. It's that awful sensation of standing inside a vacuum as every remaining molecule of oxygen is stolen from his lungs like an eager thief.

It becomes a simple and yet inelegant reminder screaming decisively over the din; it says that a person has lost a thing once held precious, and while they weren't paying attention, it slipped away from the living like a vapor escaping through open cracks in the ceiling. The words might sound genuine enough as they ricochet inside the skull, hitting one wall only to bounce to another, but they linger and reverberate there. Like an echo working through the hollows of a brain as each tiny pause between words becomes its own unbearable existence. A person tries to break down the information, to chew each word into smaller and more manageable bites, one that their intellect can ultimately consume…but it's difficult.

Such was the case with Albert when at twenty-eight he received such a phone call from his sister back in the States. She'd called to say their beloved mother Carlotta passed without warning sometime in the previous night. And as he stood alone in the rectory hall frozen and silent, gripping the heavy black receiver in his viselike hands, he remembered picturing his mother's face as she must've exited one life for the next. She would have been smiling because Albert knew how closely his mother guarded her own faith, and he suspected she would be at her happiest after finally being able to stand face-to-face with her maker.

Albert felt a wave of both compassion and sadness hit him hard as he recalled his sister sobbing hysterically in the background. She'd been crying for hours, he imagined, but her wailing made it appear as if she'd just heard the tragic news herself. But that was Gisela's way. Even from childhood, she'd been a small and twitchy type of girl, one who learned to utilize her overly dramatic histrionics. It must be her personality, Albert surmised, and the only way such a tiny girl might've garnered the attention she desperately craved while living in such a boisterous large Italian household as theirs.

Although that conversation was burned into his memory, he could no longer visualize himself standing there in the rectory with a fog of disbelief plastered on his face and the first indication of a fraying around his edges like a worn-out cotton shirt that had seen too many launderings. What he did recognize that day, as he did the day Gabriel visited him, was that no matter how earthshattering the news might be, it still looked like nothing but a Polaroid reminder of someone's past in the making. Whatever pain his visitor was carrying around his neck like a millstone, it wasn't small enough that any of Albert's platitudes might grant him the peace he needed or the penitence he might've been hoping for. Whatever guilt the man possessed was surely a heavy burden, and yet Father Kait was a believer in his faith. And as he'd tell his congregation each and every Ash Wednesday, "Remember we are all born of dust, and it's dust that we're all returned to in the end."

BEHIND THE TINY screen in Gabe's booth, the air then was pregnant with new and unfamiliar emotion. He was unburdening himself in ways he'd never done before. Not even with Chris in Seattle. They'd assumed everything would be laid bare over time. But Gabe still had secrets he'd never disclosed. And having the opportunity of releasing them and freeing them into the ether was giving him an autonomy he'd never felt before. Not in any of the interviews back in the hotel or any of the discussions they'd shared over dinner or drinks in a bar. This priest was becoming more important than any father confessor he'd ever known.

"I'm here to ask a question?" he began in a slow methodical way, showing he'd played out this scenario somewhere previously in his mind. "I wondered if it's possible that if you'd done some terrible things, even though you'd done them all in the name of God, you'd still be offered mercy, or any sanctuary and forgiveness, after the fact?"

A LONG PAUSE dragged by while Kait considered what the man was asking.

"Any life, whatever life you desire anyway, will only happen after complete absolution. If you don't ask for it, then you won't get it. And whatever sins you think you've committed can only be forgiven after your honest confession before the Lord. If you don't ask for help from anyone above, you risk that those sins will scar over the soul and damage it in ways you couldn't have fathomed."

Seconds turned into minutes until the silence became a vast forge and finally whispered through the blackness, "Does that help, young man? Does it offer you any guidance?"

The next sound he heard was a scraping of the confessional door as it opened abruptly, and then a burst of daylight invaded Father Kait's side of the partition. He realized his confessor had slipped out without responding, and as the priest stood up quickly in an effort to stop the man's departure, he saw only the chapel doors behind drawn closed as the man left the church without a word. Alone in the cathedral, he felt unnerved, like staring into a black void and expecting it to be God's face looking back and then being surprised when he only felt a cold chill and dark emptiness staring back. Frightened without completely understanding the reason, he then noticed how his legs were trembling and standing was difficult, causing Albert to have to reach for a nearby pew for support.

SITTING IN HIS car, Keen scoured through the file on Shea Baltimore. Having already spoken to her coworkers, he was at a loss as he tried to construct a list of known friends or associates, those who might've actually cared for the girl. Social media had given him nothing to draw a bead from, and he was beginning to wonder how much of a loner this pitiful young woman might have been. Clearly, she was another product of a broken home, and he thought his best shot in understanding Shea would come by speaking to her father. He didn't have girls yet, and the idea they might end up like Shea sent shivers down his back. He'd always known raising a child would be a challenge, but seeing this girl's life encapsulated in a file of the few things he was able to gather about her personality made him sad and a little frightened of the future he might have in store.

He'd found DeWayne Baltimore easily enough, and after gently knocking on his door, he noticed how long it took Mr. Baltimore to answer. He looked shabby and unshaven, and after a brief introduction, Keen was allowed in and saw the dank crap hole DeWayne called home, a residence that desperately needed a proper cleaning. Keen saw how much he'd given up; it was painfully detectable through the bloodshot eyes and spider veins stretching across his bulbous nose, indicating both alcoholism and abject misery.

A lounge chair sat centered in front of a television: one of those hunchback models manufactured years prior to the advent of flat screens. There was a tiny side table littered with beer cans that'd been drained of any alcohol and an overflowing ashtray that needed emptying. There was an acrid smell which reminded Keen of a nest of tattered papers that a common mouse might've called a home. Dust was settled everywhere and dishes sat piled in a sink. DeWayne unapologetically retook his chair and snubbed out a smoldering cigarette left smoking in the bowl.

"I've already talked to the police and the detectives, so why the visit?" he asked with a raspy smoker's grumble in his throat.

"We are still investigating the death of your daughter, Mr. Baltimore. I was hoping you might offer some insight into Shea's life; her friends, any men that she might've been dating at the time...things like that."

"I'd love to help out, but she hadn't been living in that shit hole for very long, it would've been her first apartment," he said sadly. He detected loss oozing off the man and understood the grief he was suffering, but it wasn't hard to imagine that his personality had curdled long before this singular event of tragedy.

"Was Shea seeing anyone at the time of her death?" Keen regretted how he phrased it the second it escaped his lips.

"Naw, Shea was too shy. All she ever wanted to do was paint and draw. She could've done that here—she might still be alive."

DeWayne coughed loudly, causing him to lean forward to regain his raspy breath. Even someone not in the medical profession might hear a rattle of emphysema or lung cancer in its early stages. If the alcoholism didn't take the liver first, he noted. Recalling the notes he read from one of the first reporting detectives, her apartment was covered with sketches and paintings and there were ample painting supplies and easels in each corner.

"I was told she was a promising artist," the detective lied, trying to sound sympathetic at the man's loss. "Are there some friends you can remember by name?"

"May have been some from her job; I never met any. Shea wasn't like normal girls her age...a real loner that one."

Keen suspected if she had close friends she might've wanted to keep them from meeting her father. What others thoughtlessly assumed was a shy, self-effacing young woman, might have been someone who didn't want others to witness the tragedy of her home life. This poor fool had no idea, the detective figured. He was surprised when he asked to see Shea's old bedroom and DeWayne readily agreed, waving his hand still gripping a fresh beer and declaring, "Back bedroom on the right... hasn't been touched."

Keen presumed it would be a testament to a young artist in the making, with charcoal drawings pinned to the wall and sketchpads and colored pencils strewn around the room. And in that regard, he wasn't disappointed. It appeared a little like a sanctuary, a shelter of a bedroom with a palpable sense of a young girl and all her desperate angst. And without exhibiting it outright, it also showed a modicum of regret in the absence of any maternal figure in her life. It told him volumes about his victim and left a twinge of *what could've been,* filling the empty room like smoke. He understood why she wanted and needed her freedom. Just meeting her father was proof of that. But then the horrible CSU images came rolling back into his head, and as he turned to leave, he couldn't help but wonder about the cruelties of life and the loss of someone so young.

He thanked Mr. Baltimore for his time and departed. He felt gratitude that the Seattle sun met him at the door, lifting the proverbial cloud of despair that he just exited. He figured that DeWayne Baltimore was not long for this world either; not by the red splotchy skin he noticed, or the petechial fading from one who recently abused too much alcohol. There'd be no one to mourn him now, Keen thought. It appeared the Baltimore family was destined to get wrapped in bitterness from before Shea's murder, and for long after. Eventually he ended up back at the precinct and that unending printout of names as his only clue going forward.

Chapter Eleven

IT IS NOT widely known, but the Bible mentions the name Gabriel as angel in both the old and new testaments, but never as *archangel*. His name is littered throughout other religious writings from the Quran to the book of Enoch as being one of God's archangels, specifically as the *revealer* and who is set over the repentance unto hope of those who inherit eternal life. In Jewish mythology, it is the angel Gabriel who reaches down into the *Guf*, or the treasury of souls, and pulls out the first one within his grasp to establish a life. In the book of Enoch, Gabriel is the fifth angel of five who watches and guards and sets man against man "that they may destroy each other in battle: for length of days shall they not have."

Little Gabe heard the narratives, back when his family took him to St. Ignatius Parish. Although he'd been too young to understand all the stories, he remembered his mother squeezing his tiny hand whenever the subject of angels came bellowing from the pulpit in yet another charismatic sermon delivered on Sunday. He took special account of when this occurred because he enjoyed Sissy's loving gaze as well as the warmth of her fingers clutching his.

As an adult, he'd never much thought about the connections. He was still a boy sitting in wonderment of the world around him, and too easy to forget how a bond existed silently with his mother, based upon such a tiny string of intangible fabric. Gabriel Church had indeed become the *revealer*, drifting into town and locating the white-lighters who fortuitously crossed his path. Igniting them up into some preordained glory and sending their souls heaven bound to face God.

As he sped away from St. Joseph's that afternoon, his insides were twisted in anger. He'd said too much; that he understood. He was cursing himself for confessing to a priest. He felt shame for doing it at all, and particularly to someone he genuinely liked such as Father Kait. If Chris had been here, he might not have needed to walk into a church and confess his sins to a complete stranger. Then again, he would never have described Chris as being a religious man, and whenever Gabe described his kills and the reasons for each one during those long interviews, it had become clear Chris couldn't comprehend his calling. He'd seen the glassy-eyed confusion creeping across the writer's face. He knew that Chris learned not to judge him, but any celestial rationale he'd tried to explain seemed to escape his understanding. Even from such a worldly, learned companion as Chris seemed to be. Like explaining politics to someone from a different culture—it didn't translate well.

Although the killer and the writer had never spoken the words aloud, both knew they were bound to one another. They would protect each other whenever the need arose. The same way Gabe knew that Chris would never turn him in. He would lie, refuse to cooperate, or simply remain silent on the matter of his lover and any crimes he may have committed before they ever met. That was the only reason Gabe felt comfortable enough driving out of Seattle and leaving his greatest witness behind and alive. If things had been even slightly misaligned, he would have felt the need to murder Chris as well and wash any contact from his hands in true Macbethian style.

It became that lack of human contact which drove him into St. Joseph's in the first place, his loneliness and a need to confess to practically anyone how fucked up he felt. He just didn't mean to allow the words to spill out as effortless and random as they did. And even though he knew the priest could break his bond of confession and tell the police all he'd heard, he didn't think he would. Naturally, he couldn't be certain about Kait, but the old dude seemed constructed by steadfast moral bricks and a strong conviction to serve those needing his care. Another reason he decided instantly that he liked the man and enjoyed his gentle way with words.

When Gabe noticed the fuel gauge and realized that he needed to gas up, he started scanning for the closest station. Then by sheer chance, like it'd always been, he caught a wayward glimpse of the next white-lighter in his life. Chance and Fate always ruled supreme in Gabe's life. It'd been his belief in a fatalistic destiny that always guided him to the next town, the next bar, and next circumstance which made up his very existence. Chance was the one who allowed him to cross paths with the writer. Chance made them would-be lovers, just as it had been chance that barreled him forward into the arms of all his fucks and in the intersection of every white-lighter he'd ever dispatched. And chance played another round again, after he observed a small-figured man getting out of a newer model Dodge Neon to head into the Gas-N-Sip on that same afternoon, and that exact moment when Gabe pulled in to refuel.

The man appeared to be in his mid to late twenties. With a radiance surrounding him that Gabriel locked onto as he pulled the nozzle from its housing at the gas pump. The glow emanating from the stranger would have been perceptible to him even from a distance. This was much like Gabriel witnessed before in many others, starting with a green and yellow luminosity inches off the body, then becoming even brighter as it escaped. Like some eerie glow-in-the-dark smoke dancing around a form before turning into a bright bleached shine before evaporating into nothingness and back into the ether of the real world. It could only be another white-lighter; there was little question in Gabriel's mind.

It'd been a while since he last saw one, and to him it stood as an inescapable truth that divulged this man was separate from any other patron at the Gas-N-Sip. Gabe tossed a ten on the counter before heading back to the pump. Now he hoped he filled his tank before the man exited the store and got into his red Neon and drove away. He wanted to follow this one, the same as he'd followed others, and regardless whether the ten was used in the tank or not, he knew he'd be behind the wheel exactly when he needed to be.

Chance intervened again, and he was able to pull his truck out of the way of oncoming cars and wait for his quarry to leave the convenience store. As the man exited, Gabe could see how young his face looked, his wispy, adolescent attempt at facial hair, and his grunge-style wardrobe, bordering on failure. He had that inexperienced, awkward continence of a virgin. Someone who might claim to love music a lot but really only liked select bands, ones he thought others might think were cool. Gabe wondered what this man-child could have done to warrant becoming a white-lighter. Maybe it wasn't something he'd done, but something he was meant to do. Because Gabriel never divined the complete wherefores of his life mission, nothing beyond seeing them revealed in the glow that designated them as being special...at least to his twisted thinking. Gabe followed the red Dodge Neon out of the parking lot and then trailed behind, confident he wouldn't lose him.

THE WHITE-LIGHTER'S name was Matt Alan Rakes. He was twenty-three years old and currently worked as a customer service rep for a publisher of instructional manuals specializing in the aeronautics field. He had no girlfriend but surrounded himself with the close friends he'd made during his days in high school. He spent far too much time playing video games on weekends, going well into the night with his geek squad of high school companions, surviving off heavily caffeinated Jolt cola and fat-laden snacks. Matt had used one of his breaks to make a run to the convenience store only a few blocks from the office building where he worked.

He had no idea that a serial killer had taken an interest in him or that he was currently trailing behind in a two-tone Dodge pickup. It became his oblivion to the uncanny circumstances surrounding him that changed everything—like the blanched, tinted glow bouncing off him in a halo that only Gabriel Church could see.

Since neither vehicle needed to enter the on-ramp to the nearby expressway, Gabe followed easily. The man only took residential streets to reach his office park and then entered through a back warehouse door, a burrito and a big soda gripped in his hands.

Gabe parked in an unsecured lot across the street and waited. He was willing to stretch his patience by sitting there for the remainder of the day watching that same door for his quarry to exit...as he'd done many times before. He was a man without constrictions to his time and with no place in particular he needed to be. He knew how this would go and settled in for an extended period behind the wheel, alternating from listening to the radio and reading from an old book he'd once crammed behind the driver's side of the bench seat a long time ago. The words on the paper were only a distraction but allowed him to appear more normal to strangers than what he truly was. Life on the road had taught him the fortitude of waiting and the need for patience whenever stalking his prey, and so he sat alone without being lonely because he had a new mission to occupy his brain.

Checking the time, he saw 5:15 p.m. on the clock in his truck. This was as employees began to filter out, but it was the youthful, small-framed figure Gabe had been watching for who held his gaze. He walked out with a group of similarly aged men and women, and the sounds of muffled laughter crept across the road and into Gabe's open truck window. Ostensibly everyone was headed home and walked in separate directions to their respective vehicles. But then the Neon's driver opened his door and waved casually to someone, and it prompted Gabe to turn the ignition and fire up the Dodge.

He once again followed the white-lighter, weaving through lines of rush hour traffic, careful not to lose sight of the Neon's bumper as he drove. Within twenty minutes his prey had reached a destination, turning into what Gabe assumed was the young man's residence. The Dodge slipped into a parking space in front of a length of single-story apartment units stretching along poorly manicured sidewalks. Every unit displayed the same unattractive air conditioners from a bygone era crafted into vinyl sided walls, the same matching single pane glass in a front vista window, and each had the same inexpensive vinyl blinds in a sad, systematic row of boring uniformity. It must be all the young man could afford, Gabe presumed, not that he could question another's choice in residences, having none himself since leaving Tennessee and becoming his own form of aimless drifter.

With his truck idling across the street, he watched as the young white-lighter exited his car and walked inside a unit with the letters FOURTEEN neatly painted on the placard right above the doorway. He couldn't bear to sit and wait there until his opportunity arose, having spent too much time behind the wheel. Since he now knew the car and gained an address, he could sneak away to grab a bite for dinner and stretch his legs. Gabe would be back soon, he merely needed time to decide how to handle the upcoming situation. He'd not let a white-lighter slip through his fingers so far, and he had no intention of this one becoming his first. He was, after all, a patient and careful hunter.

Cramming a burger down his throat, Church stared out the window of a Burger King only minutes from the white–lighter's rundown apartment. He thought about Chris, remembering conversations and the laughter of male companionship—he'd laughed in a way he hadn't in years. He recalled one lengthy interview where they indulged in too many cocktails and discussed things not pertinent to the book. At some point, they'd sat on the floor and leaning against the sofa in the suite at the Mayfair. They were relaxed and enjoying their conversations, even when they took on a darker, more personal side.

GABE WAS NAKED, and Chris was in nothing but his underwear. They fucked earlier and were now relaxed as they chatted about old dates and high school days. Christian regaled Gabe with some of his failed dates in college, which amused both men to no end. Undoubtedly the alcohol assisted with their frivolity because Church made idle jests about seeing Chris with a woman and pantomimed the awkward dance of a shy, graceless young man, which was supposed to be a clumsy version of Christian Maxwell asking a girl out. They both found it amusing and laughed until tears filled their eyes.

"I never asked girls for dates..." Gabe chimed in. "I simply told them they were going out with me."

"Well, I don't like telling people what to do...*unless I'm naked.*" Chris arched his back and burst into raucous laughter, which Gabe joined until they were practically rolling on the floor together with that image darting through their brains.

It took a few minutes, but eventually the merriment dwindled down, and Gabe regained enough composure to stare over at Chris and whisper, "Well, you're not naked now, but you should be."

With a sly grin and a twinkle rising through bourbon-bleary eyes, Chris stood up and stripped himself of his tighty-whities, then turned and headed to the bedroom for another game of sweat-inducing pleasure. Gabe was quickly on his heels catching him before he could reach the bed and swallowing him in a body-hugging motion from behind. Drinking always brought his libido out and the growing swell in his cock assured him he was ready for round two.

It'd been a strange time. All of that had been new and should've felt unaccustomed and alien to him. But somehow it seemed comforting in a way he wouldn't have guessed, that was, if he'd spent any time thinking on it. He hadn't ever considered himself queer before then, but there he was, naked and full of zeal, his body reacting to every stimulus as if it'd always desired what was happening in that moment. At the time he wasn't sure if he could attribute that to Chris or not, being with another man hadn't really crossed his mind before their night shared in the hotel. But being in his company and laughing and enjoying it as he had, made perfect sense in retrospect; exotic, freeing and the sex being incomprehensible to anything he'd experienced in his youth.

GABE CAUGHT HIS reflection in the glass of the Burger King window and noticed he was smiling. The recollections always brought him pleasure. Memories of Chris and those few days were pivotal changing points to his life. He'd been with men sexually since leaving Seattle, as many men as he had women, but nothing ever seemed to eclipse that time he'd spent with the writer and no fuck ever seemed as sweet as it had back then. He knew he'd been chasing dragons and tilting at ridiculous windmills thinking they were giants, but he was certain that it had altered him in a multitude of ways. And for that he was glad. But his memories, however saccharine they had become, always brought the bitter, and he seemed sadder when the minute finally passed. Chris had given him as his final gift he supposed, that ball of heavy iron chained to his ankle and preventing him from running free as he'd done before they'd first met. All those strange and awkward feelings had become more than a passing notion.

Pushing it all aside, he got up from the table and drained his cola with a single long swig before tossing the cup in the trash bin. As he headed to his truck, he knew he could force out any of those bitter memories by concentrating on the job at hand. He had a mission to complete and trained his mind to that end alone. He parked on the side of the road nearly a tenth of a mile past those motel-looking apartments. He surveyed the white-lighter's car, and then the door marked fourteen. *Still at home*, he thought, which was good. But he knew it would've been too dangerous to attempt a break-in at that tiny rat hole the lighter called home. Someone would easily hear such a noise, so he never even considered the risk.

Gabe decided to drive around the neighborhood, knowing that every keyhole had its own particular form of access, and one only had to look closely to see it. He found his when he crossed a bridge a half mile from the white-lighter's residence. As his truck passed over the viaduct, he could hear the rumble of heavy current, even over the creak of his axles and the thump of his tires across wood and concrete. It interested him enough that he pulled to the side of the road and stopped his vehicle. Stepping out he could see the spray-painted graffiti and the dark stain of rust running along the sides from every rivet used to construct the bridge. *This was a place schoolchildren hung out and teenagers drank beers and fondled their first titties, desolate and bordering empty grazing fields overgrown by sage and thickets of tall thorns.*

The roadway seemed to connect one residential area to another and must've seen its share of speeding cars where no police usually patrolled. Peering over the railing, he was surprised at the fast flow of the current. Waves rolling over one another making frothy tiny tides, spilling into even smaller eddies and whirlpools as they surged forward. Gabe had expected nothing but a trickling creek under the bridge, but far from being so fainthearted. It must be runoff from a lake, he suspected, even though he knew of no body of water that could support this rushing current. Deeper than he'd imagined, even in the fresh light of the afternoon, he couldn't see the canal's muddy bottom. He watched as empty cola bottles and rubbish sped along with the undercurrent, and his first flashing idea seemed to be that this was the ideal spot for dumping a body.

Church knew that even a short while spent in this current would cleanse any remains of DNA and telltale fibers. The mucky waters would easily add more than they took away and staring down at the dreck bouncing atop the black oily waters of the canal, a serial killer became suddenly inspired. This is where the white-lighter's body would end up.

Church witnessed the familiar radiant glow exploding around the white-lighter upon his death, much as he had before. A victim he never knew by a proper name. He'd felt the same heady satisfaction as the glowing light rose a few feet above the body, right before exploding like fireworks and then ascending skyward. The murder occurred under a beautiful and expansive San Antonio sky. Stars were twinkling overhead, and a chilly clearness existed in the air, even being so close to the downtown lights of the city. The man's whimpers and tear-stained face fell away under the taut stretched rope Church used to silence his screams. The following sound came only as the body hit the water and began its fast journey downstream.

MATT RAKES'S WATER-drenched remains turned up a week later and over a mile away from the tiny bridge where it had been so casually tossed by Church. His disappearance hadn't even become public knowledge before two young boys made the grisly discovery of a corpse washed up and trapped under a tree stump along the edge of the canal. Bloated from the elements and appearing like so much typical river debris, it nearly went unnoticed. Authorities already performed a wellness check at Matt's apartment after he'd failed to report to work for two consecutive days, but they discovered nothing that might've indicated foul play. The disappearance barely made the five-o'clock news before patrol officers fished out his body and the coroner made her initial decree at the scene.

Recognizing the strength of the water's current and the proximity to Matt's apartment, police suspected the viaduct almost immediately. CSU teams had combed the area but years of teenage partying, with its mountains of waste transported along the creek bed and piling into mounds around the rocky terrain of the bridge's underpass would make finding any clue all but impossible. Any traces of a crime scene were made invisible under the accumulation of beer cans, used condoms, and general rubbish caught between the broken concrete slabs and rocks. Too much sin traveled the same path downstream and no one at San Antonio PD even guessed the bridge might prove beneficial in finding his killer.

They would also search for a motive but find nothing there as well. It wasn't a drug deal gone awry; no jealous lovers to interview, nor was there any money to be made by someone's death. There was no apparent cause for Matt Rake's murder at all. How could they have seen the randomness of the killing without learning what twists and turns were in his killer's mind? Detectives couldn't have known that it happened at night. That he'd been surprised from behind as he headed from his apartment door to his car and taken by force to an isolated spot where he was shoved to his knees and in blind confusion had to listen to his killer's rants about religion and not understand. Or even that he'd begged for his life over tears of shock and horror but found no mercy from his killer. A medical examiner would later say was ligature strangulation by someone using strong influence, having nearly severed his tracheal windpipe quite unnecessarily.

The amber-blue lights of police cars attracted residents from their homes: gaping, curious spectators from the area traveling in small groups along the rural stretch of blacktop. All to watch as the CSU teams turned up nothing of any evidentiary value. From the outside, it remained a seemingly nondescript location, which would eventually become more legend than former crime scene. A scarce number might sense a quasi-ill feeling as they passed over that venerable bridge headed to work or off to go shopping, but they couldn't remember what event may've prompted a change in their mood. An unexplained cold air remained, long after the body was pulled from the water's edges. Mothers hollered out to their children from kitchen windows and back doors: "Steer clear of the bridge now…ya hear!" But even those stories would fade with passing time, as teenagers found the allure of an ideal secluded spot to sneak a few beers or smoke their first cigarettes. It would again become a place hidden from the outside world where they may congregate and escape the pressures of being young.

But to Church, it would always be that spot where Matt Rakes coughed blood into his mouth, turned blue from his lack of oxygen, and his eyes bulged red under the constraint of Gabe's rope. It would be the spot where he died and then went face-first into the inky black water before disappearing from sight altogether.

Chapter Twelve

CHRISTIAN MAXWELL NOTICED the little red blinking light on his answering machine as he walked through the door of his apartment but went straight to the kitchen to pour a glass of wine without checking the messages. He'd long given up thinking that Gabe would have called so it could wait. Christian had taken a new job, after his dream of writing that one great crime novel was shattered into nothing when Gabriel drove out of Seattle, leaving him sad and confused. And sucking out his soul, even while paying the bills and giving him something to concentrate on. But here, alone at night, he couldn't stop the memories.

Shea's murder had come as a shock to him, as well as a constant reminder that he'd unwittingly caused her death. Had he not visited her at her apartment or felt that burning jealousy twisting his insides into tightly wound knots, she might be alive today. It frightened him to realize he'd become somehow complicit, not only in her murder but in any Gabriel might have done after their first casual meeting at that trendy little coffee house in the arts district. The guilt and shame intermingled with regret over allowing him to become romantically involved with a serial killer in the first place.

But he saw Gabe in ways that no other person could. He saw the tormented childhood, and he read between every line that he'd been so unsuccessful in penning to paper. He'd seen the good in the man and been brought to his knees by Gabe's gentle nature and forthright charisma. On the other side, he'd been as justifiably frightened with all the stories he heard about murder, been confused with Gabriel's insane rationale about religion and personal mission statements from God. Gabriel Church was far more than an enigma: he was complicated in indescribable ways...clockwork of wheels and gears that fascinated Chris, who always felt as if he were balancing on a blade's edge, between affection and fear. That was when it came to the killer turned lover. That ringing, continual question bounced in his head, *can you love the man and hate the things that made him cold?*

Chris had taken no other lovers since Shea's death. He hadn't even gone out socially...not once. That may have been because he possessed a quality of humanity he suspected Gabriel lacked. His remorse and guilt for the things he'd done, which had all turned sour and gotten that mousy, frail, but artistic girl dead. When dead was what she shouldn't be.

To his credit, Christian had found the tools to go on, basic, fire-starting tools we're all gifted from birth. The same ones he'd thought all his life he lacked in comparison to others. Surprisingly, *life goes on!* He put Shea's murder alongside those images of a naked Church, back on the dusty shelves in the farthest recesses of his mind...as far back as they would allow themselves to remain abandoned.

But occasionally, far too frequently in truth, pictures of Gabriel lying seductively naked on those expensive rugs of the Mayflower, or flashes of smiles he remembered from their time spent walking the tourist district together came flooding back. And whenever they did, they dragged Shea's body behind them. Christian had only known she'd been murdered after Gabe confessed to it. Then later of course, when he'd heard the insignificant tidbits of information blurted out on television by an attractive news anchor, but he never knew the full details. He'd never wanted to learn the details. He lived with a persistent fear that the authorities would contact him and that they would know of his involvement with the killer. Or that he would be arrested or hauled in for questioning. He wasn't like Gabe. He couldn't lie or feign any lack of involvement. It wasn't in his nature to be so callous. He would have likely dropped to his knees and confessed to everything he knew with very little provocation. No, he wasn't like Gabriel in that regard at all.

Finishing his stiff drink, Christian pushed away from the kitchen counter and stopped in front of the landline to listen to what was probably another funeral insurer trying to sell him a plan. But when he played the voicemail his every fear became even more tangible and his hands began to tremble as he listened.

This is Detective Scott Keen of the Seattle Police Department trying to reach out to a Christian Maxwell. Your name came up in our investigations as a potential witness to a crime, and we are asking for assistance in this matter. If this number belongs to Christian Maxwell, 35, who owns a 2012 Mercury Sedan, or owned one recently, we are asking that you contact our offices at your earliest convenience.

The voice was male, authoritative, but sounded disinterested when he rattled off the number where the detective could be reached. It sounded bland enough that it shouldn't have caused anyone that much concern or consternation, like he was reading from a long list of names and each one was less important than the last. But Christian knew that this call wasn't by chance. Whoever this detective was, he wanted it to sound that way, simple and meaningless. He was probably working off some unknown list of names and yet trying not to alert a possible killer, Christian suspected. But that guess only unnerved him more.

Then it dawned on him that the detective asked about his car. This meant someone could've seen his vehicle at, or near, the scene. He had to remind himself that he hadn't killed Shea himself, hoping that would stop the tremble in his hands or quash the rising bile in his throat, which threatened to explode onto his polished floors if he didn't regain some semblance of control. But what if they asked him why he'd been there?

He had zero answers for those types of questions, and he knew he couldn't even fabricate a lie because he was simply not capable of that type of deception. How the hell could Gabriel choose to live like this? He wondered. How could someone be so guilty and yet retain such a cool outside demeanor as he'd seen in the man? It seemed unnatural for one so used to being truthful with others in his day-to-day existence. It wasn't in his nature...even though he hadn't been completely truthful with himself. Like when he tricked himself into believing he was straight, or when he questioned those odd stirrings that awakened his crotch and burned in his gut when he sat across from Gabriel at the coffee house downtown.

Then the reality hit him cold like a slap to his cheek. The police wanted to speak to him about Shea Baltimore's murder. He was, at the very least, guilty of being acquainted with her *and* her killer, which created new and fresh images of him paddling upstream atop a turbulent river of shit. He expected his usual luck to hold true to form, which meant he was about to lose his one and only paddle, ultimately to become stranded in the middle of that crap-filled current he was navigating. That flash of bitter realization only made him smile, without even being aware he'd been grinning. All he could do was watch dumbfounded and powerless as his metaphorical oar slipped below the surface, leaving him with his customary what-the-fuck expression plastered on his face.

Well, you either find the humor or find yourself crying in the dirt. What else was left to do?

He had no idea what his next steps should be. Should he contact this Detective Keen and try to make up something, or should he run? He suddenly wanted to talk to Gabe about it because he knew that he'd tell him what he should do. Gabe was confident and sure, in a way that Chris wasn't. He may have been a murderer, but he was someone Maxwell could count on, possibly the only one when it came to this. But Gabriel had never carried a cell when he knew him. Even if he had he wouldn't have given Chris the number. Gabriel merely wanted to protect his lover. He'd made that clear when he chose to leave Seattle to protect the writer for whom he'd grown to have affection. Chris had seen the regret behind those pale gray-blue eyes as he turned and walked out of his life forever. He hadn't been blind to what the man was doing, and he agreed with everything. Even if that meant that he'd never see him again. It'd be for the best; they both understood that well, even without having to utter the words aloud.

He didn't even know if Gabriel was still alive. Given his circumstances, he could've been arrested, killed, or have even committed suicide. People couldn't always tell what he was thinking at times, but Gabe always said that whatever future lay ahead of him was going to end up explosive. It reminded Chris of something his own mother had said to him once, when she had asked why he was getting an apartment so soon after college. She thought he should come home to stay while he looked for a new profession that would be sufficient to pay his bills and secure his new place. Chris, in all of his stupid, youthful jubilance simply replied, "Well, Mother, if I don't land a job in time, then I suppose I'll be evicted. But at least I'll go down big."

His mother's stoic retort had been telling of her character, straightforward and absent any maternal affection. "Always remember, son, that you don't ever go down *big*, you only go down."

Chris listened to the message on his voicemail twice, so he'd absorb it all and then wrote down the return number and extension for the detective. He wasn't sure what his next step would be, but he wouldn't be in a rush to call back, that much was certain. He had to mull it over. He had to screw up the courage to lie, or tell the police something that resembled the truth, while avoiding admitting he not only knew the real killer but had sucked his dick on multiple occasions and simply forgotten to contact authorities when he first learned of the young woman's death.

For the first time in a long while, he decided he needed to go out and get a drink. A strong drink he figured, one that could either carry him down his crap river and away from reality or give an insight on what steps he might consider taking next. A double bourbon and Coke might begin to cease the tremble in his hands and push the pitted knot growing in his stomach downward, minimizing it into a smaller, more manageable portion. Grabbing the jacket he'd thrown over the back of his couch and patting his pocket to ensure he had his phone there, he raced out the door without even checking to ensure it locked behind him.

The weeks limped along until two months had passed since Gabriel walked out of his condo, leaving him to deal with all the ramifications and destruction that remained. He'd since changed jobs, pointed his ship to new starry horizons, and attempted to carry himself forward. But then a voicemail on his machine had yanked him backward with blinding speed. And now, as he sat alone at the bar in the first place he came to, he could only see Gabe's face staring back at his. There were flashes of Shea mixed in there as well, along with memories of research he'd done on his serial killer's murders back in the early stages of their involvement together. Pictures he'd pulled from newspapers and off the Internet, articles he'd clipped and pinned to his walls. All in some idiotic effort of understanding the depths of his killer's actions, a ridiculous attempt to understand his subject, long before he recognized that he had feelings for the man.

Chris sat drinking alone for over an hour, until his perceptions became skewered and foggy in his brain. The bartender seemed to see he was a patron with a great deal on his plate and made sure to keep his glass filled, thankfully without making that unnecessary chitchat that increased his tips. He was no closer to figuring out his next move, but he was closer to falling into a stupor.

Chris wasn't a stupid man. He knew if the devil came knocking at his door he wasn't going to see a figure with cloven hoofs, nothing bent, deformed or ugly. He wasn't going to be holding a scythe in one leathery hand, nor would he stand apart from the curtain of sulfur and brimstone billowing in his wake. He would, after all, be a thing of beauty, beyond anyone's previous comparison. Because it is only the attractive ones who can lure the innocent and insipid flocks away from their gods. And he knew Gabriel was such a man. To Chris, he was a tantalizing image of power and perfection, blinding him from the horrors in the man's past. And he did all that with nothing more than a crooked smile and a twinkle from those incredible eyes of his.

He knew Gabriel Lee Church and he were bound together, even across the expansive miles separating them. They were two different men who shared one particularly hideous secret. They were comingled by their passions, and it'd altered them for better or worse forever. And just then, as if in reply to a question never asked, Chris felt the vibration in his pocket from his cell phone ringing. It tore him from his dark thoughts the moment he was rising from his barstool to leave. When he answered, he heard the one voice he hadn't expected to hear.

"Babe, are you someplace where you can talk freely? Is it safe, I mean?" Gabriel asked

There was a long pregnant pause as Chris pulled in the oxygen to accept this unexpected reality. But the silence lingered too long, and an impatient Church demanded.

"Well...is it?"

"Yes," Chris stammered out, "Sorry, I'm a little in shock is all. I didn't figure I'd hear from you...not so soon."

Or even at all, he thought without voicing his singular fear aloud.

Whatever tensions he'd been living under previously were replaced by a new sensation. A relaxing, creature comfort that he'd always known only appeared after a substantially long period of separation. Absolute security and it came from hearing a familiar voice on the other end of a line. It washed over his body and turned every muscle into stringy loose fibers, like stepping into a warm sauna after a long, hard day. And just the masculine strength of Gabriel's voice made him unwind.

It almost made him want to cry. Not that he'd ever have allowed that to happen. He never wanted Gabriel to see him in that kind of state. He would've detested a weak, pussy display in him. The bourbon may have calmed his nerves from the earlier message on his machine, but now it became a forced assault to his senses, and regardless how tranquil Church's gravelly voice made him feel, his hands shook violently enough that he worried he might drop his phone altogether. He was barely able to contain himself as he pulled out two crumpled twenties from his wallet, then tossed them on the counter as he headed out the door of the pub, his cell fixed to his ear like glue.

"I've wanted to call you many times." Gabe's voice was a hoarse, sexy whisper. "I didn't because we couldn't risk it, but you have crossed my mind many times."

Choking back strong emotions, Chris only said, "Me too, but I couldn't have called you anyway; you don't carry a phone around." He chuckled slightly to cover the awkward silence.

"I'm calling you now from a pay phone. I was glad I remembered your number."

"Where are you anyway?" Chris asked, seconds before regretting the words as they spilled out.

"It doesn't matter, not close to you," he said flatly. "This way if anyone asks, you won't have to lie because you'd undoubtedly be a horrible liar, Chris." And then more softly Gabriel added an afterthought, "The good ones never are."

Lord...Chris thought. *It is almost like he can read my mind...even from whatever distance separating us, or whatever hole he's currently hiding in. Yes, this shithead has some magnetic hold over me...not that I'm complaining.*

"I'm really glad you called." He measured out the words to ensure they sounded sincere without sounding sappy. He knew how Gabriel would hate that. Gabriel saw life in black and white, even when it came to the two of them. "Mostly for myself," he continued, "but I wanted to let you know something happened today, only hours ago actually."

Chris couldn't have prepped him any easier with his news, so he simply lumbered forward. "I got a call from a detective at the Seattle PD. He wants to talk to me. He left a message, but I haven't had a chance to call him back. Not that I would've, not before speaking to you about it first."

The quiet came like a rolling thundercloud over distant hills, a vacuum of emptiness, dark and ominous. Gabriel's deadfall silence seemed to speak volumes for Chris. Reminding him he was about to face an inevitable squall but could do nothing but brace for the impact.

"You will," he said calmly. "But whatever happens, protect yourself. We don't need both of us running from the police. You might have to make something up, but you can do it; you're the writer, remember? Make it up good, and if you have to tell them about me, tell them I threatened you if you went to the police. That I promised to harm you if you confessed to even knowing my name."

"I think someone saw my car when I visited your apartment, or else back at Shea's. At least it sounded like that when they phoned. I'm nervous about it and really glad you called."

"You can't second-guess them, Christian," Gabe whispered. "That's not how to play the odds. You have to presume they know more than you think they do and work backward from there."

"I don't want to talk about that now." Chris blurted out, wanting to have that conversation in the safety of his place or where others couldn't listen in. "I want to talk about us."

"Not now, it's not safe to talk...but soon."

Chris felt that twinge of excitement he remembered from their last encounter. A new prospect entering into the equation that he might see Gabriel sooner than he'd expected. The word *sooner* seemed to swing like a pendulum through his brain.

Can it be true? Will I get the chance to see him face-to-face?

"I want to see you again," he blurted out. "There are things I wanted to say to you that I never had a chance...about us...about what this all means; but mostly, I want to see you and hold you again." He could almost sense Gabriel smiling then, like a refreshing gust of air suddenly blown across his face. And he knew with certainty that Gabe felt the same.

He knew that whatever city his lover visited would later discover there'd been a sudden and violent increase in the population's mortality. He knew Church wasn't exactly a good man, he was someone damaged beyond recognition, but in that particular second, it didn't matter, because he was able to wash it from his memory and feel the wind upon his cheeks. It brought new promise and told him he might salvage Church, reassemble him from scratch and repair the damage the world had done so cruelly.

Maybe they were only pretty lies, he told himself.

And even now he had to confess, if only privately to himself, that he still didn't know the cause or the catalyst that had started it all, the thing which had driven Gabe down his tragic path. He knew most of the symptoms but couldn't fully grasp the disease. It could've been his father, Bennett, or his religious ideologies, or even those long and lonely miles and years of self-imposed isolation. But for reasons he couldn't fathom in the moment, none of that mattered anymore.

Hell, it could be from something as simple as the pain he carries like a stone. The veiled grief and guilt he wallows in because he abandoned his mother and sister back in Tennessee. Chris spent enough time with him to see how he often pretended his family had little bearing on those choices he made, but he knew different. He'd seen Gabe's eyes, watched him shaking off the memories and feigning his lack of concern. It didn't take a genius to see past his subtle lies...only someone who loved him enough to want to look behind the curtain.

He pictured Gabe at a pay phone, near some no-name bar or cheap diner, holding a receiver with hands as wet and clammy as his own, and that rush of urgency as it began to swell. He desperately needed to feel Gabriel's bearded face raking across his cheek, needed to feel the safety he felt whenever the man was standing at his side. Then he became aware how his own knees were shaking, how they threatened to buckle under his weight like muscle converting into marshmallow and melting over an open flame.

"We had our first drink somewhere; remember the spot?"

Then quickly he blurted out, "Don't say it aloud—but where we had our first meeting. Look for me there in one week's time...around the same time when you first introduced yourself. You can surely avoid calling the detective for a week."

Then more forcefully, Gabe spat the words out, "Tell no one where you're going and for fuck's sake, make sure you're not followed. Take a seat close to where we did that first night...but don't look for me. I'll be nearby. I promise. I'll make it known I'm there as soon as possible. And understand this, Chris: I really wanna see you too. Probably even more than you want to see me."

After Gabriel's cryptic demand, the line suddenly went dead. Although the advent of cell service eliminated that nasty dial tone ringing to show the call was disengaged, it was almost as if he could hear it anyway. The blasting pitch shoved into his head like a screwdriver being stabbed into his brain, a ghostly reminder telling him although he might be holding a phone in his hand, the connection between them was suddenly severed with the precision of a sharp blade and over too quickly. Gabriel might have been worried about being recorded or the line being tapped, forgetting how random the call was and that it originated from a pay phone to a cell and those were the kinds of calls not easily tracked. But Church had successfully outrun the law for nearly two decades. He'd remained one step ahead because he'd been vigilant and careful. Chris couldn't second-guess him now, even though it felt like the rug was being pulled rapidly from under his feet, sending him toppling to the pavement below.

Chapter Thirteen

LATER THAT NIGHT, before he slept, Christian beat off. Perfect images of a naked Gabriel and him having copious amounts of sex ran rampant like unchecked wildfire through his brain. And even with Detective Keen's worrisome voicemail bouncing echoes inside his skull he still reached a glorious orgasm. His brief conversation with Church served to transform his shaft into a rigid mast, refusing to even consider going soft until he was fully satiated. It inspired secret fantasies to come to life and eventually he reached a satisfying, and all too necessary, climax, leaving proof of Gabriel's magnetic hold over him seeded atop his chest and stomach.

Masturbation was a sham facsimile of what he truly wanted but gratifying to think about those broad shoulders and masculine chest hair peppering him from crotch to neck, inching along that massive body and trailing down his well-defined biceps. It would have been impossible to have gained any sleep that night, not at least until he'd found some relief by evoking mental pictures of Gabe's impressive erection or imagining tiny drops of perspiration falling from that towering figure and massing over his.

Breathy and exhausted, he eventually found his slumber. And he'd been happier in those moments than in many weeks. He'd finally heard Gabriel's voice. He'd learned that his former lover still walked among the living. Even more importantly, he'd been shown how much Gabriel had been thinking of him, in as much as he'd been trying to forget all those honeyed memories spent together. But he knew in his heart they were recollections he would never escape. His dreams were fitful, and his body wrestled inside a cocoon of sweaty sheets, but he was content, that much he knew, even while in his unconscious state.

GABE HAD TO admit the devil into his circle to get to know his true name, but he was different than most sociopathic killers. And although he'd felt no remorse for those *celestially- driven murders,* he *had* killed for baser human reasons in his lifetime. His first kill outside the city limits of Dallas had been a no-name trucker who'd offended him. It became retribution and revenge that propelled him to murder in the first place. In Seattle he killed Shea, but only because she represented a real and tangible threat to Christian. Something the would-be writer was just beginning to comprehend. It had been solely to safeguard his companion because he never wanted his only friend to get pulled down into that same sinking mire. In his eyes, he'd done the unthinkable simply out of love and devotion.

During his long interviews with Christian, it had been those murders he hated discussing more than anything else...as if those stories placed him smack dab in the middle of a long list of other better-known killers. Their felonies weren't his, he reasoned. His were never that ugly, not as vile or gruesome as the wrongs committed by others. Their work was strangely beneath him, he concluded. Those men weren't doing God's work. Naturally he had to describe the first kill to Chris, who with his degree in abnormal psychology would have required the specifics for his novel, the one that would never see publication. And later it became clear why the last murder in Seattle had been necessary in his twisted perceptions.

Placing the pay phone back in its cradle, Gabe felt an unfamiliar fluttering, like dancing butterflies in his gut. He only guessed Christian felt the same rumblings, and with that thought, a crooked smile made its way across his face. He'd felt tentative, yet determined after pulling over at the Suds-N-Spin Laundromat on the corner of North Olive and finally making the call. He'd been uncertain as to what type of response he'd receive, but he knew one thing, he had to at least try. This had always been the call hovering like a dark wraith around his head, whispering in his ear, telling him the writer moved on. Disembodied voices reminding him daily that Chris didn't want to hear from a lowlife killer such as him ever again.

He'd fought the good fight for as long as he could. Until a recognizable voice from a distant friend seemed the only medicine he might swallow that could help him finally move forward. And it all but consumed him. He'd heard the statement, Chris mentioning that he'd received a call from the Seattle PD, but Gabe's mind had been so focused on hearing those familiar, dulcet tones from Christian's words from so very far away that none of it seeped in. Not at first.

Their exchange rejuvenated him and gave him a warm, enveloping sensation. For him, it appeared the butterfly wings had been replaced by tiny embers, and all he could think about was how good he felt in those first few seconds after hanging up. Even his transitory conversation with Chris had stoked fires inside his core. And for him, nothing else mattered. Except maybe, by learning Chris had been as desperate to see him, as he was desirous of running his palm along the writer's body, even now, after everything that happened to separate them.

Deciding to spend money he knew he shouldn't, Gabe steered his pickup truck in the direction of the airport, searching for an inexpensive motel and the incentive of a long, hot shower. It would be his gift to himself, he figured, having found the courage to make a phone call he'd once dreaded. He felt giddy at the prospect, but he wasn't sure if it came from sleeping on clean sheets or being able to stretch naked on a mattress as an unfamiliar change of pace, or if it had been hearing a pleasant voice from his past whisper in his ear.

"Look for me there in a week's time," he'd said to Chris. Almost as if he'd formed a plan.

But regardless, he knew he'd be there, once he pulled together sufficient food and fuel money to make the trip. He knew the risks involved in going back to Seattle, but at least he wasn't bumming around and aimlessly chasing any direction. He may not have had a plan, but he had a destination, which was more than he usually carried with him in his rundown Dodge. He caught his reflection in the mirror and noticed he was smiling before turning on the truck's stereo in time to hear the last chorus of one of his favorite old country songs.

CAROL, HIS WIFE, phoned the station just as Keen rose from his desk in his tiny office to head home. Cradling the receiver between his shoulder and neck, he yanked his suit jacket from the hanger on the door and wrestled his way inside.

"You almost missed me, babe," he said. "But why didn't you call my cell?"

"Because I knew you'd still be at the precinct. Always remember, doll, I understand you as well as I know myself."

He could hear the lilt in her voice. It always pacified him, even when all the difficult tragedies he saw daily seemed to weigh down on him. She was his light at the end of a long dark tunnel, and even though they'd been married five years earlier, he was as much in love with her now as the day he dropped to his knee and proposed. She laughed uncomfortably at the silliness of the tradition, covering her mouth to stifle her own embarrassment. He instantly regretted the gesture from the second he was down there, but he was at least thankful he hadn't done it in a restaurant or publically like at the waterfront where they liked to stroll sometimes.

"I'm leaving now." He smiled. He was eager to get home to his lovely wife.

"Figured," she said, "but I was hoping you could stop by the market and grab a gallon of milk. I need it to finish your dinner, and I forgot to pick it up last week."

"Well, you dumbass," he said with a grin, "Then what are you good for anyway?"

"Well…you might be able to find out once you get home." Her voice had taken on a sensual tone. "It might not be just your dinner I'm keeping warm for you."

God, how he loved her.

"Be there in half an hour," he promised, hoping her tone implied they would have sex before eating. They'd been so much in love when they met that they hadn't wanted to have kids right away, but after five wonderful years of marriage, and much to her parent's delight, they'd finally begun to try. So far the stick showed only negative results. But both were confident it wouldn't be long before children were running around and filling their home with noise. So they weren't worried; they knew they had plenty of time. *Maybe tonight's the night.* He found his pace quickening as he headed out to the parking lot.

The detective made quite a bit of headway on the report of vehicle owners' names, leaving messages occasionally and crossing some off his list whenever he finally spoke to someone. So far he'd found all to be unworthy of becoming the next "suspect-slash-witness," or even anyone he felt required a face-to-face interview. The worst part of his investigative work was the drudgery of reaching out to witnesses and trying to make magic by pulling a rabbit from an old hat. But it'd be his last resort, and the one thing still available he could yank from his finite bag of spellbinding tricks.

He was beginning to doubt his original path. Keen never believed he'd find the killer from what the landlord offered alone. He was, however, hoping to find a witness. Someone who'd met the killer personally, because he suspected no one was stupid enough to drive their car to the exact spot where they were going to commit murder for the entire world to see. But he was grasping at straws because in his line of work, straws were all he had.

Chapter Fourteen

BORN IN KENTUCKY but later moved to Tennessee when Bennett could no longer find proper employment in the hill country, Gabriel Church was a boy with very few friends. He liked his early memories of Kentucky, with its rolling knolls of swaying bluegrass and wooded timbers where he could run and play alongside his family's two hunting dogs, Ace and Dolly. It'd always surprised him that Bennett ever allowed anyone in the family to have pets. He was such a cruel man who seemed forever trapped in a prison of what he considered to be very masculine precepts, which even to Gabe appeared confining and unnecessary back then. For Bennett, pets were an extravagance he normally would have disagreed with, and Gabe figured out early it must have been because they were bloodhounds and made good hunting dogs, even though he'd never once seen his father sling a rifle over his shoulder and head out to do any shooting of pheasant or quail. Even chained to his outdated principles of what a man was supposed to be, somehow having hunting dogs was an acceptable trade.

The family acquired Ace and Dolly as a lot of rural people obtained pets—they simply came with the house. They inherited the hounds along with a whitewashed clapboard frame with three bedrooms and an expansive wraparound porch. Bennett was the one who found the house, then signed the rental papers while Sissy and the kids waited in the car. He wasn't cognizant how such an action might appear to strangers, like the agent assisting him. He'd never consulted anyone in the family for big decisions before and thought there was little reason to alter the tradition now. The owners were moving out of state and couldn't take the dogs. Bennett begrudgingly accepted ownership of the homeless mutts, as Gabe heard him lying through his artificial smile and flashing his pearly enamel as he mentioned how he'd always been fond of dogs, and they'd make great pets for his children. At the time, he'd bent down and was rubbing a sweet spot behind one of Dolly's big saggy ears and making idle pleasantries. Gabe remembered that tiny gesture, but throughout his childhood, he couldn't remember a single time he ever saw his father show even the smallest of affections to those old black-and-copper hounds, even though both were considered long-term members of the family.

Young Gabe was excited to welcome the dogs into their world. He instantly fell in love when they bounded around his feet and slobbered him with wet affections. He recalled how thrilled he'd been as they pulled into the driveway in their dusty old Pontiac wagon, pulling a U-Haul trailer loaded to the top with all their possessions locked inside. The dogs were good companions for Gabe and somehow became worthy substitutions for other boys his age, which at the time seemed perfectly normal. He could escape his father's angry admonishments by running into the woods with his two best—and often only friends—trailing behind him and feel unbridled freedom and safety. They'd raise their nostrils and sniff the breeze before racing away to locate fresh game, with Gabe never far behind. His determination forced him through creek beds or splashing through the pools of stagnant waters and past termite-infested tree stumps rotting into pulpy, dry husks.

When work dried up and the family was forced to leave Mercer County to find employment in Tennessee, it broke Gabriel's heart to leave Ace behind with the new renters. Dolly had passed away the previous year on a particularly chilly morning from old age. It'd been a young Gabe who found her dead, and the first time he remembered seeing anything lying cold and lifeless, tacked like glue to the frost-covered earth. He'd come rushing into the barn and unexpectedly discovered her next to the old paint cans and sacks of moldy seed, which no one had ever taken the time to toss out. The images of Dolly lying achingly still and not breathing became ingrained into the walls of his psyche and seemed to follow him for many years to come. He remembered running into the woods with his remaining pal by his side and crying the entire day away. He hugged Ace tightly for comfort as he wiped away his tears and stared out over an open field of saw grass blowing in the breeze. He'd been worried that Ace might miss his longtime companion, but later he noticed Dolly's absence wasn't nearly the same wound for old Ace that it seemed to be for Gabe. He plodded along as if he had some foresight or understanding that all their days were numbered. And her passing, though acute, was something awaiting us all. The creaking arthritis in his joints and small tumors of cancer along his chest were his constant reminders of how long he'd already lived.

If losing Dolly had been a life lesson for Gabriel, then pulling out of that same short driveway they'd crossed only four years earlier, staring out a back window of their old Pontiac, and watching Ace disappear in a cloud of red clay dust was a far greater blemish on the young boy's soul. He'd begged his father to take Ace with them, but Bennett would have nothing of it. Gabe could only ball his fists into blue hammers and bite his lip hard to keep from crying. His sadness seemed overwhelming, to the point he thought it would become more than he could bear, but he never wanted to let his father see him cry.

He pushed all the frustration and turmoil he felt down into a dark place in his heart and made a mental image of him squashing it into a tiny sphere. As if all that anger and frustration might be easily confined and crushed into something more manageable. Even then the boy knew how old Ace was. He knew he didn't have long to live, but no matter how he implored his father or pleaded with him to take Ace with them, he found only gritty, stubborn male pride returned in Bennett's stare. It wasn't the first time he'd hated his father, but in that instant, his hate and resentment found their first true path forward. Gabe recognized then he'd never have any feelings for Bennett Church other than the ones he felt in that moment. And even if he or Bennett wanted more, there was nothing either of them could ever do which might change that.

A year and a half later, after Bennett found electrical contract work in the drier, unforgiving bottoms of Tennessee, the same telling lessons came back to haunt Gabe. He hated moving out of Kentucky and hated Tennessee for stealing the good parts of his childhood, as it had in that image of Ace getting smaller in the distance. He hated and blamed the entire state for his sadness. It'd been doomed for him from even before he could unpack his clothes and put his toys on shelves in his room. He never acclimated to his new surroundings and learned to exist by walking ghostlike through life, determined even then, that as soon as he grew into legal age, he'd curse Tennessee and put the shitty state in his rearview. And as it turned out, he kept that promise he made to himself, because that was what he ended up doing after all.

The other kids in school struck him as backward and unkind, and even though he'd never been any good at making friends and this place seemed unwelcoming and alien. The older boys seemed to relish bullying the younger, smaller ones, but to little Gabe's fortune he finally hit his growth spurt and sprouted up, then out, until he was little no more. As his height and weight increased, he learned to fit in better by conforming to the crowd. He did this best by becoming a bully himself, until his cruelty and cavalier mercilessness were unmatched by any other boy in his class.

Stepping off the school bus one day at the same place where he met it daily, Gabe started down the quarter-mile journey of dirt road headed home. He was surprised to hear a barely audible whimpering sound coming from the bushes and stopped to investigate. Beneath the underbrush and timber, he discovered a small, orange tabby cat staring up in terror. She was all alone and too young not to be a part of a litter. Realizing it had been either abandoned by its mother or left behind as she was moving her brood to some safer location. The boy instantly felt his heart swell and reached out his hands to pluck her from her hiding spot. The kitten tried to show herself as quite the aggressor, hissing and spitting with upraised claws extended. But she was too tiny and frail to offer any resistance, and Gabe scooped her up inside his balled-up jacket and raced home as quickly as he could. She fought hard to escape, leaving scratches of bloody spiderwebbing along his forearms, but he never even felt the pain. Bounding into the kitchen, he displayed his find for his mother as she was washing dishes in that same tired routine of hers.

As the door slammed shut behind him, the boy presented his prize with more excitement than his startled mother had seen in him in many years.

"Look, look!" he screeched out. "Isn't she great? Can I keep her Mom? I can, right?"

Sissy smiled at her son's innocent treasure, then offered it a bowl of milk all while trying to keep her calm with quiet, soothing words of praise.

"Well, honey, I don't think her mother would care for that too much. I'm sure you scared the poor thing off. She's probably out there searching for her cute little baby right 'bout now."

Sissy stroked the back of the kitten as Gabe held her tightly. He was trying to keep her from tearing at his mother's fingers and leaving the same matching red scratches and whelps that already covered his forearms and hands. As his mother cooed and smiled at the tiny creature her son had found, Gabe looked into her eyes and felt his twangs of disappointment rising to the surface once again. *She was weak, actually only covering for my father*. Gabe knew he would have plenty to say on the subject of a new pet. Even if Bennett allowed him another animal as a replacement for Dolly or Ace, he would never permit the boy to have a cat. He'd surely call him names and curl his lip with disdain as he spat out his regular indignities, one after another.

Get rid of that ugly thing before you both become pussies and weaklings. Or, leave it to my son to pick out a cat as a pet. You must be thinking about becoming a fag. Is that it boy? Is that what you want, he asked sternly, as the spit flew out in all directions from his generous bit of verbal humiliation.

His mother had been trying to spare him from that, he supposed. He could see the kindness there in her eyes and her smile, but she was weak, and it finally dawned on him how much she'd changed over time, gradual enough that he'd barely noticed the transformation, but she was getting weaker in her husband's company, and that disgusted him. Gabe watched her conversion, but he hadn't seen it as plainly as he did now. She was a woman who loved her children and the pinnacle of a proper wife and mother. But she was becoming more of a shadow of herself with each passing year, and there was only one person he could blame for his mother's growing translucence and frail demeanor. If it weren't for him and his sister, he thought, she might disappear altogether, fading into nothing and all because she'd allowed her husband's continued abuse to fester and sour her spirit, forever changing her once jubilant personality.

Gabriel knew his future—getting as far away as possible. But he couldn't see his mother's or sister's and didn't much care what became of his dad. He was a boy on the verge of becoming a man, far earlier than he should have. He was witnessing how time was changing in those seconds and astutely saw that those few skirmishes he had with his father would never end his war, and whatever he'd thought his future would be, suddenly began fading like smoke into the nothingness around him, even without him ever doing anything to change that.

"Baby, I know you wanna keep her, but I really think it best if you took her back to wherever you found her. Let her mama find her and keep her with all her little brothers and sisters."

His mother's words sounded as sweet as sugar cane, and she was smiling kindly as she stared into the depths of his eyes in complete wonderment. Even he could see how he was salvation to her, and with her eyes beginning to fill with tears, he'd fought through the urge of racing from the room in shame. There were a lot of things she would never get to say to Gabe, but somehow the words didn't need to be spoken aloud. Some things they simply knew as fact, and those became secrets which bound them together, at least until they unraveled and lost their tensile strength to hold.

"Whatcha say, Gabe honey?" she asked. "Besides, I'd always heard if you wanted something, like this little girl here, you should set her free. If you were truly meant to have her, then she'll come back to you. Have you ever heard the story, son?"

Gabe's head drooped low as he turned quietly to leave with the kitten still screaming loudly to be set free and bundled up in his jacket like a prison. He resigned himself to letting her go, even though he was already wrestling with names he might have given her. He dropped her off right where he found her, and she scampered away into the brush as his mother's words came back to remind him that if he set her free and he was meant to have her, then she'd be back. But as he watched her disappear into the thicket, he also remembered something their neighbor mentioned to his father one day when he came over for a visit.

He was a crotchety old man who Gabe never liked, but he made regular calls on the Church family, mostly to spew out the latest gossip or to borrow a tool from Bennett, which he was always slow to return. He could never remember the old man's name. Mostly because he never gave any indication he wanted to meet the Church children or even Bennett's wife much better than he already did. But he liked Bennett and called his mother *ma'am* and joked how the kids were only ankle biters and something to be ignored.

"How's the missus doing?" he would ask as he strolled over to the fence line separating their properties. Gabe always wondered if he ever cared to hear the answer anyway.

He stopped by one afternoon while Gabe was in the backyard and Bennett was busy cleaning out their tool shed. Resting his tall, stringy body against a fence post, he leaned in and announced, "Best be careful for the wee ones, Bennett old man! I was talking with John Holloway down at the feed store, and he told me coyotes took down some of his livestock. I even heard they killed his dog as well." Bennett looked astonished as he strolled over to chat, likely grateful to get pulled from his mundane errands.

"Whatcha think has gotten into those scoundrels 'cause I can't rightly remember a time when they were as bold as they are now?" the neighbor inquired. "Might be a tad bit rabid, best keep eyes on the young'uns, and make sure you don't leave any food or trash out because once they find a food source, it's damn near impossible to get 'em run off. Ya might consider carrying a rifle around like I do. Coyotes are much better predators than most people understand." Then he spat on the ground near Bennett's feet and continued, "I aim to take me down a couple of them curs with half a chance. Well, I guess the predators are at our doors, Bennett ole man!"

Gabe, who'd been listening to their conversation, was intrigued and felt a cold chill from being in the old man's presence. There was nastiness in him, and he seemed to enjoy trying to scare people with his outlandish stories.

"The coyotes are here, neighbor, and they're unafraid. I figure they'll be scratching at the door to be let in soon enough...Whatcha think?"

Then the laughter returned, so loud the frail and cantankerous man began to cough, until it became a violent raspy wet sound as if he might choke out a lung. But he eventually regained some composure and wiped his mouth on his dirty sleeve and chuckled again. Gabe watched as his father and the old man talked for a brief time longer, and then the neighbor trekked across his big lawn and headed inside his own house. His father returned to his chores, and Gabe continued to play, but it created a synapse spark that flashed back now as a memory, and he remembered it like it had just happened. He was transfixed, but the sight of the orange-and-white tabby dashing away for her freedom pulled him back. He heard the movement she made over the dead leaves and foliage grazed aside. He watched until she couldn't be seen, and he sat on his haunches wanting nothing more than to cry.

As it turned out, the kitten's mother never returned for her offspring. He'd stumbled over the ragged remnants of hair and bone, which was all that left of a once beautiful, orange-colored cat, now covered by a ghastly red wash. There was very little left of her then, only small vestiges of skeleton and loose fur, and smaller scavengers and insects were already hard at work with removing anything else that endured. The feline had fallen there, where a hunter became another creature's quarry. And there she'd lie, to dry and crumble under the midday sun until nothing else remained. This was life, he thought. How every struggle existed and then ended on this spinning rock we called a home.

But the incident changed Gabriel in ways he failed to see at the time. The mother he'd thought he loved was disappearing, just like a cat racing to seek shelter from the elements after the first loud crack of thunder. He knew that was because she was too frail, too weak, and he learned to despise her for all the things she lacked. He wouldn't end up like her. That much he knew. And even though he still felt an unexplainable affection for Sissy and his younger sister, he knew if he made it out, and when he'd finally gained his freedom, it'd all be because of Bennett...the man who'd started him running in the first place.

The predators are finally here...and they'll be scratching at the door and hoping to get let in soon.

Chapter Fifteen

THE NEXT FEW days for Christian were a nightmare. He kept looking back over his shoulder whenever he left his condo. Apprehension trailed him like a shadow at grocery stores or walking through the parking garage at work as he headed to his car. He knew his nerves were only playing out each and every ugly scenario possible like a detective stopping him to ask about Shea Baltimore, or inquiring what type of relationship he'd had with the victim. He only felt worse when he thought about Gabriel stepping out of the shade of a building's outline and surprising him by coming into town early.

His anxiety came in not knowing what he would say to the police when asked. No subterfuge he created seemed to work to explain his presence at her apartment, which he suspected was the reason for their call. In his mind, he manipulated version after version but found no justifications that might sound plausible. He hoped Gabriel might be able to help because he had more experience in countersurveillance, he figured. If he hadn't been good at that, he would have surely been caught by now; that much stood to reason.

Chris was acting like a gumshoe or a covert operative in a foreign county, trying to look as inconspicuous as possible, making sudden stops at store windows to see if anyone was trailing behind him or scanning his gaze to see if others stood out as strangely unfamiliar with their surroundings. It felt unsettling, and he wondered how people lived under such paranoia. He tried to avoid Detective Keen for a whole week. He lied to himself by pretending he hadn't heard the voicemail. He needed Gabe to make it back into the city if for no other reason than to offer him guidance.

Inside, dread mingled with excitement as the time got closer to reach him. He holed up in his apartment for the remainder of the week, trying to keep his brain occupied with books and work; difficult because he couldn't focus thoughts for long before they were yanked back by pictures of Gabriel, which excited him as much as it became unnerving. But then imagery of jailhouse doors slamming closed or cold interrogation rooms broke through the haze, and he could feel the sweat building under his pits whenever he allowed those images to linger for too long.

Being around people was excruciating. He caught himself craning his ears to hear the murmurs swirling around his ears. Nervously he watched the chitchat among the strangers, listening intently to see if anyone used hotspot words like *murder* or *Church*. If he'd thought he heard anything alarming, he'd been mistaken. Theirs was idle conversation from a mass of uninformed unwashed public. More often than not, he found his only solace was when he was curled on his sofa, an afghan comforter at his side and a book in his hand. But anxieties came in flooding waves then; knowing he'd eventually see the face of the man he once doubted he'd ever see again. He wondered how long Gabe would stay, questioned whether he'd ask Chris to run away with him, and that made him contemplate his own motivations. *Naturally I'll go*, he reasoned, matter-of-factly. *How could I not?* Even given the discernable dangers such a decision entailed, he knew the pull Church had over him was simply too strong to contest.

How insensitive he must be, sitting there pondering his upcoming joy, and the excitement of seeing Gabe again. Particularly when there were larger morality issues that needed his deliberation. He saw that memory of Gabriel and him standing in that apartment and remembered how low his heart sunk when he heard those stinging words: "You cost Shea her life, you know."

Chris had felt the buckle of his knees after Gabe's unexpected accusation. He recalled blurting, "You're suggesting I killed her?"

Even though Gabe said nothing and eventually admitted he wasn't supposed to make it out scot-free anyway, he did confess to doing the unthinkable. If only to make sure Shea didn't go to the police or involve Christian any further in his personal crisis. He knew in his heart Gabe was speaking the truth: that his hands weren't clean, and he willingly chose to bring his lover's sins into the conversation. He knew how awful all that looked, how jealous and nasty it appeared, and how Gabriel had never had to witness this flaw before. Not that it worked anyway; he still lost the man he loved in the end. For such a traditionally standup guy who apparently was living a normal existence prior to any of this, he certainly had his own dark edge, he ruminated. What a shame he couldn't have been a better fugitive. But if the last few days taught him anything, it'd been his lack of nerve. And his tittering sanity was all he could afford to be struggling with at the moment. Yes, he would've made for one lousy outlaw. That was Gabe's gift, not his.

Sipping chardonnay, he snickered at the picture of a sedentary or conventional life spent with Gabriel. Somehow, he couldn't visualize a life where that man would hold down a nine to five or their home would be complete with two Lhasa Apso pups or they'd spend their weekends entertaining and having chic dinner parties with other male couples. The allure of sitting across from a formidable and dangerous man might have been the draw in the first place. He'd found the place where gods met disillusionment and masters were confined to the privacy of the bedroom. Sometimes people fall in love with the least expected souls, he mused. And he'd always hated the phrase, *"Well the heart wants what the heart wants." But* he understood its meaning now more than ever before.

GABE SAT IN a lot of poker games that week, trying to use whatever he'd learned from his life on the road. All to rake in enough winnings for a trip back to Seattle.

Wasn't it your dad who was supposed to teach you how to play cards?

But for his part, he'd never learned anything of value from his father, so why then did he assume others would've been luckier than he was? The only thing he was offered in the way of an education was the possibility he could end up the same way: a cruel, merciless man without even the smallest measure of understanding of his place in the world. Remembering an incident when he was around fourteen or so, he recalled Bennett watching TV in his usual chair one evening as Gabe sat on the sofa across the room, the glow of the Panasonic enveloping his silhouette. His face was beginning to show the first signs of puberty. And the shadow of a wispy, immature beard could be seen in its infancy. Bennett also noticed the stubble and his face turned suddenly sour like he'd tasted curdled milk on his tongue, Gabe turned to see his typically disapproving scowl flashing past beer-induced bleary vision. The patterns had always been there, he believed, just waiting to get carved from the stone.

"Boy, you're beginning to present yourself like you don't give a damn how you look. Do ya need me to teach you to shave, or do you think you could find a razor all by your lonesome?"

The boy smiled yet said nothing as he got up and left Bennett for the privacy of his bedroom. No, Gabe didn't make it easy for his father; that might've been true. But his disgust and resentment become something of a heavy millstone that seemed compulsory he carry it around daily as if it were an unspoken punishment.

Sitting across from a man like Church at a poker table might be intimidating for some. He could easily demonstrate a country boy smile as he first took his seat, but before long any opponents trying to assess the quality of his cards or the hand he was holding would see only a calculated frozen stare as recompense. He was unreadable. Anyone who tried to crack his exterior might observe how friendly he appeared and how he could joke and tease with the best of them. But it was just as likely Church could rise up in anger then upend the table or attack any or all of the players as coins and folded fives and tens scattered the floor. Whenever he did look up, the absence of a tell was clearly a gift. His luck was running thinner than usual, though, and even targeting a stranger whose wallet he could lift, or a purse he might rifle through was scarce bounty. He needed a fast haul with positive results if he intended to make it to Seattle by week's end. He even thought about selling the Glock, but only as a last resort. Although he never used it, he found a substantial comfort in knowing it was always close. Strange, he thought, how the weighty grip of a pistol could do that to a man. Like cupping one's own cock through denim, it became a constant reminder of just what type of predator he knew he was becoming.

He loved his Glock 9—mainly because it weighed a mere thirty ounces but had an uncanny ability of boosting a man's confidence and testosterone. Gabe was smart enough to realize he could never buy or register a firearm. But it'd been a trophy from a card game many years earlier, one with exceedingly high stakes. He'd sat across from the gun's owner in a friendly game and listened to the man's drunken boastings of his vast collection of weapons and became intrigued. Seeing an opportunity, he paid for the next few rounds, making sure everyone was sufficiently buzzed while making a concerted effort to lose one hand after another. He watched as the gun's owner crossed into an oblivious state of euphoria and turned his skills to winning more pots than losing them. He could barely hide his excitement when the sucker's piles of cash began to dwindle.

It wasn't hard to imagine his portly player would be stowing a travel piece somewhere inside his vehicle. And after the liquored-up old fool felt he finally had a surefire hand, Gabe pounced. He spotted the beads of perspiration appearing now on the fat man's brow and watched as his pudgy fingers turned white against the tight grip of his poker hand. It became clear to other players as well, but it'd been Church who goaded him on, jokingly admonishing him that he should put up one of his guns as substitution for his dwindling cash or risk be turned into a winner's unlucky little bitch for all eternity. He always had a knack for reading others, particularly men. He could push their buttons. He tested the borders of another male's insecurity by sullying their masculinity whenever possible. After stepping away victorious, he followed the blubbering loser to the parking lot and retrieved his prize. And what man would have begged or balked with honoring his debt, particularly when in the company of such a formidable and daunting a figure as Gabriel Church?

He was most assuredly a human predator but using his new gun on a white-lighter was never his plan. The 9mm was ever only intended as security because he always swung on a slim hope that he could outdraw or outlast whoever faced him. The gun was his guarantee, should he find himself backed into a corner or staring out at limited routes of escape. But he needed to make it back to Christian at whatever the cost. His sanity seemed to balance on an unseen edge, and he assured himself his presence was required. He wanted to charge in on a white steed and whisk his paramour up into the saddle, to become the savior he secretly wanted to be. This was a new sensation; a desire to protect someone other than himself and fast becoming etched into his character. Somewhere along those long rambling highways between Washington and Texas, he saw it grow, changing him greatly as every old habit fell off his shoulders like rain.

He hadn't raised enough money to make it all the way back to Seattle, but this was a start. He knew he could rely on his transient education, apply old habits and routines to get whatever he needed along the way. Church liked the idea of being a self-sufficient vagabond with his honed skills and street smarts learned from years of isolation. *If Bennett could have seen that, would he have been proud, or more disappointed?*

Then again, he didn't really give a fuck what others thought about his choices, except possibly one. It was time to hit the highway, putting San Antonio behind him. He remembered he hadn't an opportunity of visiting the Riverwalk after all, but he wanted to make one last stop before he did. As he forced the clutch pedal to the floor and ground the stick into third, he noticed dark clouds rising over the horizon. *Damn, looks like I'm going to be hitting a downpour.*

CHRIS WAS ON a beach atop a ragged towel. Through black Ray-Bans he could see a white smoky exhaust trail from a tiny jet plane, though nearly obscured by a blinding sun at its peak. He could hear the lapping of waves as they stroked the sandy lip of a nearby shoreline. Although it was a crystal-clear day, every image he saw appeared as if he'd been looking at it through the bottom of a thick cocktail glass. He saw Gabriel exiting the water with a frothy billow of white-crested surf dancing around his knees. His heart seemed to stutter with the visage of how beautiful the man was. That brown hair plastered to his head, his chest hair matted dark and dripping along his perfect torso. Looking like Burt Lancaster emerging from the sea in *From Here to Eternity*, only more handsome that he'd been. And that made him wonder, was he supposed to be the lovely Deborah Kerr in this version? He stared back, noticing that Gabriel looked happier than he'd ever seen him before.

Gabriel was calling him, but he was too far away to be heard. He began racing back from the water, collecting sand on the soles of his wet feet as he jogged up. His pale eyes shined brighter than Chris remembered, and his joyous exuberance felt somehow out of place in the sphere of all he could recall about the man.

"Get your ass out here with me, bud," he said. "It's not nearly as much fun bodysurfing alone." He shadowed over Chris, allowing the excess of ocean water to splash like falling rain over his friend's sun-drenched body.

"Hey, I'm trying to get some rays here!" he screeched, sitting bolt upright. Gabriel was laughing, which sounded alien and strange to Chris's ears. Grabbing a folded towel from the tote bag at his left, he dried himself and then tossed it up for Gabriel to use.

"There's plenty of time for that." Gabriel was smiling. Sitting in the coolness of his newly established shade, Chris watched as he rubbed his underarms and rib cage dry, staring down at him with a mischievous grin and a bright halo of light surrounding his face. *He really was an angel, or at least angelic and looking as if he was his own personal deity.* But if he were an idol to be revered, then Chris knew he'd be demanding more than religious worship whenever he placed his hands on Chris's shoulders and gently forced him to his knees.

"Worship this..." he would say, as he guided an impressive shaft past his lover's lips.

The beachfront was empty. In his head, he thought it odd how he couldn't rightly remember where they were exactly. The sandy stretch was pristine of litter, and the dunes behind them void of the usual tourists. His insides seemed too big to be contained, and the only way he could describe that moment was in absolute contentment. Before he could languish in it for long, though, the images crashed into shards when a screaming noise he couldn't place invaded his brain. He learned this had been his phone. With that, the pleasing images of Gabe and him were suddenly pulled apart as in an explosion, and the noise he heard was coming from his nightstand. It took a second before he realized he was waking in his own apartment, and that he was bitterly all alone.

Shaking the fog from his head and yet hoping he'd remember it later, he scrambled across the mattress and yanked up the receiver to discover his mother was calling.

"No, of course not," he said. "You didn't catch me asleep. I was just getting around."

He should've known it would be her since she was the only one he knew who still used the relic of his landline. Rubbing crusty sleep from his eyes, he made small talk until he could find true bearing.

"How's the professor doing? Is he all right these days?"

"He's already gone, son. It's nearly nine, and he's always at the university before all the other instructors," his mother replied, with the hint of a chastising tone to follow.

"See...I knew I'd caught you asleep. I could swear!"

There it was. That chilly wind blowing cold against a body once drenched by imagined warmth from an afternoon in the sun.

"So," she began, "why aren't you at work? Oh heavens, did I catch you at, hmmm...a bad time?"

He knew this was her way of asking if he was alone. They hadn't discussed his orientation before then, but he knew she suspected something. However, this was a well he didn't wish to plumb in his current state, particularly not while his focus was torn between his love of a serial killer, recent murder, and a new job.

"If you're asking if I'm alone, mother, I am. I'm running a little behind this morning."

"Your father is always up by five every morning as you should remember, and usually he's out the door by six forty-five."

"Well, if that'd been me, you'd be chatting with my voice mail about now, and we wouldn't have the joy of this conversation, would we?"

"Don't get smart with me, young man," she said through a smile even he could hear across the line. "I wanted to phone to ask you if you were coming over this weekend for dinner. It's been far too long, and your father misses you."

"Well, tell *father*—I miss *her* too," he offered with warm sarcasm. "But apologies, I can't make dinner for a few days. Something came up at work and it's requiring a great deal of my time."

The lies were becoming easier. Maybe this was due to him accepting his true self and no longer having to feel the weight of expectation dragging him like a heavy chain. He understood how that "indelicate conversation" was well overdue, but he wasn't looking forward to having it. He didn't have a fiancé. And his parents knew there wasn't perfume scenting his pillows at night, but if he confessed to all the gory details of his current situation, he knew they'd no doubt suddenly freeze in place, then likely both would just explode simultaneously, leaving nothing more than a cloud of lemony goodness from his mother's gin cocktail, while his father's solemn regrets dissipated through the ether like a fog. He couldn't ever begin to think about the discussions he feared most. He didn't relish talking about his recent "male" lover and how much his own life was changing with tales about his lover's dirty past and a constant specter looming over his shoulders. He needed to force a talk sometime soon, though, because he might just need to call on them for financial help in finding a good criminal attorney in the not-so-distant future. But now wasn't the time for that discussion, and maybe not ever.

"I promise you a rain check darlin'," he whispered. He needn't worry about her disappointment. He understood how strong she was, how resilient she could be despite her dispassionate party-manner exterior. It no doubt became the single greatest quality she possessed, the one he admired more than any other.

"Then remember to call your father," she said huffily. "He might like to know that his only namesake is still alive and well after all. You can explain to him your busy work schedule or the reasons you never visit."

Guilt was a weapon she'd chosen to employ for as long as he remembered; more than any shield or armor it became her favorite sword and lance. It became clear she knew how to push his buttons, yet she still managed to maintain a balance with every jab of her attacks. She had an innate wisdom, able to hedge each honeyed word as she doled out her gifts of contrite shame and regret. But she always knew the exact second to withdraw. She never left a bloodied mark or scar, not for her son anyway.

Even strong women want to see their children. And it'd been far too long since he'd made the drive up to visit or spend a few days. But, certainly this wasn't the time to consider that distraction. Their conversation would have to wait. Gabriel was coming, and Chris currently had more on his plate than he needed. These were perilous times. And nothing mattered more than seeing Gabe. Yes, his serial killer lover was about to blow into town and he could feel the ache in his belly that suggested his growing excitement. Sick idea, he mused. There were many possible outcomes ahead, but the lack of seeing them clearly was just about the most thrilling thing Chris could even imagine.

Chapter Sixteen

HIS GUT WAS tying into knots as he pulled his truck in the front of St. Joseph's Cathedral. A shiny bauble at the end of his fishing line, fixed there to attract and to lure. He couldn't rightly explain the sense he'd felt, but Gabe suspected it must be closure he'd been searching for, or at least answers he thought only Father Kait may supply. He still had beer on his breath and his five-day growth of facial hair he hadn't tended to, but he doubted the priest would mind his appearance in the end.

Surprisingly, he found the tiny chapel empty of parishioners and Father Kait nowhere in sight. *Well since you're here, you might as well light a candle and say a prayer for your lover, Christian*, a disconnected voice uttered in his head. It startled him, causing him to stop dead in his tracks and crane his neck to see if someone was coming up from behind. Whose voice had he heard? Had it been Sissy Church's or possibly Shea's? No, it sounded too baritone. A man's words, yet certainly not Bennett's. If his father had cause to use that phrase, he would've spat out the words "for your lover" like venom he'd sucked in to stall the flow of poison from reaching a heart.

Standing in the center aisle of the chapel under a vent of chilly, recirculated air, Gabe began to wonder what his father might say if he knew his only son allowed another man to hungrily gobble on his dick. He smiled a dark and sadistic grin, picturing a time when he'd fucked Christian on the floor of that fancy schmancy hotel. He'd shoved an open palm in the center of Chris's spine, forcing his face against the white Berber carpeting. The act was animal and sensual at the same time. Chris had moaned and writhed and presented his lovely ass. Images of entering Chris came flooding back as if the sluice gates were sprung wide, surprising him, given the sanctity and reverence of where he was standing. He thought if they could be captured in a photograph, it would've been something he needed to slide across their old kitchen table to his father to see Bennett's expression of shock and dismay and to see his revulsion at the thing he created. That would serve him right.

There was an elderly woman sitting inside a glass-enclosed anteroom, who Gabe presumed to be a church volunteer. Well, someone's got to answer the phones. And if four hours a day of unpaid labor could get one further inside Saint Peter's good graces that was surely an insignificant price to pay. In a hushed tone, he asked where Father Kait might be, hoping he was simply walking the halls in that labyrinth of rooms which seem so guarded from all the nonbelievers.

"I believe he is still in the rectory," she said with a pleasant smile, adjusting her Coke-bottle glasses to the bridge of her nose.

As he turned to leave, he felt a little despondent he'd not get to see the priest before leaving town. Church had felt an instantaneous connection with Father Kait. He was older than his priest from Ignatius, which made him less threatening. And for a boy of eight or ten, the black robes and austere veneration he received from parishioners didn't give him comfort like normally someone from the clergy should. Kait was different. His eyes twinkled with wisdom, and the way he moved sparked a decided lack in judgment Gabe was unaccustomed to.

He seemed to be everything a priest should be. A kind hand extended with affection. Much as if he'd been a shepherd tending a flock he sincerely adored, and not the fire and brimstone ranting I heard as a child.

He got the impression Father Kait wanted to help him, even after his last confessional turned sour. He'd been forced to exit fast before he disclosed too much, but the priest wasn't here now, so Gabe decided to get on the road again. As he opened the door of his pickup and heard the creak of metal against metal, he took one final look back. He was surprised to see Father Kait coming down the walkway in the distance. He was leaving a separate building and was headed in the direction of the main church. He was right at the spot where the yellow poplar stood, so tall and vigilant, as if patiently awaiting the inevitable rapture. Where Gabe mused it surely would burst into flames and burn a fiery orange to signify the birth of the coming Armageddon.

"Father Kait!" he called out across the grounds, astonishing himself in his own awkward gesture.

Looking up, the priest gave a quick nod of recognition, but Gabe noticed he wasn't smiling in that infectious way he remembered from before. Suddenly he thought the whole trip across town was going to be a waste, and a twisting knot began to build in his stomach. But then Kait turned on his heels and strolled across the lawn to greet him, his hand thrust forward and a faint smile emerging. It seemed an odd picture to witness. A clergyman in full Eucharistic vestments sauntering casually across the grounds and still trying to keep his stride inside the grassier areas so as not to muddy his pristine robes.

"I was hoping you'd visit again," he said sweetly, shaking Gabe's hand in a ceremonial gesture of friendship.

"I had to stop by to apologize..."Gabe began. He felt humbled in Kait's presence and his tone didn't belie the fondness he felt as his head drooped slightly with growing humility.

"What for?" Kait asked sheepishly. "Running off so darn fast and preventing us from chatting a little more?" Then leaning closer into Gabe, he whispered, "Some folks around here think I'm a pretty fair-minded priest. I certainly have been around awhile, and figure I've learned a little along the way. I might be the right one to offer up some good advice. That is, if you wanna bend my ear for a bit."

Grabbing Gabe by the arm, he ushered him along toward the entrance of the church, without even waiting for his acceptance. "And lucky for you, it seems I find myself with some spare time I need to burn off, and not to brag, but I can always tell when a man such as yourself is sorely in need of some good conversation."

With the elderly man still clutching Gabe by the elbow, they ambled down a corridor he hadn't noticed before. "This is my office," the priest announced. "I thought we needed the privacy and maybe I could offer you a cup of my favorite tea in the bargain."

The small room seemed less austere than Gabe expected. There were books lining tiny shelves and bric-a-brac gifts from church members given throughout the years. Although they were drawing dust, they appeared as loving mementos Gabe assumed Kait somehow cherished.

Motioning to the sofa, Kait said, "Make yourself at home, young man, I'm going to drop a couple of teabags in water. Why don't you tell me a little about your last congregation and church? As I recall, you mentioned how you are new to our fair city."

Gabe felt strangely comfortable confiding to Father Kait, somewhat amazed how easily the words slipped off his tongue. He trickled out stories of his childhood back in Kentucky and Tennessee and spoke long about St. Ignatius and what it meant to him. He told how, even without his knowledge, the church made a vital impression on him. And he even felt no hesitation or compunction in admitting he hadn't much cared for the former priest back at St. Ignatius.

He'd already begun a pot of water brewing in an ancient Mr. Coffee sitting across the room. As the stream announced it was finally done, Kait rose from his chair, making a grunting noise of discomfort and telling Gabe his friend was a man with arthritic joints. He gingerly poured water into two cups of fine bone china, then tossed a Lipton bag into each one.

"There's sugar and a spoon over there, young man. We don't stand on pretense here so help yourself." Then as an afterthought, he added, "Like the good Lord intends we do, each and every day."

Before he could rise to help the elder man, Kait had already turned and was gingerly carrying a cup back to offer his guest. Gabe could see his hand tremble slightly and wondered if he'd misjudged the old priest's age from the beginning or whether he was witnessing the onset of Parkinson's in its earliest stages.

Gabriel rose to spoon some sugar into his cup and heard the tinkle of silverware against old china. Retaking his spot on the sofa, he stared into the Father's eyes and blurted out a question that'd been haunting him. "Father, I may be a lapsed Catholic and well, I haven't always been the best man I could be. But I always believed in a deity who understands me—"

Before Gabe could finish, Kait interrupted him; he could see the struggle and recognized the war raging in his new friend. "We all make mistakes, son. Even old priests can trip over their own vestments. They might even lose their sanctity in their fall...but forgetting you've sinned in the past, I have to ask, is your faith still strong?"

"It's not faith which bothers me, Father; its forgiveness, if I find out I've been wrong from the beginning."

Kait was impressed with his guest. He saw the image of a farm boy grown strapping and strong. One he pictured would naturally be dumb as dirt. But he would've been wrong. This one questioned his morality, asked loftier demands. His mind was precise and unexpectedly cerebral. It wasn't difficult to see he was a coin, with kindness and civility on one side and something darker and dangerous on the other. He rabbited before he could confess too many of his sins. And he saw how much Kait wanted to help him as he bolted for the door. But he needed to be careful, to remember to speak in generalities and metaphorically.

"Gabriel, that's one of the things they never covered in the seminary. They expect faith from the onset. Me, well, I guess I was born from a rebellious mother, and I suppose I was trouble from early on. But I asked those same questions once: 'What if we're all wrong? What if we're simply fooling ourselves?' I suppose, son, it's a matter of faith."

Albert wanted to learn more about his visitor and was genuinely interested in getting to know his newfound friend, from the roots to the stalk, as his own mother had been fond of saying.

Bringing the cup to his lips, Gabe watched Kait blow a cooling breath across the steam. He hadn't noticed it before, but the priest's eyes were nearly as gray-blue as his own. Then again, they might have lost some of their luster along the years. But they twinkled back nonetheless and shone like unpolished diamonds buried in white sand.

"I've done things, terrible things, Father. Sins I want to atone for, even though they came through God's name, by his own decree. It's a thing I never questioned before, but there is someone out there who makes me question it for the first time. It's created a wedge between us, and nothing appears as solid as it did before."

Kait turned and gingerly held his teacup in wobbly hands. Leaning forward for emphasis, he said, "Conscience isn't something all people are born with, Gabriel. Sometimes we find it during our journeys through life—and usually in places we never thought to look." He smiled warmly at his tiny wisdom and sipped another drink from his painted china cup. He was the image of someone truly kind and lovingly paternal. His lined face and wispy gray hair only reminded Gabe that he'd missed out on the whole grandparent experience. He'd never known Sissy Church's parents since they'd never much cared for their daughter's choice in husband and made no effort to hide their disdain for Bennett or the marriage. His father's mother died before little Gabe was even born, and her husband followed her quickly to the grave merely eight years later when the boy was barely out of diapers.

Gabe was hanging on every word the old man uttered. He felt the rush which comes from being in the presence of one close to God, someone with insight and understanding. He was washing the feet of a future Dalai Lama, and wouldn't pass that opportunity by.

"Sounds trite, but sometimes all one can do is follow their heart," Kait said quietly. "If your spirit, or your good nature, is brought along for the ride...well then, so be it—that's not such a bad thing." The old man's face was beaming, but with every smile, the crevices lining his mouth and jaw were enhanced. "It sounds as if your 'one' who might be a suitable influence. You should cherish 'his' friendship."

With that, Gabriel leaned back and cupped his big hand around the fragile china. He'd caught the father's inference and wondered if it'd been his own calculated jab from another disapproving priest. He couldn't recall mentioning anything that might have told him Gabe was referring to another man, nor had he used Christian's name even once during their conversation. But there it was. He was surprised to see Father Kait's expression never wavered, though. There didn't seem to be any shame or judgment in those cloudy irises of blue, just the usual gentle kindness Gabe came to expect.

They both smiled and sat in silence as each man took an awkward sip of their tea, but it was the priest who broke the quiet by asking Gabe to tell him more about his childhood. Then he leaned closer to the table to rest his cup and Gabriel could see how badly his hands trembled when performing such an easy task. Kait appeared to be preparing to hear a great story, one requiring his full, undivided attention.

He asked about growing up in Tennessee and then asked about Gabe's mother. His eyes became soulful when he nudged forward apologetically to ask, "She's still with us, I take it?" Gabe nodded back quickly yet said nothing to indicate he was really unsure. He then inquired about Gabriel's relationship with Sissy and Bennett, both as a boy in the backwater sticks of Tennessee and how it was today. And though he asked politely, with his usual graciously civil manner, there was still a surgical precision with every question. It felt like being interrogated by a Harvard-educated psychiatrist because Kait possessed the skills of breaking down the minutia without a person even being aware it was happening. He could expose another's deeply hidden secrets with nothing more than his smile as a utensil. Indeed, he was a great listener, as those in the clergy are apt to be.

And at that moment the killer lifted the veil, revealing him in ways he'd only ever done with Christian. He was honest about his childhood, though his answers were guarded and came stinted like the point of a blade across flesh. But when it came to the present bond he shared with family, he spoke only lies. And even his falsehoods were cut with the same brevity.

It was nearly an hour before Church realized they'd spent the entire time chatting. He was more than a patient on a trained psychiatrist's couch because he'd asked Father Kait nearly as many questions as he'd been grilled. He was just as intrigued and needed to learn all he could about the clockworks of the man sitting across from him in his quaint and homey study. It was more than interrogation, however; it was a kinship of souls, a uniquely odd connection and a friendship between two very different men who couldn't have been more dissimilar if they tried. Nor could they have begun to comprehend just how apart they actually stood from one another.

Then a phone in the priest's study began to ring, reminding Gabe that even a compassionate elderly priest had duties that needed tending to. Gabe stood and slowly placed his china cup on the table nearby, then thanked Kait for his time and mentioned he'd had a real pleasant visit. He even promised to stop by again very soon as he gently clasped the old man by his elbow and assisted him to the door. Gabe knew it was nothing more than another lie escaping his throat. They weren't meant to meet again; that much he felt certain.

It was typical banal civility that made separating easier, and as they parted, Father Kait flashed another weathered grin before saying, "And next time I think we're gonna try something stronger than Earl Grey," surprising Gabe with his twisted lack of reverence. Then, with a chortle, he whispered, "Don't laugh, young man...I enjoy more spirits than the holy ones every now and again."

After thanking him profusely, Gabe walked out the heavy doors and into the failing sunlight as Father Kait watched him depart. At first, he considered how much time he'd lost at St. Joseph's and worried he might have to drive through the night because of it. But as he glanced back and saw the priest waving from the steps, he reconsidered he hadn't really lost any time at all because he'd found some resolutions he hadn't expected to find there in the priest's company. Something to consider, he thought, as he turned on the stereo and gripped the stick shift and headed toward the nearest on-ramp out of town.

Chapter Seventeen

KEEN'S LIST WAS dwindling fast, and the investigator was beginning to doubt the viability of any suspect buried in its pages. For the last few days, he'd been calling names and crossing off those he considered unviable suspects. If the vehicle was registered to a little old lady from the suburb of Delridge, he could draw a line through her information and move on. Making side notes of those he'd called and been forced to leave messages, he was able to see how many names remained, but he secretly wished there were more warm bodies to throw at his mundane chore.

It wasn't his only task, though. Keen already requested phone records for his victim and he was surprised to learn something the earlier agents missed during their inquiry. Shea's outbound calls were few. Fewer, in fact, than one might've guessed for such an attractive young woman as Miss Baltimore. But besides thinking how sad that sounded when he skimmed the numbers, he was more interested in the cross-referenced data he'd found once her work and father's telephone numbers had been excluded. After highlighting each remaining number, he set those aside and noticed there weren't any police background sheets in his file, ones to coincide with every name he'd found unchecked. He concluded this was a serious misstep by the prior investigators.

To the untrained, it may've appeared a back-ass way to work, but as any seasoned detective knew, this was protocol. A good investigator understands their first obligation was to run down names of any and all parties to check for arrest records or outstanding warrants and for which states. You did this prior to initiating an interview. Its leverage and it was how you understood the suspects inside your investigation, pocketing information to catch liars in the act. And long before you ever asked the big questions such as, "So where were you on the night in question?"

With the remaining names from his vehicle registration list declining, he knew he could work the same process on those tomorrow. It was all going to take time, and he'd manage to work the list by scratching off enough names to see some light at the end of the tunnel. But that was a task for tomorrow because he was tired and hungry and wanted nothing more than to escape the harsh fluorescent bulbs of his office and crawl in bed with his wife.

Keen was actually closer than he could have imagined. He was on the right track, anyway, and the only question remaining was if he would reach out to Christian Maxwell before the killer of Shea Baltimore made it back into the city. Lives could be like string that, if not careful, could get entangled and knotted into a ball. He had a laser-pointer way of looking at things, forcing him to consider only a murderer in Seattle who was currently getting away with his crime and the marked determination he had in finding that faceless killer.

Christian sat at his desk, feeling pangs of guilt because his mind wouldn't focus on the work at hand. He stared out his only window and watched dust motes sparkle like gems through a tangible shaft of light. The rays of an afternoon sun were peeking through the clouds, shooting a bright ribbon across his carpeted floor and capturing all his attention. Mostly because he was already allowing his mind to wander in and out as he played out old memories he couldn't seem to nudge aside.

He had taken a position as a marketing director at a major university, yet he felt his biggest contribution was copy editor and managing their online presence, which to him seemed far beneath his education and training. This was a job he'd never have accepted on a normal basis, but these were troubling times, where strange circumstances abounded. He knew he had to keep his mind occupied and sometimes the distractions alone were more necessary than pay.

Still, recollections had their secret ways. And if a need were there, they could slip beneath the doorframes or shimmy through the keyholes. In those particularly listless moments, Chris remembered his stay back at the Mayflower Hotel. He smiled as he remembered starched white linens and satin comforters, thinking back to all the times they'd been stained dark from sweat when he and Church were fucking. He recalled how Gabriel's breaths seemed sweeter from the bourbon on his tongue, and he'd tasted it in every kiss they shared. What had happened there at the hotel had been a thing of beauty. Some awe-inspiring level of passion he'd never experienced before. And with every past reflection, it triggered a new sensation, one that expanded his shaft and caused it to fill with blood and anticipation.

He wondered whether it was a one-time deal he experienced, or whether it'd be as miraculous the next time they'd meet. But whichever way it turned out, it became another experiment he desperately needed to try again.

Being overtly anxious from the detective's call, Christian decided when Gabriel did arrive in town, they wouldn't go back to his condo. This meant another salacious stay in a fine hotel, he thought, absently wetting his lips in some faraway distraction. He'd told himself if he could relive that brief time he'd shared with Gabriel once again, then he could die happy. They were sweet moments but bordered on being tentative and painfully fleeting. They'd been alone together the entire week, fucking in the suite or dining at whatever eatery pulled them off the sidewalks. They'd talked endlessly, trying to get to know each other in ways Christian never tried to do with any other lover. He'd told himself this was due to all former lovers being female, and not solely because Gabriel fascinated him so much or brought out all the hidden desires he never realized he'd been concealing.

A hotel stay protected him from picturing events where he and Gabriel might be rolling around naked on his bed when they heard the crashing sounds of his front door being kicked in and of men in suits rushing in, guns drawn. He could almost hear their shouts as they commanded both men to drop to the floor and place their hands behind their heads and interlock their fingers. It was an unpleasant thought, and one he preferred to avoid by checking into some surreptitious lodging downtown, and he might even use an assumed name if he could get away with that.

Christian's mind didn't work like Gabe's. He would've known exactly what to do to avoid the police altogether. While his own brain questioned how one pays with cash for a hotel suite without needing identification, his lover would've simply handled the situation. And in the same cool, reserved manner that kept him off their radar in the first place. Odd for him to admire that quality in another person, yet secretly he did. Gabriel might represent that dangerous side of his personality, one he'd always been taught by convention to bury deep inside. But he found an uncanny freedom in playing the unrestricted rebel and taking those risks he wouldn't have ever considered before they met.

He thought about Gabriel's fearless nature and how coming back to Seattle was not only a bad idea but a dangerous one. But he was coming back for him, because a threat existed, which made him feel protected, as if it were Gabriel's job to safeguard him from those menacing outside forces.

He remembered lying with his head on Church's rib cage one night and hearing his irregular heartbeat pounding. Then the killer disclosed his childhood diagnosis of Atrial Septal Defect. ASD had left a hole in his heart from his birth and hung like Damocles sword over Gabriel's perilous existence. Later, Christian made it a point to learn about the condition, but he'd known something was amiss from the second their lovemaking was over and the uneven beating in the hollow of his lover's chest suggested an abnormal rhythm.

Gabriel could live out his days with the hole intact, or he could double over from a massive heart attack one day and fall face-first dead on the ground. Christian figured this had been his Achilles heel; like the vulnerability of Sampson's hair, once removed he became powerless. The only weakness he could see in the man. That was, if he disregarded the cruel streak he knew was there but concealed from him during their time spent together. He saw it as bravery against a fated existence because the man understood the risks and yet lived his life as if the hole had never been there. He fucked harder than most. He'd probably run from the police in harrowing or nerve-racking car chases. And he'd likely felt a cold tightening in his chest whenever he took a life—and all that simply added to the risks. But he powered on, accepting it as his own twist of destiny, or that curse bestowed him by whatever God he believed in.

Gabriel never mentioned his ASD again, yet he could never seem to let it go completely. After learning the defect existed, he sensed a familiar shadow creeping in every time they made love. That loud beating of Church's heart was like a hammer in his chest, and more deafening when the two were fucking... his own "Tell-Tale Heart.". Like the story by Poe, where he described the ominous pounding under the floorboards, it resonated with its own form of foreboding and pulled other sounds into the background, like a watch enveloped in cotton. It reminded him how close death was, waiting around every corner.

It must've been the reason Gabriel perspired so much. He trained his ear and listened for the rhythms of the beating of the killer's heart as he dismounted. Watched him as he fell backward and stared at the ceiling tiles while sweat collected around his chest hair. Gabriel seemed to struggle for air, in those seconds after sex, and for Chris, it became his constant reminder of exactly how tenuous life truly was. That even in the afterglow of their lovemaking, it might only take a second and he'd lose the man forever. And he'd know that somehow, it'd been his fault.

It appeared Gabriel's biggest Kryptonite came from his sexual appetite. As shocking as that may sound to some, it had its own form of comic relief, because despite whatever efforts the state police or FBI might've undertaken, he knew there was equally as much risk that it would be his own cock that did him in for good.

Well, his dick, Chris mused, but at least my ass as the accomplice. He grinned when he considered that his own superhuman gift lay somewhere near his bunghole, and that alone might result in his power to end this murderous saga once and for all.

His fantasies were shattered by a knock on his door, another minor associate stopping by with papers requiring his signature. He smiled warmly at the young woman, grateful she at least appeared to be working with the shuffle of documents littering his desk.

Christian hadn't worked there long enough to know many people in his office, and it wasn't a job he enjoyed. Simply a necessary evil he endured to pay his bills. He never made the effort to get to befriend anyone, nor did he visit the break room or join in the holiday celebrations. He'd politely refuse their invitations because he knew that baby showers and birthday cakes were boredoms he might never survive. He suspected his job was simply a mile marker in his road, and no one would even remember his name when he finally moved on.

Six months ago, he'd thought himself a writer, hoping that novel he was supposed to pen about a serial killer would have allowed him to become something more. But the book wasn't only incomplete—it was gone. He'd never even given it any more than a bare outline, although he'd spent hours on his research, which ultimately proved futile. Gabe changed all that, and with the rug pulled from under foot, he was left to find another course for his life. Smiling pleasantly, he thanked Gail for dropping off the papers, but before she left she asked rather timidly if Christian wanted his door open or closed.

Bitch! It was closed when you invaded my privacy, so fuck yeah. He offered a bland nod but noticed her dubious expression when she closed the door behind her, leaving him to his solitude. Right outside his office were lines of cubicles housing various support staff. It created the illusion he was somehow more important than they were and thus deserving of more privacy, not merely that chasm from those with privilege, to those without. A thing his two degrees assured him and something they didn't possess.

Turning his head, he noticed the sun already disappeared behind a cloud, and that shaft of light with its glistening particles of dust was gone. His mind strayed to the moment when he'd reunite with Gabriel at the coffee house where they'd first met, and almost like a telepathic command, he heard Gabe's voice telling him, *Get yourself all shiny, boy, 'cause I'm headed your way, and I'm antsy at the thought of fucking you soon.* He smiled at his imagined vernacular but then forced himself to concentrate on the brochures scattering his desk. He had to do some work since they had to be approved before leaving the office today.

THE SLAPPING NOISE from the windshield wipers made a soothing rhythm against the backdrop of country music playing on his Dodge's radio. Along with the rain came a chilly breeze and Gabriel sensed an unseasonal cold creep in, while listening to the steady thumping sound of tires bouncing on uneven blacktop. Dark clouds were settling in the distance ahead, making it clear he was in for even worse weather for his drive.

Even with that, the hours passed uneventfully, as the stream of farmhouses changed to more of an open, urban sprawl. Homes and billboards at his left became nothing more than blurs of things that didn't interest him. His mind was elsewhere, playing out unnerving scenarios and giving him pause and trepidation in dealing with Christian's new problem. When necessary he'd stop to grab a bite or fuel up, but he saved his limited funds by finding rest stops and parking under the cover of a line of eighteen-wheelers. It was the only way he could obtain any shuteye, but sleep was hard to find. It was, however, the only relief from the numbing deadness in his ass cheeks from hours of continuous driving.

It should have taken no more than a couple of days to make his destination, but he knew he needed to pull over and suspend the journey, if for no other reason than to assess things properly and figure out each and every angle. He needed cash, which is why he told Chris it would take a full week to reach him. Though he decided not to divulge how he'd acquire said funds. His lover spent too much time measuring his character and didn't need any additional ammo. Besides, he thought, I'm clever. I'll work out the details of making it to Seattle in less time than that.

The rain beat steadily against his windshield, driven by the strong updraft winds from the Gulf. He couldn't see it yet, but he was the perfect storm flashing over a distant horizon and bringing torrential flooding in his wake. Along with him came the flotsam, jetsam, and debris. Everything would soon be tide rushed to the shoreline and all because there was a serial killer headed their way. As he shifted gears with a free hand, his eyes fixed ahead toward his destination; he was oblivious to the fact he was dragging trouble along with him close behind.

Chapter Eighteen

ONE NIGHT WHILE they were downing the remains of a bottle of bourbon they carried back to their suite at the Mayflower, Gabe mentioned that being able to put one over on everyone gave him a delicious feeling of superiority. He'd become many people during his travels, using aliases even when they weren't necessary. Partly because he liked drifting in and out of all those lives he could've had yet didn't. He'd built the walls surrounding him out of a need to protect his life, but along the way, they'd kept more than just invaders out. They isolated him and made it impossible for anyone to get close to him. Not that anyone had ever tried as hard as Christian Maxwell.

He had toiled before in many a rustic town, long enough that some lonely girl would invariably try to find a way through the cracks of his impenetrable exterior. But if anyone tried, they might've found a heart as tough as leather. No matter how pretty she may've appeared, or innocent her motives were, their resolutions were preordained before they'd even begun. Few could breach those impenetrable ramparts. Whenever he felt one pushing, he simply slipped out quietly under the cover of night and never looked back. Anyone who went to a honky-tonk to fish for women could always find an attractive girl shadowed by horny men. They offered to buy her drinks and then strutted and cock walked around her, all the while trying to cut her from the herd of other interested males.

This was a great deal of posturing, because a man may rarely open up to a woman until he had her alone. It was usually only then he'd drop the façade or speak tender, honest words on his life and aspirations. In the end, who really knew how much was truth and how much was only bait on the line. But for a man with an abundance of patience like Gabe, it never took long to find an evening's distraction. He was, after all, the picture of imposing masculinity. It was then he'd spin his tales and fill in the gaps with precision, fraud, and a well-practiced ruse. Reasons for why he couldn't take her back to his place, or go to hers, instead choosing the nearest inexpensive motel blocking his immediate path. And with that, the inevitable lies he crafted of what he did for a living and where he'd spent his childhood was complete.

Christian was the first soul he'd allowed entrance into the fortress. Possibly because the lies no longer felt necessary or because he'd reached a limit to his deceptions after seeing them spill out and flood the floor around his feet. Whatever the reasons, Gabe confessed to every truth, expecting nothing from the writer in return save for his acceptance. They talked long into every night and they found a connection. They joked and mocked each other as men did, and because he'd been granted a ticket at the door, Chris became the single most important aspect of Church's life. And this surprised them both for very different reasons.

After he pulled into dusty Albuquerque, Gabriel spotted his next white-lighter. He hadn't chosen Albuquerque exactly, and it was never meant to be anything but a pass through town and where he might pick up a few wallets or purses before topping off the tank then heading out. He hadn't expected to find a white-lighter there. Then again, he never did. He was always surprised when he stumbled onto one—it happened rather abruptly and without forewarning and always stopped him dead in his tracks.

But this was the second white-lighter he'd seen and targeted in a relatively short period of time, and he wondered if it was a sign or an indication of things to come. If true, he hadn't seen it clearly enough, which meant more to him than anything. It represented contradiction to his instinct and flew against the face of everything he thought was real and trustworthy. For him, it became an idea that left him cold and disconcerted... and just another fissure in his crumbling wall of doubt.

At the corner of Fifth and Route 66, while Gabe was looking for a venue he might exploit, he saw two younger men crossing against the light. Both were boys of eighteen or nineteen. One wore a letterman jacket with a yellow eagle emblazoned on the back, a pointless display of his glory days at Eldorado High, no doubt. Days that Church knew he'd never be able to recreate again.

Well at least he got his jacket, Gabe thought, as he watched them cross the street.

But it was the other one, the one without a jacket, who interested him more. The lankier of the two: the one who seemed content and still oblivious he'd been engulfed in a glow of bursting oranges and paler greens. He was far more special and his light all too familiar.

He craned his neck sideways, watching as the boys jaunted across the street to beat the traffic. Yet in those first seconds, he could only focus on that discernible amber glow radiating from his target. Then a faint tug from his insides grew stronger, an urge barely containable, and he hit his blinker and turned the Dodge left in quick pursuit.

If he'd been there, Christian would have begged him to stop; telling him this awful act would mean he was giving his soul to the devil. Gabe knew it was an unworthy transaction for the likes of that dark master since his contract was with the other one. It had already been forged, stamped, and filed. If successful, this wouldn't be the youngest life he'd taken, but even for him, it was a detestable thing he secretly hated doing. *But you can't fight the compulsion or the calling that comes with it*, and then he slowed his vehicle to watch the boys as they entered a hardware store midway down the block.

Both were strapping men, and Gabriel had to wrestle with the notion of retrieving the Glock from its secured hiding spot. But no gun could be used, and each victim had to have the randomness of a unique MO and cause of death. Naturally, he'd used the same techniques over and over throughout his long career, but he tried to keep it unpredictable and whenever two happened in the same state, he made sure to alter his method. It was a necessary evil if he wanted to stay ahead of the authorities. This particular man could represent a physical challenge he preferred not to risk. Surprise would be his greatest weapon, and Gabe's greatest aptitude was in his patience. He waited until the white-lighter was alone in a place where he could be taken.

Parking in an empty space just ahead of the hardware store, Gabe watched the entrance through the rearview mirror and waited for the stranger bathed in that typical radiant glow to exit the building. His truck sat conveniently in front of a sport's equipment and athletic store, a tiny mom and pop operation. Jumping out of his truck, Gabe ran inside and quickly found what he was looking for: what he knew would be near the front of the shop. He spotted an oaken barrel with red sale tags and the multitude of inexpensive bats nestled inside. He chose a Louisville Slugger carved from ash out of all the possible choices crammed into the cask. There were aluminum and other alloy bats, but the wood one was cheaper, and he suspected it would work fine for his hellish purposes. He quickly grabbed up the Louisville then headed to the counter. It seemed an appropriate choice of weapon since the white-lighter wasn't an adult and his buddy wore a letterman's jacket; it was almost fated choice he'd park directly in front of a store that'd no doubt stock the perfect implement for his needs. It was apropos, given the whimsy of his circumstances and how it fit perfectly with his hastily-formed plan.

As the high school kid at the counter rang him up, Church's eyes were trained on the hardware store. He couldn't quite see the door from his angle, but he'd certainly spot anyone as they left. He didn't worry he might miss him, because he couldn't ever remember losing a target before. No one ever slipped through Church's fingers once he caught them in his steely gaze. He was just that determined. In truth, he could be somewhat rabid or animalistic when he first caught a scent. It reminded him of that old dog Ace from those halcyon days spent at the farm. He'd admired Ace's unyielding devotion to maintaining the trail and would watch as he dashed excitedly in circles with his nose high and sniffing for fresh game to chase. Dolly equally was an excellent tracker, but no beast compared to Ace's single-minded obsession of the hunt.

Pulling out a crumpled twenty and then tossing it on the counter, he whisked up his purchase and pocketed the receipt. With a breathy and barely audible "Thanks, fella," tossed at the pimple-faced teenager at the register, he sprinted back to his truck. He wanted to make it outside before his boys could exit and escape into the crowd. He wouldn't have this target as the one who shattered his record and broke apart his winning streak. It would not be this boy who prevented him from being able to boast that nary a single white-lighter had escaped his grasp.

Yes, it may have looked a little odd, he thought, a man his age racing into a sporting goods store hell-bent on nothing but the cheapest bat he could find. But if others noticed, he didn't have the time to reflect on that. He hadn't strolled down the aisles nonchalantly or ran his fingers through the racks of paraphernalia, nor had he priced baseball jerseys or pitcher's gloves, that was true. He could only hope he appeared like some haggard, divorced part-time dad racing off to the ex's house with a hastily purchased present for his son.

As he waited in his truck some minutes longer, he reasoned that if a body was discovered in such a small place, someone there might end up being clever enough to see that the victim had most likely been assaulted with a bat, and he worried that it wouldn't take long for police to look into who had recently purchased one. Even police there in Albuquerque had to be given some due, and besides, the string-haired pothead at the counter might remember him and be able to offer a description, or he might have witnessed his vehicle drive away. *Yes, I have to consider all the possibilities.*

Gabe had never used a bat before, and knives were a rarity for him. Although they were a tool he found to be effective, they could easily be the messier choice. He liked that they were quiet as opposed to other killing instruments. They weren't definitively traced and could be disposed of with the tiniest flick of a wrist as the pickup rumbled across any remote bridge he found along the way or dropped effortlessly into a sewer grate where he could watch it be carried in the flow of water drainage and debris as it headed off to God knows where, rinsed clean of DNA and forensic evidence as it journeyed out.

Guns were typically out of the question, apart from the 9mm he stowed in the broken air vent of his Dodge, a reminder it should only be used as a last line of defense when all other efforts for a successful escape were exhausted. It was his own form of black, metal security blanket, and he found comfort in knowing it was there whether he rarely used it or not

Strangling someone was easy for a man his size and had become the fallback method he'd utilized more than not. He understood how gruesome it appeared from the outside, but he thought it was still more merciful than others, simply because their end came so quickly. He'd beaten one white-lighter to death and burned up another inside the very car he lay unconscious in after Gabe had popped up unexpectedly from his backseat and choked him until he blacked out. He'd even drowned a couple. The methods altered, as did the faces of each victim. What remained constant was that it'd been done as rote, a repetition of the grisliest chore. How their lives were extinguished wasn't nearly as important as maintaining the blind replication and monotony in each kill. He protected the malleable walls inside his brain by performing each task in an automated uniformity that never allowed the door to become ajar and any of his own assessments of his sanity to slip inside and therefore make the task impossible to complete.

The bat wasn't a typical weapon in his arsenal, but it spoke to a simplistic truth somewhere in his being. The glistening white polish of the ash and the soft curvature of the bat felt comforting to hold, and he caressed it gently as if it were his lover's thigh. He began spinning the bat in tiny circles to occupy his hands. It seemed to quash the rising storm in his chest as he patiently waited for the boys to exit the store.

When they stepped out into the afternoon heat, they were still engrossed in a very animated conversation, as young men their age were prone to do. He could tell they'd made a purchase by the paper sack one carried. Nails possibly, screws or batteries; it didn't matter. It might even be a can of paint for a project, or a spray can meant to vandalize the local water tower or a building at their school. He remembered doing that very thing as a boy. He'd painted graffiti of vulgar words on a water tower a half mile from his house once. Although he remembered climbing out his bedroom window late one night and how unseasonably cold it had been, he couldn't remember why he'd done the act in the first place; maybe nothing more than unsophisticated teenage angst and his unspoken desire to leave a mark—or his way of telling others that he'd existed once, he too possessed a voice. He told himself other children did those same pranks and gestures of mischief, but he was clever enough to see he did them because any voice he should have had was being pulled from others before the words could ever reach the surface.

When the two boys crossed the street headed back to where Gabe first picked them up, he turned his ignition and pulled out to follow. He trailed them with the same tenacity that Ace would've expended. And when they eventually parted ways, he watched as his white-lighter got into an old Mustang and his friend headed to another vehicle parked in the lot behind those storefronts. Gabe never knew the comforts of having many male friends when he was growing up. He'd missed out on the camaraderie and the usual taunts guys bore from buddies that they'd never have suffered willingly from a stranger. Not a lot of drinking games or long conversations in the dead of night about pussy, or masturbation, or laughing raucously after someone accidentally farted. He'd never double-dated with a couple or didn't get an opportunity of deflowering his prom date. He didn't even get the chance of going to his prom. Looking at the kid, he instantly felt a wave of resentment wash over him. He possessed a life Gabe would've only dreamt possible.

So as not to alert the driver, Gabe maintained a proper distance between the Dodge and Mustang. By the time the Ford finally turned off the main thoroughfare and onto a rural road he felt the heat in his belly maturing into a slow burn. It reminded him how close the deed was to completion and birthed a volcano in his insides, just as the excitement began to build to its inevitable eruption. Having no idea where his lighter was going, he could only hope to overtake him before he pulled into a driveway, where any number of witnesses could observe their exchange. He increased his speed and began closing the gap while noting a line of houses coming up along the horizon line and realized then this was probably where the young man was headed. Choices around there were as few and far between as the farmsteads themselves. Gabe knew he couldn't allow him to reach his destination, so he punched the accelerator and quickly scanned the surrounding area for any spot that'd make for an ideal killing venue.

After overtaking the Mustang, he noticed the kid's expression as he sped past and observed a look of confusion on his face. He must've thought it odd that anyone in his neighborhood would race their engine and then elbow their way around his locally distinguishable machine. Neighbors around had to know the Mustang at first glance; they'd no doubt seen it barreling down the road all hours of the day or night. His countenance seemed to suggest he wasn't acquainted with the driver of the truck. The furrowed brow on the young man's face told Gabe he'd searched his database of nearby residents and come up empty. No one he knew drove a tan over white, beat-up old Dodge, and the brawny driver wasn't anyone he recognized. Seeing a slight bend ahead and noticing he was still at a point where grazing pastures were on either side and those houses were still nearly a mile up the road, he knew intuitively it would be now or never.

When he'd gauged there was sufficient distance between vehicles he slammed his foot on the brakes and careened the Dodge into a wild arcing spin of gravel and billowed dust. He didn't want to get T-boned by mistake, but he did want that element of surprise. This unexpected maneuver startled the other driver, forcing him to stomp on his brakes just as Church had, hastily spinning his steering wheel to the right just to prevent a collision.

Springing out of the driver's side, Gabe raced toward the Mustang even before the dust had settled or the acrid scent of burnt rubber against hot blacktop dissipated. Sheer surprise had done most of the labors; the inexperienced skills of a fledgling driver, and those small-town notions ensnared his white-lighter in the crosshairs, perfectly positioning him for Church's vicious assault. If this had been the city, one might've concluded this was a road-rage incident and possibly been more prepared for the unknowable. And awful things like that did transpire in the big city every day. But this was the backwoods country and deep in the sticks; where people generally knew all their neighbors and where bad things rarely chanced to reality. If the kid had the time to think of anything before being hauled out of his vehicle, it was probably that the truck ahead had simply swerved to evade an animal scurrying across the asphalt, or a deer who'd foolishly strayed onto the road dangerously. He had no reason to expect otherwise, or to understand what was about to occur. This worked well to Church's advantage—just as he'd planned.

Tearing open the driver's side door, Gabe grabbed the young man by his shirt collar and then hauled him from his seat while still holding the slugger with his free hand. The seventeen-year-old was clearly caught unaware and his knuckles still shone white from gripping his steering wheel so tight. He hadn't time to utter a single defiant word before Gabe roughly tossed him effortlessly to the ground with a thump of his boot on his back for good measure.

He finally began to scream at his unknown attacker, but Gabe couldn't hear anything above his burgeoning rage. It filled his eardrums with coursing blood like stuffed balls of cotton. It wasn't that he possessed hatred for the youthful bumpkin scampering around his boots; it was just was how it was, as it needed to be. It was thrilling in a weird way—the danger, and the unexpected outcomes. All of it created a heady intoxication, at least for a man like Gabriel Church. Lifting the Louisville into the air, he brought it down with a single, wild, brutal strike against the back of the young man's skull. Whatever words of retaliation that might've been escaped his lips suddenly were lost in the noise of shattering bone and red gore flying out in all directions like a grisly spigot suddenly released. Scalp wounds can bleed profusely. And his young cranium was no exception. He gurgled something inaudibly as his mouth began to fill rapidly with blood, but Gabe continued assailing the frightened man with more and more wallops. Blood drained down his face like a red dishrag had been wrung out over his head and any sounds he might've made were drowned out by the sound of the next few critical and final blows.

Fortunately for him, he'd slipped into warm unconsciousness after that second or third clap of white ash against bone and his vital organs. It sent him into a merciful oblivion lest he feel every painful strike. Church shattered bone on his second draw of the slugger and a crimson fissure in the man's hairline gushed blood for minutes on end, until his labored breathing became too unbearable to continue and he gasped one final time before expiring at Church's feet. He never knew his attacker, was never privy to his motives, and never understood why he'd been destined to die alongside that rural road on a late afternoon in early October...without even a witness to the crime.

It was over as quickly as it started, Gabriel stood for a full minute on the side of that farm-to-market route, in some *backassward* little town, absorbing everything that'd happened over the course of twenty or thirty minutes in full. It wasn't out of reach to call how he felt a "rush," but it was the most accurate description he knew. The pounding in his chest and anxiety of potentially seeing another car creeping up behind him during the throes of his attack could be electrifying. But only if he accepted it as the welcomed risk it was and adjusted his better reasoning to be able to stop and fully enjoy the moment for what it was while the exhilarating sensation was still at its peak.

He'd sent another blessed soul homebound to God, gift-wrapped and ethereal. And while he stood in the shadows of those impressive Sandia Mountain ranges, he soaked in the sensation of irrevocable finality and a job complete. He remembered enough high school Spanish to know *sandia* translated in English meant watermelon and holding the bat as that bloodied symbol of unencumbered youth, he felt a special kinship with every delicate and earthly element that makes up our insignificant lives. Every cell in his body seemed to scream out with joy, and every particle that once had fashioned him became charged with immediacy, with vibrant colors of gold and Tahitian blues.

A distant cry from a white-tailed kite circling the skies above finally brought him back to reality. Church looked up from the road when he heard the screech of the bird and smiled. Yet another predator on the hunt, he figured. It appeared she was making nothing more than lazy, haphazard loops through the air. But he knew her vision was unmatched; she'd been scanning the ground for foraging rodents or disturbances among the tall scrub grasses. She'd become an unexpected witness to everything that happened below and there was little she wouldn't have seen with her gifted sight and her safe vantage overhead. Gabe wondered if she might've noticed the rising specter once he'd released it, allowing it to ascend into the sky as he passed her in the air and then rose upward towards its heavenly domain.

He wondered if animals knew more than humans ever gave them credit for, possibly understanding death in ways we never would. *We are much alike*, he whispered to himself as he watched the kite with his hand up as he shielded his eyes from the sun's glare. *We are both hunters and killers alike, but still there isn't malice in the things we are meant to do.* His smile eventually faded, and he looked down at the carnage and blood at his feet. He realized the body had to be moved and began to formulate a plan for disposal before any hayseed residents came barreling down that dusty road and upended his mission altogether. And most of these folks carried guns in their cars and trucks. Even a trip to Walmart could prove fatal for someone if they got their ire up.

Hoisting the dead man's body gently, he placed it in the passenger side of his truck and calmly slid behind the wheel of his victim's car. He needed only to make it a half mile or so, just to remove it from the actual crime scene. They wouldn't search the whole road for clues, so if he inadvertently left something behind, he was improving his chances it wouldn't get picked up as evidence. He cautiously wiped any prints from the dash, stick shift, handles, and exterior. Although he'd never been booked anywhere, and to his knowledge never left anything to match to, he knew it was because of that attention to detail that enabled him to maintain his freedom. *Better to be safe than sorry*, he remembered his mother saying once. Popping the hood and latching it into place, he then began that long walk back to his truck. He hoped that it would appear that the Mustang stalled with mechanical problems and had stranded the driver who apparently had walked to reach a phone or to find assistance. It might give him a little time, he thought. And there were times when even twenty minutes or so can make a world of difference in survival as one is racing out of the city with the police hot on their tail. Before he reached the spot where his white-lighter fell, he'd pulled a thorny bramble up from its roots and used it to rake the pavement and soft earth of any tracks to hide what struggles had occurred there. He needed to find a good place to hide the body. Someplace where he might remain undiscovered for a few days while hoping a strong rain might arise and destroy any remaining DNA he left behind. But he knew he wasn't an amateur, he'd left nothing for them to trace back to him; that much he was certain. Remembering the purpose of all this, he pulled out the young man's wallet and emptied it of any cash. *Robbing the dead wasn't much of an offense*, he thought, not when it was relative to homicide. Besides, every little bit helps to get him farther in his journey. Finding a whopping sixty dollars via crinkly fives and with a solitary twenty was lucky. Since this stemmed from his need for fuel, he knew what he gained was plenty to get him started on the highway.

Within an hour he was again back on the interstate heading northwest. Turning on the stereo, he reclined into his seat and mentally prepared himself for what he knew was going to be hours behind the wheel...god willing. The music soothed his jangled nerves, and before long he'd all but forgotten the last white-lighter in his mission and found his distractions turning from what'd transpired in Albuquerque to the bright lights of Seattle and that first glimpse he'd have of Chris.

One can't even begin to be a successful serial killer while still weighing out the insignificant consequences of their actions. And if anyone were to sit right next to Gabe that night he drove from New Mexico, they might've spotted the difference in kind that he couldn't see. But only if one paid close attention to all the words he spoke and listened intently to the ramblings of all his twisted philosophies. Although he'd have enjoyed the company of a stranger in his truck and found the distraction a welcome way to pass the time, it might not be as pleasant for them. It couldn't be easy listening to a killer as he rationalized through all the evil things he'd ever done. It must surely sound like the hefty clank of manufactured iron, like doors of a vault being slammed shut. They might even have said to themselves how much wiser it was for those dark thoughts to become locked away and hidden behind the heavy metal doors of laden steel.

Chapter Nineteen

EVERYBODY ON KEEN'S list had been contacted and then crossed off or circled for a follow-up. Every name had been run through a criminal background check and Keen saw nothing noteworthy in the dwindling list that remained. Still, he felt sure the vehicle he'd been searching for lay buried somewhere among those names. Whoever owned it either knew Shea Baltimore or was possibly her killer.

As he lay in bed that night with his wife, he'd voice his frustrations. He didn't like sharing the grisly details of his investigations, but he enjoyed Carol's sharp mind. She'd become his favorite sounding board, and he knew the importance of hearing another angle presented. He knew how easy it was to get lost in the minutia of an inquiry; without even being aware you were drowning in it. Carol might look up from the book she'd been skimming on her lap as she prepared to turn in. She'd been listening to her husband as he droned on and complained about his fruitless day of interrogating suspects, and she'd surprise him by innocently mentioning an obvious thing he'd overlooked.

"Well I don't know, hon," she'd say as if she hadn't been paying attention.

"But if it were me, I'd talk to the girls who didn't particularly like your victim. Start with girls from school who weren't close with her, the ones who didn't hang around her but knew her from chem class, or field hockey, or those after-school events. People not close can sometimes be the most beneficial," she'd say. And then she might nonchalantly offer some great wisdom like it was coming from a prophet sitting atop a mountain. *"You know, baby sometimes our **frenemies** have the deepest secrets about us...more than those we normally confide in. If the poor girl had anyone like that, I'd begin there."*

Carol often supplied Scott with an unexpected clarity. Call it the female brain, or just another way of seeing the same things he saw, only different. She was more than his wife in those times - she was his *partner*. And it was just another reason to love her, he thought – another great thing about sleeping with a woman with such a bright and energetic mind. Not to mention someone with a delicious body. Grabbing the open book from her lap, he might toss it carelessly onto the floor beside the bed and then roll over to begin ravishing his spouse as payment for her insight into his investigation. The next morning he'd happily exploit her suggestion by taking another swing as those souls he overlooked the first time. He found over the years, that Carol, although not a detective, could be more accurate than most of the cops at his precinct. Another reason he loved her, he knew.

Shea Baltimore's murder wasn't the only investigation he was running at that moment, but remembering her attractive, lifeless body or the way she'd been discovered with her eyelids still open unnerved him; that milky, distant gaze of a death victim was something a good detective saw many times, but for Keen it was something he could never fully shake, no matter how world-weary and jaded he felt he'd become. Miss Baltimore wasn't famous, she wasn't a notable artist on the rise, she had a meaningless go-nowhere job and supported an alcoholic father...but she was still someone worthy of killing. And this meant that someone out there thought she either knew too much, or had seen something she shouldn't have, or had inadvertently become an integral part of a mystery in the making. So with that aspect, Shea Baltimore was one of the most important people in Seattle at that moment. She was evidence, a clue to a crime Scott intended on solving. The Baltimore investigation wasn't the only one on his plate at the time, but it was quickly evolving into the one that drove him the hardest.

Carol Keen saw her husband's dilemma and recognized when a case was burrowing under his skin. She'd always been empathetic to his brooding and knew he felt regret for many of the victims he encountered in his daily grind. It may have been because the girl had been so young, she figured. Or possibly because family members weren't calling with inquiries as to the status of the case—she couldn't rightly tell. But her husband was a man of great character. That she knew without question. He'd carry the investigation around like a millstone until he solved it—if not for the victim's family, then for himself. In the faint bedroom light, she could see that Scott's eyes were open and he was staring at the ceiling instead of sleeping. All she could do was comfort him and offer him solace, so she rolled over on her side and placed a palm on his chest and said nothing. She listened to his breathing, imagining the gears turning inside as he searched his brain for new avenues and forgotten clues.

The following morning Keen chose one of his better suits to wear. He was going to track down the few remaining names from his list and surprise them with a visit. Remembering what a former partner of his was fond of spouting off: "When all else fails, go and rattle their cages." Well, he would rattle a few today. With a serious absence of leads, he had nothing else to pin his hopes to, and as he headed out that morning with a kiss on Carol's cheek and a steaming cup of coffee in one hand for the drive in, he felt a renewed sense of direction. If the names gave him nothing, then he'd go back to Shea's apartment and use a more threatening personality as he interviewed every resident as well as that fat shit who managed the complex. He would take the complete Baltimore file with him and toss out the grisly photos if that was what it took, because someone was going to give him something viable today, or there was going to be hell to pay. And it would be paid forward.

By the time he got to his desk, someone was waiting there. It was Dennis Gilroy, another homicide detective that Keen knew on sight, but one from the CSI unit. He was a rising star in the agency, having utilized DNA trace evidence to skyrocket the city's solve ratio of murders from their already impressive figure of eighty percent to a staggering ninety percent. He'd done that primarily by opening the cold case file boxes and sending out forensic samples to the crime lab. Most detectives thought his glowing reputation was a little unfounded. Anyone can put a stamp on an outgoing mail pouch, they'd say in hushed whispers, dripping with envy.

"Keen, my man, how's it going, buddy?" he asked with his hand thrust out and a self-congratulatory grin on his face.

"Dennis. What brings you down to the Subzero?" Keen asked with a self-effacing tone. The "Subzero" had been the nickname of the first floor for as long as Keen could remember. It housed most of the first-tier detectives, like Narcotics and Homicide. The second story and subsequent floors above were where the upper echelon had been stationed. This included the Special Crimes and High-Risk Victims Unit, as well as Forensics and Computer Crimes. Even the Canine Unit and Harbor Patrol had offices on the second and third floors. For most this never made much sense. It also received its moniker because of the faulty air conditioning on the first floor. The unit maintained a temperature that kept it as cold as an English dungeon and all because the upper floors complained. And in this old building, nothing really worked right, nor had it for years. Heat rose, and as everyone else knew, shit still rolled downhill. It created a chasm between Homicide and all other departments, but Keen wasn't about to play that game with Gilroy.

"I come with offerings from upstairs," Gilroy said with a grin that could slice through timber. "I know you're on that Baltimore murder, and I hear it's dragging just a bit."

"Well you might be listening to the wrong people, Dennis," Keen said calmly as he took off his suit jacket and hung it on the door. "I have a few leads I'm working on at this very moment," he said, trying to make the lies sound more authentic. In truth, he had squat, just some random names to run down, and a faint suggestion of hope that a clue was concealed somewhere in that list.

"Well I thought I might help since I had some free time," Gilroy offered. "I took the initiative of pulling video footage from street cams and nearby businesses on the day of the murder. I knew you'd be asking for it soon enough…and I think I found something."

The heat under Keen's starched collar was rising, but that last sentence hastily brought it under control. Gilroy was clearly questioning his ability to investigate a crime, but even he had to concede that he hadn't considered that possibility. The case was already stale by the time it hit his desk, so he reasoned that any footage would've been taped over or lost entirely.

At least that was what he was telling himself. Any less and he knew he'd be losing a lot of sleep tonight—and that nearly full bottle of vodka tucked in a cabinet at home was holding the risk of never surviving the night.

Maybe it wasn't just the Greeks you needed to worry about because even assholes come bearing gifts. "Great, Whatcha got?" Keen asked, trying to sound nonchalant as he took his chair, restacking the skewed files on his desk, and trying to keep his face from showing elation.

"I have the clips upstairs in my office," Gilroy said, reminding Keen of his place in the precinct's hierarchy. "But I found a vehicle pulling onto the street that sparked my interest. We caught it leaving the crime scene the day before the victim was discovered, then caught it again on the red-light-running cameras." Gilroy was using the full vernacular of what was commonly just called a red-light cam, and Keen wondered who the fuck he was trying to impress.

"So what sparked your interest with this one vehicle?" he asked intrigued.

"Well, let's be frank and say the victim lived in a rundown shit hole, and most of the other residents drive cars from the mid-to-late nineties. This car was brand new, and we got a pretty good shot of the driver. He didn't look suspicious at all, which to a good detective can mean just as much, you agree?"

"I'm currently running potential vehicle owner's names," Keen offered honestly. "I found a witness, and I'm nearly finished. So your man is probably one that I'm visiting today." Keen boasted to save face and ignored Gilroy's question altogether. "But I'm surprised at your interest in the case."

Keen watched as the detective raised an eyebrow and plopped his butt on the edge of the desk. He appeared to be a slight degree friendlier and a huge amount more conciliatory. "I'm not here to breach my presence into your investigation," Gilroy said soothingly. "I knew you'd be asking TCIS for the video soon enough, and I just wanted to lend a hand wherever I could."

To his credit, Gilroy was correct, at least in the fact that Keen thought about the video as a possible lead, he would have gone to the Traffic Collision Investigative Unit upstairs to inquire whether footage existed, but it didn't bode well he hadn't considered it. Even though he'd racked his brain the night before trying to unearth a lead he'd felt he'd overlooked.

Dennis wasn't a man who offered a hand so freely, though, especially when it hadn't been requested. Shades of doubt began to surface that his captain doubted his skillset with this particular investigation or feared it would be heading to cold storage if he hadn't asked a *more seasoned investigator* to look into it. He may have done it on Keen's behalf, but the lack of forewarning suggested there was something else working the mix. The idea ruffled his feathers even further but didn't quell the excitement he felt with finding a new lead, regardless of where the good news would come.

"Then let's take a look at it together, Dennis. I'd love to see what you found."

There was time to hate this shithead later, he thought, because the footage was calling him. He probably did need the leg up, he reasoned. The real goal was in solving Ms. Baltimore's murder after all. Grabbing his printout and the investigative file, he rose and followed Dennis to the elevator. As they waited for a car to arrive, they chatted in that casual way coworkers do whenever they're backed into a corner and forced to smile congenially and make nice, even though the two men didn't share any type of bond, more than working as detectives in the same city who were roughly the same age.

The video was surprisingly clear and the man's face was easily distinguishable. The tags and full images of the vehicle were captured spot-on. Looking closely, the driver's face was easy to see, and it appeared he'd been upset about something. Keen even thought that he saw the man pound his fist on the dashboard once, and not because there were any nearby drivers who'd cut him off in the flow of traffic or seemingly impeded his route. The man appeared furious about something, and whatever caused him to hit his own dash and squint out in an angry private outburst occurred very recently. People failed to realize how much our individual lives could be captured on film, or that even our most confidential moments can become public viewing and fodder for the masses. It seemed, to Keen, that the Internet hadn't really taught us anything.

The make and model of the car did seem out of place, even to Keen. Given that particular area of town, with its diseased infrastructure and decaying buildings, it seemed a rather educated call on Gilroy's part and quickly becoming one of the dirtier sections of the city which most sane people avoided whenever possible. A place where dealers squatted on trash-littered corners and waited for addicts to pull up in beat up autos before thrusting two crumpled twenties out a window like a fast handoff at a drive-thru window. But it wasn't burgers and colas they opted for, these were baggies of meth rocks and expensive cocaine.

"Your perp is, umm...a Christian Maxwell," Gilroy said systematically as he retrieved the information from the chicken-scratched notes off his desk. Continuing, he offered, "He lives on Lancaster in one of those old restored condo buildings they began refurbishing a few years ago. More gentrification for the urbanites, I suppose. Check your list. You have a Christian Maxwell in there?"

Trailing his fingers down the list Keen found what he was looking for and circled the address, and wrote 'see this one' in red next to Christian Maxwell's name. "I was just heading there this very morning. It seems we were both getting to the same place. But I appreciate your help; really, I do," Keen said, finding some truth in his own words.

They might have met in the middle, but Dennis surprisingly brought something to the table. And he couldn't hide his gratitude in the subtle stains of his earlier dislike of the man. "I don't know how busy you are this morning...but wanna take a ride with me? I mean, after all, you brought the first pics of a possible witness, and he might turn out to be a suspect we like for the crime in the end."

Somewhere in his gut, he knew the offer would come back to bite him in the ass. Gilroy would take an undue amount of credit and gossip around the station would surface that the case would've gone stone chilly without his better efforts. Scott could almost see his puffed out chest and that look of superiority brewing in his expression whenever he told the story of how he solved the Baltimore murder, even though it'd never officially been assigned to him.

Well, there it is. Just when I thought I could tolerate this asshole, images come back to remind me I was right all along. This fucker is a grade-A douchebag!

But those were Keen's images and no one else's. He'd just failed to see that in the heat of the moment. Quite unexpectedly, and somewhat graciously, Dennis agreed to tag along for the ride but quickly interjected, "Sure, I'd love to, but this is your investigation, not mine. But, hells yes, I'll go. I suppose I'm a little curious whether it produces a lead or not."

Dislike or not, Keen had to concede that Dennis was a good detective, despite the ill-gained reputation of solving many cases solely by dumb luck, as in merely licking a stamp or being in the right place at the right time. His personality was the problem. And other investigators didn't enjoy his company, complaining to anyone who listened how off-putting Dennis seemed to be. Even Keen could see that, and therefore he understood why it'd been so difficult for Dennis to make friends. Like when he *permitted* the more seasoned detective to tag along. It was this type of false bravado that gave him his reputation, and it reminded Keen of the poor kid on the playground who had to work extra hard just to make friends, someone too eager and overtly excited when others asked him to join in their reindeer games.

GABE WAS CLOSING in on the outskirts of Seattle and bordering on reaching the city limit signs. He'd driven throughout the night and made as few stops as possible to reach his destination. He was, as he'd expected, arriving earlier than he'd told Chris he could. He wondered if he should ring him up to hear the excitement in his voice, or to take a day to survey the man's movements before reaching out to him.

Gabriel hadn't remained one step ahead of his pursuers by being stupid or making spur-of-the-moment decisions. In his mind, his pursuers were very real, tangible figures. They may have been cloaked in dark obscurity, but they were ever-present and always watching. Sadly, for the loved ones of his victims, the decidedly painful lack of progress regarding the apprehension of any killer must be an albatross dragging at their hull. Because his MO had been altered and twisted outside of recognition, and because the murders crossed state lines in an arbitrarily meandering fashion, no one had even begun to suspect a serial killer was making his way cross-country or even guessed that he'd done that trip from coast to coast and back again more than once. There'd been no task forces assigned to examine the carnage Gabe left in the cities behind him. The deaths were all local investigations, and all unsolved as far as he knew. If the police arrested anyone for one of his crimes, they'd chosen poorly.

Christian Maxwell was different from anyone else in that respect. He set out to find a serial killer for a book he'd intended on writing. He began with a simple inquiry line; one that inadvertently hooked Gabriel Church and brought a prospective writer, face to face with a murderer. Though it seemed an easy, albeit tedious, task Chris may've done the impossible. Or at least more than other more seasoned investigators who'd ever worked his case from coast to coast. He'd seen the patterns most overlooked and then made concerted determination that the crimes were committed by someone wandering aimless across these United States, and it became the randomness of it all that stumped most detectives. But for Chris, there was a murderous design he saw more clearly than most. At least after he'd researched the multitudes of homicides and then placed them on his whiteboard, even ones others missed because they were outside certain jurisdictions.

While profilers and other authorities were looking for a Modus Operandi, Christian was looking at dates and victim recounts. He could almost trace a line of crimes with a finger until he could see it spanning its way from one location to another as Church traveled through a state, making grisly work of dispatching strangers along the way.

Chris fully expected to find a raving lunatic by the time he sifted through the clues long enough to find, not where Church once had been, but where he was heading. When Gabriel took the seat across from him at the coffee house for their first meeting, he was shaken and disturbed by what he saw. The killer was calm, polite, and above all handsome. As a society, we tended to give allowances to the attractive. We make incorrect judgments based upon someone's appearance. Even though he knew better, Chris was dumbfounded with how someone with so much going for them could actually be a murderer. He'd expected to see obvious signs of psychosis and was petrified thinking when he did meet the man. He expected to observe a rabid foaming mad dog and was pleasantly surprised when Church appeared as normal on the outside as any other patron at the café. There was an edge of something untoward in his beautiful eyes, but it wasn't enough that Chris's first inclination was to jump up and run from the restaurant in fear for his life.

Though their first conversation was brief, the game plan and rules were laid out and done so in public surroundings. Gabriel didn't worry that Christian Maxwell was working with the authorities, some plant for the FBI or some such shit, because unknown to him, Gabe had surveilled him for two full days prior to the meeting. Christian foolishly gave the killer just enough information to learn his identity and once known, was simply a matter of time and patience to Church; two things he possessed in copious amounts. He needn't have worried it could be a trap. The most bewildering aspect of their introduction was why he'd chosen to meet in the first place. Who would be rash enough to willingly confess to a stranger some of the most horrifying crimes that any man could commit on another? What were his motivations?

It made sense to him to repeat the process, since trust was something he never had in much abundance. He trusted Chris, more than anyone, but there was no telling what kinds of promises and lies the authorities could have drawn from their armory to push Chris to turn in his old lover with his freedom from prosecution and his moral duty to the dead white-lighter's families. Even waving the flag in front of him and spinning tales of the greater good and all. They could use any number of techniques to force Christian to do the unthinkable. So in his mind it was settled. He would shadow Chris for a day before making his presence known. He would watch to see if he made contact with anyone who might yet pass as police or the FBI and wait to see if his movements implied their relationship wasn't all he had thought it should be.

Gabe's arrival in the city was under sunny skies with a cool breeze blowing off the Elliot Bay. He wasn't riding in on a white steed as he'd hoped, just a dusty Dodge pickup had seen too much mileage and was on a permanent risk of breaking down. Gabriel had seen more towns in his travels than he cared to name, but even he was forced to admit just how splendid the views around Seattle were. He liked the Northwest—it suited him. Hearing the distant horns from ferries as they made their way from shore to shore or watching the flocks of sandpipers, plovers, and gulls crisscrossing the pale sky was something Gabe hadn't experienced until becoming a man. And once he met Christian Maxwell, he even considered for a moment settling in Seattle.

It'd been foolish daydreaming and an unlikely end to his running. There would be no white-picket fences surrounding Cape Cod style cottages anywhere in his future. Once he'd murdered Shea, it sealed his fate with Chris and pushed him back onto the road to make his escape. He was forced to leave this beloved city behind, just as he was leaving the only other person he thought understood him. He'd chosen Texas, partly because the highways were in control of his destiny and partly because it felt as far away as he could run to put Seattle in his rearview. He could have run from one coast to another, but inside he knew the cries of seabirds and the sounds of boat engines humming across the water only reminded him of Washington. Central Texas was dry and vast, and the openness guaranteed that anyone could get lost among the small rural towns and long stretches of vacant grassland. No, it wasn't anything like Washington, which may've been the point, and the only reason he'd ended up there.

Sun-bleached houses dotted the hillsides of Seattle, and on a clear day, one could see from the Space Needle all the way to the hazy outline of Mt. Rainier. There was industry here. And residents of Washington were a private class of people who minded their own business, with that hippy way of life that encouraged others to live however they saw fit— minus the typically harsh judgments and acrimony he'd noticed in other places. He'd become accustomed to the picturesque surroundings, realizing now how this'd become the first destination he'd ever found where he thought it had the power to tempt him into stopping for good...of planting his feet on solid soil and building a future with a man he admired. This was a city of promise. The only one he'd thought could lure him off that endless series of no-name little towns he'd suffered through the years. And even driving through the city's heaviest traffic, he still felt as if he were heading home for the first time in years. Though that by itself wasn't stopping that nervous ball of twine in his belly from becoming tighter the closer he got to Chris and the Lancaster. *But even good homes can have their shadows.*

Chapter Twenty

DETECTIVE KEEN BEEPED his car door open and sat behind the wheel. In his mind, this was his investigation and he intended to take the lead. Gilroy seemed all right with that and illustrated it when he walked over and took the passenger side door without questioning who was in charge and therefore driving their inquiry. Conversation during the drive was cordial enough. Dennis asked about Carol and ribbed Keen about when he'd finally get around to giving his wife some babies to care for. Gilroy didn't realize that he and Carol had been trying to get pregnant lately, but so far the stick hadn't turned that pale shade of blue. Dennis was married with two of his own and one on the way, but Keen couldn't visualize what type of woman would have chosen him to spend the rest of her life with.

Of the two detectives, Gilroy was the only one with a regular partner, so Scott asked him about that, being a minor subject he could make idle conversation about without becoming too personal. He could see the detective thought quite highly of himself and listened to his pious ramblings as he talked about shaky turf where one person was just beginning to learn the other's idiosyncratic ways. He confided it had been a little hard early on, but now he was learning to appreciate having a colleague he could rely on. Keen suspected Gilroy's partner, a man named Hollingsworth, was doing more of the grunt work in that arrangement than Dennis was, but he smiled and nodded as the detective threw out his range of insights, as if anyone really cared that he and he alone could see the big picture at play. Keen had been saddled with a temporary partner, but he couldn't regret it, he knew he was one of the few detectives not currently assigned one, so he took that burden in stride. Just part of the game and something he could suffer through for the time being. Gilroy had been correct about the neighborhood, though. There had been a complete gentrification of the area, which might have gone another way had it not been for those who saw money bubbling to the surface with the renovation of a once-failing section of the city. Developers had slipped in, then refurbished, remodeled, and salvaged the overall feel of the district. It was quickly becoming quite cosmopolitan, and every corner seemed to house a new coffee house selling exceedingly high-priced beans from around the world and trendy boutiques sporting more name than they did merchandise.

The once busy warehouses of seaside commerce had blossomed into spacious lofts and tiny apartments. Storefronts sat at street level, with most buildings turning to residential housing above those. Sidewalks were all freshly paved and well-lit with benches at the intersections where buses and trolleys met their passengers. It could've easily become a place that turned stale and lifeless or even dangerous once the sun set. The type of streets people tended to avoid at night. Instead, the area was salvaged and transformed because of industry and gentrification. It thrived with new activity under a bright and fresh façade. Awnings stretched along the blocks and pedestrians found it a safe and inviting a place to walk, even after dusk. Streets where cheap bars and liquor stores could be ostensibly converted into the height of fashionable sports taverns and vegan eateries.

As Keen turned onto Lancaster Street, he wondered about the people who chose to live there, because it was a district that Carol and he might've found alien to their lifestyle. Nice place, he thought, but no place to raise children. Even the pet owners had been forced to replace their big chocolate Labs and German shepherds with smaller Shih Tzu's, and everyone was required to take freight elevators or the back stairs down to the tiny manicured courtyards, just to allow their pets to do their business outdoors. It seemed to him that the urbanite sprawl, which seemed to swell with new growth, somehow made everyone's daily life smaller and tidier by comparison. He couldn't see the reward in living in such a place. No room to stretch, particularly when babies entered the picture or kids got old enough to attend public schools. He felt that familiar twinge of melancholy, remembering he had yet to give Carol what she most wanted, and what she deserved to have: a family to call her very own.

"There it is," Gilroy blurted out, "the Lancaster Square Lofts, and I think it is unit 213, if I'm remembering correctly."

The Lancaster building was a stately remodel, but without the frill of its nearest neighbor. Brown brick with its multitude of windows facing out from every direction, it sat comfortably in the hub of the city's elite. Not far from the popular Pioneer Square, it was within casual walking distance for many theaters and dining establishments and quickly becoming a desired residency for an up-and-coming generation of Seattle's most erudite.

"Wonder what this Christian Maxwell dude does for a living?" Gilroy asked unashamedly.

"We'll ask him that," Scott replied quietly as his eyes searched the streets for available parking. "Maybe if they're hiring, I could apply and finally afford to take Carol on that vacation to the islands she's been dreaming of." He chuckled.

After circling the block and finding no place to park at street level, Keen pulled into the underground lot and flashed a badge to the attendant in lieu of an explanation. The young man opened the gate with a dumbfounded expression. It must've been a rare occurrence to have the Seattle police stopping by the Lancaster, Keen mused.

Standing outside Christian's door, they knocked politely, but when they weren't immediately invited in, he said, "Mr. Maxwell, I'm Detective Keen and this is my associate, Detective Gilroy of the Seattle Police Department." Again he flashed his badge for anyone peeking through the peephole. "We were hoping we might have a moment of your time regarding a crime you may have been a witness to."

In the building's long history, first originating as a port access and warehouse for a thriving river trade, and eventually to being developed into posh, exposed brick and mortar residential lofts, no tenant had ever heard those terms spoken in the barbered halls of the Lancaster. People talked and neighbors liked to gossip, so phrases beginning with words like "detective" or "Seattle police" were not typically heard by those residents choosing to live in such a prestigious downtown condo.

Christian had heard the knocks, heard the detective as they made their introductions through the closed door of his unit. Mostly because he'd been listening on the other side while nervously holding his breath, uncertain of whether he was supposed to answer to pretend not to be there. He'd figured someone might come to call, particularly after he'd avoided the phone messages for as long as he had. He'd just wanted Gabe to get there before it happened. To offer him some form of guidance with how to handle it. He was an intelligent man, but way outside his depth, specifically to those types of challenges. He relied on Gabe to be his Sherpa through this new life of recent subterfuges and lies. He was playing out ridiculous scenarios in his head—like they might be carrying a warrant, or about to kick in his door only to find him cringing in a corner and cowering in the darkness. But he was relieved when after a minute, he heard another knock, quieter than the first and he noticed through the peephole they were shaking their heads in disappointment. Clearly they were giving up and about to leave, he hoped. He did catch his first glimpse of Detective Keen though, recognizing it was the same voice he'd heard from his machine days earlier. And this was the same voice of the man currently threatening to break his slackly tethered world apart.

With the detectives gone, he felt he could finally breathe again and do his best to contain his growing anxiety. *Where the fuck was Gabe when I needed him?* he wondered, before thinking how bad it might have been had he been in his apartment in that exact moment the police showed up at his door. For the rest of the evening, Chris sat in the living room with the lights off, sipping from a glass of wine to help calm him down. Thinking every shadow had a face, and picturing a car filled with detectives sitting on the streets below in some crazy stakeout of his apartment.

GABRIEL SAT ACROSS the street, watching the windows of his lover's apartment. Chris was at home. He'd been spying on him long enough to see him pass by those same windows, moving from room to room. Chris rarely closed his blinds or curtains. He'd once told Gabe he lived on the second floor and didn't give two shits what others witnessed while he was in the privacy of his own domain. It was the reason he felt comfortable walking around naked on those few times Gabe visited there, and they'd engaged in some superb sex. Gabriel wondered what Chris was doing up there in the dark, it being so early in the evening. He even suspected Chris might be up there fucking someone.

The notion of being jealous seemed incongruous to his nature, and odd such an idea could pop up in his noggin. He himself had fucked quite a few people since departing Seattle, and he naturally assumed Chris had gone on with his life in much the same fashion. But even as unaccustomed as he was to these new emotions of suspicion and envy, he couldn't seem to stifle the resentful thoughts brewing that Chris might be unfaithful, if only to his memory. In Gabe's twisted reasoning, he could do whatever sick thing he desired, but he fully expected Chris to remain chaste and despondent over the loss of his one true love.

Suddenly the idea of sitting in the cab of his truck for hours on end and worrying about what he didn't know rather than what he could feel and touch seemed like an unbearable task to continue. And even though he knew it'd be more intelligent to conduct surveillance on Chris a little longer, if only to appease himself with Chris's true intentions, the battle in his mind was waging something fierce and seemed foolish to just ignore. Throwing caution to the winds, he turned the Dodge's ignition headed out in search of one of those most elusive items: an operational, free-standing pay phone.

THE RINGING OF his cell phone startled Christian. It sent a tremor coursing through his body, which for him felt far too much like voltage. As if he'd been sitting in an electric chair at the moment the switch was pulled. He jumped off the couch like it'd miraculously burst into flames under his ass, turning his head this way and that as he tried to remember where he'd seen it last. He didn't think it would be Gabriel calling, not this early. It might be one of his few girlfriends calling to ask him out for drinks or even a late dinner. Finding his phone on the kitchen counter, he stared at it for a full second as he weighed his decision to answer, thinking it might be that Keen fellow trying to reach him, yet again, but he answered anyway. He was genuinely surprised to hear Gabriel's sexy voice on the line. His heart skipped a tiny beat when those raspy, breathy words asked, "It's me, you alone?"

"Well, yes," he said, a slight confusion evident in his tone. "I'm so fucking glad you called. You won't believe it, but that detective I told you about was just at my door."

Gabriel seemed calm, though there was still a beat pause of hesitation between his last question and his next. "Well, did you let him in or talk to him?"

"No... I was too fuckin' freaked out. I'm not even sure exactly what he wants, or even what I'd say to him."

"That's good," Church said in reply. "We can talk about that later, but at this moment my cock is aching sumpin' fierce, and I'd like nothing more than waking up next to you on clean sheets...any ideas? But not at your place, that's far too dangerous."

Chris's nightmare of police as they forced their way into his home was looming heavy in his mind. "I've thought about it already, and I found a nice hotel not far. I didn't make any reservations, though, since I wasn't sure when you'd arrive, but I imagine we could get a room without one." He was surprised he was sounding so normal with his heart beating out of his chest at the unexpected prospect of seeing Gabriel so soon. "The question is," he said quietly for effect, "how do I get out? Don't you think they might be watching or following me?"

"It's doubtful, babe." Gabriel sounded confident, and suddenly Chris felt a blanket of comforting protection wrap around him. It allowed his longstanding anxieties to finally ebb from his pores like toxins in a dry sauna.

"You have a back entrance to your place, don't you?" Gabriel asked? "I mean, it's not impossible for you to make it out to the streets unseen. You'll have to leave your car, though. I can drive us, or we can walk the distance. Didn't you say it wasn't far?"

For Chris, walking the sidewalks of Seattle with Gabe was fast becoming a glorious recollection he never intended to lose. Slowly they walked Pioneer Square together, strolling along the arts district and eating small meals from vendors they passed along the way. It'd been a wonderful time: a period of respite between the harsh interviews at the Mayflower and a chance to learn a few things about one another when it didn't feel so clinical or serious. They even managed to hit a few clubs and share some fond times joined by laughter.

Not all occasions were remembered fondly, though. One time they'd found themselves walking along the shoreline, near the seawall that faced out at the endless rolling waves coming in off Elliot Bay. He remembered it had been a particularly gray morning back then. After a long night of talking, with occasional fucking or drinking in-between, they'd walked close beside each other, hands nearly touching. They were close because each man had to speak loud just to be heard over the sounds of lapping waves breaking against the rocks and the cacophony of seabirds and distant boat horns. It was different than other times they'd been together. Chris remembered those times, though they seemed difficult now to recollect with perfect clarity. It was a time when Chris was becoming overwhelmed with every new side and awful truth he was learning about Gabriel's past and what that could mean as a future. Gabriel had turned his back and abruptly stormed off in a huff, leaving Christian to question whether he wanted to ever see his lover again. He had, and after that, most times were special and relaxing, a bonding experience for two men learning how to shed the shackles of their old lives and adjust to loving each other despite their tragic and uncertain odds. Christian had never felt the ease of being in another man's company as much as he did Gabriel's.

That night Christian felt like a cat burglar, peering apprehensively through the peephole before slinking into the empty hallway—all while expecting the worse. He crept out his door half imagining he'd be blitzed by

SWAT officers hell-bent on taking him down. To his surprise, he made it all the way to down the hall unmolested. He raced to the stairwell and gripped the doorknob with sweaty palms, turning only for an instant to tell Gabe he'd meet him at the cafe at the end of the block. As he flew down the fire exit his heart hammered nails in his chest. It reminded him of Gabe's arterial defect. He wondered abstractly if simply sleeping with a killer who shared his type of imperfection was enough to alter his own organ. Maybe from some fucked-up sense of a body's sympathy, like when a man has pregnancy pains even as his wife stares daggers in his direction; a scornful expression to imply she was about to unleash a tirade on the ridiculous dickhead she'd chosen to marry.

He pushed the safety bar on the exit leading toward the sidewalk and hurried outdoors. He remembered how they'd once called them "panic bars." They became standard regulation code after a multitude of citizens lost their lives in a disastrous fire in the 1930's. People are reactive, and they are fools, he thought. Somehow in the blink of an eye, and under duress, they can lose the ability to navigate the simplest of things, like exits or doors as they scrambled for freedom. *Panic bars seem an appropriate name since that is what's rising in my chest.* But he didn't care. He was finally close to seeing Gabriel Church, and to him, nothing else mattered.

As the cool night air hit him, he considered his actions as he ran with his arms stretched wide to embrace a serial killer. He raced through the open courtyard out back and circled the building through a passage between it and its adjoining neighbor, too big to be considered an alleyway, yet too small to allow vehicles to navigate. Making it to the front of the Lancaster Square Lofts, he dropped his head and focused his gaze toward the pavement below.

Coming up onto the cross street, he scanned the night folks who were loitering at the corner café. The area had become artsy and upscale. Most nights, whenever Christian was pulling his car into the garage, he would observe the young crowds there and pictured them smoking clove cigarettes and railing on about a failing economy that they had no real knowledge of. A straight pub was located on the same block midway down, and a trendy coffee house just two doors down from that. He suspected there was also a gallery nearby, from all the well-dressed people he saw milling about. It was an ideal meeting place for their ilk: those who had more money than sense and too much time to kill. He'd previously imagined how many of them were there solely to meet strangers they'd encountered on dating websites or even Craigslist. It was a great place to hook up. It was public and well lit. And if one found out their rendezvous had lied, either about their looks or their age, there were still a few escape routes one could choose. He skimmed the array of attractive smiles with breathy anticipation, but he was interested in seeing just one face.

The smell of gasoline seemed strange to him then and spinning around to find the origin of the odor, he saw Gabriel standing directly behind him. *What now? Rush over to throw my arms around him or just stand here dumbfounded until he says the next thing to shatter this awkward feeling?*

"Did ya miss me, babe?" Gabriel closed the gap between them.

It felt like a lifetime since their last meeting. He was wearing that same faded ball cap he seemed to love, green and threadbare with the Louisiana State University logo embedded on the front. Chris had always wondered where the hell Gabriel had picked it up along his travels. He was in a plaid shirt with a light-brown jacket over his faded denim jeans. His beard appeared heavier and unkempt and scraggly. But it was those eyes of his. Those pale, determined eyes he remembered so well with every image he recreated of the man. Gabriel's gift had always been that gaze of his. It had the uncanny ability of melting forged steel under the intensity of a blast furnace. It left Christian puddled on the floor at his feet, like molten steel transformed into wet slag.

"You just get into town?" he muttered, not catching Gabriel's question because of the numerous sparks igniting throughout his brain.

"Just now," Gabriel replied. It was an introduction made uneasy by the bustle of people passing them at their right and left, almost brushing their shoulders as they shoved past them heading to wherever people went when they weren't trying to interrupt a private moment between friends. Gabriel moved toward him, but stopped, probably knowing a more intimate gesture would only draw unwanted attention to them both.

"It's crowded here, but you did mention something about a hotel nearby, right?" A twinkle flashed in Gabriel's eyes and his crooked grin indicated he had other plans in mind.

"Well, if there's time." Chris smiled sheepishly.

"Hon, there's always time," Gabriel whispered back, and with a nod, their unspoken contract sealed itself.

For Chris, it brought visions of the sweat-filled fun he had in store, where a big gun banged under a loud discharge. If he was lucky, he thought with a grin, he'd hear the reports of many blasts—depending on how much time they had to spare.

Turning north, they headed down Euclid Street in the general direction of downtown and to where Chris knew the Olympia Hotel was located. As they walked, Chris had to fight the urge not to reach out his hand and grip Gabriel's like school kids. Christian for one wanted nothing more than to have Gabriel's arm slung over his shoulder. But they seemed to be on the same wavelength, refusing to acquiesce to their base desires. Christian was acutely conscious that a car might be creeping slowly up behind. Loaded down with married cops or detectives and laughing at the picture they created of *the cute little faggots in love.*

"So, assuming they have a suite even available, how do we do this?" Chris asked. "I mean, do I give them my driver's license as ID or what?"

"You pay, and we can use my ID. Well, not mine actually but someone's. And it'll work, with no problem. I promise."

"You carry false identifications!" Chris exclaimed, sounding incredulous.

"Wouldn't you?" Church offered with a smirk.

"I figured you'd know how to handle this," Chris nearly stuttered. "I suppose you're getting pretty good at it by now."

"I just heard what you said and remembered to bring along a phony ID. I don't generally carry them, but they are stored in a spot in the truck. They've come in handy a time or two."

Church spoke in whispers as they walked, which brought his Tennessee drawl to the surface more than was customary. He was truly a rural, country-born boy at heart. It was all part of his undeniable charm. Charm he knew Gabriel was all too prepared to utilize just to acquire whatever it was he thought he needed at the time. Necessary and critical tools he could steal or cajole right out of someone's pockets, without them even finding out he had procured them. Anything he could pull that might get him farther down the long, dark road he'd been forced to travel on.

And it would have been stupid not to respect that. Or anyone like him, who seemed so amply fortified with all those very basic, fire-starting tools Christian felt he lacked in comparison, and which Gabriel Church seemed to have overflowing from any pack he carried.

Chapter Twenty-One

GABE WAS ASTONISHED with the lobby of the Olympia. It was an oasis of cherry paneling, bright light, and polished surfaces. The clarity coming off the parquet flooring was akin to staring directly into a mirror. At first glance, Church thought he could slide across the expansive floor as if his feet were skis. Not that he would've tried. It was far grander than the Mayflower Park, which had been the nicest hotel, to date, he had ever stayed in. Though his pride would not have let him freely admit that to Chris at the time. As they passed the doorman, wearing his black jacket and tails, complete with red piping at the edges and a matching silk square neatly tucked in the breast pocket, Church realized how underdressed they both were for such a place.

"Lord, this place is the do," he whispered to Christian as the doorman smiled and then whisked the outer doors open with a flourish. "Do we tip the prince over here or not?" he asked under his breath, unsure of his actions. "Do you even have enough money for a room?"

"I pulled sufficient funds out of my account when I made inquiries here last week. Now stop with all the questions, Gabe. I can handle this part. Give me the identification card you wanted to use...quick now. And for heaven's sake, be discreet," Christian muttered back with a decidedly fake smile breaking across his face.

Once he had passed over the ID, Gabe watched as Chris strode up to the concierge desk with renewed confidence, his former biographer suddenly falling into his own. He wondered if Chris had acted in some school play or something as he watched him assume a different persona as he pretended to make a call on his cell, raising his voice enough that the concierge and anyone in the lobby could hear the one-sided conversation into a dead line.

"No, Blake, I decided to cancel the res at the Alexis Hotel. The paparazzi were already piling up at the front."

He saw Chris looking down at the identification card Gabe had subtly palmed him and paused as if listening to someone speaking.

"Not at all, buddy. I decided a last-minute stop at the Olympia was in order. It's a smallish place off Euclid, but nice. It'll suffice," he said a bit too loudly. Gabe looked over at the reception desk and saw the attractive young woman at the front counter was avidly piqued with Chris's performance.

"Yes, I'm getting a suite for Jimmy now." He paused again for effect. "Now you see why I'm the best talent manager in the business. And that's the reason my clients always come back to ole Abe Schmidt, one step ahead of the photogs at every turn." He closed his portrayal with a hearty laugh before pocketing the cell and breezing to the counter.

"We don't have a reservation, but I need to obtain a suite for the night for my client, Mr. Whitehall," Chris said, as if that name was supposed to mean anything to the wide-eyed young ebony princess standing so meticulously at the ready. Then leaning in, as if sharing a confidence, Gabe heard him whisper, "I'll be paying in cash as well since we'd like to keep this transaction private. And I am certain the staff at the Olympia can be discreet with their patrons' stays." Chris sounded stern, and Gabe stifled a laugh, not ever having seen this side of him before. "One would never want photographers showing up around the entrance and blocking the way for other residents."

"Certainly, sir," the young woman said under her breath, and she began clicking away at the keyboard. He could see the wheels turning in her mind, trying to remember the name James Whitehall from the identification card Chris skimmed across the mahogany counter, yet she was expectedly coming up blank.

Christian knew she'd be googling the name later, trying to find someone famous who fit the bill, but it would happen after he signed in and wouldn't matter once they were in the room.

He tried to stifle the choke rising in his throat when she said, "That'll be twelve hundred dollars, sir, and we have a room available for Mr. Whitehall waiting on the fifth floor, if that's amenable?"

He nodded politely, then turned back to Gabriel and grinned. He'd been trying to mask the fact his lover's jaw was dropping open, like some country hayseed flabbergasted with the exorbitant price the young woman quoted him. Chris could see the nervous shifting of Gabriel's weight from one leg to the other, and he slowly dipped his head and smiled again, as if saying, '*Keep your composure, lover. I got this.*'

After paying and accepting the access card, he then scribbled out an illegible signature on the paper she'd slid across the counter. He waved off the bellhop with an act of superiority and chortled, "Not necessary, my good man. No luggage tonight since we're only here for a couple of hours."

He knew it was a lie, but even Christian had never paid twelve hundred dollars for a suite, and only for a single night's stay. It had come as a surprise to him as much as it obviously had to Gabriel. He figured a better plan would have to be considered for the next few nights if Gabriel stayed much longer. He only allowed his mounting tension to dwindle after he'd pushed the button for the fifth floor. When they were finally alone in the elevator, he expelled an exasperated discharge of oxygen and bent his waist and gripped his knees tight. He noticed then Gabriel was leaning against the wall, smiling in true admiration.

"Just who the hell are you, dude?" he asked with a surprised laugh. "You're cool as a cucumber, son. You might've been an asset on the road, after all."

The swishing sound of the elevator doors as they opened could not diffuse what he'd heard. Christian caught the subtle inference Gabriel had let slip. He had, at one time at least, considered taking Chris with him when he left the city that first time.

At first sight of the inside of the room, Gabriel whistled. Chris stood just inside the door in awe. The suite was a study in earth tones: beige walls and exquisite yellow furnishings, all made from a polished maple, clearly designed by craftsmen who probably charged accordingly. The suite was stunning in its simplicity, and though smaller than Chris had earlier imagined, it was perfect. The bed sat high off the floor, which was covered in a Berber carpet the color of mushrooms. The throw pillows were rust and faded reds, and a flat screen television was mounted above a sleek dry bar cut in the same maple.

"*Fancy schmancy,*" Gabriel mumbled. He had a look of adoration on his face, one that showed his rustic upbringing. "But I can't believe you had money to pay for it. I felt sure we were about to be run out, like we were skipping the bill at a Cracker Barrel."

Christian could have confessed how high the bill had been, that it hadn't been planned or he'd dipped too deeply into his savings to guarantee them privacy. But instead, he chose to accept the expense and wallow in the luxurious opulence like a sponge drawing in clean water. He was finally alone with Gabe and away from prying eyes. And Gabe seemed to match his mood perfectly as he too walked through the suite taking in every extravagance with a bent smile. It was clear he was unaccustomed to such sumptuous good fortune displayed.

"It's a far cry from the dingy motel rooms you might be used to staying in," he said with a grin.

"That's when I even have enough money to stay in those shit hole dives." Church did not look ashamed in the slightest. Then that country boy from Tennessee peeked back to the surface, and he threw himself on the king-sized mattress, rolling around happily, like some sheepdog that'd found a dead, rank smell to wallow in.

"What do you want to do first?" Chris hoped he knew the answer already.

"That's easy—*shower*!" Gabriel yelled as he raced to the bathroom, while simultaneously yanking off his jacket and shirt. In no time, he was standing naked under the heat of the water as Christian watched the steam billow out from the open door.

"I needed this!" He heard Gabriel call out. And Chris tended to agree, noticing the funk and gasoline smell emanating off him during their walk back to the hotel. He couldn't blame him, though. It was obvious he'd spent too many nights sleeping in the cab of his vehicle. And long miles behind the wheel left their mark.

"I still need someone to soap up my back, though," Gabriel blurted out as he popped his head from behind shower doors and grinned seductively.

"Ya don't have to ask me twice." Christian slipped out of his own clothes and sprinted to the bathroom.

The sex was as scalding as the water, and when Gabriel wrapped his arms around him, Chris noticed his cock bounce with a rigidity he hadn't seen it possess in a long while. They fucked quickly as a necessity, knowing there would be much more to follow. Then he soaped up a washcloth and standing behind Gabriel, he began lovingly and meticulously cleaning the expanse of the man's broad back.

He felt like a priest adoring the body of a saint in ablution. Like Christ washing the feet of his apostles. It was a religious worship for him, ceremonial and purifying in a way he could never have described. He loved Gabriel's form. Every crease and every crevice housed a spot that required his touch. And running his palms over every muscle, he'd felt that he might explode in ecstasy so recently after the last time, spilling whatever still remained onto the tiled floor of that shower stall. No matter how relaxing it might have been for Gabriel to have that veneration from someone he desired, it could never surpass what reverence Christian felt in his soul as he scrubbed his lover down and drifted in and out of blissful pleasure.

The next few hours were reminiscent of their time spent at the Mayflower. They talked about everything that had happened in their lives after they parted ways. Christian brought up his new job, and Gabe told humorous stories about his life on the road. But there were things he was sure Gabriel omitted. He said nothing about any white-lighters he might have encountered or lives he'd taken, and Chris steered any topic as far away from Shea Baltimore as he could.

Sitting very unabashedly naked atop the Olympia's fine lounge chairs, their moods were light and joyous. As they talked, each man frequently caught himself interrupting the other and cutting a good tale in midstream. They were like high school buddies who hadn't seen each other in years and couldn't seem to fully contain their exuberance. They only broke up their discussions when Church grabbed his bottom boy by the hand then pulled him to the bed for another furious fuck session.

They were sweaty and exhausted before long, breathing hard between the tangle of a satin comforter and rumpled sheets. Then a grumbling noise escaped Church's empty stomach, shattering the silence with an awkward growl. Both men rolled over and stared into each other's eyes, then let out a hearty laugh at the same time. They knew they'd soon be enjoying dinner and drinks together. Though inside, each regretted having to get dressed and go anywhere in public.

After evaluating the price of the room, Christian was certain they wouldn't be calling in for any room service.

After finding a place they both liked, only three blocks from the hotel, they ordered quickly. Chris could tell Church was ravenous and felt a twinge of pity in thinking his lover had been forced to live like an animal more often than not. It had to be a hand-to-mouth existence with his meager funds. He only had the vaguest of notions of how Gabe got by at times. *How long has it been since he even allowed himself to have a decent meal?*

Choosing steaks with substantial side dishes, they drank cocktails while they waited and began the conversation he'd hoped they could avoid for longer.

"So what's our play?" Chris asked, sounding far too much like a Sam Spade character trapped somewhere outside of time.

He could see the amusement on Gabriel's face as he sheepishly asked, "Whatcha mean our play?"

"Oh come on, babe," Chris chided. "You know what I mean. I'm asking whether we run or whether you want me to actually meet the detective.

Because, as you've already witnessed, I'm not the best of liars, and just the thought of going toe to toe with a detective is...well, scary!"

"You haven't done anything wrong—not really," Gabriel assured him. "So you don't have anything to worry about. He's probably working a tip that you knew Shea...and you did!" Gabriel said the last part like an adult reminding a child, like he wasn't staring into a line of trees and seeing the view obstructed for the fucking forest.

"You weren't even there when it happened," Gabe whispered, as if those last two words were a painful release he needed to expel from his lips. "Tell the dude you met Shea through a friend, but that you can't remember who by name now. Tell them she'd been dating someone around the time of her death, but that you only met the guy once. You never knew his name, and you can even give 'em a generalized description if you want."

"That's not going to throw them off my scent, is it?" I mean, what if they follow me or something and spot you?"

"Throw them off your scent? How many old gangster movies have you been watching lately, son?"

Chris smiled and stared down into his glass of bourbon as Gabriel leaned over the table and reminded him, "Ya know what FEAR stands for, don't you?" he offered with a grin. "Forget everything and run, and that's good advice for just about anyone. Keep it in your head, 'cause one day it might save your life."

"Then you don't think that visit by the police is something I need to worry about?" Chris asked.

"Worthy of spending a few minutes in deep reflection," Gabe replied quietly, his gaze drifting to the images outside the window. He was clearly concerned, but Christian could see he was trying to appear otherwise. And just as he completed his thought, the waitress showed up with their dinner. Gabriel didn't stand on ceremony and dived in hungrily. "Been a while since I had a steak," he said as he began cutting into his T-bone. His darker mood evaporated as he savored his meal, but Chris couldn't shake the glimmer in those pale eyes. They sent shivers crawling across his flesh and reminding him of a nursery rhyme his mother sang to him as a child:

Crisscross applesauce,
Spiders crawling up your back,
Cool Breeze,
Tight squeeze
Now you've got the shivers!

He'd felt that rising tide of things to come in Gabriel's distant gaze and gripped his fork tightly, like he was holding a talisman to ward off some growing evil. Gabriel looked up from his plate, confusion clear when he saw Chris not eating.

"What's up, babe? Aren't you hungry?"

Caught in his distraction, Chris blurted out, "No! I am. I was just lost in thought." He began cutting into his steak, which reminded him just how famished he was. And for a few minutes, both men were so absorbed with their meals they didn't say much of anything to each other. The only sounds emanating from their table came from the utensils scraping ceramic, and Gabriel's occasional grunts of pleasure as he enjoyed his meal.

WORKING BACK LATE at the precinct, Keen was ready to call it a day when the cell in his pocket began to ring, startling him slightly and forcing him to instinctively reach for his gun holster. The ringtone told him that it was Carol. He'd assigned the musical theme from *Psycho* as her ringtone. It had been a shits and giggles kinda thing, and he'd done it on a lark thinking the other detectives would get a kick out of it. He was forever losing his cell at home. He would find it crammed between seat cushions or laying on the kitchen bar or stuffed in his suit jacket pocket when he'd forgotten to pull it out for its nightly charge.

It became a regular occurrence in the Keen household, him asking Carol to ring his number from her phone so that he could track down his misplaced cell. She would watch him comically scurrying around, frantically searching for the ring before racing out the door already late for work. The first time she'd called his number and heard the theme from *Psycho* playing from his jacket pocket hanging in the hall, she came into their bedroom with an absolute evil glare plastered on her face. She'd been holding both phones in her hands, and at first, he assumed he was in deep doo-doo with her. She stood at the door with a blank, confused expression just as his cell was blasting out that familiar tune. It only highlighted his prank, and all he could do was stand there, shamefaced and apologetic. Fortunately for him, Carol wasn't that type of spouse to be offended, and he was instantly relieved when she grinned slightly, right before tossing his cell on their bed and turning with a huff and heading back to the kitchen, the word "asshole" still toxic on her lips. It was just another shared moment between the two and another reminder of exactly why he truly loved his wife.

"I'm just leaving, hon," he said as he answered the call.

"Figured that," she laughed. "I just wanted to remind you of our plans for a barbeque cookout this weekend. So, you might want to stop on your way home and pick up more beer for you and your buddies."

"Got it—be home in thirty," Keen said, then clicked the call off and turned back to Gilroy who had accompanied him back into his office.

"The wife's daily reminders in my 'honey do' list," he said with a conciliating shrug of his shoulders in Dennis's direction.

"Mine isn't any better," Gilroy said with a deliberate nod of understanding. "Janet calls me no less than five times a day, so I feel your pain."

Keen thought about inviting Dennis and his wife to the cookout they'd planned for the weekend, as some act of gratitude for his help with the Baltimore murder. The picture of the two men being forced to make idle conversation, staring at chickens broiling over an open flame, had less appeal than any obligation required. He decided against extending the offer.

He'd put in a new deck off the back patio last summer and was quite pleased with it. Once completed, he'd found he became more socially engaging with their friends. It'd been his wife's decree that they needed to entertain more, and he was finally ready to accommodate that wish, standing proudly atop the stained timbers of his most recent achievement. He liked the image it created of him wearing a BBQ apron with his silly grin, tongs in one hand and a cold beer in the other. He'd often suspected his work had its own way of isolating Carol from the other wives in the neighborhood and seeing her through a crowd of their gathered friends or carrying a pitcher of iced tea or tray with hors d'oeuvres only made him smile. It completed a picture he'd long desired they'd someday reach. Putting on his suit jacket, he asked the detective, "I'm gonna have to go back to the Lancaster tomorrow. If you have the time, you can always tag along. I owe you that much."

"Call my desk before you head out, Scott. If I can slip away, I might just take you up on that."

It was the first time Keen noticed he detective called him by his first name. A shudder ran down his back with the supposition, and he could only hope Dennis didn't think they were now becoming fast friends. He had a bad enough rep among all the other detectives at the Seattle PD, that he didn't need additional rumors and gossip, or the pantomimed kissing and smacking sounds behind his back with everyone thinking the two were quickly becoming BFFs.

Despite his age and profession, Keen understood he worked in an office filled with juvenile, mean-spirited fuckers. Thanking Dennis again for going with him to the interview, he headed out to his car alone. The visit to the absent Christian Maxwell may have come up empty, but the gnawing in his gut told him otherwise. It might be his detective's instinct, but every fiber in his body was telling him this man was intimately connected with his investigation. More than just being a possible witness or a minor associate of the victim's. And for the first time since receiving the file, Keen felt he had a snowball's chance in solving the murder of Shea Baltimore, giving him a renewed sense of hope.

Chapter Twenty-Two

AFTER DINNER, THE two headed back to the hotel. Gabriel sighed and said he longed for some undisturbed sleep on crisp, clean sheets—his recompense for a long drive across country and a well-deserved change from his customary routine. He took another shower once they arrived, shucking his clothes as he ran for the bathroom.

Chris could see he was thrilled with having the convenience of another hot shower and very much needed to shed the road dirt and weary miles from his body. While Gabriel languished in his purifying heaven, Chris phoned downstairs for a taxi. He must have gotten the same concierge who registered them because the woman sounded unexpectedly cold on the line. No doubt she'd completed her Google search and found nothing to substantiate her new guests were anybody of note, as she might've hoped they'd be. But she curtly agreed to call for a cab, and then Chris popped his head into the bathroom to announce his intentions.

"Gabe, I'm going to step out and grab us a bottle of bourbon for tonight," he called out over the pleasant sound of humming against the splashing.

All he could see was a dark shadow behind the opaque glass of the shower doors. Steam was quickly overtaking the small space and producing a hazy, dreamlike quality blurring his vision. But what he couldn't see, he knew to imagine. His brutish lover positioned under the nozzle as water raced in long soapy strings down the length of his impressive frame. As the sensual streams outlined every naked curve and mound of Gabriel's body, Chris could smell the perfumed scent of white gardenia and lavender hitting his nostrils. He even wondered for a minute if it was indeed water trickling down and tracing through the dark stain of damp hair or whether it had somehow become his open palms. He visualized the swirling pools at Gabe's feet as they circled then disappeared down the drain. Why anything would want to escape that tiled heaven so readily, he couldn't even begin to fathom. His emotions had become tactile and carnal, and he grinned with every hallucination he conjured. It made his own cock dance excitedly in his jeans, and he felt the swell of anticipation building as the blood coursed southward.

Gabriel poked his head out, smiling his infectious grin, his hair dripping the last remnants of his shampoo. "Hey, great idea. I guess that's becoming a tradition for us, isn't it, stud?"

Smiling back, Chris felt a growing reassurance with his newly given pet name. It was a seemingly small gesture, but one for him that had a power beyond measure.

"That's just what I was thinking." He turned happily and left the suite.

As he strolled toward the elevator, he began to consider how much his life was becoming a type of purgatory. Where on one side was the love and devotion he felt for Gabriel, the other housed all his anxiety, along with the ominous threat of danger he knew existed around every corner. He'd been caught in-between two realities, but neither world held any real substance for him. They were each just ghostly probabilities, and each side was waiting patiently for his foot to waver to where Chris would find himself standing in the middle no longer. He was smart enough to understand it wouldn't take much to shatter the barrier dividing his worlds but seeing a thing clearly and choosing to do something about it wasn't a decision he felt he was ready to undertake.

The rest of the evening was spent as a carbon copy of their time at the Mayflower, mere days after their first introduction at the coffee shop. They lounged naked without shame and drank bourbon from complimentary hotel glasses, finely cut with crystalline sharpness. They talked and curled up beside each other on the bed, Chris feeling a contentment he'd not experienced in quite some time. They screwed, naturally, but only once. But even that single experience was exquisitely hot.

Christian was amazed at the pitiful, animal sounds escaping his lips as Gabriel pounded for release against the mounds of his ass cheeks. Sweat landed on his back as the grinding and guttural noises of pleasure completely filled the space inside their room. Christian wanted to take the copious seed forced inside as proof of the fact he was more than just a single night's fuck. Someone worthy of being remembered by a man he, at times, thought quite godlike.

Then Chris saw Gabriel's eyelids growing heavy, and he suddenly remembered how far he'd traveled on very little sleep. He'd sent out a lonesome call, and Gabriel had done his best to accommodate, driving through the night to make it back to Seattle in time. Clicking off the lights and crawling in next to his lover, he knew he'd not be able to sleep. Through the half-open curtains, he could see the reflection from the city's skyline dancing on the floor beside their bed. *It is my city and the place where I first met Gabriel.* But regardless, he'd called it home for most of his adult life. He knew he might have to leave it all behind if Gabriel suddenly announced it was necessary.

Even through the scant lighting he could see Gabriel's chest rise and fall with every breath. He snuggled closer, hoping to hear the man's irregular heartbeat. It seemed amazing that a thing which earlier unnerved him, now only served to remind him just how tenuous life could truly be, it felt comforting in an odd way. Like learning to become accustomed to the train sounds off in the distance, with their rumbling and chugging steel wheels. Yet finding out how sleep wouldn't come once the familiar noises were no longer there.

Gabriel slept hard, occasionally muttering an indistinguishable word or an inaudible phrase during a restless REM state. It made Christian wonder what types of dreams sifted through a killer's head at night. Eventually he too drifted off, and they lay tangled in each other's arms until morning. When Chris woke to the first rays of light hitting them square in the face, he felt a strong urge for caffeine. But even before that could be offered, Chris detected a stabbing pressure on his backside and recognized Gabriel's morning erection demanding attention. Rolling over, he forced his tongue into Gabriel's mouth. They kissed wetly and passionately for only minutes before he felt an open palm nudging his head downward. He made the journey lovingly all the way to the thick cock bouncing atop Gabriel's abdomen and begging to get sucked.

Chris straddled a prone Gabriel then rode his way to a furious and mutually fulfilling orgasm. Falling to his side, he was still breathing vigorously as Gabriel bounded up and out of bed. He watched his lover as he headed for the shower, an impressive swinging piece of meat dangling pendulously between his thighs.

"Care to join me, stud?" Gabriel called out without looking back. But to his ears, it sounded less like invitation and more like a stern mandate. Hopping up, Chris followed quickly, as any good pup would do who was anxious to please his master.

Within the hour they were sitting at the same café at the corner of Chris's block along Lancaster. The same café he'd only ever purchased a cup of coffee to go or an occasional pastry.

"You don't seem upset or even concerned about the police," Chris began, whispering the word police so as not to be heard from those who might be conversation dipping from another table.

"Upset no, concerned yes." Church was staring into his coffee. "What was the detective's name, the one who called you?" he asked, cold and plain. Chris could almost see his gray-blue eyes change with a shadow clouding once radiant pupils like a summer sky suddenly overtaken by stormy weather.

"Keen," he mumbled. "Why? What's going through your head, Gabe?" He could imagine mechanical gears turning behind those eyes and suspected the man was formulating a plan to save them both. And that scared him.

"Just curious," Gabriel said, as he sipped his coffee and stared at a couple who were in that moment crossing the street and heading to their same café. They were laughing and holding hands in the middle of some shared conversation. From the outside, they appeared to be very much in love. Turning back to his companion, Gabriel couldn't hide the inner workings of his mind. He might have if it'd been anyone else, but not him. They had shared too much and were too intricately bound together. Gabriel's eyes flickered like a cobra's darting tongue. He was vainly trying to disguise what was racing through his mind, but his coconspirator already began to suspect something was amiss. One could almost smell the scent of burning rubber, wheels spinning frantically on a muddy basin road as his gaze became locked and fixed into the distance. He was suddenly the only passenger on his indistinguishable train of thought.

"Aren't you scared?" Chris muttered, breaking the man's concentration.

"What do you think?" Gabriel asked flatly.

Chris saw a flash in those pale eyes and understood completely just how differently his life could've gone. Yes, his upbringing had left their scars, and he was a killer tried and true. But surely, he hadn't grown up as one of those boys burning anthills with magnifying glasses or torturing neighborhood cats for the pleasure of it all. He had seen the man behind the irregular heartbeat and knew there was goodness in him. He had just become bent with his own sick ideologies. Warped by some misconstrued, religious dogma he'd picked up somewhere along the way. The expression on that face bordered on a dark, brewing evil. And Christian was surprised that he'd even been there to witness the transformation.

"Whatever you're thinking, put it out of your head," Chris said to Gabriel.

"I think it's wise we know who's sniffing about. Do you think you can get back to your place unnoticed and bring your laptop back?"

"Possibly, but for what reason?" His inquisition was bearing little fruit.

"I want to learn everything you can find out about this Detective Keen of the Seattle PD."

"To what end? It's not like he's doing anything but his job. Why would you want to know anything about him?" In his excited confusion, he placed his coffee down too quickly and sent droplets flying out onto the table. "I figured once I told you he'd come by that you'd just show up and we'd hit the road together."

"Why are so ready to run away from your life? Particularly since you haven't done anything wrong," Church asked coolly. His level-eyed glare was almost accusatory, and though it stung, Christian knew the question was valid. It reminded him of those crisscross spiders still playing along his spine. Gabriel wasn't waiting for an answer as he brought his coffee cup up and drank deeply, wetting those luscious lips of his and staring back featureless, without emotion.

Christian finally nodded and then pushed his chair back and turned to leave. Slipping back between the buildings as he'd done the night before, he pushed the iron gates open in the courtyard at the rear of his building. During the daytime hours, he knew there was an unlocked exit for residents to walk their pets. He wouldn't have to enter through the fire door and risk any alarms sounding. He wasn't thinking about the detective in that moment, but what Gabe had asked. He was probably right—he was just too ready to depart Seattle and escape the mundane existence he'd created, ever since first meeting the killer. He had to admit to himself that he'd felt trapped lately. Gabriel represented danger. But that danger could also be thrilling. Certainly there was no denying he was one sexy fucker. Had he become the equivalent of a bored housewife taking up a lover, all to free her from the tedium of housework, chores, and chauffeuring the kids to soccer practice then back again?

Gabriel had no family to worry about him, but he did. *Could I disappear and leave them all behind without an explanation? Just how much of this was the result of the erections Gabriel gave me or the warm tingling embers in my belly whenever I watched the man walking around naked, as if it was something normal. Could I live with myself if I allowed my libido to shatter my ordinary life into shards?* They were questions he never had answers for but continually asked nonetheless.

Standing at his door, he pulled out his keys and the first twinge of nervousness hit him. But he found his apartment just as empty as he had left it. He grabbed up his laptop from the dining room table and stuffed it into its carrying case, then headed back out to the hallway. He was half afraid that he'd run into Keen standing there, but in mere minutes he was back at the café where Gabriel sat comfortably with a new cup of coffee, scratching his scruffy face with a relaxed expression.

"Use your nimble fingers and find out all you can about this Detective Keen," Church said. "You know I haven't a clue about using computers."

"I imagine not. You haven't even mastered the cell phone yet," Chris teased, smiling. He pulled out the laptop and began searching the Internet for stray facts, beginning with the SPD website. Naturally, he didn't find personnel photos of homicide detectives, but he was able to pull the police report of Shea Baltimore's murder via their site, although heavily redacted. He jumped to Facebook and other miscellaneous social media outlets, grateful he'd remembered the detective's first name had been Scott. As he worked, Gabriel sat close, seemingly transfixed by the process. His drifter life had never given him much occasion to use a computer, nor had he ever owned a laptop. To Christian that display of innocence was refreshing. He was glad the dark shading had finally disappeared from his eyes and was now replaced with the bright twinkle of his curiosity.

"It's so fucking amazing how much you can learn about people by using a computer these days," Gabriel said to him, awestruck.

"Welcome to the twentieth century, baby," Chris chimed in, "but you're right. People don't understand how just much privacy they've lost in the new world order."

Christian's fingers deftly worked the keyboard. After almost an hour of searching, he had learned a great deal about Detective Scott Keen, as well as many cold and analytical aspects to the Baltimore homicide investigation via the SPD website. Ones he would have preferred not seeing. He'd retrieved footage of news reporters making the announcements to the public. The cameras were focused on the front of the apartment complex where her body had been found, crime tape and flashing lights in the background. He pulled segments from local broadcast news outlets and stories from the print media. As he did this, his heart sank lower in his chest. While Gabriel watched fascinated over his shoulder, seemingly unfazed by what he read.

"Why do you want to find out about Keen?" he asked again, a little fearful of the answer.

"Well, when you live on the road, you have to make quite a few decisions based solely on the person staring you down." Church's voice was very gruff as he responded finally to his question. "But whenever possible, it's best to learn all the players in the game...hence the reason I asked you to get me anything you could on the detective assigned to the case."

"What will you do with it?"

"It's just information, babe," Gabriel said, placing a comforting hand on Chris's shoulder.

"You can't afford another night at that fancy hotel," Church changed the topic. "I passed a cheaper Motel Six when I came into town. It's just off the I-5, around the Dearborn Exit. Go check out of the hotel, then head there. Get a room and use your real name if you want." Church was scribbling something on a napkin as he spoke.

"I'll meet you there. Park directly in front of your room, and you might wanna sneak back into your apartment and grab a bag. It might be a place you're gonna have to stay for a couple of nights."

"Where are you going?" Chris asked as Gabriel stood up to leave.

"Got business to attend to, but I'll be there soon," he said reassuringly. "And remember to grab whatever's left of that bourbon as well." He smiled confidently as he pushed in his chair, then gave Christian a surprisingly public air kiss, touched him gently on his back, and turned to leave.

Christian sat stunned for a minute in contemplation and watched Gabriel disappear down the street away from the café. He suspected he'd parked more than a block away and was taking a meandering path back, making sure he wasn't followed in the process.

Chapter Twenty-Three

AFTER PULLING THE crumpled napkin from his jeans, Gabe turned the ignition and the Dodge rumbled into life. Memorizing the address he'd previously scrawled there, he began to head in that general direction. As he weaved through downtown streets, he thought about Christian Maxwell, and how strange his life had evolved since their first meeting. He could admit to himself that he cared for the man. He even understood he was sexually attracted to him. At times it seemed nearly inconceivable his dick might swell as rock-solid as it had whenever his thoughts strayed to those warm, morning injections in elegant hotels and under crisp, clean sheets. For a straight dude, that was reason for confusion enough. The other thing that struck him as odd was the clear absence of any warning lights, cautioning him of an imminent breakdown ahead. Their entire relationship had simply snuck up from behind and caught him unaware. And for someone as guarded and vigilant as he was, that was surprising indeed. He'd always lived by a set of rules guaranteed very little crept up on him without his notice. It'd been the only reason he was still breathing the fresh air of freedom.

Church grew to a man without an ounce of quit inside him. Listening to Christian bring up the idea the two could just hit the highway and disappear was more than merely eye-opening, it was unsettling. He'd truly showed his ignorance at the café. He didn't understand the costs and the challenges of trying to stay one step ahead of the police. He couldn't see the damage in racing from one shadow to the next on a continual misery of his life on the lam. But in that split second at the café, he realized he was becoming fiercely determined his life would not ever become Christian's.

He had lived many years standing in a downpour. Hard rains caused by his own self-made misfortune. The years had taught him many lessons. Primarily that it was a difficult life he'd freely chosen for himself. But it wasn't something he could easily transfer to another unsuspecting soul. Few men might've found themselves strong enough to endure such a vagabond existence. His part-time lover slash would-be-biographer would never be able to lead that type of survival. Plus, of all the crimes he'd committed so willingly, none should be a debt he forced others to have to pay.

Particularly when the person was the only one Gabe had ever encountered who claimed to love him unconditionally. Despite everything he knew to be true.

The address he'd written down belonged to the SPD, specifically the precinct where Keen worked. Even Christian's nimble fingers had been blocked from finding a home address for the detective. But as Gabriel knew, there were always ways around such obstacles. What he had seen was a *selfie* posted to Keen's Facebook page. It showed Keen with his wife, Carol, where the two were dressed to the nines for some apparent function they were attending. They were holding cocktails and smiling in the photograph. They appeared happy in the instant of that captured moment. But it only served to give Gabe a clear description of his target and a way to identify a perfect stranger. All before placing him square in the sight lines of his Glock 9mm.

His trip back to the city had instigated a firestorm, where he supplied the gasoline and Christian kept the matchbook in a breast pocket at the ready. He'd considered every possible outcome though. It was the only thing racing through his mind as the blacktop flashed under the Dodge's tires during his long, dead-assed and dull night drive. This was just one scenario, although not exactly as he might've planned. His companion wouldn't agree with his next few moves, of that he felt certain. But he wouldn't let the man become another tragic participant in the maelstrom of his life.

In the back of his mind, he'd often wondered what life would be like if he just ignored the white-lighters' glowing radiance. How different it might be, if only he were able to disregard the urge he felt burrowing through his gut telling him he needed to extinguish it. It was always the same for him. First, he saw the aura surrounding them, bathing them in twinkly greens and bright fiery golds. Then, he heard the familiar rumbling sound in his ears.

The best way Gabe could describe it was like standing on train tracks, centered inside a dark tunnel carved into a mountainside. And as the rails began to vibrate and shake, he knew danger was racing toward him like a hungry predator to that very place he stood. Echoes from loud horn blasts could be heard bouncing off interior walls, the same ones that appeared to close in and surround him. Though he saw a light at each end of the tunnel, he knew one could only be a headlight of the train barreling down to overtake him. In his brain, an awful noise pounded something fierce. Then came the inescapable feeling he was just too far inside the shaft to ever make it out. The only thing he could do was stand firm and prep for impact.

His only relief came after the white light was sufficiently snubbed out and ultimately rocketed skyward. In those seconds just after a kill, quiet post-murder moments he reveled in, the rumbling sounds slowly faded. He would then feel a shiver running down his spine became the signal telling him he'd made it out alive and was finally free of that dark mountain pass. The last thing he experienced could only be defined as being pure reprieve. An amnesty of sorts for sins he may have committed in an earlier life.

That was how each murder went for him. But not having Christian's vocabulary or fine college education, he knew it was beyond his capacity to explain it to others. *Let 'em see me as a psycho.* Soon enough the police would either catch him or his heart would stop beating on its own or he'd be shot down in a crossfire of flying bullets. Nothing really mattered to Gabe. Everything was quickly becoming a fragile transparency, save Christian Maxwell. But just as he had reminded the writer once before, everything crumbles and eventually fades under the passages of time.

By the time he arrived at the precinct, it was a little after two in the afternoon. He had hours before the staff would be pulling out and heading home. He had no earthly idea how late detectives generally worked. He noticed the station sat across the street from a lush wooded area. It could have easily have been made into a park, but the abundance of uncut foliage created a dense forest with varying shades of greens from a multitude of native fauna. Everything was in full springtime bud and blossom, crowded in and becoming a tight thicket. *What an ideal place to hide a body.* He saw a uniformed officer enjoying a smoke by the front entrance before his shift and he smiled, amused. It titillated him such a place existed—so perfect for dumping a corpse—all within eyeshot of the men and women in blue.

He was happy to see there wasn't an underground parking garage like in Christian's building. That would've put a wrinkle in his plans. He circled the block and saw a lot where a sea of vehicles sat waiting patiently. Undoubtedly, patrol cars had their own lot somewhere nearby. The cars and trucks he saw parked in long lines surely belonged to SPD support staff and detectives. Somewhere in those rows of vehicles, Keen's car sat waiting for him to arrive as well.

He parked his truck near the rear doors, assuming the detective would take the route closest to his car, and then waited. He was close enough to see each face of those exiting clearly enough to distinguish his prey. He settled in for a long stay, which was something he was accustomed to. If he'd learned anything during his travels, it was endurance. He had the staying power necessary because his missionary works of killing time before killing humans was a steadfast requirement. Reaching behind the seat, Gabe retrieved the book he sometimes read to occupy time. Wiping dust from the worn and wrinkled paperback cover, he opened it to the dog-eared page and reconciled himself to accepting his fated task with his usual determination.

Looking up occasionally to see people coming and going from the back entrance, he gauged every face as those not belonging to Keen and then went back to his novel. Once he caught his own reflection in the rearview and noticed the first strands of gray hairs interwoven through his dark beard. *That's discouraging. It reminds me I'm getting older. Just when do serial killers know when it's time to retire?*

Hours passed uneventfully, and he had to reposition his ass cheeks several times to find relief. He considering stepping out and stretching his legs but thought it too dangerous. He also had to fight the urge to pull out the Glock as well. He wanted to hold it in his lap for comfort but couldn't take the risk some officer might stumble up innocently and inquire why he was parked there, only to notice a gun hidden under his book. To amuse his mind, he stared off into the distance toward the wooded area, which he'd observed as nearly perfect dumping grounds. He wondered if it was private property or public lands. Seattle was truly beautiful. The emerald and avocado greens mixed together like some image plastered on a postcard inviting tourists. He couldn't imagine why more people didn't see the need to pilgrimage to these verdant rolling hills so close to the beaches with their saltwater sprays.

Before his mind could stray too far, he looked up to see there was staff coming out the back in small clusters and chatting among themselves. It must be nearly quitting time, he suspected. Church never wore a watch, and the truck was too ancient a beast to have a working clock on the dashboard. Time held little meaning for a drifter, never having to be tied to a schedule or chained by its constraints. He scanned each face but came up short. Then he saw several men in suits exiting and walking independently to their cars. He figured it must be time for most detectives to call it a day. He squinted to shield from the setting sun, and he spotted the face he recognized from Facebook belonging to Detective Scott Keen of the SPD homicide division. Gabe grinned with pleasure at finally seeing his target in person for the first time.

He observed Keen pulling keys from his pockets, then unlocking the driver's side of a polished gray Hyundai Sonata. It was a newer model and still showroom clean. It aggravated Gabriel the detective had a newer car than he, but more so that he hadn't bought American. He glanced away as it stopped at the exit gate in the chain link-protected lot, and then turned right onto SW Webster and sped away. Turning his own ignition, Church proceeded to follow the Sonata from a comfortable distance.

Using the same skills he maintained for white-lighters, he kept at least two car-lengths between him and Keen, yet never wavered his eyes from the prize. The Dodge was a nondescript sight, but he didn't know the detective personally and wanted to give him enough space as to not alert him he was being tailed. The Sonata entered an on-ramp for the nearest expressway and Church followed suit. There may have been cold calculations running through his brain, but Gabriel looked at it as if it were any other mundane task. It became a detached mimicry to his determination. He even turned on the radio, choosing to relax his sore muscles as the two cars traveled the highway together. Scott Keen was surely headed home to Carol and his first chance of relaxing with a cold beer as she prepared dinner and Gabriel Church with his darker plans.

Within twenty minutes or so, the Sonata had exited the interstate and began meandering through the surface streets, fighting traffic as it moved along. It was in the latter stages of rush hour, which made the driving slower. This enabled Gabe to keep a visual proximity of his target without appearing out of place. He wasn't sure if Keen was going home or had other business to attend to, but these were risks he'd learned to take early on. Those who understood the importance of patience and endurance were the ones who made the best hunters.

Turning onto residential roads, Keen's car traveled its predetermined path like it knew its own way home. Church was forced to lag behind more and more or risk Keen spotting the same beat-up Dodge which had followed him onto the interstate. They passed tidy modest houses each one nestled along safe streets with traditional architecture and each one displaying a freshly mowed lawn. Gabriel knew instinctively they were close.

Just as he figured, the Sonata turned into a driveway along Park Street, directly in front of an unpretentious and somewhat conservative two-story brick and frame. Gabe surmised it had been constructed sometime in the 1980s and guessed it had been refurbished for a quick sell in the early to mid-1990s, during the economic freefall when all the banks were first starting to go under. Most Americans had suffered painfully through those first crashing waves in their economy, with a depression era looming dangerously just over the horizon. Where everyone who held a job feared they were on the verge of losing it, and along with that, their homes and property. That was everyone except Gabriel, who as he'd told himself at the time, "You can't lose what you don't own." Because of that, he never learned to offer much sympathy and solace to the meat and gristle of the corporate structure. He blamed everyone else for their capitalistic dreams. He blamed them for their sickness in trying to outdo their neighbors and their race to possess anything and everything they came in contact with.

The house itself was lovely, though; even Gabe had to admit. With its walkway to the covered porch all lined with shrubbery and established plant life, and every freshly budded flower patch in full bloom. The portico was snuggly housed under the overhang from a spacious upper floor attic. And large-paned windows gave it attractive curb appeal. It made for a homey, picturesque quality that only aggravated Gabe more in a struggle to recognize the haves and have-nots disparity.

It was the perfect place to raise children. No doubt exactly what Keen and his wife originally planned when they purchased it. And for the first time in his strategy, Church was forced to consider that children might have already come. The Keen family may have already been blessed with babies, and in that very moment, they could be playing in a room upstairs. This was something he'd failed to consider in his early planning.

Gabriel had taken the lives of younger white-lighters before but never had he done a violent act against a child. It may have been the line even he was unable to cross. But fortunately for him, that circumstance had yet to come up.

Unknown to Church, the fact that none of the lighters he'd ever encountered had been children may have been a very telling aspect of his mental defect. Had Christian been there, he might have seen this more clearly, but it was opaque and obscured from Church's perceptions. Whatever the man saw as truth and what he recognized as God's will might not have been as acutely attuned as he first believed. But that question would have to wait until later because, in that second, Church had other options to weigh.

Chapter Twenty-Four

THE MOTEL ROOM was a dive. Then again after the opulence of the Olympia, everything would have paled in comparison. Christian was thankful he didn't have a black light to shine across the dingy comforter or the two salon chairs the motel furnished for its guests because he knew he would have been forced to turn tail and retreat from whatever stains he suspected were there. But it was a sixty-nine dollar a night stay. He reminded himself what a better rate that was over the twelve hundred he'd thrown down so willy-nilly earlier. "You get what you pay for," he said to himself, but he shuddered to think what acts of depravity had gone on in the shit hole he was walking into. He'd done as Gabriel instructed without question. There was little he wouldn't have acquiesced to, whenever his man requested it.

He'd seen the enigmatic look in Gabe's eyes as left the café'. It appeared like steely determination. Christian tried to find comfort in the supposition his lover had a plan to save them both. They may have been lies to ease his worrisome fears, but he jumped at the chance to pass those fears to another person. An odd endowment, he figured. But Gabriel was a better man than he was; at least, when it came to these types of problems.

The room had a queen-sized bed and an array of awful artwork, no doubt secured tightly to the walls. *Because we couldn't have those reproduction watercolor prints ending up on the black market.* There was a clock sitting friendless on the nightstand. One of those ten-dollar jobs found in any outlet mall, and the rhythmic ticking sound coming from it was unusually loud. Tossing the duffel he packed onto the bed, he surveyed the bathroom. It was cleaner than he'd expected it to be, but either way, it was a nicer place than Gabe saw most days, he feared.

His heart had been racing when he crept back into his apartment as Gabriel instructed. Taking the back stairwell, he'd ascended the steps with an uneasy pit growing in his stomach. It was both electrifying and bothersome at the same time. It reminded him of his childhood and those times he'd sat glued to the television engrossed in one of his favorite shows, *Mission Impossible*. He loved the adventure he found in every episode. The only difference between then and now was that the characters he admired always seemed more in control than he felt tiptoeing around and trying to avoid being seen.

He suspected Peter Graves's stomach was never as irritable as his was in those moments. *It's just the coffee*, he told himself as he unlocked his front door. This was his apartment, his things, and as far as he knew, the police only wanted to ask him some questions. He didn't kill Shea Baltimore, after all. He was just allowing his mind to wander to dark places.

"You cost Shea her life!"

The words Gabriel had said were back again to haunt him, ringing in his head. Maybe it was true. It may be more his fault than Gabe's. He wondered if all of this might be by design and the judicial scales couldn't be balanced by the smallest distinction of who actually committed the deed. Racing through the condo, he began packing a bag with clothes and toiletries. He didn't want to linger there, mostly out of fear there would be a knock on his door and he'd find himself trapped in his own home.

Christian stuffed extra clothes into the duffel for Gabe's use. He'd packed so much the seams stretched and threatened to rip open. *I pack like a woman, always adding more and more, telling myself "Well, we don't know how long we're going be there."* Was this what it'd come to: a life on the lam and dashing from relative safety to the shadows at the lightest whisper of the police closing in? *How the hell had Gabe done this for as long as he had?*

Peeking into the hallway, he left he locked the door then headed down the passage toward the fire exit, just as he had once before. He took one last distant look back at his condo with sadness; realizing then how he'd probably never see it again. Gabe would likely announce that they were leaving Seattle for good together. The notion of abandoning his job, family ties, and all his possessions was a great deal to absorb all at once, but the word '*together*' was something he found comfort in. Despite the gravity of everything, he still found himself smiling as he made his way downstairs.

Once he made it to the parking garage, he tossed the duffel into the rear seat of his car and left the Lancaster in search of a motel room he'd been instructed to procure. As he stood alone facing that drab motel room, he was already hoping Gabe wouldn't desert him for very long. His anxiety was increasing due to unexpected changes in his daily routine. But he knew he'd find some relief once he was lying next to his burly savior. Even in this cum-stained shithole, there was a promise of future contentment on the horizon.

CAROL KEEN WAS in the middle of making dinner when her husband came through the door. She heard him going through his usual routine of hanging up his suit jacket and ripping off his tie like Superman transforming into his Clark Kent identity. The sound of him relieving himself of his holster and then hanging it on the coatrack always comforted her. It meant he was home safely and she could relax once again. At the least he'd made it through another day, she'd tell herself. He was home and safe, and all was suddenly right with her world.

Being married to a detective wasn't particularly an awful thing, but she doubted she could've coped as well if he was still a patrol cop. Those days had been harder on her and she was glad to have them behind her. Being a detective wasn't without its risk, but it was immeasurably less hazardous than a DUI stop or domestic violence call, and he enjoyed reminding her the only real dangers in his day-to-day would be if he allowed a paper cut to become septic. It was a conversation they'd had with intent from the very beginning. He knew Carol would never agree to start a family as long as he was working patrol. There were just too many risks and most she couldn't accept if she'd been nursing a child.

Since then they'd tried for a baby, but it hadn't happened yet. Each of them tried to stay cautiously optimistic. Without informing her husband, Carol had already visited her gynecologist for a checkup. She didn't need to worry him should she find out she had thyroid issues or other medical concerns that might prevent a pregnancy. Thankfully she'd received a clean bill of health, but that too she kept to herself for the time being. Because who wanted to have that conversation, she thought. She didn't relish the idea of now having to bring up the idea it was time for Scott to get checked out as well. However difficult, it was a talk which was fast becoming something they'd have to broach one way or another. She couldn't bear the not knowing any longer.

"Is that my big strong husband I hear coming in my door?" she called out loudly.

"No, but I'm here to huff and puff and blow down your house." Scott came up behind her and wrapped his arms around her waist, kissing her sweetly on the cheek.

"What's for supper baby?" Scott asked her, even though he should be able to see the fish cutlets already sitting in a dish on the counter, waiting to be placed in the oven.

"Fish, veggies, and rice pilaf," she muttered as she continued cutting carrots, then asked, "Tough day at the office?"

"Naw," he said, obviously not wanting to discuss his day. "Do I have time for a quick shower?"

"Knock yourself out, hon," Carol said, turning then to give him a welcoming kiss in return. "On the table in twenty, though," she reminded him as if scolding a toddler. *God, I feel like a mother already, sometimes.*

GABE HAD GONE past Keen's house, then circled around and parked in front of the next house up from the one opposite theirs. He noticed Scott wait patiently as the garage door slowly opened and then lost sight of him as the door closed again. He spotted Keen's wife as she slipped past a window, carrying a loaded plate of food to the table, and again when she was carrying a pitcher. He was there to scope out the address and to see if children's toys were present in the yard. He wanted to see the neighborhood and calculate every risk imaginable. He wanted to lay his pale eyes on his target firsthand, as was his custom. But Church wasn't there for violence that afternoon. A good hunter should learn all about his prey: how they move, where they hide, and how to get as close as possible before a gun is ever brought up to bear or an aim is leveled to find a target centered in a sightline.

Things were different now. This was no white-lighter he was tracking, but a homicide detective for the Seattle PD. Reason told him it was time to run and to put as much distance between the crime and the city as possible. The girl's murder had been a regrettable necessity, and he knew that. It was due to a growing affection stirring inside him, an unexpected emotion that came out of nowhere and held all the makings of shattering his world apart and placing him in immediate peril. *And I am doing it again.*

God, this is one fucked-up situation.

He literally mouthed the words as he pulled away from the curb, then sped down the block. Blurting them out seemed to be an appeasement to his rational-thinking brain, but even as he thought them aloud, he knew nothing was going to alter his plans. If he was a murderer, then Christian was a thief. He'd taken something Gabe had once held private and laid it bare at his feet. It allowed him to see it was nearly impossible to live alone for any length of time, buried inside his self-imposed prison.

He had never talked to anyone about his celestial mission before Chris, nor had he ever tried to see past another person's exterior facade. He'd previously felt nothing, like he was walking among the already dead and each and every face he passed became nothing more than a cardboard replica. Gabe had stopped even trying to understand people. At least after leaving Bennett standing in the dust of his spinning tires, that sour look of derision still present on his face as it became smaller and smaller in his rearview.

But Christian had done something no other person had done since then. He had simply asked to hear the tale and listened without any noticeable judgment. He had studied Church's face so meticulously the killer was left to wonder if he was trying to visibly assemble the pieces together as if he were reconstructing the man from every horrible story he'd been told.

Even though their time spent together had been brief, Chris had taken the time to get to know him in ways no other person would have. He'd moved closer whenever he spoke and nearly edged off his seat during all their whispered conversations, whether they'd been in public or in those private moments alone. He'd appeared to be so unafraid, and even to Gabe that seemed brazenly unwise.

It was not until later that he caught on it was something more than his own lack of fear. Yet that only astonished and intrigued him even more. For him finding Chris was nothing short of a godsend, a pivotal moment that hadn't just defined him but transformed him. The murder of Shea had been his protection from losing that elusive thing forever. His plans had become water, filling his head like a balloon and expanding with such a force they threatened to explode, but Gabe knew they wouldn't. He knew his newly formed strategy was just another regrettable necessity. *His plans were shatterproof.* And for that, he hated himself even more. It was an inescapable truth that meant he was headed down a path with dark, twisted outcomes, and he still might still end up losing Christian when it was all said and done.

The mooring rope had been unwound, releasing him to idly drift into those black, murky waters. But there was no turning back now because Christian Maxwell needed his help, and he'd not let the man down again by driving out of town, as he had before. Not this time, and not while he had still had the breath in his lungs.

It was nearly dark by the time Gabe arrived at the hotel where he'd told Chris to meet him. He knocked quietly, unsure if he was standing at the right door, but Christian had parked directly in front as commanded and greeted him with a grateful smile when Gabe brushed past him.

"Good man," he said before nervously pulling the curtains back to check outside. He wanted to learn if the Dodge had been followed and was relieved to know it hadn't.

"Well, it's hardly the Olympia, but it's ours for a few days," Chris began. "Now are you going to fill me in on what business you were taking care of?"

"Later maybe," was all he said. Mostly to shut off Chris's line of questioning, he pulled him closer then gave him a hard, passionate kiss. It was like he hadn't seen him in many months, and after their tongues momentarily wrestled, his lover's inquisitions were all but forgotten.

"It's a crappy room, isn't it?" Chris asked, finally breaking free of their embrace.

"You weren't spotted when you went back to your place, were you?" he asked as he plopped down on the bed.

"Didn't see a soul actually...but I really want to know what is going through your mind now. It's more than merely ducking the detective's call, I presume."

"In due time," Gabe said, a grin emerging. "But I'd rather get naked and nasty with you since we're at least going to be here for the night." He was trying to placate Chris but wasn't sure if it was working. He smiled in a lascivious way, hoping to distract Chris with his twinkling gray-blue eyes.

"I brought some extra clothes for you" Chris said, avoiding the question. "I have clean socks and jockey shorts for you too."

"Thanks, boy. It's not like I've had time to hit a laundromat recently." Gabe began shedding his outer garments without even waiting for an invitation. "We could just cuddle and watch bad TV if you'd rather do that."

"Just as long as we're together," Christian whispered. Gabe was almost sure that he wasn't meant to hear it.

Before long they were again lounging in their underwear in front of an older model television, the nearly unseen type with the cathode ray tube, now thankfully unattainable to purchase. Even the remote seemed clunky and outdated, and Gabe smiled broadly as he picked it up then pantomimed hoisting a heavy burden. They laughed briefly, then lay beside each other, relishing in the distraction from their bigger issues.

But Gabriel's mind was focused on the plans he had working in his head, plans of protecting Christian from any further harm, though he managed to hide that fairly well from his companion with each tiny gesture and raked his fingers lovingly down Chris's arm. With the man snuggled safely in the crook of his arm, they watched TV as he clicked from channel to channel but found little of interest to either of them. As if by unseen signal, Gabe rolled Christian on his back and began kissing him again. This time he wouldn't allow himself to be put off, and they made love atop the comforter as the sun set over Seattle just outside their motel room.

Chapter Twenty-Five

THE FOLLOWING MORNING Gabe woke up alone in their bed. With Christian not lying beside him, he was surprisingly panicked. Stray thoughts ricocheted like bullets through his skull, catching him unaware. Barely cognizant of his surroundings and half asleep, his first thoughts sprinted to the notion he was being *set up*. Shaking his head, he forced himself awake and called out for Chris, hoping that he was just standing under the jets of the shower. But not hearing the splash of water, he bolted to the bathroom, only to find he was alone in the motel room.

The copious miles of the highway without proper rest had taken their toll on his faculties. He hadn't heard the rustle from his partner as he'd gotten up, or heard the door being closed quietly behind him whenever he'd made that getaway. Still naked, he quickly grabbed for his jeans and had one leg inside, before noticing the black duffel sitting on a chair in the corner. It was the same one Christian brought with him when he'd arrived. He almost tripped and fell forward as he yanked his leg out, then saw a slip of paper on the television stand that hadn't been there last night.

I went for coffee and donuts, back in fifteen. Near the bottom of the scrawled message: *Don't worry, I'll be extra cautious! GET SOME REST.* And below that, a heart had been hastily drawn in ink.

Smiling, Church stumbled back to the bed, relieved, but then labored on the question of why he'd suddenly jumped to the irrational conclusion Chris had betrayed him, and then his added concern of why he'd awoken up anxious and worried by his absence in the first place. He told himself it was the effects of a tired brain and nothing more. He crawled back under the covers, then propped himself up with pillows and clicked on the TV.

I have to be prepared for anything. It was just natural instinct for him to think he'd been played from the beginning. Players always suspected the other parties of the same crimes they themselves committed, at least when they got as proficient as Gabe had become over the years. Stopping on a channel, Gabe saw a televangelist talking that he didn't recognize. The man had been ranting at the top of his lungs to his cathedral-sized congregation, consisting mostly of gray-haired older women with palatine Grecian features and vacant stares.

He raised an arm to the heavens, all to garner emphasis and effect, like some terrible actor munching up the scenery with his overacted exuberance. He devoured the stage area completely. Working his way from the left and then to the far right. He appeared there as some heavenly prominence, a gold dangly thing to hypnotize and enrapt his onlookers. It was fascinating to him, and he stopped driving through the channels to watch. There was wickedness in the twinkle hidden behind the man's artificial smile, leaving Gabe to guess that the preacher was performing his best rendition of celestial guidance for those thousands sitting alone in their living rooms. Each one he perceived as opening their checkbooks and wallets to send the cash God so sorely needed. The preacher's baritone voice was raised and lowered for showy inspiration and a killer watched transfixed, thinking maybe he'd gone into the wrong line of work from the onset.

The minister bellowed out, "Only the Lord can render punishment." A statement Gabe knew to be a lie. The plastered fake smile continued his analogy by saying, "God is the only one who can judge us. But what are we, as his loving flock, doing to make his judgments easier?" The minister didn't hesitate, after his rhetorical question sat pregnant on the same stage, continuing and driving the nail even deeper. "We should be living in God's grace every day of our lives and progressing in his good works by learning patience with kindness from his eternal love."

Well, this is bullshit! He'd never met a more intolerant group of souls than during his time at St. Ignatius. People liked to boast of their compassion and ability to extend a hand in generosity, but let it be known the distressed party was a "sexually deviated homosexual," and their compassionate grip would be wrenched away under a speed previously unseen. The congregation at Ignatius, for example, would rather have had a reformed serial murderer on death row as their personal pet project. But let a lesbian couple stand beside them and join with parishioners in hymnal singing... Well, that would just never happen.

Gabe had to admire the minister's ability to enthrall worshippers with his mesmerizing colloquialisms and rapid movements as distraction.

Never mind about the man behind the curtain, just realize you're in the presence of the Great and Powerful Oz. He laughed at the thought of it because he had been the right hand of God's punishment ever since he was a young and idealistic man. He had smote down the guilty, or sent the innocents to sit at their Father's side; either way he wasn't really sure. But he knew he'd rendered out God's decrees with his usual tenacity, and he was better affiliated with the almighty than this suited asshole imitating that onscreen.

Hearing footsteps approach from outside the motel, he bolted out of bed in preparation for a fight. He stopped short when he saw the door handle turn and figured it had to be Christian. As the door opened, he smiled pleasantly surprised. Gabe knew he wasn't alone again and found solace in that quiet truth. For a loner like him who'd never known any better, he was amazed to find how much his previous isolation disturbed him now...much more than it had when he was younger, he realized. It seemed the older he got the more he needed to hear another person in the room with him - someone else's company to stave off the voices rattling through his brain.

Christian smiled too as the door slid open to reveal a naked man blocking his path. It was a sight to see, and one he savored. A broad-shouldered man with a mat of chest hair and his short-cropped hair tousled from the bed sheets. It was an image he wanted burned into his psyche forever. The two large coffees and the paper sack became a challenge to hold as he unlocked the door, but he somehow managed. "I have treats," he announced, making sure to secure the door behind him after entering.

"Good. I'm starving."

"I was hoping you'd still be asleep. You need your rest, darling" he said, tossing the bag on the table nearby.

"I don't like waking up alone," Gabriel announced with an audible pout.

"Well you are rarely in as good a mood as when you wake up next to me, baby. I seem to have a knack to bring out your best in the mornings."

He didn't like to think about Gabriel waking up next to strangers. He knew the man had an overpowering drive to fuck, but he attempted to extinguish those images from his mind. They always led to questions he preferred not to have answers for in the end. They sat on the edge of the bed, with the white noise from the TV playing in the background and ate donuts and sausage kolaches and drank hot coffee together.

"What's the game plan for today?" Christian asked, wiping his lips of sticky, sweet sugar.

"I have business to attend to today..." Church began. "And I have a job for you as well."

"Great." Christian smirked. "I get to participate, instead of waiting by the campfire for the menfolk to return from their long cattle drive," he said in his best twangy accent. His eyes leveled across from those iridescent irises and he grinned again, feeling a fevered flush of adoration and love swelling inside his belly. And all because Gabriel flashed back his gift of a half-crooked smile under an unkempt, furry bearded face.

After eating they showered together, getting just as dirty as they'd eventually become clean. Pulling out the toiletry case he'd remembered to bring Christian tossed it on the counter for his lover. He'd already mentioned to Gabe that it was high time his face saw a razor, but secretly he hadn't cared either way. This man was a silver fox no matter how unkempt his beard grew. Steam covered the mirror as he brushed his teeth and tried to become more presentable for the public. Gabriel took up too much space in that tiny bathroom, and Chris jumped out as quickly as possible. He watched from the other room as the man shaved, wondering to himself why it was so enticing to see another man perform the same mundane task he himself performed daily. It was a sensual illustration, he had to admit, seeing Church's naked, hairy ass cheeks presented tastily as he leaned into the sink and began covering his stubble with white, lathery foam.

After getting fully dressed, Christian sat patiently on the edge of the bed and waited for his man to finish as well. He sensed those caterpillars in his stomach had burst from their cocoons and were now adult butterflies flittering around his innards. He wasn't sure what Gabriel had planned for him, but by the tempered way he'd told him he had a job for him to complete, it surely meant something big.

"I'm going to be gone for most of the day," Gabriel pronounced, "but I want you to contact the detective at that office number he'd given you in his voicemail message. You did write it down, didn't you?"

"Well, yeah! But I thought you didn't want me to contact him. I mean, hell, we've been trying to duck him for two days now," he said incredulously.

"But today you will," Gabriel said coolly. "And you will do it exactly at three thirty in the afternoon. *Not before and not any later.*"

Staring, confused, Christian seemed unable to piece the jigsaw together in his mind. He nodded blankly, but then said, "Well, what do you want me to tell him?"

"You won't need to tell him anything, because he won't be there. But you will leave the message and make sure whomever takes your call knows the exact time you called in. If you get his voicemail, you'll need to announce what time you called in the message," Church told Chris calmly. "And make up an excuse as to why you hadn't called him earlier—too much work at the office or some shit like that. Understand?"

The pieces were still scattered, but eventually a shimmer of recognition grew visible in Chris's eyes. "You're trying to fabricate an alibi for me, aren't you?"

"Not to worry, babe." Gabe was distracted, hoping those four simple words could shield him from any further interrogation.

But pacifying his boyfriend was harder than he'd imagined. Christian was a clever man, though ill-prepared for building a ruse from scratch and nothing. This was Gabriel Church's domain, and his mind continually worked his own unique set of circumstances, all to get him further ahead in whatever games he was playing. He finally just grabbed Chris's face in his oversized mitts and then forced his gaze onto his, and with his usual steely determination, he muttered, "Just trust me, boy. I know what I'm doing."

It was slightly irritating to be left in the dark. He'd never fully understood each and every ebb and flow inside the man's mind, but he'd learned a few things after Gabriel's first departure from Seattle—one being that he needed to allow himself to just let go and give someone else the faith, the trust that they knew what they were talking about. He'd successfully evaded the law for too long not to garner some respect in that arena. It was freeing in a way. To just "let go and let God," as it were. But offering the reigns to a serial killer was a hard thing for anyone to do, even one as pretty as Gabriel Church. He resigned himself to accept his task willingly and not to add insult to injury by discussing it at relentless length, which might've frustrated his lover further.

He nodded and hung his head. It showed his willingness to become participatory in Gabriel's unknown plan. *I am nothing more than a devoted domestic. There to serve and be of service...to a man I strangely consider larger and more important than myself.* Maybe it was acceptance, or maybe it had been that embrace, but whatever the reason, he suddenly felt better and his spirits began to lift.

The feeling didn't last for very long. In that small bridge of time, when a heart may beat once, possibly twice, everything quickly turned sour once again. Time seemed to drag Chris unwillingly behind it during the interval. He was forced to see all the things he hadn't permitted himself to notice earlier: hat this had been one of Gabriel's intended little gestures. It was a reminder to Chris the two was risking never meeting again. The thought racing through Chris's brain at that moment was that he may never again be able to gaze into Gabriel's radiant steel-blue eyes or experience the completeness he felt while in his company. And this was a prospect he was loath to consider.

Chapter Twenty-Six

LEAVING THE MOTEL parking lot, Gabe took a last glance back, partially hoping to see Chris's face peering out from behind the curtains as he pulled away. But he wasn't there. *Well this one takes direction well,* he thought, like the best-trained bloodhound from his childhood. And with that, memories of Dolly came flooding in like a tsunami crashing over breakers. They were bittersweet recollections of watching his beloved dog race excitedly across the meadow, dodging thickets and jumping any available downed tree or bramble of dead sage. He pictured her dancing as she'd stop and circle ahead of him, like she was begging him to keep pace and match her speed. It was the last time Gabe had any true freedom, and the images of Dolly brought a smile and a contentment he hadn't felt in a while

Before getting into his pickup, Gabe furtively reached inside the broken air vent and withdrew his Glock from its secured hiding spot. He made sure no one had seen this maneuver, especially Chris. He didn't need him to worry for the whole of the day yet felt no compunction to describe his intentions to anyone, even to him. Jumping onto the freeway, he headed back in the same direction as the night before, closer to his objective at the Keen family home, and his plan to save at least at least one person he loved from having to carry the penalty of any crimes he alone had committed, regardless of what he'd said at the time.

It was another humid Seattle morning and cerulean skies displayed puffy cumulous clouds that promised there shouldn't be any rain in today's forecast. It would be warm and lovely for most living in this part of Washington. But to Gabriel, it signified a glimmer of hope. That maybe this one day would be a beginning to alter their fortunes for the better, his and Chris's alike. It became a sensation he equated to breezing down the interstate with the truck windows down and the wind licking his face and ruffling his hair. It was reminiscent of those sunny drives along the coast when he was just reaching his early twenties and didn't have a care in the world. He'd been unrestricted, borderless and could point his Dodge in whatever direction that suited him. It was a feeling that only a true road-weary traveler might fully appreciate. He still knew it was nothing but a lie his brain had constructed to ease the discomfort he felt coming down the pike. But he didn't care. He pushed his ball cap farther back and then turned the radio on to relax during the drive to the Keen home, even with the cold Glock stowed under his jacket, lying next to him on the bench seat.

Twenty minutes later, he was parked one block down and one over from the Keen's tidy two-story residence. Stuffing the Glock into his waistband, and then putting on the jacket to hide the bulge, he stepped out into the afternoon air and began walking a dead man's route to his destination: a tan-brick home with lovely stark white-trimmed exteriors. All of his preparedness came in protecting the Dodge from being noticed, but little attention was focused on his being seen. He strolled atop the cracked sidewalks like a man without a care in the world. If there were witnesses, and they were able to describe him to authorities, it wouldn't matter. It was another unimportant part of this story to him. That was if his strategy went according to plan.

This was a street he would like to have spent his childhood on, but it was the type of neighborhood far beyond Bennett's sporadic income. It was also the type of place he might have curled his lip with distaste had he seen it that day. Like some anthropomorphized fox desiring the grapes that hung farther than its reach. It was like Bennett hadn't seen how others easily spotted the envy brewing inside his wicked soul. Or the hate he seemed to feel when others succeeded in life and where he was doomed to failure.

Every house Gabe passed seemed contained inside a bubble of traditional décor; their lawns mowed to exacting heights and porches and walkways meticulously edged and swept clean. Gabe could see how living here would represent a good place to raise a family. The Keen house fit the same mold as the others that lined this shaded street, but theirs may have been even homier by his tastes due to the brightness of the paint or possibly because of the quaint inlaid stone making up the walkway. The backyard was surrounded by a tall wooden privacy fence, the construction of which didn't appear too much a challenge for a man such as himself. Still, the adjacent homes sat closer than he'd imagined at first glance and being two stories meant anyone upstairs could watch him climb into the yard next door. It only took one nosey neighbor to topple his apple cart and turn a bad situation into something far worse.

He decided to take another approach and headed directly to the front door. Puffing his chest out confidently might've made it clear to those who knew him he was decidedly not like most criminals. He was a man who wasn't controlled by the same unease, one who rarely felt regret for things he'd done. Since his nerves were never racked with questions and indecision, he'd become transformed over time. He'd been made into something even stealthier; a predator, a man who felt comfortable inside his own deadly skin. It didn't hurt he already knew what hell or perdition awaited him on the other side. If not because of the white-lighters whose lives he'd stolen, then surely for Shea Baltimore, or that dumb, no-name fucker back in Texas.

Circling back, Gabe scanned for the alarm company's sign he knew would be there. It would be posted near the front bushes but clearly visible as a deterrent. He'd broken into enough places to learn residents fell into two typical subsets of the species: those who paid the monthly fees for home security, and those who wanted criminals to merely think they did. Since he was at a detective's home, he had to consider it would surely be the former and not the latter.

The name of the company would give him two things: the relative age of the system and the likelihood that the company possessed top grade and dedicated cellular access. Since the sign was worn out and nearly illegible from the elements, he had to work the presumption it may be operational, but it was an out-of-date relic meant to feign safety, more so than actually guarantee it.

Gabe stepped to the side of the house and immediately located the demarcation point, the metal panel found outside most houses and the box that housed most phone and security lines. It was the main hub for all Internet access and was ridiculously easy to break into. There were only four tiny screws meant to shelter the guts from the rain and bad weather, and Gabe, being a good Boy Scout who enjoyed coming prepared, pulled out his trusty pocket knife with its screwdriver attachment and went about opening the panel.

Cutting the mangle of red, blue, and yellow wires was easy enough, and almost anyone could tell the difference between phone lines versus the bulkier gauge connection of an Internet hub junction. Gabe understood if the wire was cut, the home's ability to summon police was cut off. The inside alarm may still sound but it couldn't complete the call to the offsite alarm company, and therefore no need to get authorities to make a safety check or drive by. He pulled the Internet cable free before closing the box to head inside.

Life was funny sometimes, a lesson Gabe had sadly learned far too early for his own good. Certain events had to fall exactly into place to ensure a tragedy in the making. Like a passenger aboard a flight when the plane is spinning into the Atlantic, who in that moment regretted accepting the counter agent's generous upgrade to an earlier flight.

Fate and chance have the tensile strength of a spider's web; it doesn't take much for a good day to turn terribly wrong when the strands break. Gabe wasn't worried about the noise of the alarm. He had run every option in his head prior to walking in. He knew Mrs. Keen was alone, and he knew he could take her quickly should the need arise. He hadn't heard any commotion from upstairs, and from his vantage point at the base of the stairwell, he thought he detected the sounds of running water in a bathroom above.

He pulled the Glock from his waistband and crept quietly across the space, surveying surroundings at every point and trying to familiarize himself with the layout. He didn't see a need to climb the stairs since they might creak in a house this old. Besides, he knew she'd be coming down soon enough. Standing in the living room, he looked out past the rear dining room, which had been framed by large paned windows, and out onto a picturesque backyard. It simply begged to have children playing there, and he could see why the Keen's had chosen it. It was furnished as he'd expected it to be, traditional and homey, pillows everywhere and lines of brick-a-brac on shelves above the fireplace, along with the obligatory stack of women's magazines neatly fanned atop a mahogany coffee table.

He decided he wanted something deadly and quiet to have as backup and headed into the kitchen. The first thing he spotted was a butcher's block of ready knives sitting atop the white marble counter near a gas range. Choosing a large utensil, he reflected how earlier female victims he'd come across always seemed more frightened by the body-to-body contact. Guns could be ideal whenever facing a male victim. Their reasoning seemed to better equate to how powerful and lethal bullets could be when propelled by force into a man's core, destroying organs in a mere flash. Then again, maybe it was nothing more than experience with the weapon itself. He didn't know.

Women understood knives on a level most male assailants did not. There was a basic and yet highly charged emotion to draw a knife on someone. This was why, he figured, they were more apt to reach for a knife over something else when defending themselves.

But he found where knives scared them more, the women he'd met during his life would likely lack the confidence to plunge the blade in and cause any real damage. As if they wanted all the protection they offered without having to actually harm another person in the process. He figured it must've been a throwback from a long history wrought with misogynistic males who only saw females as chattel, or simply a warm spot to bury their bone. Men like himself, who in reality were nothing but Pavlovian dogs with drooling tongues and rising fevers when confronted with a prospect of food or fucking.

He saw two doors in the kitchen; one he supposed headed out to the garage while the other appeared to be a pantry of sorts. He could still smell the aroma of brewed coffee growing cold in a pot nearby and imagined his life under more conventional scenarios. Seeing a set of keys lying on the counter, he picked them up quietly and pocketed them. He didn't need Carol reaching them and setting off her car alarm to draw attention to her plight. He heard the sound of a drawer being pulled open upstairs, noticing only then he could no longer hear the stream of water splashing across tile. Stopping to hold his breath, he craned his neck to one side, trying to discern the woman's movements before she reached the stairs.

Backing quickly into the door he presumed belonged to a pantry, he was pleased to see a line of stacked cans and dry goods shelves all around. *Two for two,* he muttered to himself with a grin. Leaving the door slightly ajar, he was able to surveil the whole kitchen and dining area. He then noticed the washer and dryer set in the rear of the walk-in storage slash laundry room. *Fuck,* he thought, *I hope she doesn't come down with a load in her arms.* But then a smile beamed across his face.

Why the hell had he thought that? He wondered. And why the shit should he care if she was doing laundry that morning? It didn't matter to him anyway. Sometimes he found little pleasures in how very random his brain could be.

Like a thump of a metronome, the only sounds he could hear then came from the beating in his own chest. Not because, like a pussy, his nerves were unwinding from their spool. He was better than that. He'd always known how much better he was at that. But after he held his breath trying to control the oxygen escaping his lungs so he could hear Carol's movements upstairs, something felt constricted.

For any other predator it might represent anxiety, but for him, it was a rush, something positively electrifying. It reminded him of a hunter pulling in the cold morning air and steadying the rifle butt firmly against this shoulder, his target sitting patiently inside the crosshairs for the bullet that would drop them. His mind raced to the security panel and the wires he'd pulled, meaning there was no panic button Mrs. Keen could push now. He took particular attention to the empty gun holster hanging on a coatrack rung by the front door. That made sense to him given the detective's line of work, but it could also mean there was another gun somewhere in the house. Most likely in a nightstand or somewhere within easy reach in the middle of the night.

He'd never met Carol Keen and couldn't be sure of the type of woman she was. But having a husband in law enforcement might mean she was proficient in gun use. Or at the very least spent some time at the range with her husband teaching her basics, like how to fire into the subject's core or how she should always continue firing until she was positive her attacker was down for the count. It was how Gabriel's mind worked; the gears and wheels whirring in his skull whenever hunting a white-lighter or prepping for the eventual kill. He spotted the frilly curtains of the front windows open a bit to allow the morning light in. This meant any passersby could see in if some commotion drew their eye. It was only calculations in his head, things to consider and precautions he needed to be aware of.

There are no perfect plans. Most of what he did could be attributed to his fast-on-his-feet thinking. No one ever willingly stepped into those exact spots where one needed them to stand. And there were ideal circumstances whenever it came to abduction and murder. His first thoughts were to come up from behind her when she entered her kitchen. This was a favored technique when subduing the female sex. But he could hear his heartbeat pounding louder in his ears, and even to him it sounded forced and painfully out of sync. That damned defect of his, reminding him how tenuous life could be. With its surging blood and infinitesimally slow closing of his arterial valve, telling him one day soon he'd fall facedown on the pavement and be dead.

But not today. Not while I have things that needed my immediate attention.

Hearing the creak of stairs as the woman descended reminded him that earlier cautions had been well founded. He could only continue holding his breath and trust the hammering sounds in his chest were not audible to her. She entered the kitchen as she would have every morning—void of any expectation that an unseen assailant might lunge from the shadows and grab her from behind. At the precise moment she was bending over to put a coffee mug in the dishwasher, Gabe struck. With the speed of a scorpion tail, he came hurtling out and nearly engulfed Carol with his immense frame. He'd naturally caught her unaware, and he felt her body stiffen in his arms, too frightened and far too surprised to utter a sound. With one hand he brought the blade's edge across her tiny throat and with the other he held her down by her arms.

"*Don't scream!*" he whispered gruffly.

AMAZINGLY CAROL KEEN was able to stifle the outburst which had risen in her throat and threatened to explode. In her shock, she couldn't move as her attacker engulfed her from behind. Her legs were liquefying, turning to molten flux. She wanted to fall to the ground in fear, like some marionette doll whose strings had been severed. But she couldn't collapse while the stranger was holding her upright in his tight grip and overpowering her. In a flash, her instinct blindly raced toward the inevitability of rape. In those milliseconds of terror, Carol was already turning the story over in her head, dissecting the trauma and the abuse and exploring every ramification. She was performing a sick play in her head where she was standing in tears as she explained what happened to her husband. She was testing the waters of his reaction and weighing the consequences even before the assault began.

As terrified as she was, Carol didn't overreact. She knew the place where that steely resolve first originated, and it came from years of being the wife of a patrol officer. When Scott started at the force and worked in his regular blues, he'd been assigned the night shift early in his career. Like most officers, he had to experience that unique responsibility before he could move up the ladder, sink or swim as it were. She'd spent excruciating evenings glancing at the door from time to time. Even from the comfort of her couch while watching TV wrapped in an old afghan, she knew too well the anxiety that spouses of police officers faced every day. Would her husband come home after his shift was over? Would another black-and-white pull up along the curb with its light bar flashing? Would she spot the Chief of Police walking to her front steps with his hat in his hand? Yes, Carol knew the tension of the Damocles' sword suspended by nothing more than a horsehair-sized thread. She knew the dangers warriors like Scott faced, and she was as familiar with the range of emotions felt by those they left behind. All the wives who tended home fires while trying hard not to imagine the worst of outcomes. With every passing day, she'd learned a little more strength, a tad more determination. She tapped into the keg in that moment and drained off whatever tenacity she needed, simply to survive that instant of panic.

This woman was no daffodil withering under a hot noonday sun. She'd heard horrific tales of her husband's work. She encouraged Scott to share his stories, and he had - though he'd been smart enough to leave many of the grislier details from of his accounts. Carol knew what it meant to carry that type of burden. She'd observed it firsthand. Scott had freely chosen his life behind a badge, and thus it had become her life by his transaction. She'd researched every aspect and chatted with as many spouses of officers that she could. Like the suicide rates attributed to his job. She knew that statistically, those working in law enforcement were more likely to commit suicide than be killed in the line of duty. It was just one more reason being a police officer had its drawbacks. Yes, Carol had read the data; she knew other wives and husbands of officers and understood all the risks involved. They were the worries you felt every time the phone rang in the middle of the night, or when you saw another UNI pulling up out front unexpectedly. It was the type of thing that freezes the oxygen inside your lungs then grips your chest tight with anticipation. She knew it was healthier to allow Scott to talk it out, to air his grievances and discuss the things he witnessed. This was her support, her way of showing how much she cared...because she was his partner in life - and that was always more significant than the partner sitting next to him in his cruiser.

The normal experiences Carol learned throughout her marriage were valuable lessons to be certain, but it was her role of being the wife of a detective that truly augmented her for the better. She adapted to change faster than most wives, due in part to every story she'd ever listened to regarding her husband's work, and the kind of people he dealt with in his chosen profession. So when a stranger broke into her home and a traditional response would be the weak-kneed predicament which always feels far too unreal to actually be happening, she was able to grasp her situation quickly. Even though the muscles in her back tightened and her spine felt like taunt cable, she bravely stood her ground while an unknown man held a knife against her carotid artery, and she calmly whispered, "I'm not screaming." And then, even heroically, she asked the one thing gripping her in her state of fear and disbelief, "What is it that you want?"

"Relax. I'm not here to rob you," the man said in cold measured words. "And even as hot as you are, Mrs. Keen, rest assured, I've no inclination for rape or humiliation."

With their close proximity, she thought she could feel his heart beating and rattling the hollow of her empty lungs. His heart seemed to race at the same speed as hers. She was trembling yet cognizant of the knife held in that dangerous place. If she jumped too rashly or didn't control her shaking, it was there threatening her, reminding her it could slice away her life with nothing more than the tiniest of moves. She knew she had to remain still and calm or any dream she had of growing old with Scott would simply disappear. There would be blood spilling on the kitchen tiles, splashing red across her white marble counters, and she would drop like a sack of potatoes with her life draining away in a puddle. She was trapped inside that awful image and could only do her best to slow her breathing and hold firm.

The stranger was far bigger than she was, and his body engulfed hers. She could feel the blade at her neck. Felt that it hadn't moved, even in the slightest. He, at least, was not shaking like she was. She could tell her attacker was powerful by the size of the arms wrapping her and holding her tight. It was amazing to her how, in that split-second, her mind began to trail away unexpectedly. Her experience as a policeman's wife and hearing Scott rant over the years about the fallibility of witness descriptions trained her in ways she hadn't known. She was busy calculating every detail she could about her attacker and shelving the information for later use, like cold storage retrieval, even outside the tangible reality of a very dreadful circumstance.

She was picturing events that hadn't happened. Her standing in a circle of detectives in her living room, giving them a description of her intruder, then listing every element of the horrors she'd survived that day. *I will be ready for that. If I can only make it out alive to see that occur.* Scott would be proud of her for being able to give such clear and accurate details to the detectives taking her statement, and how she'd remained calm and collected through it all, despite the weirdness of the situation.

"We are alone in the house, correct?" the man asked in his husky baritone.

She nodded once, and as she did, his lips brushed faintly at her ear. She could feel the humid dampness of his words as they slipped out and heard the composed masculine timber of his pitch. "Besides the knife, which is one of yours I stole from your kitchen by the way, I also have a gun," he announced dispassionately. "It's not something I want to use, so don't make me. If I release you a bit, can you try hard to not attempt an escape?"

With his huge hands clenching her neck and holding the back of her head, she could only nod and draw in oxygen with a tiny gasp, forcing her fears into another place she hadn't realized ever existed prior that moment. Even with her bravery, she felt a strange wetness welling in her eyes. But she wouldn't cry. She wouldn't give him the satisfaction of seeing how truly scared she felt. It was proving difficult for her and hard to hold back the tears looming behind her eyes, warning her how her pride was about to be compromised.

She wanted nothing more than to be inside Scott's arms right then, not this stranger's. And almost as if it were a reply to the foreboding, her intruder spun her around quickly, gripping her arms down tightly at the elbows and anchoring her in place. Her feet felt as if they were encased in concrete, and as she looked up into his eyes with abject panic, she saw a face she hadn't expected. He didn't appear the type who broke into homes and terrorized women. And then like an explosion in her brain she remembered something she heard him say. Had he really called her *Mrs. Keen* earlier?

AS CHURCH STARED into her lovely brown eyes, he could tell she was about to burst into tears. *She is verging on being hysterical.* Then everything seemed to snap into place, and her expression wasn't unfamiliar to him. He'd seen that look on his mother's face many times. And with that recollection from his youth, a brusque cold chill raced downward along his back, tensing his muscles and turning them into tight inflexible cording. When his white-lighter victims were female, their first instincts always ran to rape when he pounced from the safety of the shadows. But sexual assault was abhorrent to him. This was odd even to him, considering how frenzied his play could often get.

A killer with a conscience, he supposed, but he'd seen the look on Bennett's face whenever his little sister was innocently playing on the floor at his feet. He'd mistrusted that look from the beginning, even though he never had any proof anything ever happened, or that his father was brewing some strange sickness of the soul.

Gabe could easily stretch a woman's limits sexually. He could do the same with a man. Like when he'd bent Christian's naked body below his own then smashed his face into the carpet with his open palm and fucked him rough and hard. He found his dick would stay hard longer and become stiff enough to hurt with every grunt of submission or whimper his lovers made when under his control. But extreme sex wasn't the same as assaulting someone, and Carol Keen had nothing to fear from him in that regard.

He knew she was petrified, but he saw intelligence in her brown eyes. She knew if she tried to break free, she wouldn't make it far before he'd wrestle her to the ground and make her pay for her ill-conceived attempt to gain her freedom. Gabe could see astonishment in her eyes and suspected she was wondering why he wasn't wearing a mask or a stocking to hide his identity. She was clever, he knew, so he'd have to pacify her and do it quickly before she made the connection that he didn't intend for her to survive this.

"No," he said to calm her, "I'm not in disguise, but don't jump to conclusions, Mrs. Keen. It's not what you think."

"You know my name," she blurted out. Her confusion took full hold then and every fear she had was rapidly turned upside down.

"Not exactly, it's your husband I'm familiar with, although I hadn't the privilege of meeting you yet."

In comical insanity, the man grinned, cocking his head slightly to the side before saying, "So hello, nice to meet you." It sounded like a sadistic line coming from a twisted killer in a slasher flick, the kind Carol always hated and Scott loved. It sent shivers convulsing down her small frame and all her apprehension turned into a wild panic.

Carol was transfixed by the man towering over her. His eyes were ungodly pale, like lightly polished granite. His jaw was covered by a course, unkempt beard, yet there was something strangely beautiful and frighteningly feral inside him. He was an untamed animal capable of becoming ferocious and deadly in a flash of seconds. And yet there was something behind the pupils telling Carol there was a capacity of reasoning in him.

He seemed incalculable to her, like a man balancing the edge of his own blade. Was he a sadistic killer or only a man pushed beyond his reason? Or both, or neither, she couldn't tell. But it no longer mattered because she was shaking so hard by then she felt as if she were about to hurl. Tears finally broke through the dam she'd maintained so diligently and were falling down her cheeks. But her body wasn't racked with sobs, nor were her shoulders trembling violently, and she hadn't lost her ability to speak. Not everything was gone.

In direct conflict, the man seemed to have retained all his composure, which only unnerved her more. It was apparent he'd at least a passing acquaintance with danger, and that he'd probably done this type of thing before. She thought about Scott and wondered whether he'd arrested this man at some point in his career. Was it a vendetta? Was that the thing which drew this stranger to her home and was now trapping her inside it like some timid animal who'd inadvertently stumbled into a hunter's trap? She didn't know, nor could she have. Scott never mentioned the likes of this man before. She would have remembered. She could only stand there dumbfounded and frozen. A white marble statue fashioned by fear and surprise, with the Lord's Prayer resonating through her head. In the stillness, every second became a minute, and as they passed, she was becoming less sure those minutes wouldn't turn out being her last.

Releasing her, the man used a free hand to unzip his jacket and then exposed the Glock. "I want to talk to your husband, but I can't really visit him at the station, not like this..." he said, gesturing to the gun with a sardonic grin.

"I only want to talk to him."

"You could just call him... I can give you his number..." Carol managed to squeak out, her voice crackling with uncertainty.

"Oh, I have his number, but for me, it's better we have a conversation face-to-face. Then again you could call him for me."

Somewhere in the hollows of her fear-racked brain, Carol was seized with a new and stronger apprehension. Like waves crashing on a rocky shore it was sudden and inevitable, violent and inescapable...this man intended to kill Scott before killing her because she was a witness. What else could it be? She could think of nothing else that would fit. Because why else would someone go to these ends for want of a conversation? Her panic was rising to uncontainable levels, and she knew that any second it may boil over. That even against uncertain odds, she'd be forced to flee screaming, racing toward the front door with this man hot at her heels and close enough to catch her before she could make it to freedom.

But even as that awful movie played through her brain, she saw the futility. He'd easily catch her before she could reach the door. She would only get herself killed in the process. Then images of her being stabbed in her living room flashed like tiny detonations in her head. She could picture Scott seeing her body bathed in blood and her still in the sweatpants she'd chosen that morning. It'd be an inglorious ending and something her husband saw in his mind for years to come. Carol was gauging all this by the stranger's demeanor. *He is clearly insane, too calm to be anything but batshit crazy.* His statements were deliberate and cold, telling her everything he was doing had been planned. And it became the premeditation which scared her most.

"Here's what I was thinking..." Gabe began as if explaining to a child and not a frightened adult. "You call your hubby then ask him to come home. Make up an excuse, one that ensures he will rush home to be by your side."

He pulled out his Glock for influence, and then waved it carefree in the air, appearing much like a maestro holding a baton before his orchestra and waiting impatiently for the swell of string instruments and that sweet life of the crescendo.

"When he gets here, we can talk for a bit, and I promise I'll leave you both safe and sound. You and your detective hubby can resume normal lives unmolested. All I need is a head start... Sound simple enough?"

As he stared onto Carol's wide-eyed, fear-induced expression to see how truly lovely she was. He stopped momentarily to consider the tiny flecks of brown in her irises and the way the light streamed in from the backyard to bounce perfectly amid those eyes already welling up with tears. They resembled tiny auburn pools that had an alluring ability to draw a man in. She was an attractive woman, with a slender figure and clearly had loyalty and a fair degree of intelligence. It became obvious to Gabe exactly why the young detective had chosen her as his mate. He also saw how much she loved Keen. The evidence of that seemed to ooze from every pore and also by the way she kept looking at the wall phone mounted in the kitchen. She hadn't taken her eyes off it after he suggested she may have to call her husband home. Church felt a wave of jealousy spilling over him before reminding him that he had Christian. At least he wasn't alone. Not like he'd been all those years on the road. He too met someone who could love him unconditionally...just as Carol Keen loved her special one.

It is sad, I am about to end their relationship in order to save my own.

Chapter Twenty-Seven

"SO HOW DO you know my husband? Did he arrest you once so now you're plotting murder? Is this your version of some sick revenge?" Even with her bravery, she couldn't hide her distaste, spitting the questions out like they'd turned rancid on her tongue and required immediate expulsion. She wasn't stupid, though; she knew the risks she was taking—the chance he'd level the barrel of the big gun at her temple and fire. She could only wonder if she'd even hear the explosion before the nothingness enveloped her.

"No, your husband and I have never met. I thought I mentioned that."

He was a glass full of empty. There was an absence of malice in his words, though it was clearly present, lurking right below the surface.

"Like I said before, I only wanted to chat a bit with him before taking my leave."

Taking my leave—strange words coming from his lips. Not exactly the turn of a phrase I would've expected from this gruff and bearded figure. He turned to glance at the clock on the microwave, and she noted that was the second time he'd done that.

"Do you have somewhere you need to be?" she asked tentatively. His eyebrows rose with a pop and a twinkle crossed those slate-bluish eyes of his, but he never responded to her question.

She sat nervously, squirming frequently. The rail-back kitchen chair was uncomfortable to sit in for very long, particularly with some dangerous armed man invading her home. The big man watched her with a grin on his face. *Is he killing time? And if so, what for?* It was hard to imagine what was hiding behind those eyes of his, but in her mind, she reasoned it could be any number of possibilities.

"Nice house," the man said, turning his head to take in the homey atmosphere she'd created. "So how long have you and Scott lived here?" he asked rather offhandedly.

Was this man for real? Making polite conversation while his fingers tapped nonchalantly on the gun he pointed directly her way? Carol had seen enough crime dramas on television to understand her best chance to survive came only from humanizing herself with her captor. So she played along, even though it seemed more irrational than anything she'd ever done before.

"We moved in almost two years ago. We liked the neighborhood, thought it was the best place to start our family," she muttered. It could have been a pleasant conversation between neighbors had he not been carrying a weapon or broken in uninvited to hold her prisoner.

For an experienced predator like Gabriel Church, it was clear what she was trying to do. But he was quiet, simply nodding acknowledgment with a hint of a smile to show how normal this situation could be if they let it. This must be her valiant attempt to present herself as one deserving of life, he figured. Humanizing herself to her captor in a bond she could only describe as Stockholm syndrome. If that was the case, then so be it. It couldn't change what had to happen here today, he thought. Besides she wasn't a stellar actress and played it too loose and disconnected to be believable. Minutes passed with more silence. To occupy his time, he studied Carol more closely. She was still in sweatpants and tennis shoes, a simple top covering her braless breasts. A soccer mom in the making, he figured. Still, she had a tight little figure with gold highlights in her auburn locks, and he could see if she hadn't been so petrified, she might come off playfully innocent and fun to be around. This made him smile for reasons he didn't understand. But then he glanced back at the clock and noticed the time. It was finally ready to begin. Carol needed to make that all-important phone call. The one he needed to guarantee happened and the secondary reason for his visit.

As he occupied his time studying her, Carol was doing likewise, committing every detail she observed to memory. His build, his clothing, his accent. Even the smaller specifics, such as words he used or the mannerisms he employed. He was rustic by her description, not necessarily a native to the city. He didn't look the part of a petty criminal. He also possessed other qualities and a somewhat greater intelligence. Unless that was only her misconception, due in part to those nearly indescribable gray-blue eyes of his. Eyes that might've made him appear smarter than he actually was. Somehow he didn't quite fit the picture of a person her husband might know. Since he didn't look like a man who committed crimes as easily as he did. More like a bumpkin-would-be farmer who dogged behind pretty women in honky-tonk bars and pool halls. But whatever he was before this, now he was a man holding a gun on her, without a trace of guilt or remorse that she could see.

Just then, an ambulance screamed past the front windows, startling her and causing her to visibly jump in her chair. The flashing lights and sirens seemingly came out of nowhere, and she wondered why she hadn't heard it blasting down the street before it crossed in front of the house. Still, the man watching her hadn't batted an eye or moved a muscle. Like he already knew it was roaring down the street before she did.

"If you're not going to tell me your name, or how you know my husband, are you going to say whether you intend to kill me?" Carol asked, to break the silence.

"Not now," Church said. "But soon maybe."

"DOES IT HELP, young man? Does it offer you any guidance?"

The words came back like an echo, stained completely by Father Kait's kind, inquisitive nature as he'd been shuttered in the sanctity and darkness of that confessional booth. Gabriel wondered in that moment if the choices he'd made could've ever been undone. He wondered if they were even wise decisions at all, or irreparable, after his actions as he tried to protect someone innocent of his crimes and one he believed he loved. It could all go terribly wrong, after all, and he might not be able to save Christian Maxwell from going to prison for a crime he alone committed. But it was like struggling in quicksand. One eventually had to "let go and let God," because Gabriel could only do what he hoped would be the best. For both Christian and himself, even though those paths might not always converge.

Taking a look at the clock on the microwave again, he turned and then abruptly stood up and announced, "Carol it's time for you to call Scott home. So where's your cell phone, darlin'?"

Taking her by her elbow, Gabe casually led Carol upstairs to retrieve her phone. It lay temptingly beside the computer throughout her ordeal, too far to reach, and beyond an opportunity to utilize and call for help. Exchanging the butcher's knife for the Glock, he tapped it softly against her temple as ample explanation that should she fail to play her role effectively he would simply shoot her in the head and then secure another plan to speak directly with the detective. A large hand held her neck tightly at the base of her neck as he made the call. Gabe felt the intensity of her pulsating heart through his fingertips and detected the scent of soap and shampoo off her body from her morning shower. This time she needed to be a better actress than before, and ultimately, she played her part well.

"Hey, babe..."she began, trying to smile against any growing fear. She needed her words to sound as relaxed as possible—both their lives might rest on that. "Sorry to bother you at work, doll, but I forgot to mention it earlier. I could've used your help with something before you left."

"Whatcha need, hon?" Scott asked, confusion clouding his tone. "I mean really, I haven't been here all that long. Is it something that can wait till I get home?"

"Afraid not," Carol stammered out. "But don't you yell at me for forgetting. I need you to haul something heavy up to the attic for me. It's too damned big for little ole me."

"And it can't wait till later?" Scott asked. Carol knew he was trying hard not to make it sound harsh or that Carol was bothering him with something of little importance. That was what her husband was like. What was important to her was equally important to him.

"Well, not exactly!" she said rather abruptly, and then attempted to soften her words. "I'm cleaning and it's in my way. It's that damned old television sitting in the guest room. I'm clearing out the room and starting from scratch. I'm finally gonna start the painting today and that shitty TV has to go, so if you won't let me get rid of it by putting it up in the attic, it goes. I will have my pretty nursery, mister!"

She secretly hoped reminding Scott of the baby would turn out to be her effective tool in shutting down his opposition. One of the things she loved about him was the way Scott became so beautifully malleable whenever the merest hint of baby talk entered their discussions, or the way his eyes glazed over when he imagined their first child being born. She knew from experience Scott was picturing his wife shoving a cumbersome and heavy TV up those rickety attic ladder steps. She'd rather take risks to her safety and that of a child not yet in utero to accomplish her task, and that was an image she knew he couldn't live with.

He'd race headlong to reach her before she could attempt doing something so unnecessary. He'd show his male dominance and his ability to protect his family by moving it so she didn't have to. And besides, he'd promised her since the day they'd moved in that he was going to store the thing upstairs. Every single thing she knew about her lover only worked to her advantage, because he quickly agreed to come home for a brief break. He would do it willingly because he had a wife who was in need. He even mentioned he could take a late lunch at the house, which was something he rarely did. She felt his boasting smile creeping across the airwaves. She knew Scott was proudest when he provided for or was protecting his family.

It brought another surge of love to her bosom, and with it, concern and a swell of sadness, because she didn't know what might happen when he arrived. She thought she may be luring him home only to have it end in tragedy. She hoped that was unlikely, and the stranger hadn't been lying all along, because her betrayal of Scott would be more than anything she could bear if she were proven wrong.

"See ya soon, wife," he said right before the line went dead. She was struggling to hold back her tears again by then.

"There's a good girl," the intruder said, his southern drawl laboring with each word. He widened the distance from the gun barrel and her temple, and she was finally able to breathe again.

"You did great, darlin'. You'd make a fine film actress."

"And now we wait," he said, tapping the gun barrel against an invisible air wall commanded Carol to head downstairs. Gabe could feel waves of panic tiding in off the woman as she walked in front of him, gingerly taking the stairs while he trailed behind. He could tell she was holding her breath, expecting him to release a solitary bullet into the back of her brain. She had a sudden and nightmarish realization that he'd lied from the very beginning; he had no intention of leaving her, or her husband, safe and unmolested once this initial introduction was complete.

She had a child's fear of the unknown plastered across her face: the type of fear where children clicked off their lights and then raced for the protection of their beds, fighting the minefield of the unimaginable existed between their bedroom door and the security of cool sheets and warm comforters. That sense of dread an alien-like hand would slither from dark shadows underneath their bed only to grab their ankles in icy fingers. It was fear of rape, abduction, violence, and the cold, blackness of the unspecified. It was nameless and terrifying, and for the first time in a long while, Gabriel felt truly bad being the bearer of such apprehension.

Entering the living room, Gabriel was chastising himself, reminding his inner voice this was nothing but necessity. The same ends Keen would take to protect his family, he imagined. And he was protecting his, in a way. He had zero options but killing the detective and his wife. He had done the same with Shea, and he was learning fast there wasn't a great deal he wouldn't do to try to save Chris. But he had to wonder if this would ever change; that the bodies were beginning to pile up only to keep the writer free from prison.

God, I am so damaged. Even I can see how much the damage is visible at times. How can Chris ever look at me the same way after this?

He was careful to keep the Glock hidden as they passed by the front windows and with a small wave of the gun barrel, he directed Carol to an empty chair in the dining room.

"It's almost over," he said coolly, trying to keep her relaxed. "Does your husband keep handcuffs at the house or does he carry them daily?" he asked brusquely. His captive seemed confused by the question and thought a few seconds before answering.

"He has a pouch attached to his belt," she said as the color drained from her face with worry.

"I may need to secure you both before leaving," he said calmly. "I need time to get a running start before your stalwart husband begins his pursuit of me."

He was offering her more information than she might have needed, but he wanted to settle a few fears she had, and it seemed to do the trick. His statement gave her the small gradations of hope their murders weren't something he was planning for the near future. The blood reappeared in her cheeks after that.

"I still don't understand what you want from us," she said to him rather meekly.

"Well, Carol..." Gabe began slowly, "I am a very bad man, done many bad things as it were, and your husband, being the good detective he is, should be made aware of this."

Gabe checked the time on the microwave again. It was time for Chris to make his call to the station, and Gabriel was already guaranteeing the detective wouldn't be there to take the call. He could only pray it would be sufficient in pulling any light off his lover in the process. It was probably twisted logic, but in Gabe's head, it made perfect sense. With his anonymous assistance, police would discover the remains of a detective and his wife. The time of death would establish it couldn't have been Christian, who was calling from a cell at a location that could be verified by signal towers. Whatever Keen learned in his investigation of Shea's murder would be jotted lines in a notepad. The real story would be the homicide of one of their own and might be attributed to some poor sap Keen had arrested once; at least, this was his hope.

It held some clarity in Gabe's mind, and though he might've been working under the false assumption he couldn't be tied to the crime or that no one had anything substantial on him, it didn't matter. He knew the actions he was forced to take, like the murder of Shea Baltimore, were necessary evils for a good cause. It was his way of protecting his loved one.

Not unlike the detective he knew would be racing toward this house in that very moment. He knew Christian wasn't a guilty man; he'd simply gotten caught in the wake of his own drama. Whatever he did here today, Gabe knew he had to try to save him as best he could.

And it wasn't like he hadn't killed for him before. Christian could be many things, but at least he wouldn't be a deadly causality in a chain of tragic events. He was his indirect and intervening springboard and had allowed all that had happened to take place. And even in the aftermath of Shea's murder, Gabe felt certain he was nothing but a mere instrument, a means to the conclusion, and the one who was going to ultimately pay the tab. Because in his head he figured he wasn't the kind of man who was ever supposed to win in the end. At least, he hadn't so far.

Oh well. It's not like I didn't already see how it was going to crumble in the end anyway.

Church's hand instinctively went back to the Glock he shoved down his jeans to give Carol Keen the chance to relax. It was all down to this gun, he figured. They'd be looking for a killer with a Glock 9mm, and ipso facto they wouldn't be looking quite so solid at Chris. Just another magic trick where someone didn't notice what one hand was doing because they were staring at the other that the magician was waving around wildly, practically in a panic as if it were on fire or something. It was only a simple plan he'd rested everything on, but it was the best one he could muster in the short time he had to work with.

Intruder and captive alike sat facing each other for nearly twenty-five minutes. Carol's fear hung like radio static in the air as she fidgeted nervously on the sofa where Gabe forced her to wait. Her hands moved constantly, going from her lap to the throw pillows at her sides before returning to her lap once again. She'd been wringing them in her unconscious anxiety and then folding them back in demure, female fashion. Even from across the room, Gabe could see how white they'd become because of how tightly she was holding them. Clearly she'd been trying to contain herself, or possibly prevent the stranger from seeing how much she was actually trembling. Her breathing was coming harder, faster with every tick of the second hand from the clock on the mantle above the fireplace. Her brown pupils darted uncontrollably right and then left. It was the foreboding inevitability of her husband's arrival troubling her. She knew his car was getting closer and closer, and with every mile, the dread rose to meet it with the thought of the danger he'd face once he crossed the threshold of their door and entered her nightmare.

Chapter Twenty-Eight

QUITE ABRUPTLY, THE sounds of Scott's squeaky axels as he pulled into the drive altered the tension inside the Keen home. The stalemate of emotions the intruder skillfully crafted to maintain Carol's peace of mind was instantly shattered, like a wine glass falling unexpectedly to the hard tile floor and destroying the silence. Her eyes went wide as she gulped in air in anticipation of something that she couldn't quite grasp. No longer able to control her fear, Carol's hands began involuntarily shaking like rice paper in a strong breeze. She was about to stand in some automatic reflex of greeting her husband at the door, but the man quickly waved her back down to the sofa with the smallest of gestures of his pointed barrel.

Carol turned to the entryway, and the man stood up quickly and moved to a spot across from her but out of sight of the door. Carol couldn't help her reflex action, raising a hand over her mouth to suffocate an audible gasp from escaping, but she wasn't successful. In her rising panic, she was considering now how the stranger might fire his gun at Scott the minute he was inside their home, and then he'd turn the gun on her after that. Killing them both without her ever learning the explanation of why it happened in the first place.

How could I have been so fucking stupid? Why had I believed he hadn't been completely lying from the first minute he surprised me in the kitchen? What seemed unimaginable to her was that she'd been the bait he'd used to lure her husband home. Now Scott was at the hands of this asshole and whatever fate he alone intended for them. And it would all be her fault.

Her brain was reeling with brand new consequences, and she began to perspire. She could feel her heart beating inside her throat, stifling her breathing and preventing her screaming to warn Scott before his hands turned the doorknob. She was suddenly afraid she might never learn what her husband had done to this man to warrant any of this. Everything inconceivable before that second had become something real and deadly.

Even if he allowed her to stand, she knew her knees would've buckled under her weight, and whatever he'd been planning was now about to transpire. Carol knew the only thing she could do was brace for the impact and pray it'd be all right in the end.

CAROL WAS TERRIFIED. She couldn't hide it on her face, and Scott Keen recognized it the instant he closed the door and saw his wife sitting so rigid with a well of fear in her pupils. His homicide detective instincts may have kicked in by then, but he hadn't the time. As cold realization struck him with the force of a hammer, he knew something was terribly amiss in his home...right before he felt the barrel of a gun at the base of his skull and heard the breathy sounds of an armed intruder at his back. His hand automatically reached for his holstered gun. It was a reflex arc he couldn't have controlled even if he'd chosen to, but a large hand stopped him short, grabbing him in a viselike grip and holding him firmly and confidently, interfering with the action of protecting his wife.

"Now, now, detective...let's not go there," the man uttered over his shoulder. Keen paused long enough to absorb his words. Even though the split second he had would never be ample time to fully comprehend it all, he'd heard the word detective, which meant a home invasion was an unlikely scenario. His ears were busy trying to decipher the accent in those few stray words, and he was already attempting to gauge the man's height and weight as any trained officer might do. He looked over at Carol, who again placed a hand over her mouth to stifle the scream threatening to explode from her at the sight of her husband with a gun to his head. She was pale and wide-eyed but appeared unharmed as far as he could tell. She had never risen from the sofa, no doubt instructed to remain there by the intruder.

Were there additional intruders in his home, he wondered, as he slowly dropped his arms to his sides to show that he was fully ready to acquiesce to the man's demands.

"I EXPLAINED THIS to your wife, and now I will tell you," Church began as he took a quick glance outside and realized he needed to move his captive away from the windows and any view from the street.

"Let's all sit down at the table for a minute, because I don't want this 9mm going off unexpectedly. And as I promised Carol earlier, I only want to talk to you for a minute and that is all."

Nudging the detective with the gun barrel, he walked him to the table and the same empty chair he'd jumped out of when he heard the car pull into the drive.

"Who the hell are you, and what the fuck do you want with me and my wife?"

"In time, Detective Keen, in time," Church said flatly as Keen took the chair next to his wife and then reached out and gently touched her hand to comfort her.

The detective stared at him, blue eyes glaring daggers. Was he angry? Yes, naturally. But he was surveying the intruder from top to bottom, committing every detail to a skilled and trained memory.

Through all of his years, with every crime he'd committed, Gabe had been able to remain a faceless figure, a man void of motive for every murder. But now this was a new game. And should he escape the city unharmed, his life would never be the same again. Ever since the murder of Shea Baltimore, he'd been born a new man with a new mission, committing violence and murder out of immediate need, rather than his usual celestial direction. He regretted having to take Shea's life and equally regretted having to take Carol's and the detective's. It wasn't something he'd planned, and for him, the planning had been everything and the reason why he'd never gotten caught. He told himself he wasn't any different than Scott Keen, wanting to protect someone he loved at any cost, but he'd been made the bad guy in this scenario, and he was going to play out his part. He'd fight like other monsters, there in the dirt of his life and to whatever ending it created. He knew no other way because monsters played by different rules.

With the Glock trained directly onto Carol Keen, Gabe bent slowly and methodically and withdrew Scott's gun from the holster strap under his suit jacket. If the detective had thoughts of trying to overtake him, they were quickly disregarded. Both men knew a stray bullet from such a close proximity would easily take her life, and he was forced to begrudgingly allow himself to be unarmed.

"Who else is here?" Scott asked gruffly as his head spun around looking for other strangers to come storming in from every door.

"Just us, detective, your wife can attest to that. I only wanted to introduce myself, once I'd heard you were searching for me."

Gabe saw the detective's eyes darting around the room. He could see that he'd started his gears to turning and figured correctly that the investigator was calculating whether this was connected to an active homicide or a cold case he'd been assigned but never solved. Even now, with all his difficulties, he was still working it as a case; running a lengthy list of suspects through his mind, but far too long to be of any immediate help.

"I'm here because of Shea Baltimore," Church announced, as if recognizing the laundry-list of horrors skipping through the detective's head. There wasn't any worry about confessing to that, he knew, because he had no intention of leaving any witnesses behind. He was suddenly flooded with guilt and an image of Father Kait standing in the rectory with his palsy hand outstretched in his goodbye. It all came crashing into his brain like a tsunami because out of all his multitude of kills, that one had been the only one he'd ever truly regretted. He and Chris had never really spoken about Shea's murder. The guilt was ample burden enough and something they both understood was better left unsaid and quickly forgotten. But now he had his own captive audience and could release his soul for spiritual cleansing. Maybe in the back of his mind, he wanted Carol to see at least once in that second before he placed the barrel of the Glock to her heart and ended her existence that he hadn't been such a bad man after all.

"I killed Miss Baltimore, strangled her with these very hands," he told them, looking down remorseful. He stared at his hand holding the gun, clearly remembering that fated evening when that same grip was tightened around her frail throat.

"Her murder hadn't been planned, but she spurned my sexual advances," Gabe said with a practiced, steady gaze of an experienced liar. "I guess I got too worked up and looking back at it now, I regret it immensely. But I did it, nonetheless." It was a lie, naturally, but he didn't need complete honesty to garner any sympathy; he only wanted to finalize it like the last sentence of a suicide note.

He wanted to give something back to Shea. Something he'd stolen from her when they fucked back at her apartment. He figured she thought she saw something good in him, like the two had a possibility to date or something. He was nothing more than a monster that'd only seen her as his next fast screw, though, and somewhere between the partial lies and painted truths he'd created around her as memory, the truth was always there, staring back like a hideous mask of deniability. He should never have involved her. Never gotten close to her or made eyes at her simply to get laid. If he'd only kept his distance, she might still be alive today, and Carol and the detective might have had the chance to start the family they always wanted.

"After she died, I gently placed her on her sofa...surrounded by all the pictures she liked to draw. She was fairly talented, as far as artists go." Church wanted to paint a picture for the detective, knowing the details of her living room or how her remains were discovered would be proof of his confession. He knew all too well there were holdbacks police routinely kept from the papers. He wanted the detective to see him standing there in her bare flat, maneuvering her body on the sofa and draping her hair back from her face in that way only her killer would know. It was insanity, though. There was no point in explaining any of that now. These were doomed souls who didn't need the pretense or his made up lies. But the floodgates were open and the rush of it could no longer be contained.

"I ran across her in town, and we ended up at her place. But she was a frigid little thing, and I had drunk a lot of booze that night."

It was almost like Gabe fully believed his own deceptions. He was spinning the weave of a silly fabrication, and for two people who no longer mattered to him. But sometimes even lies can sound cathartic, if allowed to work their magic. He wasn't thinking about Chris at that moment, and to his ears, it sounded like a more plausible story—a story where a killer inadvertently murders a young woman because of sexual fever and his overconsumption of alcohol. If someone was born under a bad sign, a corrupt seed like him just waiting to flower, then that was a tale anyone could buy. Not that he'd done it to save a cocksucker who'd fallen under his spell.

"I left the city after that..." he added, almost as an afterthought. "But I came back only so the police would understand that it was a horrible, but unintentional, disaster. And I do feel bad about it!"

Looking into Carol's eyes, he thought his ruse might work on her. She looked as if she almost believed him when he said he was a tortured soul, living his past with regret, but the detective was another issue altogether. He'd have sat inside numerous tiny interrogation rooms. He would have listened while suspects claimed for hours they had nothing to do with the crime they were questioned on. He would've seen how they broke under the strain and heard them eventually recount their part in the murders giving lurid and accurate details. Scott Keen would see the same deception in his eyes and realize he was as jaded.

"So, you killed Miss Baltimore. What does this have to do with me or my wife?" Keen blurted out angrily, still gripping Carol's fingertips in his.

"I needed to confess," Church said decisively, as images of Father Kait, still wearing his priestly robes, came flooding back. "I wanted you to know how it happened and the sorrow that I feel."

CAROL FELT FROZEN with every word the man said, yet strangely she was still thinking back to her younger self, and those Sunday school lessons she'd learned in church. If her lessons, or her faith, taught her anything, it was that the *Great Deceiver* wouldn't come as any red horned figure with his spiked tail and cloven feet as depicted in cartoons. She remembered reading scriptures that described him quite differently. He was supposed to be an angel named Lucifer after all, gifted with great beauty and perfection...at least prior to his eventual fall from grace. And while listening to this madman prattle on, all she could do was stare unconsciously transfixed, as if she been made into a zombie and held viselike inside a spell.

She hadn't even been aware how hard she'd been staring. Maybe it was because he was so handsome, she thought...because he was. Even more than that, he was striking. In that sickly dangerous way, she presumed. That was why it felt so alien and unreal to her because he certainly didn't appear the type to be holding them hostage or scaring her to the point where she couldn't stop her trembling.

Yes, the devil has to be beautiful. How else could he tempt away his stolen souls from those he visited? It wasn't like they'd offer up such a treasure simply because they were asked by someone old and withered ugly or even shabbily dressed. She was reminded of that as she glared at the man across the room. The devil and he had to share those same eyes. Depthless, cold, and yet still lovely, eyes that possessed a power to pull someone in and hold them trancelike, despite all their efforts to wriggle free. There were the same malice and danger lurking in his eyes, something born from an awful and painful past.

Then without warning, she saw him transform. The visible remorse he showed while describing the killing was invariably falling away like shards of clay, the mask figuratively disintegrating before her very eyes. She saw a dark cloud creeping in and taking hold, and in that instant, her intruder became even scarier than before. As if that were even possible.

She could tell that Scott had seen his moment to act. She watched as he dove forward and grabbed the stranger's hand with both of his as he attempted to wrestle the Glock free. She knew her husband well enough that she understood his only concern was pointing the weapon away from his wife. But the intruder was bigger in size and apparently quite strong. She saw them scuffling across the floor knocking over everything in their path but tragically couldn't offer any help of her own. At one point she feared the stranger might prevail as apparently had Scott because he managed to scream over his shoulder with a command that Carol hated to hear.

"Run!" he yelled, "Get out now!"

And with that instruction, she jumped up and fumbled past the two brawling men in her living room and raced for the front door and an opportunity of freedom.

CHURCH HADN'T EXPECTED this act of defiance and was paralyzed in his surprise. He hadn't gauged how desperate the detective was or that he'd make an unexpected lunge forward while he still had Carol in his crosshairs. He was forced backward and struggled to regain his footing. The detective was no match for him, but this came so unexpectedly that it caught him unaware. And his opponent was using that to his every advantage. Stepping on his heels, Gabe shoved one fist into Keen's chest with sufficient force to rail the detective backward and each weightless ounce of air became instantaneously expelled all at once. Keen staggered off balance as he tried to pull in enough air to inflate his lungs and grab instinctively for any nearby support. His arms flailed as he went for the nearest chair or table to support his fall.

Gabriel heard the panicked sound of Carol's breathing as she struggled to get the door unlocked. But he'd remained clearheaded when he surprised Scott Keen at the foyer, and with one hand he'd latched the door behind his back while the other hand held the gun against the back of Keen's skull. He knew she might make it out before he could stop her, so with his considerable strength, he reached high into the air and brought the gun handle down on Scott's head with a loud wallop. He'd always intended to silence his shots with one of the throw pillows Carol had been nervously fingering as she sat on the sofa waiting for her husband, but now he knew he had no choice. He took a calculatedly aim and let a single bullet to flying, creating an explosion that seemed deafeningly loud in that tiny space.

The woman screamed in pain as the bullet tore into her back and invaded her lungs. A sickly wet noise escaped her body as tiny splatters of blood were ejected. They appeared to hang slowly in the air for a split second, like dime-sized red globules suspended in time. The force of the shot shoved her body forward, almost as if she'd been kicked by an angry mule. She was thrown hard against the doorframe, and even from across the room, Gabe could sense all the oxygen leaving her at once. Out of the corner of his eye, he caught her wrenched and tragic expression as she skidded down the wood like a carelessly tossed sack of onions hitting the ground with a thump.

KEEN WAS ONLY stunned by the killer's blow and witnessed the bullet scorch his wife's back and drop her to her knees. In his unfathomable disbelief and through blurred vision, he watched as Carol fell.

Any daydreams Scott Keen may have once had about growing old and retiring from the force, or buying a little place near the ocean with his one true love at his side, simply shattered into nothingness at that very second. No amount of sacrifice was ever going to make it end any differently. In his panic and despair, he simply forgot about the killer still poised over him and began blindly crawling to reach his wife before it was too late.

Hands and knees scrambled and contorted as he raced crablike, awkwardly trying to get to Carol before she slipped beyond his grasp. He was no longer a seasoned detective with training and skills most citizens didn't possess. He'd simply become nothing more than his own all-consuming need. The stalwart efforts to reach Carol and shelter her had made him sadly and irrevocably oblivious to anything else around him.

It may have been his single-minded focus racing through his brain that prevented him from ever feeling the bullet as it seared into his back and tore apart vital organs that once sustained him. In a span of time less than seconds, the flash and the whispering hint of cordite from the gunfire laid waste to those arteries feeding his heart and opening chambers of his lungs like bloody tissue paper. Forever ending his life and any of the dreams he shared with his wife of starting a family and building a life they could be proud of.

GABE WAS MOTIONLESS as he looked at the carnage in front of him. The detective had never fully reached his wife before dying only a foot from her motionless body. His arm lay stretched like a tether, as if he'd been trying to pull the woman he loved back from imminent death. Gabe stood for a minute trying to regain his composure, then realized the noise could've alerted neighbors on either side. He'd done what he'd come here to do, he figured, and it was well past the point where he needed to become a ghost.

He knew he'd been sloppy, unlike other times he'd killed, and he could almost identify a coppery aftertaste on his tongue, could feel bile rising and threatening to explode from somewhere in his gut. He attributed that to the image of Carol lying so frail and bloodied by the door. She'd nearly gained her freedom. That would've been the true shame, he figured, because if she made it out the door, he wouldn't have run after her. He knew how strange and foolish that sounded, but she'd have won her freedom fair and square. Sadly though for her, she'd only come tragically close.

That gesture made Church's mind wander and may have been why he hadn't thought to check for a beating pulse or if there was any breath from either of his two victims. Had he done this, he surely would have detected a faint, yet ever-present pulse in Carol's wrist. It would have told him this woman was a fighter from the start, and that she was still clinging to life by the smallest of filaments. Just what this misfortune might mean would be speculation. But it was the kind of mistake Gabriel Church had never made before and certainly not since. It was a cost for him he may never learn, or find out when it was too late to act. Should Carol Keen live, he'd be leaving behind a witness, someone who could finger him for two homicides, at least; not to mention her own attempted murder. Yes, Church would be royally fucked; that was certain, and it went against the grain of every plan he'd set out to achieve.

Chapter Twenty-Nine

GABRIEL LEFT THE Keen's home by the sliding glass door that opened onto the backyard. He easily jumped the fence without much effort and stood in the alley separating the rows of upper-middleclass homes he knew he'd never be able to afford. It was a messy backstreet where the only traffic came from work vehicles and the garbage trucks making weekly stops for empty refuse and recycling bins. It was the hidden part of their lovely street, where homeowners needn't look at the rubbish directly. The rank odor of spoiled food hit his nose, and he stepped gingerly to avoid the piles of coffee grounds and old rotten fruit that littered the road. He was careful not to leave any tracks behind as he calmly headed down the side street undetected.

He knew this wasn't a route dog-walkers or door-to-door salespeople would normally take, so he felt comfortable that he wouldn't be spotted trying to get down the block to circle around and back to his truck. His ears strained to listen for the distinct wailing sirens he suspected would be screeching down the main street...though none came. But there were no sirens, no choppers circling overhead, nothing but the sounds of birds chirping in the trees and the distant rumble of cars from an unseen nearby expressway.

CHRISTIAN WAS ALONE in the motel room. His eyes were fixed on some recently rain-damaged tiles in the upper corner of the ceiling. They were discolored a rusty shade and made an odd array of shapes. He found himself becoming obsessed by the shapes, as he struggled to make out recognizable objects and animals from the silhouette and stains. He wondered why no one had ever replaced them. Or why they hadn't painted the walls in a dog's age. Then again, this wasn't the Olympia; remembering how much that short stay had cost him financially. This was a shithole motel; the kind of place you rented by the hour in a ridiculous reckoning called *Nap Rates*. He was anxiously awaiting Gabe's arrival and not certain how he should feel about any of this. He didn't know exactly what his lover was planning for the afternoon. At least that was the lie he'd been telling himself all day. But Church wasn't the type of man who you questioned his authority. He knew he'd have to wait patiently and do as he was told until this bad spell was behind them in the rearview.

With the TV off and no background noise, say for the whir of an old air conditioner by the bed, his mind could wander aimless and undisturbed. He thought back to that call from the detective and the message that began his latest drama. He'd acquiesced to Gabe, done what he'd suggested and phoned Keen back with a made-up alibi and a ruse to protect them both.

No, you didn't question a man like Church. Gabriel wasn't up for being second-guessed by anyone, and particularly one as inexperienced as he was in those matters. It had always been Gabe's confidence and the near certainty in his convictions that initiated Chris's interest in him. Even prior to their budding physical attraction, it had been how calculated his reasoning seemed, how unassailable his beliefs were, even if he stood alone in those beliefs. Even crazy people could still be admired for strength of character. Above all, Gabriel Church knew exactly how disturbing the words sounded once he spoke them aloud. He simply didn't give two shits what others might think.

Chris remembered a psychology class he'd taken his sophomore year, and a quote attributed to Aristotle rattled around his recollection: "There was never a genius without a tincture of madness." It seemed altogether appropriate given what he knew today and about as responsive a description of Gabriel as any he'd come up with himself. Madness seemed a thing Church knew more intimately than most—with everything he'd done and seen in a single lifetime.

Hearing the jingle of the doorknob twist sparked an electrical current along his spine, and he was amazed at how relieved he felt after seeing Gabriel enter. He couldn't contain his pleasure and showed it with a triumphant smile.

"You're back!"

"Were you expecting someone else?" Church asked amused.

"I was... Well, I was worried," Chris stammered out nervously. He was grateful that his lover returned safely and rose to hug him, choosing instead to throw his arms around Gabriel's neck, wanting to never let go. When the man didn't reciprocate his affectionate gesture, Chris sensed a change for the worse occurred in his absence.

"Did everything go as you planned?' he asked quickly, prodding him for details and stepping back to survey the man and look for signs to explain his mood.

Chris was well acquainted with the moods Gabriel could shift between. He'd known others he worked with who sauntered through the halls at his job with perpetual scowls on their faces no matter what the season or climate outside. To him it seemed they'd been born in a bad mood and nothing ever occurred in their lifetimes to affect a change for the better. Gabriel could be dark and brooding at times, secretive and elusive about whatever icy rivers were currently running through his brain, but he could also be joyous. Like a kid running into the front room on Christmas morning to see all the open presents and the toy cavalry soldiers lined up ready to do battle.

Gabriel looked at life as a gift, which was a quality Chris could appreciate. But not in that moment, not standing together in that dismal tiny motel room. Gabe had taken his chillier personality back, and the tension in his shoulders could be felt as something tangible. Perceivable to Chris when he reached to hug the man's neck, solid cable-like muscles refusing to go soft in his embrace, the absence of his arm gripping him around his waist or that open palm gently supporting his back—none of it was there. He was the serial killer Gabriel Church once again. The man first introduced to him at a coffee house in the arts district months earlier.

He wasn't playing nice, Chris thought. This wasn't fair because a person couldn't just shed the man they'd become as easily as turning up a collar to protect their face from a blast of cold winter wind.

"I don't mean to play devil's advocate, but did something happen today that we should be talking about?" Christian asked, turning from the man and then slinking back to the bed to sit on the edge.

He wanted to draw out Gabriel's mood. It was his typical practice whenever he saw darker clouds roll in. He knew his best options came by either seeking shelter from it or extracting it before dissecting it together in the radiant light of exposure. It'd become his way with Gabriel, digging out the problem, then hoping he might change his temperament somewhere along the way.

"You're using that wrong," Gabriel said emphatically. "And besides, did you know the title of devil's advocate was originally a church-assigned function?" he asked with a lilt, sidestepping Chris's question with a purpose.

"The Catholic church would use one priest to speak against the canonization of a particular saint. His real title was 'Promoter of the Faith,' but somehow everyone started calling it the 'Devil's Advocate.' Few people today even know that."

"And you know that because...?" Chris asked wearily, dragging his fingers in the air as a gesture to indicate Gabriel should continue. It was a shade more sarcastic than he would've liked, but he was sure some valuable news was being left out of the story someplace.

"Years of listening to a fucked-up priest back in Tennessee," Gabriel said, rather matter-of-factly. "And quite possibly, I'm not as dumb as I appear."

"Never said you were," Chris replied with a hint of a smile covering his earlier harshness. Gabriel could come off a particular way, but he was astute and well-read, if you took the time to see that quality about him. It was something most people missed, due in part to his scruffy bearded face and sinewy arms poking out of wife-beater tanks or camouflaged behind his worn-out plaid shirts purchased off the rack.

"I once fancied myself a writer, but now you're correcting my phrasing. What's next, my grammar?" he asked with a chuckle and a defeated nod of his head. "But you didn't answer my question. Did something happen after you left? You look like something's bothering you."

"No!" Gabriel said, shortly. "Did you do what I asked and make your call?"

His silence became the only acknowledgment, because Gabriel wasn't looking directly at him then and wouldn't have seen him nodding any approval with his back turned anyway.

"Detective Keen understands now that you didn't have anything to do with Shea's murder..." Church began. It was the first time he'd used her first name in a long while. It sounded wrong coming from him now, like a betrayal that shouldn't be.

"He will know you were in the process of calling within minutes of him finding out who really murdered the girl. It's not a perfect solution, but it's workable."

CHURCH HAD NO difficulty in lying about what really happened in the Keen home. He wanted Chris to believe he was better than he was. That he could fix almost anything and not have to resort to his usual method of murder as he'd done with Shea. "Yeah, I did my best imitation of a killdeer, I suppose."

When Chris only stared back confused, Gabe remembered the man hadn't been raised in the hills of Kentucky and Tennessee. "Where I come from we have a bird called the killdeer. It's a plover bird, mostly found nesting around fields where cattle graze. After laying eggs, they become very overprotective. Should an intruder come close to the nest, they begin to screech and caw. They hobble with a wing slung down as if it were broken and baiting themselves as easy prey for any unsuspecting predators. Their dance of distraction is mere survival, at least for the lives of their chicks or the future lives of unhatched eggs." Church was pleased with himself for knowing a thing that his more educated friend hadn't.

"AND DIRECTING THE heat to where...to you?" Chris's voice was rising, edging on becoming hysterical. Although he was an intelligent man, he hadn't truly looked at it for what it was. Or maybe he had, and simply been too afraid to recognize it for what it was from the very beginning; Gabe's plan to protect him and bear the brunt of the bullet he figured was already loose in the air.

"We did what we had to. Face facts, boy. You and I are not cut from the same cloth. You wouldn't have made it long living on the lam." And then more emphatically, "You are not me, Chris. You'd never have survived with a life on the road, always running from the law...and besides, you'd only slow me down."

"Slow you down." Christian measured each word as it fell off his lips like poison he needed to spit to the ground. He suddenly realized why Gabriel had said what he had - that somehow this had been his plan all along; a workable conclusion that would save him while practically burying Church in the process. His heart sank lower in his chest than he'd ever remembered it had.

The images of passing buildings streaked by from Chris's passenger window, a gray collage of concrete, steel, and parking lots and all meant absolutely nothing to him and they drove until he couldn't remain awake any longer. Early morning fog was beginning to roll in off the water, and the rumble of the Dodge's engine roused him from his restless slumber. He woke sitting next to Gabriel, who sat hunkered behind the steering wheel and was grinning mischievously at his sleeping beauty

His muscles ached from sleeping in an upright position with his head propped against cold glass, but he remained content. He felt safe in Church's company, and he couldn't be less concerned about where they were heading or who might be trailing them. He knew his lover would protect him. Like a shepherd watching over his flock, he'd become that pillar of strength and support he'd so desperately required in his life, a yin to his yang as it were.

But before he could linger there long enough to satisfy his mood, he noticed that ripples were forming. Waves and eddies were breaking his pleasant picture apart. They were tiny swells at first, undulating from its center like the effects of tossing a stone in the middle of a pond with a still water's surface. Gabriel was talking somewhere in the background, though he couldn't quite make out the words. It was too hard to comprehend, because every time he spoke, those self-induced images began to shatter and dissolve even more. They were replaced with black nothingness and an unfamiliar chill racing up and down his spine.

He was no longer sitting in the cab of the Dodge with Gabriel by his side, he was in a motel room, and the bigger man was gripping him by both his shoulders. His stare was squinty yet intense as he fixed his gaze directly into Christian's pupils. He appeared as if he were about to shake him violently while trying to reinforce some understanding to the jumbled words he was still speaking. But all Christian sensed was his knees growing weaker as they turned soft like congealed gelatin.

It became clear he was being dumped by the roadside once again. And that he'd be forced to watch as Church pulled away in that beat-up truck of his and disappeared down some long highway. He'd be left to pick up the pieces and begin again as he went through the motions of his pantomimed, cardboard existence. Chris suddenly felt too old to fight about it or even try to plead his case. It was a battle that he knew he'd never win with Gabriel, so he slumped down and out of his grip and back onto the mattress's edge with a resigned and stoic expression on his face.

"I'm not saying we can't be together. We just have to take a break till the heat dies down. We'll work out a way to talk regularly," Gabriel said softly, taking a seat beside Chris and trying to comfort him by placing his arm around his neck. "We'll have to be cautious about it for a while."

Christian heard the promise made in that statement but couldn't help remembering that he'd heard similar words spoken once before. And they hadn't proven to be any more solace to him than either.

"We'll get a prepaid cell phone for each of us. I can call you from the road, but we have to wait till the dust settles a bit," Gabe said as a tiny spark grew in strength somewhere behind those gray-blue eyes of his. "We'll meet up somewhere along the way. I promise you, babe."

Just like before, huh, living a life where the dust never seems to settle around a man like Gabriel Church—never even in the smallest of amounts.

""Sure," he replied, sorrowfully shaking his head. Even with all he knew, he'd still lost the war—and regrettably before the battle had ever begun.

Well, hope still springs eternal, he thought.

Chris rose from the bed and crossed the room to grab his bag from the chair. "Well I suppose you can drop me back at my place on your way outta town."

It wasn't a statement or a question; it was clarity; personal and deeply profound. And Gabriel knew it. Chris understood this was why his lover felt that need to reach over and pull him into his arms. They stood there in a long embrace while neither said a word. They both knew the futility of rehashing the obvious. And sometimes the silence can often say it better than words ever could. Chris felt miserable beyond measure, but once you realized how much a bitch reality could be, you knew you could either drop to the ground crying like a baby until your tantrum was over, or force yourself to stand and walk out that door with your head held high. Because some chasms are just too damned expansive, Chris reflected...some are just too impossible to ever cross.

Epilogue

IT WAS DIFFICULT leaving his lover standing on the corner of Lancaster and Euclid with a duffel slung over his shoulder. And Chris had tried to disguise his lovelorn puppy-eyed expression plastered across his face. But he wasn't very successful. If Gabe hadn't pulled away as fast as he had, he knew it could've turned ugly. He presumed the writer might lose it right there in public, whimpering like a child as cars passed by, curiously unaware of why a man would be crying on the sidewalk in broad daylight. Their goodbyes had been said in private because they were just that: private. Their declarations were meant to appease one another, but they still reminded Christian of the epitaphs carved into headstones, resolute and wretchedly final. As much as Chris seemed ready to break down, Church was hardly a pillar of masculine strength himself. If he hadn't forced his gaze outward, he too might've lost any control. He didn't need Chris seeing his lips quivering like a pussy, or tears welling behind his eyes like a dam on the verge of collapse. If he had to admit it openly though, he understood why he was going to be so affected by their separation. Their relationship had always been him being a little more gone than ever physically there. He could watch as Chris stood there on the corner appearing like a kid who'd recently lost their parents. He appeared abandoned and confused by the pain in his eyes. He may as well have been in short pants, holding a teddy bear by its paw and bawling like a fool.

They'd stopped at a neighborhood pharmacy on the way back to his condo and purchased two prepaid cellular phones. It would be their only contact with one another for quite some time, Gabe explained. He tried to lighten the mood by promising him he would call later that evening once he'd gotten miles out of the city safely and found a secure location where he could pull over to get some rest. Chris accepted everything he'd been told stoically, acknowledging everything with the slightest of nods and a begrudging smile that belied all his sadness.

There wouldn't be any friendly waves of goodbye like old high school chums separating after an enjoyable trip down memory lane. He simply watched Christian in the side mirror as he stood alone and isolated. It made him appear smaller and more fragile in the backdrop and shadows of those tall city buildings. It wasn't until he was speeding along the interstate that he finally wiped those first trails of wetness away from his cheeks.

He'd told himself they would stay in touch, and that he'd keep the promises he'd made to Christian like he'd always tried to do in the past. But it was only the first inklings of yet another lie creeping in and taking hold. He suddenly began to wonder why the single deity he'd been so devoted to throughout his entire life had so royally screwed him in the end. He could feel the discomfort; like having a celestial shaft plunged deeply into his ass where every stabbing, thrusting motion seemed to be screaming at him from over his shoulder in a loud booming voice: "Fuck you, princess, 'cause I got the reins now...and I'm the jackass who's now controlling your shitty future!"

It somehow reminded him of all the times he and Chris made love—whether it was in those fine hotels or the dimly lit, cum-stained motel rooms that made up much of their time together. He could only thank the stars that he was born a top, as if he'd some choice in the matter of how twisted his sex would later become. He didn't like the particular feeling he was left with and wondered how anything so painful might be so pleasurable to someone else.

Gabriel tuned the truck's stereo to a station he hoped might have fewer sad songs in their selection, songs that wouldn't remind him of the regrettable memories he now possessed of a life that had slipped through his fingers. He drove with a purpose and determination, almost hell-bent in his speed to escape Seattle. He wanted to leave every gentle face he'd seen and every little hurt he'd known—to bury it beneath a stone somewhere, hidden in the dark rich soils of the Northwest never to be unearthed again.

Sometime between the last rays of dusk and the first gloomy pitches of night, as Gabriel Church drove that long highway out of Washington, a particular priest was grasping his chest from the immense pain brought on by a sudden and tragically unexpected coronary. He'd dropped to his knees just as he was entering the chapel of St. Joseph's. And just as he hit the carpeted floor, his first thoughts ran to the prospect of finally seeing his mother and father's faces again, and he found a small slice of comfort from the pain. He would stand in the presence of God Almighty he knew, he'd finally feel the white light of holy embodiment and he would find solace there. He could almost envision himself with his hand extended upward, like greeting a familiar old friend who'd been absent from his life for far too long. His grip was tenuous however and he succumbed to his own mortality right there in the cathedral of the church he called home.

There was no way Gabriel could have known this of course, not that they shared that exact flash of an instant, he behind the wheel thinking about his God, Albert falling to his knees before his savior. It wouldn't have made a difference if he had been aware, but it created a strange coldness in the air that both would feel even across that vast distance. It was like someone strolling across your grave. After a minute Gabe felt the shivering chill and decided to roll up his window to escape the cold. He stared blankly ahead at the white painted lines as each one became nothing but a dot racing alongside the Dodge. He decided it was best to put away any future thoughts he had of the struggles that lay ahead. His not-so-distant future, as he had to remind himself with a smirk, and all because of the recent actions he'd taken willingly and in the so-called name of sacrifice and love.

While he was saying that to himself, he noticed, rather abruptly, that he was already weeping, and that fact caught him by some surprise. He was forced to steer to the side of the road to park because it was simply too dangerous driving while simultaneously bawling like a baby. Gabe couldn't believe what was happening to him there in the darkness, but he knew he was helpless to stop it from continuing. He planted his face in his hands and rested his head on the steering wheel and openly cried, without an ounce of his typical bravado that masked his feelings. His only distraction came from the headlights of passing cars, shining like blinking strobe lights across his face and lighting up the belly of the Dodge's interior.

About the Author

Rodd lives in Dallas, TX, yet originated in the back hills and sticks of Oklahoma. To learn more one merely has to visit his online presence at RODDCLARK.COM. A fan of mystery and suspense, he is drawn to the journey as much as the tale itself. With deeply rich characters, all bent and misshapen by circumstances beyond their control, he enjoys taking his readers on often dark and disturbing flights of fantasy. He began his books with the Brantley Colton Mysteries and evolved into the critically acclaimed series The Gabriel Church Tales. He's enjoyed writing since long before he could legally drink and likes making new friends and fans along the way.

Email: roddtx@usa.net

Facebook: www.facebook.com/rodd.clark.96

Twitter: @RoddClark

Website: www.roddclark.com

Other books by this author

Rubble and Wreckage

Also Available from NineStar Press

Connect with NineStar Press

Website: NineStarPress.com

Facebook: NineStarPress

Facebook Reader Group: NineStarNiche

Twitter: @ninestarpress

Tumblr: NineStarPress